Everyman, I will go with thee,
and be thy guide

THE EVERYMAN
LIBRARY

The Everyman Library was founded by J. M. Dent in 1906. He chose the name Everyman because he wanted to make available the best books ever written in every field to the greatest number of people at the cheapest possible price. He began with Boswell's 'Life of Johnson'; his one-thousandth title was Aristotle's 'Metaphysics', by which time sales exceeded forty million.

Today Everyman paperbacks remain true to J. M. Dent's aims and high standards, with a wide range of titles at affordable prices in editions which address the needs of today's readers. Each new text is reset to give a clear, elegant page and to incorporate the latest thinking and scholarship. Each book carries the pilgrim logo, the character in 'Everyman', a medieval mystery play, a proud link between Everyman past and present.

THE SECRET SELF 2

Short Stories by Women

Selected and Introduced by

HERMIONE LEE

'One tries to go deep –
to speak to the secret self we all have'
Katherine Mansfield

EVERYMAN
J. M. DENT · LONDON

This selection first published in Great Britain by
J. M. Dent 1987
Reprinted 1989

First published in Everyman's Library 1991
Reprinted 1993, 1994, 1995, 1997

J. M. Dent
Orion Publishing Group
Orion House
5 Upper St Martin's Lane, London WC2H 9EA

Printed by The Guernsey Press Co. Ltd, Guernsey, C.I.

British Library Cataloguing-in-Publication Data
is available upon request.

ISBN 0 460 87349 0

CONTENTS

NOTE ON THE EDITOR

Hermione Lee grew up in London and read English at Oxford. She has lectured at the College of William and Mary in Virginia, at Liverpool University, and at York University, where she is Professor of English Literature. She is well known as a critic, broadcaster and reviewer. Her books include *The Novels of Virginia Woolf* (1977), *Elizabeth Bowen: An Estimation* (1981), *Philip Roth* (1982), *Stevie Smith: A Selection* (1983), *The Mulberry Tree: Writings of Elizabeth Bowen* (1986), *Willa Cather: A Life Saved Up* (1989) an edition of Willa Cather's stories, and editions of Virginia Woolf's *To the Lighthouse* (1992) and *The Years* (1992). She is now working on a new life of Virginia Woolf.

INTRODUCTION

Hermione Lee

The Secret Self/2 is my second anthology of stories by women writing in this language in this century, but these stories are not my second choices. On the contrary, they came crowding in at me, all the writers I had reluctantly omitted from the first volume, and very many more. The choices were just as difficult. I have left out some of my favourite writers from the first anthology—Willa Cather, Grace Paley, Jean Stafford, Elizabeth Taylor—because I needed the space for different names. But I have included one story by the writers who seem to me to be the very finest artists of this genre—Elizabeth Bowen, Flannery O'Connor, Katherine Mansfield, Eudora Welty, Nadine Gordimer, Alice Munro—because I had found it extremely hard to select from their work the first time round, and because they give such strength and interest to the new anthology. I am still conscious of many excellent writers and stories excluded. This is an overwhelmingly rich area; inexhaustible, it began to seem, when I started to look more intensively for stories from the last twenty years, which make up, as a development from the first *Secret Self*, over half this volume.

Like the first, it takes its title from a remark made by Katherine Mansfield in a letter of 1921 about the writing of 'At the Bay'. Her description of herself as a writer trying to 'go deep', to 'speak to the secret self we all have', made me perceive a link between the very different stories in the first anthology. Looking for connections other than the fact that I liked them all (and in the end it's hard to justify selections on any wider grounds than personal enthusiasms), I began to see a consistent quality. This was, I thought, the disclosure of a private, alternative imaginative vision in some ways alien to the 'normal' socialized world, but, as Mansfield implies, made recognisable and authentic. Many of the stories involved some form of conflict: between what Eudora Welty has called 'secret imaginings' and 'an unwelcome realism', between consolatory dreams and hostile circumstances, between childlike or social individualities and adult expectations and demands—and, of course, between women and men. I don't mean to suggest by this that women's stories are characteristically frail, self-concealing and unworldly. The first *Secret Self* contained some ferociously assertive, comical, robust, political writing. But I do mean that one of the few common denominators I could find was a resistant, energizing tension between a personal fantasy and the existing (often brilliantly described) conditions.

Not to be able to discern definable, consistent attributes of women's writing, while reading and choosing stories by women, puts me at odds with a powerful school of feminist thought. *L'écriture féminine*, both as a description of and a prescription for women's writing, has been an influential concept in French feminist criticism since the 1970s. The utopian idea of an alternative feminine speech which infiltrates male-dominated language has been joyfully developed by writers such as Hélène Cixous and Luce Irigaray. Cixous said of woman in 'The Laugh of the Medusa' (1975): 'Her language does not contain, it carries; it does not hold back, it makes possible.' Woman's language, according to this school of thought, subverts the official, traditional ways of writing; it is associated with the evasive, the discontinuous, the multiplicitous; it expresses the rhythms of the female body itself.

These ideas have been hotly contested, particularly by feminist critics who find *l'écriture féminine* insufficiently political and even reactionary (since it seems to reinstate the old tyranny of an essential difference between men and women). Still, the idea of a definable woman's language is a tempting one, and might be justified, I think, by a few quotations from these stories:

> Far away lightning flutters—flutters like a wing—flutters like a broken bird that tries to fly and sinks again and again struggles.

> She was some nameless, tiny bell, growing in a stream, with a stalk as fine as hair and a human voice.

> I haven't seen Andrew for years, don't know if he is still thin, has gone completely grey, insists on lettuce, tells the truth, or is hearty and disappointed.

All these sentences are rhythmical, allusive, fluid, suggestive, in a way which could easily be identified as 'feminine'. But exactly the contrary could be proved by another set of examples:

> We surmount the skyline; the family come into our view, we into theirs.

> The majority of the people had lived off crops, but for two years past they had all returned from the lands with only their rolled-up skin blankets and cooking utensils.

> They sat listening to Saturday night, all round them, pressing in upon the hollow cement units of which the house was built.

These are, I think, neutral formulations: there is no discernible mark of gender in the syntax or the vocabulary. The search for what Virginia Woolf called (writing of Dorothy Richardson) 'the psychological sentence of the female gender' can never be conclusively resolved.

My examples were unfairly weighted, of course: the first three phrases are subjective and impressionistic, and so might be identified more with the 'feminine'; the last three are more formal, impersonal and general. Perhaps it is reductive to look for evidence of a woman's language only in selected phrases. But if the whole shape of each of these stories is considered, it quickly becomes apparent that general rules can't be applied. Some, certainly, work through fluid rhythms, suggestiveness, refusal of closure: look, for example, at the free association in the Jamaica Kincaid and Antonia White stories, or at Elizabeth Spencer's tender, garrulous fragment of married life. But others, like the Edith Wharton or the Marjorie Barnard or the Flannery O'Connor, are formally constructed, firmly defined, shaped towards a climax, in a quite different way.

Even if 'content' were to be separated from 'style', these stories couldn't be lined up neatly under the heading 'women's subjects'. There are a number of adulteries, bullying husbands, suicidal wives, daughters leaving home, mothers travelling to find their daughters. But there is also social prejudice, the diaspora, apartheid, emigration, war, ghosts, reincarnation—a range of subjects not determined by gender. My sympathies are with Nadine Gordimer, in her introduction to the *Selected Stories* of 1975: 'When it comes to their essential faculty as writers, all writers are androgynous beings.'

I don't believe, then, that a literal-minded search for a consistent woman's language or subject will be rewarded in this selection of stories. But there is, possibly, an intensification of the conflict between the aberrant and the socialized which I recognized as a theme in the first *Secret Self*. Elizabeth Bowen considered 'fantasy' to be a crucial ingredient in her short stories. When she made a selection of them in 1959 she said: 'More than half of my life is under the steadying influence of the novel, with its calmer, stricter, more orthodox demands: into the novel goes such taste as I have for rational behaviour and social portraiture. The short story, as I see it to be, allows for what is crazy about humanity: obstinacies, inordinate heroisms, "immortal longings".'

The stories in *The Secret Self/2* allow even more for 'what is crazy about humanity'; in the words of the mother matter-of-factly telling an English ghost story in the West Indies, in Jane Gardam's 'Weeping Child', they are 'not I think usual'. 'I couldn't remember a situation like this in any of the stories I had read', K.Arnold Price's baffled boy narrator says. Likewise, these stories all create their own very unexpected conditions and possibilities. Strangeness, fantasy, the unfamiliar, hallucination, myth, dream, memory, co-exist with the verifiable world, so that in many of the stories it feels as if one can have, simultaneously, more than one life. This imaginative duplicity may be expressed, ironically, as a vulnerable escape-route, like the young wife's invention of King Lappin and Queen Lapinova in the Virginia Woolf story, or the stoical husband's memories of England while abroad with his invalid wife, in the Katherine Mansfield, or the paralysed financier's dream of a nickel mine in the cruel, startling story by Rose Tremain. It may provide the sense of infinite alternatives, as in Elizabeth Jolley's mysterious series of possibilities for the old Viennese mother's visit to her 'paper children', the daughter she feels guilty for having let go as a baby and the Australian son-in-law she fears to meet. In Alice Munro's moving, brilliantly controlled, apparently leisurely narrative of a family journey, what might have happened has as much force as what did happen.

Or, the imaginative duplicity establishes two concurrent worlds, separate in real time and place, but drawn dramatically together through the obscure actions of the mind. So, in Rachel Ingalls's 'Third Time Lucky', pitched at a disconcertingly low key, the 'curse' on a modern woman, Lily, whose two husbands have died, very gradually takes shape as the re-enactment of an Ancient Egyptian myth. Lily used to think 'what a waste it was that people had only one life, that the choices were always so few, that you couldn't lead several lives all at once or one after the other. But now it seemed to her that what remained of the past was just as much where she belonged as was the present. In fact, you couldn't help living more lives than one.' In Cynthia Ozick's 'Levitation', the Gentile wife in the room full of Jewish intellectuals, their voices levitating on 'the glory of their martyrdom', has an alternative 'illumination': a vision of Mediterranean, pagan goddess-worship, a natural celebration to set against the suffering, intoning patriarchs. And in Elizabeth Bowen's magnificent story 'The Happy Autumn Fields', the bereft, de-natured violence of a modern existence—an unhappy, nervous woman lying in a bombed London flat—is set in contrapuntal antithesis to the lost, rich, slow-moving innocent world of Victorian Anglo-Ireland, its illusion of safety ('Nothing would fall or change') betrayed by the wartime scenes. Mary, who speaks for the narrator ('How are we to live without natures? . . . All we can do is imitate love or sorrow') is haunted, through a box of papers she has found, by the Tennysonian lives of Sarah and Henrietta. So this is a kind of ghost story, poised between Mary's sense of the lost past and the Victorian girls' anticipation of an unimaginable future. Though the story has an ending, and a bitterly sad one, it also seems not to end at all: the two times, made to co-exist by the force of the imagination, refuse to be closed off, and continue to haunt us. The alternative or double world in these stories sometimes—and startlingly—takes the form of a surreal retreat into delusions. Antonia White's 'The House of Clouds' and Anna Kavan's 'An Unpleasant Reminder' are two of the most alarming, exact presentations of madness and alienation I have read. By contrast, the fantastical journeys in Jamaica Kincaid's and Patricia Highsmith's stories are oddly alluring, and eccentric obsession takes on splendidly malevolent, farcical form in the Ruth Rendell. Like the hieroglyphic picture-writing seen in Lily's Egyptian dream in the

Ingalls story, some of these narratives cannot be solved. They use language to describe an untranslatable world. 'We can't hope to understand other peoples' lives', says the humane father in K. Arnold Price's quietly powerful 'The White Doll'. 'Lives are really very private. They are mysterious. They are hermetic . . . '

Though I find the strange, alien narratives very alluring, I want to resist a characterisation of women's stories as essentially sealed off, solipsistic, escapist. It is true that there are women here whose lives are circumscribed or isolated. Edith Wharton's painfully formal account of a mistress trying to see her dying lover, and driven back by a killingly conventional resistance from his sister; Fay Weldon's ferocious cartoon satire on an exploited housewife's weekend in the country; Kay Boyle's sad, elegant characterisation of a pathetic governess, ill-at-ease in an eccentric, cultured family; Julia O'Faolain's devastating tale of a havoc-wreaking male chauvinist, told by an edgy feminist in exactly the right strained tones; Henry Handel Richardson's sad, eloquent sketch of two young women lovers in a hostile society; Marjorie Barnard's unimaginative husband's version of his wife's brooding, long-planned revolt: all these are stories in which the women are threatened, enclosed. They are hard put to it to withdraw into or take strength from their 'secret selves'.

And there are damaging pressures in many of the stories. The weight of family life is powerfully felt: preventing mothers, legacies of recurring behaviour, networks of surveillance and censorship. Flannery O'Connor, with magnificent comic savagery and economy, tells us everything we need to know, in her scene on the bus, about the son's smug liberal revolt, the mother's stupid, human prejudices, the history of their reduced gentility, the insoluble racial conflict of the South. 'They don't give a damn for your graciousness,' Julian said savagely. 'Knowing who you are is good for one generation only. You haven't the foggiest idea where you stand now or who you are.' The absurd, painful conflict between son and mother opens out and out into the surrounding darkness. Mavis Gallant's self-deceiving Canadian in exile carries on his back the whole inheritance of a spoiled Presbyterianism; he's been left 'the rinds of income, of notions, and the memories of ideas rather than ideas intact.' The story is a whole cultural history. In the Eudora Welty and the Caroline Gordon, individuals who belong to the complex, watchful, gossipy families of the American South have to fight for survival, so as not to be 'petrified' within the repetitions, however rich and reassuring, of local history.

But for all these pressures, many of the stories take the form of energetic games and battles, in which voices of great style and vigour are in charge of events. Some of these narrators—Toni Cade Bambara, Anne Leaton, Stevie Smith and above all Eudora Welty—take my breath away with their unstoppable ebullience, recklessness and panache. Their voices go on in my head after the stories are finished. Even if their subjects are painful, the narrators are triumphantly assertive and in control. They fall on their feet, like some of the victorious heroines—Kate Chopin's lovely, sexy Calixta, or Suniti Namjoshi's whistling princess, cocking a snook at all but one of her suitors.

These writings resist constriction and oppression in other ways too. Because they are short stories (not, I think, because they are written by women) they tend to deal with the particular and the personal. Even the most political writing in the collection, the stories from Africa by Bessie Head and Nadine Gordimer, focus their bitterly truthful historical accounts on a particular family. Gordimer's black housewife, making her own political choice in a situation forced on her by men who are themselves victims of a system, is a fully felt character. And Bessie Head's magnificently stark story of famine, the most generalized and universal of all my choices, is full of telling, tender details, like the games played by the little girls.

But stories which don't at once declare themselves as 'historical' may open out much further than might be anticipated. Several of the stories of families and marriages I've already mentioned—Cynthia Ozick's, Mavis Gallant's, Flannery O'Connor's, Elizabeth Jolley's—encompass, by the end, complex cultural histories. And the same may be true of the most eccentric, idiosyncratic writers. Inside the offhand quizzical brusquery of the Stevie Smith, for instance, is a formidable attack on male bullying, war, and Christianity (with its frightening 'de-moting and upgrading, the marks and the punishments and the smugness') which makes the links between them quite clear.

These are all stories of conflict—some pleasurable, exciting, funny, some extremely disturbing, some mysterious, some unresolved. But the 'secret selves', the deep or hidden imaginative lives, are always in negotiation with experience, time, history, responsibility. Even if the characters hold back, like the son in Flannery O'Connor 'postponing from moment to moment his entry into the world of guilt and sorrow', the story always marks a point of entry: a moment of change, recognition, acknowledgement; something understood.

This selection is for
Jenny Uglow

KATE CHOPIN

The Storm

I

The leaves were so still that even Bibi thought it was going to rain. Bobinôt, who was accustomed to converse on terms of perfect equality with his little son, called the child's attention to certain sombre clouds that were rolling with sinister intention from the west, accompanied by a sullen, threatening roar. They were at Friedheimer's store and decided to remain there till the storm had passed. They sat within the door on two empty kegs. Bibi was four years old and looked very wise.

'Mama'll be 'fraid, yes,' he suggested with blinking eyes.

'She'll shut the house. Maybe she got Sylvie helpin' her this evenin',' Bobinôt responded reassuringly.

'No; she ent got Sylvie. Sylvie was helpin' her yistiday,' piped Bibi.

Bobinôt arose and going across to the counter purchased a can of shrimps, of which Calixta was very fond. Then he returned to his perch on the keg and sat stolidly holding the can of shrimps while the storm burst. It shook the wooden store and seemed to be ripping great furrows in the distant field. Bibi laid his little hand on his father's knee and was not afraid.

II

Calixta, at home, felt no uneasiness for their safety. She sat at a side window sewing furiously on a sewing machine. She was greatly occupied and did not notice the approaching storm. But she felt very warm and often stopped to mop her face on which the perspiration gathered in beads. She unfastened her white sacque at the throat. It began to grow dark, and suddenly realizing the situation she got up hurriedly and went about closing windows and doors.

Out on the small front gallery she had hung Bobinôt's Sunday clothes to air and she hastened out to gather them before the rain fell. As she stepped outside, Alcée Laballière rode in at the gate. She had not seen him very often since her marriage, and never alone. She stood there with Bobinôt's coat in her hands, and the big rain drops began to fall. Alcée rode his horse under the shelter of a side projection where the chickens had huddled and there were plows and a harrow piled up in the corner.

'May I come and wait on your gallery till the storm is over, Calixta?' he asked.

'Come 'long in, M'sieur Alcée.'

His voice and her own startled her as if from a trance, and she seized Bobinôt's vest. Alcée, mounting to the porch, grabbed the trousers and snatched Bibi's jacket tnat was about to be carried away by a sudden gust of wind. He expressed an intention to remain outside, but it was soon apparent that he might as well have been out in the open: the water beat in upon the boards in driving sheets, and he went inside, closing the door after him. It was even necessary to put something beneath the door to keep the water out.

'My! what a rain! It's good two years sence it rain' like that,' exclaimed Calixta as she rolled up a piece of bagging and Alcée helped her to thrust it beneath the crack.

She was a little fuller of figure than five years before when she married; but she had lost nothing of her vivacity. Her blue eyes still retained their melting quality; and her yellow hair, dishevelled by the wind and rain, kinked more stubbornly than ever about her ears and temples.

The rain beat upon the low, shingled roof with a force and clatter that threatened to break an entrance and deluge them there. They were in the dining room—the sitting room—the general utility room. Adjoining was her bedroom, with Bibi's couch alongside her own. The door stood open, and the room with its white, monumental bed, its closed shutters, looked dim and mysterious.

Alcée flung himself into a rocker and Calixta nervously began to gather up from the floor the lengths of a cotton sheet which she had been sewing.

'If this keeps up, *Dieu sait* if the levees goin' to stan' it!' she exclaimed.

'What have you got to do with the levees?'

'I got enough to do! An' there's Bobinôt with Bibi out in that storm—if he only didn' left Friedheimer's!'

'Let us hope, Calixta, that Bobinôt's got sense enough to come in out of a cyclone.'

She went and stood at the window with a greatly disturbed look on her face. She wiped the frame that was clouded with moisture. It was stiflingly hot. Alcée got up and joined her at the window, looking over her shoulder. The rain was coming down in sheets obscuring the view of far-off cabins and enveloping the distant wood in a gray mist. The playing of the lightning was incessant. A bolt struck a tall chinaberry tree at the edge of the field. It filled all visible space with a blinding glare and the crash seemed to invade the very boards they stood upon.

Calixta put her hands to her eyes, and with a cry, staggered backward. Alcée's arm encircled her, and for an instant he drew her close and spasmodically to him.

'*Bonté!*' she cried, releasing herself from his encircling arm and retreating from the window, 'the house'll go next! If I only knew w'ere Bibi was!' She would not compose herself; she would not be seated. Alcée clasped her shoulders and looked into her face. The contact of her warm, palpitating body when he had unthinkingly drawn her into his arms, had aroused all the old-time infatuation and desire for her flesh.

'Calixta,' he said, 'don't be frightened. Nothing can happen. The house is too low to be struck, with so many tall trees standing about. There! aren't you going to be quiet? say, aren't you?' He pushed her hair back from her face that was warm and steaming. Her lips were as red and moist as pomegranate seed. Her white neck and a glimpse of her full, firm bosom disturbed him powerfully. As she glanced up at him the fear in her liquid blue eyes had given place to a drowsy gleam that unconsciously betrayed a sensuous desire. He looked down into her eyes and there was nothing for him to do but to gather her lips in a kiss. It reminded him of Assumption.

'Do you remember—in Assumption, Calixta?' he asked in a low voice broken by passion. Oh! she remembered; for in Assumption he had kissed her and kissed and kissed her; until his senses would well nigh fail, and to save her he would resort to a desperate flight. If she was not an immaculate dove in those days, she was still inviolate; a passionate creature whose very defenselessness had made her defense, against which his honor forbade him to prevail. Now—well, now—her lips seemed in a manner free to be tasted, as well as her round, white throat and her whiter breasts.

They did not heed the crashing torrents, and the roar of the elements made her laugh as she lay in his arms. She was a revelation in that dim, mysterious chamber; as white as the couch she lay upon. Her firm, elastic flesh that was knowing for the first time its birthright, was like a creamy lily that the sun invites to contribute its breath and perfume to the undying life of the world.

The generous abundance of her passion, without guile or trickery, was like a white flame which penetrated and found response in depths of his own sensuous nature that had never yet been reached.

When he touched her breasts they gave themselves up in quivering ecstacy, inviting his lips. Her mouth was a fountain of delight. And when he possessed her, they seemed to swoon together at the very borderland of life's mystery.

He stayed cushioned upon her, breathless, dazed, enervated, with his heart beating like a hammer upon her. With one hand she clasped his head, her lips lightly touching his forehead. The other hand stroked with a soothing rhythm his muscular shoulders.

The growl of the thunder was distant and passing away. The rain beat softly upon the shingles, inviting them to drowsiness and sleep. But they dared not yield.

The rain was over; and the sun was turning the glistening green world into a palace of gems. Calixta, on the gallery, watched Alcée ride away. He turned and smiled at her with a beaming face; and she lifted her pretty chin in the air and laughed aloud.

III

Bobinôt and Bibi, trudging home, stopped without at the cistern to make themselves presentable.

'My! Bibi, w'at will yo' mama say! You ought to be ashame'. You oughtn' put on those good pants. Look at 'em! An' that mud on yo' collar! How you got that mud on yo' collar, Bibi? I never saw such a boy!' Bibi was the picture of pathetic resignation. Bobinôt was the embodiment of serious solicitude as he strove to remove from his own person and his son's the signs of their tramp over heavy roads and through wet fields. He scraped the mud off

Bibi's bare legs and feet with a stick and carefully removed all traces from his heavy brogans. Then, prepared for the worst—the meeting with an over-scrupulous housewife, they entered cautiously at the back door.

Calixta was preparing supper. She had set the table and was dripping coffee at the hearth. She sprang up as they came in.

'Oh, Bobinôt! You back! My! but I was uneasy. W'ere you been during the rain? An' Bibi? he ain't wet? he ain't hurt?' She had clasped Bibi and was kissing him effusively. Bobinôt's explanations and apologies which he had been composing all along the way, died on his lips as Calixta felt him to see if he were dry, and seemed to express nothing but satisfaction at their safe return.

'I brought you some shrimps, Calixta,' offered Bobinôt, hauling the can from his ample side pocket and laying it on the table.

'Shrimps! Oh, Bobinôt! you too good fo' anything!' and she gave him a smacking kiss on the cheek that resounded. '*J'vous réponds*, we'll have a feas' tonight! umph-umph!'

Bobinôt and Bibi began to relax and enjoy themselves, and when the three seated themselves at table they laughed much and so loud that anyone might have heard them as far away as Laballière's.

IV

Alcée Laballière wrote to his wife, Clarisse, that night. It was a loving letter, full of tender solicitude. He told her not to hurry back, but if she and the babies liked it at Biloxi, to stay a month longer. He was getting on nicely; and though he missed them, he was willing to bear the separation a while longer—realizing that their health and pleasure were the first things to be considered.

V

As for Clarisse, she was charmed upon receiving her husband's letter. She and the babies were doing well. The society was agreeable; many of her old friends and acquaintances were at the bay. And the first free breath since her marriage seemed to restore the pleasant liberty of her maiden days. Devoted as she was to her husband, their intimate conjugal life was something which she was more than willing to forego for a while.

So the storm passed and everyone was happy.

Katherine Mansfield

The Man Without A Temperament

He stood at the hall door turning the ring, turning the heavy signet ring upon his little finger while his glance travelled coolly, deliberately, over the round tables and basket chairs scattered about the glassed-in veranda. He pursed his lips—he might have been going to whistle—but he did not whistle—only turned the ring—turned the ring on his pink, freshly washed hands.

Over in the corner sat The Two Topknots, drinking a decoction they always drank at this hour—something whitish, greyish, in glasses, with little husks floating on the top—and rooting in a tin full of paper shavings for pieces of speckled biscuit, which they broke, dropped into the glasses and fished for with spoons. Their two coils of knitting, like two snakes, slumbered beside the tray.

The American Woman sat where she always sat against the glass wall, in the shadow of a great creeping thing with wide open purple eyes that pressed—that flattened itself against the glass, hungrily watching her. And she knoo it was there—she knoo it was looking at her just that way. She played up to it; she gave herself little airs. Sometimes she even pointed at it, crying: 'Isn't that the most terrible thing you've ever seen! Isn't that ghoulish!' It was on the other side of the veranda, after all . . . and besides it couldn't touch her, could it, Klaymongso? She was an American Woman, wasn't she, Klaymongso, and she'd just go right away to her Consul. Klaymongso, curled in her lap, with her torn antique brocade bag, a grubby handkerchief, and a pile of letters from home on top of him, sneezed for reply.

The other tables were empty. A glance passed between the American and the Topknots. She gave a foreign little shrug; they waved an understanding biscuit. But he saw nothing. Now he was still, now from his eyes you saw he listened. 'Hoo-e-zip-zoo-oo!' sounded the lift. The iron cage clanged open. Light dragging steps sounded across the hall, coming towards him. A hand, like a leaf, fell on his shoulder. A soft voice said: 'Let's go and sit over there—where we can see the drive. The trees are so lovely.' And he moved forward with the hand still on his shoulder, and the light, dragging steps beside his. He pulled out a chair and she sank into it, slowly, leaning her head against the back, her arms falling along the sides.

'Won't you bring the other up closer? It's such miles away.' But he did not move.

'Where's your shawl?' he asked.

'Oh!' She gave a little groan of dismay. 'How silly I am, I've left it upstairs on the bed. Never mind. Please don't go for it. I shan't want it, I know I shan't.'

'You'd better have it.' And he turned and swiftly crossed the veranda into the dim hall with its scarlet plush and gilt furniture—conjuror's furniture—its Notice of Services at the English Church, its green baize board with the unclaimed letters climbing the black lattice, huge 'Presentation' clock that struck the hours at the half-hours, bundles of sticks and umbrellas and sunshades in the clasp of a brown wooden bear, past the two crippled palms, two ancient beggars at the foot of the staircase, up the marble stairs three at a time, past the life-size group on the landing of two stout peasant children with their marble pinnies full of marble grapes, and along the corridor, with its piled-up wreckage of old tin boxes, leather trunks, canvas holdalls, to their room.

The servant girl was in their room, singing loudly while she emptied soapy water into a pail. The windows were open wide, the shutters put back, and the light glared in. She had thrown the carpets and the big white pillows over the balcony rails; the nets were looped up from the beds; on the writing-table there stood a pan of fluff and match-ends. When she saw him her small impudent eyes snapped and her singing changed to humming. But he gave no sign. His eyes searched the glaring room. Where the devil was the shawl!

'*Vous desirez, monsieur?*' mocked the servant girl.

No answer. He had seen it. He strode across the room, grabbed the grey cobweb and went out, banging the door. The servant girl's voice at its loudest and shrillest followed him along the corridor.

'Oh, there you are. What happened? What kept you? The tea's here, you see. I've just sent Antonio off for the hot water. Isn't it extraordinary? I must have told him about it sixty times at least, and still he doesn't bring it. Thank you. That's very nice. One does just feel the air when one bends forward.'

'Thanks.' He took his tea and sat down in the other chair. 'No, nothing to eat.'

'Oh do! Just one, you had so little at lunch and it's hours before dinner.'

Her shawl dropped off as she bent forward to hand him the biscuits. He took one and put in his saucer.

'Oh, those trees along the drive,' she said. 'I could look at them for ever. They are like the most exquisite huge ferns. And you see that one with the grey-silver bark and the clusters of cream-coloured flowers, I pulled down a head of them yesterday to smell, and the scent'—she shut her eyes at the memory and her voice thinned away, faint, airy—'was like freshly ground nutmegs.' A little pause. She turned to him and smiled. 'You do know what nutmegs smell like—do you, Robert?'

And he smiled back at her. 'Now how am I going to prove to you that I do?'

Back came Antonio with not only the hot water—with letters on a salver and three rolls of paper.

'Oh, the post! Oh, how lovely! Oh, Robert, they mustn't be all for you! Have they just come, Antonio?' Her thin hands flew up and hovered over the letters that Antonio offered her, bending forward.

'Just this moment, Signora,' grinned Antonio. 'I took-a them from the postman myself. I made-a the postman give them for me.'

'Noble Antonio!' laughed she. 'There—those are mine, Robert; the rest are yours.'

Antonio wheeled sharply, stiffened, the grin went out of his face. His striped linen jacket and his flat gleaming fringe made him look like a wooden doll.

Mr Salesby put the letters into his pocket; the papers lay on the table. He turned the ring, turned the signet ring on his little finger and stared in front of him, blinking, vacant.

But she—with her teacup in one hand, the sheets of thin paper in the other, her head tilted back, her lips open, a brush of bright colour on her cheek-bones, sipped, sipped, drank . . . drank . . .

'From Lottie,' came her soft murmur. 'Poor dear . . . such trouble . . . left foot. She thought . . . neuritis . . . Doctor Blyth . . . flat foot . . . massage. So many robins this year . . . maid most satisfactory . . . Indian Colonel . . . every grain of rice separate . . . very heavy fall of snow.' And her wide lighted eyes looked up from the letter. 'Snow, Robert! Think of it!' And she touched the little dark violets pinned on her thin bosom and went back to the letter.

. . . Snow. Snow in London. Millie with the early morning cup of tea. 'There's been a terrible fall of snow in the night, sir.' 'Oh, has there, Millie?' The curtains ring apart, letting in the pale, reluctant light. He raises himself in the bed; he catches a glimpse of the solid houses opposite framed in white, of their window boxes full of great sprays of white coral . . . In the bathroom—overlooking the back garden. Snow—heavy snow over everything. The lawn is covered with a wavy pattern of cat's-paws; there is a thick, thick icing on the garden table; the withered pods of the laburnum tree are white tassels; only here and there in the ivy is a dark leaf showing . . . Warming his back at the dining-room fire, the paper drying over a chair. Millie with the bacon. 'Oh, if you please, sir, there's two little boys come as will do the steps and front for a shilling, shall I let them?' . . . And then flying lightly, lightly down the stairs—Jinnie. 'Oh, Robert, isn't it wonderful! Oh, what a pity it has to melt. Where's the pussy-wee?' 'I'll get him from Millie.' . . . 'Millie, you might just hand me up the kitten if you've got him down there.' 'Very good, sir.' He feels the little beating heart under his hand. 'Come on, old chap, your missus wants you.' 'Oh, Robert, do show him the snow—his first snow. Shall I open the window and give him a little piece on his paw to hold? . . .'

'Well, that's very satisfactory on the whole—very. Poor Lottie! Darling Anne! How I only wish I could send them something of this,' she cried, waving her letters at the brilliant, dazzling garden. 'More tea, Robert? Robert dear, more tea?'

'No, thanks, no. It was very good,' he drawled.

'Well, mine wasn't. Mine was just like chopped hay. Oh, here comes the Honeymoon Couple.'

Half striding, half running, carrying a basket between them and rods and lines, they came up the drive, up the shallow steps.

'My! have you been out fishing?' cried the American Woman.

They were out of breath, they panted: 'Yes, yes, we have been out in a little boat all day. We have caught seven. Four are good to eat. But three we shall give away. To the children.'

Mrs Salesby turned her chair to look; the Topknots laid the snakes down. They were a very dark young couple—black hair, olive skin, brilliant eyes and teeth. He was dressed 'English Fashion' in a flannel jacket, white trousers and shoes. Round his neck he wore a silk scarf; his head, with his hair brushed back, was bare. And he kept mopping his forehead, rubbing his hands with a brilliant handkerchief. Her white skirt had a patch of wet; her neck and throat were stained a deep pink. When she lifted her arms big half-hoops of perspiration showed under her arm-pits; her hair clung in wet curls to her cheeks. She looked as though her young husband had been dipping her in the sea and fishing her out again to dry in the sun and then—in with her again—all day.

'Would Klaymongso like a fish?' they cried. Their laughing voices charged with excitement beat against the glassed-in veranda like birds and a strange, saltish smell came from the basket.

'You will sleep well tonight,' said a Topknot, picking her ear with a knitting needle while the other Topknot smiled and nodded.

The Honeymoon Couple looked at each other. A great wave seemed to go over them. They gasped, gulped, staggered a little and then came up laughing—laughing.

'We cannot go upstairs, we are too tired. We must have tea just as we are. Here—coffee. No—tea. No—coffee. Tea—coffee, Antonio!' Mrs Salesby turned.

'Robert! Robert!' Where was he? He wasn't there. Oh, there he was at the other end of the veranda, with his back turned, smoking a cigarette. 'Robert, shall we go for our little turn?'

'Right.' He stumped the cigarette into an ash-tray and sauntered over, his eyes on the ground. 'Will you be warm enough?'

'Oh, quite.'

'Sure?'

'Well,' she put her hand on his arm, 'perhaps'—and gave his arm the faintest pressure—'it's not upstairs, it's only in the hall—perhaps you'd get me my cape. Hanging up.'

He came back with it and she bent her small head while he dropped it on her shoulders. Then, very stiff, he offered her his arm. She bowed sweetly to the people on the veranda while he just covered a yawn, and they went down the steps together.

'*Vous avez voo ça!*' said the American Woman.

'He is not a man,' said the Two Topknots, 'he is an ox. I say to my sister in the morning and at night when we are in bed, I tell her—*No* man is he, but an ox!

Wheeling, tumbling, swooping, the laughter of the Honeymoon Couple dashed against the glass of the veranda.

The sun was still high. Every leaf, every flower in the garden lay open, motionless, as if exhausted, and a sweet, rich, rank smell filled the quivering air. Out of the thick, fleshy leaves of a cactus there rose an aloe stem loaded with pale flowers that looked as though they had been cut out of butter; light flashed upon the lifted spears of the palms; over the bed of scarlet waxen flowers some big black insects 'zoom-zoomed'; a great, gaudy creeper, orange splashed with jet, sprawled against a wall.

'I don't need my cape after all,' said she. 'It's really too warm.' So he took it off and carried it over his arm. 'Let us go down this path here. I feel so well today—marvellously better. Good heavens—look at those children! And to think it's November!'

In a corner of the garden there were two brimming tubs of water. Three little girls, having thoughtfully taken off their drawers and hung them on a bush, their skirts clasped to their waists, were standing in the tubs and tramping up and down. They screamed, their hair fell over their faces, they splashed one another. But suddenly, the smallest, who had a tub to herself, glanced up and saw who was looking. For a moment she seemed overcome with terror, then clumsily she struggled and strained out of her tub, and still holding her clothes above her waist, 'The Englishman! The Englishman!' she shrieked and fled away to hide. Shrieking and screaming the other two followed her. In a moment they were gone; in a moment there was nothing but the two brimming tubs and their little drawers on the bush.

'How—very—extraordinary!' said she. 'What made them so frightened? Surely they were much too young to . . .' She looked up at him. She thought he looked pale—but wonderfully handsome with that great tropical tree behind him with its long, spiked thorns.

For a moment he did not answer. Then he met her glance, and smiling his slow smile, '*Très* rum!' said he.

Très rum! Oh, she felt quite faint. Oh, why should she love him so much just because he said a thing like that. *Très* rum! That was Robert all over. Nobody else but Robert could ever say such a thing. To be so wonderful, so brilliant, so learned, and then to say in that queer, boyish voice . . . She could have wept.

'You know you're very absurd, sometimes,' said she.

'I am,' he answered. And they walked on.

But she was tired. She had had enough. She did not want to walk any more.

'Leave me here and go for a little constitutional, won't you? I'll be in one of these long chairs. What a good thing you've got my cape; you won't have to go upstairs for a rug. Thank you, Robert, I shall look at that delicious heliotrope. . . . You won't be gone long?'

'No—no. You don't mind being left?'

'Silly! I want you to go. I can't expect you to drag after your invalid wife every minute. . . . How long will you be?'

He took out his watch. 'It's just after half-past four. I'll be back at a quarter-past five.'

'Back at a quarter-past five,' she repeated, and she lay still in the long chair and folded her hands.

He turned away. Suddenly he was back again. 'Look here, would you like my watch?' And he dangled it before her.

'Oh!' She caught her breath. 'Very, very much.' And she clasped the watch, the warm watch, the darling watch in her fingers. 'Now go quickly.'

The gates of the Pension Villa Excelsior were open wide, jammed open against some bold geraniums. Stooping a little, staring straight ahead, walking swiftly, he passed through them and began climbing the hill that wound behind the town like a great rope looping the villas together. The dust lay thick. A carriage came bowling along driving towards the Excelsior. In it sat the General and the Countess; they had been for his daily airing. Mr Salesby stepped to one side but the dust beat up, thick, white, stifling like wool. The Countess just had time to nudge the General.

'There he goes,' she said spitefully.

But the General gave a loud caw and refused to look.

'It is the Englishman,' said the driver, turning round and smiling. And the Countess threw up her hands and nodded so amiably that he spat with satisfaction and gave the stumbling horse a cut.

On—on—past the finest villas in the town, magnificent palaces, palaces worth coming any distance to see, past the public gardens with the carved grottoes and statues and stone animals drinking at the fountain, into a poorer quarter. Here the road ran narrow and foul between high lean houses, the ground floors of which were scooped and hollowed into stables and carpenters' shops. At a fountain ahead of him two old hags were beating linen. As he passed them they squatted back on their haunches, stared, and then their 'A-hak-kak-kak!' with the slap, slap, of the stone on the linen sounded after him.

He reached the top of the hill; he turned a corner and the town was hidden. Down he looked into a deep valley with a dried-up river bed at the bottom. This side and that was covered with small dilapidated houses that had broken stone verandas where the fruit lay drying, tomato lanes in the garden and from the gates to the doors a trellis of vines. The late sunlight, deep, golden, lay in the cup of the valley; there was a smell of charcoal in the air. In the gardens the men were cutting grapes. He watched a man standing in the greenish shade, raising up, holding a black cluster in one hand, taking the knife from his belt, cutting, laying the bunch in a flat boat-shaped basket. The man worked leisurely, silently, taking hundreds of years over the job. On the hedges on the other side of the road there were grapes small as berries, growing wild, growing among the stones. He leaned against a wall, filled his pipe, put a match to it . . .

Leaned across a gate, turned up the collar of his mackintosh. It was going to rain. It didn't matter, he was prepared for it. You didn't expect anything else in November. He looked over the bare field. From the corner by the gate there came the smell of swedes, a great stack of them, wet, rank coloured. Two men passed walking towards the straggling village. 'Good day!' 'Good day!' By Jove! he had to hurry if he was going to catch that train home. Over the gate, across a field, over the stile, into the lane, swinging along in the drifting rain and dusk . . . Just home in time for a bath and a change before supper. . . . In the drawing-room; Jinnie is sitting pretty nearly in the fire. 'Oh, Robert, I didn't hear you come in. Did you have a good time? How nice you smell! A present?' 'Some bits of blackberry I picked for you. Pretty colour.' 'Oh, lovely, Robert! Dennis and Beaty are coming to supper.' Supper—cold beef, potatoes in their jackets, claret, household bread. They are gay—everybody's laughing. 'Oh, we all know Robert,' says Dennis, breathing on his eyeglasses and polishing them. 'By the way, Dennis, I picked up a very jolly little edition of . . .'

A clock struck. He wheeled sharply. What time was it. Five? A quarter past? Back, back the way he came. As he passed through the gates he saw her on the look-out. She got up, waved and slowly she came to meet him, dragging the heavy cape. In her hand she carried a spray of heliotrope.

'You're late,' she cried gaily. 'You're three minutes late. Here's your watch, it's been very good while you were away. Did you have a nice time? Was it lovely? Tell me. Where did you go?'

'I say—put this *on*,' he said, taking the cape from her.

'Yes, I will. Yes, it's getting chilly. Shall we go up to our room?'

When they reached the lift she was coughing. He frowned.

'It's nothing. I haven't been out too late. Don't be cross.' She sat down on one of the red plush chairs while he rang and rang, and then, getting no answer, kept his finger on the bell.

'Oh, Robert, do you think you ought to?'

'Ought to what?'

The door of the *salon* opened. 'What is that? Who is making that noise?' sounded from within. Klaymongso began to yelp. 'Caw! Caw! Caw!' came from the General. A Topknot darted out with one hand to her ear, opened the staff door, 'Mr Queet! Mr Queet!' she bawled. That brought the manager up at a run.

'Is that you ringing the bell, Mr Salesby? Do you want the lift? Very good, sir. I'll take you up myself. Antonio wouldn't have been a minute, he was just taking off his apron—' And having ushered them in, the oily manager went to the door of the *salon*. 'Very sorry you should have been troubled, ladies and gentlemen.' Salesby stood in the cage, sucking in his cheeks, staring at the ceiling and turning the ring, turning the signet ring on his little finger. . . .

Arrived in their room he went swiftly over to the washstand, shook the bottle, poured her out a dose and brought it across.

'Sit down. Drink it. And don't talk.' And he stood over her

while she obeyed. Then he took the glass, rinsed it and put it back in its case. 'Would you like a cushion?'

'No, I'm quite all right. Come over here. Sit down by me just a minute, will you, Robert? Ah, that's very nice.' She turned and thrust the piece of heliotrope in the lapel of his coat. 'That,' she said, 'is most becoming.' And then she leaned her head against his shoulder and he put his arm round her.

'Robert—' her voice like a sigh—like a breath.

'Yes—'

They sat there for a long while. The sky flamed, paled; the two white beds were like two ships. . . . At last he heard the servant girl running along the corridor with the hot-water cans, and gently he released her and turned on the light.

'Oh, what time is it? Oh, what a heavenly evening. Oh, Robert, I was thinking while you were away this afternoon . . .'

They were the last couple to enter the dining-room. The Countess was there with her lorgnette and her fan, the General was there with his special chair and the air cushion and the small rug over his knees. The American Woman was there showing Klaymongso a copy of the *Saturday Evening Post*. . . . 'We're having a feast of reason and a flow of soul.' The Two Topknots were there feeling over the peaches and the pears in their dish of fruit and putting aside all they considered unripe or overripe to show to the manager, and the Honeymoon Couple leaned across the table, whispering, trying not to burst out laughing.

Mr Queet, in everyday clothes and white canvas shoes, served the soup, and Antonio, in full evening dress, handed it round.

'No,' said the American Woman, 'take it away, Antonio. We can't eat soup. We can't eat anything mushy, can we, Klaymongso?'

'Take them back and fill them to the rim!' said the Topknots, and they turned and watched while Antonio delivered the message.

'What is it? Rice? Is it cooked?' The Countess peered through her lorgnette. 'Mr Queet, the General can have some of this soup if it is cooked.'

'Very good, Countess.'

The Honeymoon Couple had their fish instead.

'Give me that one. That's the one I caught. No, it's not. Yes, it is. No, it's not. Well it's looking at me with its eye, so it must be.

Tee! Hee! Hee!' Their feet were locked together under the table.

'Robert, you're not eating again. Is anything the matter?'

'No. Off food, that's all.'

'Oh, what a bother. There are eggs and spinach coming. You don't like spinach, do you. I must tell them in future . . .'

An egg and mashed potatoes for the General.

'Mr Queet! Mr Queet!'

'Yes, Countess.'

'The General's egg's too hard again.'

'Caw! Caw! Caw!'

'Very sorry, Countess. Shall I have you another cooked, General?'

. . . They are the first to leave the dining-room. She rises, gathering her shawl and he stands aside, waiting for her to pass, turning the ring, turning the signet ring on his little finger. In the hall Mr Queet hovers. 'I thought you might not want to wait for the lift. Antonio's just serving the finger bowls. And I'm sorry the bell won't ring, it's out of order. I can't think what's happened.'

'Oh, I do hope . . .' from her.

'Get in,' says he.

Mr Queet steps after them and slams the door . . .

'. . . Robert, do you mind if I go to bed very soon? Won't you go down to the *salon* or out into the garden? Or perhaps you might smoke a cigar on the balcony. It's lovely out there. And I like cigar smoke. I always did. But if you'd rather . . .'

'No, I'll sit here.'

He takes a chair and sits on the balcony. He hears her moving about in the room, lightly, lightly, moving and rustling. Then she comes over to him. 'Good night, Robert.'

'Good night.' He takes her hand and kisses the palm. 'Don't catch cold.'

The sky is the colour of jade. There are a great many stars; an enormous white moon hangs over the garden. Far away lightning flutters—flutters like a wing—flutters like a broken bird that tries to fly and sinks again and again struggles.

The lights from the *salon* shine across the garden path and there is the sound of a piano. And once the American Woman, opening the French window to let Klaymongso into the garden, cries: 'Have you seen this moon?' But nobody answers.

He gets very cold sitting there, staring at the balcony rail.

Finally he comes inside. The moon—the room is painted white with moonlight. The light trembles in the mirrors; the two beds seem to float. She is asleep. He sees her through the nets, half sitting, banked up with pillows, her white hands crossed on the sheet. Her white cheeks, her fair hair pressed against the pillow, are silvered over. He undresses quickly, stealthily and gets into bed. Lying there, his hands clasped behind his head.

. . . In his study. Late summer. The virginia creeper just on the turn. . . .

'Well, my dear chap, that's the whole story. That's the long and the short of it. If she can't cut away for the next two years and give a decent climate a chance she don't stand a dog's—h'm—show. Better be frank about these things.' 'Oh, certainly. . . .' 'And hang it all, old man, what's to prevent you going with her? It isn't as though you've got a regular job like us wage earners. You can do what you do wherever you are—' 'Two years.' 'Yes, I should give it two years. You'll have no trouble about letting this house, you know. As a matter of fact . . .'

. . . He is with her. 'Robert, the awful thing is—I suppose it's my illness—I simply feel I could not go alone. You see—you're everything. You're bread and wine, Robert, bread and wine. Oh, my darling—what am I saying? Of course I could, of course I won't take you away . . .'

He hears her stirring. Does she want something?

'Boogles?'

Good Lord! She is talking in her sleep. They haven't used that name for years.

'Boogles. Are you awake?'

'Yes, do you want anything?'

'Oh, I'm going to be a bother. I'm so sorry. Do you mind? There's a wretched mosquito inside my net—I can hear him singing. Would you catch him? I don't want to move because of my heart.'

'No, don't move. Stay where you are.' He switches on the light, lifts the net. 'Where is the little beggar? Have you spotted him?'

'Yes, there, over by the corner. Oh, I do feel such a fiend to have dragged you out of bed. Do you mind dreadfully?'

'No, of course not.' For a moment he hovers in his blue and

white pyjamas. Then, 'got him,' he said.

'Oh, good. Was he a juicy one?'

'Beastly.' He went over to the washstand and dipped his fingers in water. 'Are you all right now? Shall I switch off the light?'

'Yes, please. No. Boogles! Come back here a moment. Sit down by me. Give me your hand.' She turns his signet ring. 'Why weren't you asleep? Boogles, listen. Come closer. I sometimes wonder—do you mind awfully being out here with me?'

He bends down. He kisses her. He tucks her in, he smooths the pillow.

'Rot!' he whispers.

Virginia Woolf

Lappin and Lapinova

They were married. The wedding march pealed out. The pigeons fluttered. Small boys in Eton jackets threw rice; a fox terrier sauntered across the path; and Ernest Thorburn led his bride to the car through that small inquisitive crowd of complete strangers which always collects in London to enjoy other people's happiness or unhappiness. Certainly he looked handsome and she looked shy. More rice was thrown, and the car moved off.

That was on Tuesday. Now it was Saturday. Rosalind had still to get used to the fact that she was Mrs Ernest Thorburn. Perhaps she never would get used to the fact that she was Mrs Ernest Anybody, she thought, as she sat in the bow window of the hotel looking over the lake to the mountains, and waited for her husband to come down to breakfast. Ernest was a difficult name to get used to. It was not the name she would have chosen. She would have preferred Timothy, Antony, or Peter. He did not look like Ernest either. The name suggested the Albert Memorial, mahogany sideboards, steel engravings of the Prince Consort with his family—her mother-in-law's dining-room in Porchester Terrace in short.

But here he was. Thank goodness he did not look like Ernest—no. But what did he look like? She glanced at him sideways. Well, when he was eating toast he looked like a rabbit. Not that anyone else would have seen a likeness to a creature so diminutive and timid in this spruce, muscular young man with the straight nose, the blue eyes, and the very firm mouth. But that made it all the more amusing. His nose twitched very slightly when he ate. So did her pet rabbit's. She kept watching his nose twitch; and then she had to explain, when he caught her looking at him, why she laughed.

'It's because you're like a rabbit, Ernest,' she said. 'Like a wild rabbit,' she added, looking at him. 'A hunting rabbit; a King Rabbit; a rabbit that makes laws for all the other rabbits.'

Ernest had no objection to being that kind of rabbit, and since it amused her to see him twitch his nose—he had never known that his nose twitched—he twitched it on purpose. And she laughed and laughed; and he laughed too, so that the maiden ladies and the fishing man and the Swiss waiter in his greasy black jacket all guessed right; they were very happy. But how long does such happiness last? they asked themselves; and each answered according to his own circumstances.

At lunch time, seated on a clump of heather beside the lake, 'Lettuce, rabbit?' said Rosalind, holding out the lettuce that had been provided to eat with the hard-boiled eggs. 'Come and take it out of my hand,' she added, and he stretched out and nibbled the lettuce and twitched his nose.

'Good rabbit, nice rabbit,' she said, patting him, as she used to pat her tame rabbit at home. But that was absurd. He was not a tame rabbit, whatever he was. She turned it into French. 'Lapin,' she called him. But whatever he was, he was not a French rabbit. He was simply and solely English—born at Porchester Terrace, educated at Rugby; now a clerk in His Majesty's Civil Service. So she tried 'Bunny' next; but that was worse. 'Bunny' was someone plump and soft and comic; he was thin and hard and serious. Still, his nose twitched. 'Lappin,' she exclaimed suddenly; and gave a little cry as if she had found the very word she looked for.

'Lappin, Lappin, King Lappin,' she repeated. It seemed to suit him exactly; he was not Ernest, he was King Lappin. Why? She did not know.

When there was nothing new to talk about on their long solitary walks—and it rained, as everyone had warned them that it would rain; or when they were sitting over the fire in the evening, for it was cold, and the maiden ladies had gone and the fishing man, and the waiter only came if you rang the bell for him, she let her fancy play with the story of the Lappin tribe. Under her hands—she was sewing; he was reading—they became very real, very vivid, very amusing. Ernest put down the paper and helped her. There were the black rabbits and the red; there were the enemy rabbits and the friendly. There were the wood in which they lived and the outlying prairies and the swamp. Above all there was King Lappin, who, far from having only the one trick—that he twitched his nose—became as the days passed an animal of the greatest character. Rosalind was always finding new qualities in him. But above all he was a great hunter.

'And what,' said Rosalind, on the last day of the honeymoon, 'did the King do today?'

In fact they had been climbing all day; and she had worn a blister on her heel; but she did not mean that.

'Today,' said Ernest, twitching his nose as he bit the end off his cigar, 'he chased a hare.' He paused; struck a match, and twitched again.

'A woman hare,' he added.

'A white hare!' Rosalind exclaimed, as if she had been expecting this. 'Rather a small hare; silver grey; with big bright eyes?'

'Yes,' said Ernest, looking at her as she had looked at him, 'a smallish animal; with eyes popping out of her head and two little front paws dangling.' It was exactly how she sat, with her sewing dangling in her hands; and her eyes, that were so big and bright, were cetainly a little prominent.

'Ah, Lapinova,' Rosalind murmured.

'Is that what she's called?' said Ernest—'the real Rosalind?' He looked at her. He felt very much in love with her.

'Yes; that's what she's called,' said Rosalind. 'Lapinova.' And before they went to bed that night it was all settled. He was King Lappin; she was Queen Lapinova. They were the opposite of each other; he was bold and determined; she wary and undependable. He ruled over the busy world of rabbits; her world was a desolate, mysterious place, which she ranged mostly by moonlight. All the same their territories touched; they were King and Queen.

Thus when they came back from their honeymoon they possessed a private world, inhabited, save for the one white hare, entirely by rabbits. No one guessed that there was such a place, and that of course made it all the more amusing. It made them feel, more even than most young married couples, in league together against the rest of the world. Often they looked slyly at each other when people talked about rabbits and woods and traps and shooting. Or they winked furtively across the table when Aunt Mary said that she could never bear to see a hare in a dish—it looked so like a baby; or when John, Ernest's sporting brother, told them what price rabbits were fetching that autumn in Wiltshire, skins and all. Sometimes when they wanted a gamekeeper, or a poacher or a Lord of the Manor, they amused themselves by distributing the parts among their friends. Ernest's mother, Mrs Reginald Thorburn, for example, fitted the part of the Squire to perfection. But it was all secret—that was the point of it; nobody save themselves knew that such a world existed.

Without that world, how, Rosalind wondered that winter, could she have lived at all? For instance, there was the golden-wedding party, when all the Thorburns assembled at Porchester Terrace to celebrate the fiftieth anniversary of that union which had been so blessed—had it not produced Ernest Thorburn?—and so fruitful—had it not produced nine other sons and daughters into the bargain, many themselves married and also fruitful? She dreaded that party. But it was inevitable. As she walked upstairs she felt bitterly that she was an only child and an orphan at that; a mere drop among all those Thorburns assembled in the great drawing-room with the shiny satin wallpaper and the lustrous family portraits. The living Thorburns much resembled the painted; save that instead of painted lips they had real lips; out of which came jokes; jokes about schoolrooms, and how they had pulled the chair from under the governess; jokes about frogs and how they had put them between the virgin sheets of maiden ladies. As for herself, she had never even made an apple-pie bed. Holding her present in her hand she advanced toward her mother-in-law sumptuous in yellow satin; and toward her father-in-law decorated with a rich yellow carnation. All round them on tables and chairs there were golden tributes, some nestling in cotton wool; others branching resplendent—candlesticks; cigar boxes; chains, each stamped with the goldsmith's proof that it was solid gold, hall-marked, authentic. But her present was only a little pinchbeck box pierced with holes; an old sand caster, an eighteenth-century relic, once used to sprinkle sand over wet ink. Rather a senseless present she felt—in an age of blotting paper; and as she proffered it, she saw in front of her the stubby black handwriting in which her mother-in-law when they were engaged had expressed the hope that 'My son will make you happy.' No, she was not happy. Not at all happy. She looked at Ernest, straight as a ramrod with a nose like all the noses in the family portraits; a nose that never twitched at all.

Then they went down to dinner. She was half hidden by the great chrysanthemums that curled their red and gold petals into large tight balls. Everything was gold. A gold-edged card with gold initials intertwined recited the list of all the dishes that would be set one after another before them. She dipped her spoon in a plate of clear golden fluid. The raw white fog outside had been turned by the lamps into a golden mesh that blurred the edges of the plates and gave the pineapples a rough golden skin. Only she herself in her white wedding dress peering ahead of her with her prominent eyes seemed insoluble as an icicle.

As the dinner wore on, however, the room grew steamy with heat. Beads of perspiration stood out on the men's foreheads. She felt that her icicle was being turned to water. She was being melted; dispersed, dissolved into nothingness; and would soon faint. Then through the surge in her head and the din in her ears she heard a woman's voice exclaim, 'But they breed so!'

The Thorburns—yes; they breed so, she echoed; looking at all the round red faces that seemed doubled in the giddiness that overcame her; and magnified in the gold mist that enhaloed them. 'They breed so.' Then John bawled:

'Little devils! . . . Shoot 'em! Jump on 'em with big boots! That's the only way to deal with 'em . . . rabbits!'

At that word, that magic word, she revived. Peeping between the chrysanthemums she saw Ernest's nose twitch. It rippled, it ran with successive twitches. And at that a mysterious catastrophe befell the Thorburns. The golden table became a moor with the gorse in full bloom; the din of voices turned to one peal of lark's laughter ringing down from the sky. It was a blue sky—clouds passed slowly. And they had all been changed—the Thorburns. She looked at her father-in-law, a furtive little man with dyed moustaches. His foible was collecting things—seals, enamel boxes, trifles from eighteenth-century dressing tables which he hid in the drawers of his study from his wife. Now she saw him as he was—a poacher, stealing off with his coat bulging with pheasants and partridges to drop them stealthily into a three-legged pot in his smoky little cottage. That was her real father-in-law—a poacher. And Celia, the unmarried daughter, who always nosed out other people's secrets, the little things they wished to hide—she was a white ferret with pink eyes, and a nose clotted with earth from her horrid underground nosings and pokings. Slung round men's shoulders, in a net, and thrust down a hole—it was a pitiable life—Celia's; it was none of her fault. So she saw Celia. And then she looked at her mother-in-law—whom they dubbed The Squire. Flushed, coarse, a bully—she was all that, as she stood returning thanks, but now that Rosalind—that is Lapinova—saw her, she saw behind her the decayed family mansion, the plaster peeling off the walls, and heard her, with a sob in her voice, giving thanks to her children (who hated her) for a world that had ceased to exist. There was a sudden silence. They all stood with their glasses raised; they all drank; then it was over.

'Oh, King Lappin!' she cried as they went home together in the fog, 'if your nose hadn't twitched just at that moment, I should have been trapped!'

'But you're safe,' said King Lappin, pressing her paw.

'Quite safe,' she answered.

And they drove back through the Park, King and Queen of the marsh, of the mist, and of the gorse-scented moor.

Thus time passed; one year; two years of time. And on a winter's night, which happened by a coincidence to be the anniversary of the golden-wedding party—but Mrs Reginald Thorburn was dead; the house was to let; and there was only a caretaker in residence—Ernest came home from the office. They had a nice little home; half a house above a saddler's shop in South Kensington, not far from the Tube station. It was cold, with fog in the air, and Rosalind was sitting over the fire, sewing.

'What d'you think happened to me today?' she began as soon as he had settled himself down with his legs stretched to the blaze. 'I was crossing the stream when—'

'What stream?' Ernest interrupted her.

'The stream at the bottom, where our wood meets the black wood,' she explained.

Ernest looked completely blank for a moment.

'What the deuce are you talking about?' he asked.

'My dear Ernest!' she cried in dismay. 'King Lappin,' she added, dangling her little front paws in the firelight. But his nose did not twitch. Her hands—they turned to hands—clutched the stuff she was holding; her eyes popped half out of her head. It took him five minutes at least to change from Ernest Thorburn to King Lappin; and while she waited she felt a load on the back of her neck, as if somebody were about to wring it. At last he changed to King Lappin; his nose twitched; and they spent the evening roaming the woods much as usual.

But she slept badly. In the middle of the night she woke, feeling as if something strange had happened to her. She was stiff and cold. At last she turned on the light and looked at Ernest lying beside her. He was sound asleep. He snored. But even though he snored, his nose remained perfectly still. It looked as if it had never twitched at all. Was it possible that he was really Ernest; and that she was really married to Ernest? A vision of her mother-in-law's dining-room came before her; and there they sat, she and Ernest, grown old, under the engravings, in front of the sideboard . . . It was their golden-wedding day. She could not bear it.

'Lappin, King Lappin!' she whispered, and for a moment his nose seemed to twitch of its own accord. But he still slept. 'Wake up, Lappin, wake up!' she cried.

Ernest woke; and seeing her sitting bolt upright beside him he asked:

'What's the matter?'

'I thought my rabbit was dead!' she whimpered. Ernest was angry.

'Don't talk such rubbish, Rosalind,' he said. 'Lie down and go to sleep.'

He turned over. In another moment he was sound asleep and snoring.

But she could not sleep. She lay curled up on her side of the bed, like a hare in its form. She had turned out the light, but the street lamp lit the ceiling faintly, and the trees outside made a lacy network over it as if there were a shadowy grove on the ceiling in which she wandered, turning, twisting, in and out, round and round, hunting, being hunted, hearing the bay of hounds and horns; flying, escaping . . . until the maid drew the blinds and brought their early tea.

Next day she could settle to nothing. She seemed to have lost something. She felt as if her body had shrunk; it had grown small, and black and hard. Her joints seemed stiff too, and when she looked in the glass, which she did several times as she wandered about the flat, her eyes seemed to burst out of her head, like currants in a bun. The rooms also seemed to have shrunk. Large pieces of furniture jutted out at odd angles and she found herself knocking against them. At last she put on her hat and went out. She walked along the Cromwell Road; and every room she passed and peered into seemed to be a dining-room where people sat eating under steel engravings, with thick yellow lace curtains, and mahogany sideboards. At last she reached the Natural History Museum; she used to like it when she was a child. But the first thing she saw when she went in was a stuffed hare standing on sham snow with pink glass eyes. Somehow it made her shiver all over. Perhaps it would be better when dusk fell. She went home and sat over the fire, without a light, and tried to imagine that she was out alone on a moor; and there was a stream rushing; and beyond the stream a dark wood. But she could get no further than the stream. At last she squatted down on the bank on the wet grass, and sat crouched in her chair, with her hands dangling empty, and her eyes glazed, like glass eyes, in the firelight. Then there was the crack of a gun. . . . She started as if she had been shot. It was only Ernest, turning his key in the door. She waited, trembling. He came in and switched on the light. There he stood tall, handsome, rubbing his hands that were red with cold.

'Sitting in the dark?' he said.

'Oh, Ernest, Ernest!' she cried, starting up in her chair.

'Well, what's up now?' he asked briskly, warming his hands at the fire.

'It's Lapinova . . .' she faltered, glancing wildly at him out of her great startled eyes. 'She's gone, Ernest. I've lost her!'

Ernest frowned. He pressed his lips tight together. 'Oh, that's what's up, is it?' he said, smiling rather grimly at his wife. For ten seconds he stood there, silent; and she waited, feeling hands tightening at the back of her neck.

'Yes,' he said at length. 'Poor Lapinova . . .' He straightened his tie at the looking-glass over the mantelpiece.

'Caught in a trap,' he said, 'killed,' and sat down and read the newspaper.

So that was the end of that marriage.

Edith Wharton

Atrophy

I

Nora Frenway settled down furtively in her corner of the Pullman and, as the express plunged out of the Grand Central Station, wondered at herself for being where she was. The porter came along. 'Ticket?' 'Westover.' She had instinctively lowered her voice and glanced about her. But neither the porter nor her nearest neighbours—fortunately none of them known to her—seemed in the least surprised or interested by the statement that she was travelling to Westover.

Yet what an earth-shaking announcement it was! Not that she cared, now; not that anything mattered except the one overwhelming fact which had convulsed her life, hurled her out of her easy velvet-lined rut, and flung her thus naked to the public scrutiny. . . . Cautiously, again, she glanced about her to make doubly sure that there was no one, absolutely no one, in the Pullman whom she knew by sight.

Her life had been so carefully guarded, so inwardly conventional in a world where all the outer conventions were tottering, that no one had ever known she had a lover. No one—of that she was absolutely sure. All the circumstances of the case had made it necessary that she should conceal her real life—her only real life—from everyone about her; from her half-invalid irascible husband, his prying envious sisters, and the terrible monumental old chieftainess, her mother-in-law, before whom all the family quailed and humbugged and fibbed and fawned.

What nonsense to pretend that nowadays, even in big cities, in the world's greatest social centres, the severe old-fashioned standards had given place to tolerance, laxity and ease! You took up the morning paper, and you read of girl bandits, movie-star divorces, 'hold-ups' at balls, murder and suicide and elopement, and a general welter of disjointed disconnected impulses and appetites; then you turned your eyes onto your own daily life, and found yourself as cribbed and cabined, as beset by vigilant family eyes, observant friends, all sorts of embodied standards, as any white-muslin novel heroine of the 'sixties!

In a different way, of course. To the casual eye Mrs Frenway herself might have seemed as free as any of the young married women of her group. Poker playing, smoking, cocktail drinking, dancing, painting, short skirts, bobbed hair and the rest—when had these been denied to her? If by any outward sign she had differed too markedly from her kind—lengthened her skirts, refused to play for money, let her hair grow, or ceased to make up—her husband would have been the first to notice it and to say: 'Are you ill? What's the matter? How queer you look! What's the sense of making yourself conspicuous?' For he and his kind had adopted all the old inhibitions and sanctions, blindly transferring them to a new ritual, as the receptive Romans did when strange gods were brought into their temples . . .

The train had escaped from the ugly fringes of the city, and the soft spring landscape was gliding past her: glimpses of green lawns, budding hedges, pretty irregular roofs, and miles and miles of alluring tarred roads slipping away into mystery. How often she had dreamed of dashing off down an unknown road with Christopher!

Not that she was a woman to be awed by the conventions. She knew she wasn't. She had always taken their measure, smiled at them—and conformed. On account of poor George Frenway, to begin with. Her husband, in a sense, was a man to be pitied; his weak health, his bad temper, his unsatisfied vanity, all made him a rather forlornly comic figure. But it was chiefly on account of the two children that she had always resisted the temptation to do anything reckless. The least self-betrayal would have been the end of everything. Too many eyes were watching her, and her husband's family was so strong, so united—when there was anybody for them to hate—and at all times so influential, that she would have been defeated at every point, and her husband would have kept the children.

At the mere thought she felt herself on the brink of an abyss. 'The children are my religion,' she had once said to herself; and she had no other.

Yet here she was on her way to Westover. . . Oh, what did it matter now? That was the worst of it—it was too late for anything between her and Christopher to matter! She was sure he was dying. The way in which his cousin, Gladys Brincker, had blurted it out the day before at Kate Salmer's dance: 'You didn't know—poor Kit? Thought you and he were such pals! Yes; awfully bad, I'm afraid. Return of the old trouble! I know there've been two consultations—they had Knowlton down. They say there's not much hope; and nobody but that forlorn frightened Jane mounting guard . . .'

Poor Christopher! His sister Jane Aldis, Nora suspected, forlorn and frightened as she was, had played in his life a part nearly as dominant as Frenway and the children in Nora's. Loyally, Christopher always pretended that she didn't; talked of her indulgently as 'poor Jenny'. But didn't she, Nora, always think of her husband as 'poor George'? Jane Aldis, of course, was much less self-assertive, less demanding, than George Frenway; but perhaps for that very reason she would appeal all the more to a man's compassion. And somehow, under her unobtrusive air, Nora had—on the rare occasions when they met—imagined that Miss Aldis was watching and drawing her inferences. But then Nora always felt, where Christopher was concerned, as if her breast were a pane of glass through which her trembling palpitating heart could be seen as plainly as holy viscera in a reliquary. Her sober after-thought was that Jane Aldis was just a dowdy self-effacing old maid whose life was filled to the brim by looking after the Westover place for her brother, and seeing that the fires were lit and the rooms full of flowers when he brought down his friends for a weekend.

Ah, how often he had said to Nora: 'If I could have you to myself for a weekend at Westover'—quite as if it were the easiest thing imaginable, as far as as his arrangements were concerned! And they had even pretended to discuss how it could be done. But somehow she fancied he said it because he knew that the plan, for her, was about as feasible as a weekend in the moon. And in reality her only visits to Westover had been made in the company of her husband, and that of other friends, two or three times, at the beginning . . . For after that she wouldn't. It was three years now since she had been there.

Gladys Brincker, in speaking of Christopher's illness, had looked at Nora queerly, as though suspecting something. But no—what nonsense! No one had ever suspected Nora Frenway. Didn't she know what her friends said of her? 'Nora? No more temperament than a lamp-post. Always buried in her books . . . Never very attractive to men, in spite of her looks.' Hadn't she said that of other women, who perhaps, in secret, like herself . . .?

The train was slowing down as it approached a station. She sat up with a jerk and looked at her wrist-watch. It was half-past two, the station was Ockham; the next would be Westover. In less than an hour she would be under his roof, Jane Aldis would be receiving her in that low panelled room full of books, and she would be saying—what would she be saying?

She had gone over their conversation so often that she knew not only her own part in it but Miss Aldis's by heart. The first moments would of course be painful, difficult; but then a great wave of emotion, breaking down the barriers between the two anxious women, would fling them together. She wouldn't have to say much, to explain; Miss Aldis would just take her by the hand and lead her upstairs to the room.

That room! She shut her eyes, and remembered other rooms where she and he had been together in their joy and their strength . . . No, not that; she must not think of that now. For the man she had met in those other rooms was dying; the man she was going to was some one so different from that other man that it was like a profanation to associate their images . . . And yet the man she was going to was her own Christopher, the one who had lived in her soul; and how his soul must be needing hers, now that it hung alone on the dark brink! As if anything else mattered at such a moment! She neither thought nor cared what Jane Aldis might say or suspect; she wouldn't have cared if the Pullman had been full of prying acquaintances, or if George and all George's family had got in at that last station.

She wouldn't have cared a fig for any of them. Yet at the same moment she remembered having felt glad that her old governess, whom she used to go and see twice a year, lived at Ockham—so that if George did begin to ask questions, she could always say: 'Yes, I went to see poor old Fraülein; she's absolutely crippled now. I shall have to give her a Bath chair. Could you get me a catalogue of prices?' There wasn't a precaution she hadn't thought of—and now she was ready to scatter them all to the winds . . .

Westover—*Junction!*

She started up and pushed her way out of the train. All the

people seemed to be obstructing her, putting bags and suitcases in her way. And the express stopped for only two minutes. Suppose she should be carried on to Albany?

Westover Junction was a growing place, and she was fairly sure there would be a taxi at the station. There was one—she just managed to get to it ahead of a travelling man with a sample case and a new straw hat. As she opened the door a smell of damp hay and bad tobacco greeted her. She sprang in and gasped: 'To Oakfield. You know? Mr Aldis's place near Westover.'

II

It began exactly as she had expected. A surprised parlour maid—why surprised?—showed her into the low panelled room that was so full of his presence, his books, his pipes, his terrier dozing on the shabby rug. The parlour maid said she would go and see if Miss Aldis could come down. Nora wanted to ask if she were with her brother—and how he was. But she found herself unable to speak the words. She was afraid her voice might tremble. And why should she question the parlour maid, when in a moment, she hoped, she was to see Miss Aldis?

The woman moved away with a hushed step—the step which denotes illness in the house. She did not immediately return, and the interval of waiting in that room, so strange yet so intimately known, was a new torture to Nora. It was unlike anything she had imagined. The writing table with his scattered pens and letters was more than she could bear. His dog looked at her amicably from the hearth, but made no advances; and though she longed to stroke him, to let her hand rest where Christopher's had rested, she dared not for fear he should bark and disturb the peculiar hush of that dumb watchful house. She stood in the window and looked out at the budding shrubs and the bulbs pushing up through the swollen earth.

'This way, please.'

Her heart gave a plunge. Was the woman actually taking her upstairs to his room? Her eyes filled, she felt herself swept forward on a great wave of passion and anguish . . . But she was only being led across the hall into a stiff lifeless drawing-room—the kind that bachelors get an upholsterer to do for them, and then turn their backs on forever. The chairs and sofas looked at her with an undisguised hostility, and then resumed the moping expression common to furniture in unfrequented rooms. Even the spring sun slanting in through the windows on the pale marquetry of a useless table seemed to bring no heat or light with it.

The rush of emotion subsided, leaving in Nora a sense of emptiness and apprehension. Supposing Jane Aldis should look at her with the cold eyes of this resentful room? She began to wish she had been friendlier and more cordial to Jane Aldis in the past. In her intense desire to conceal from everyone the tie between herself and Christopher she had avoided all show of interest in his family; and perhaps, as she now saw, excited curiosity by her very affection of indifference.

No doubt it would have been more politic to establish an intimacy with Jane Aldis; and today, how much easier and more natural her position would have been! Instead of groping about—as she was again doing—for an explanation of her visit, she could have said: 'My dear, I came to see if there was anything in the world I could do to help you.'

She heard a hesitating step in the hall—a hushed step like the parlour maid's—and saw Miss Aldis pause near the half-open door. How old she had grown since their last meeting! Her hair, untidily pinned up, was gray and lanky. Her eyelids, always reddish, were swollen and heavy, her face sallow with anxiety and fatigue. It was odd to have feared so defenseless an adversary. Nora, for an instant, had the impression that Miss Aldis had wavered in the hall to catch a glimpse of her, take the measure of the situation. But perhaps she had only stopped to push back a strand of hair as she passed in front of a mirror.

'Mrs Frenway—how good of you!' She spoke in a cool detached voice, as if her real self were elsewhere and she were simply an automaton wound up to repeat the familiar forms of hospitality. 'Do sit down', she said.

She pushed forward one of the sulky armchairs, and Nora seated herself stiffly, her hand-bag clutched on her knee, in the self-conscious attitude of a country caller.

'I came—'

'So good of you,' Miss Aldis repeated. 'I had no idea you were in this part of the world. Not the slightest.'

Was it a lead she was giving? Or did she know everything, and wish to extend to her visitor the decent shelter of a pretext? Or was she really so stupid—

'You're staying with the Brinckers, I suppose. Or the Northrups? I remember the last time you came to lunch here you motored over with Mr Frenway from the Northrups'. That must have been two years ago, wasn't it?' She put the question with an almost sprightly show of interest.

'No—three years,' said Nora, mechanically.

'Was it? As long ago as that? Yes—you're right. That was the year we moved the big fern-leaved beech. I remember Mr Frenway was interested in tree moving, and I took him out to show him where the tree had come from. He *is* interested in tree moving, isn't he?'

'Oh, yes; very much.'

'We had those wonderful experts down to do it. "Tree doctors", they call themselves. They have special appliances, you know. The tree is growing better than it did before they moved it. But I suppose you've done a great deal of transplanting on Long Island.'

'Yes. My husband does a good deal of transplanting.'

'So you've come over from the Northrups'? I didn't even know they were down at Maybrook yet. I see so few people.'

'No; not from the Northrups'.'

'Oh—the Brinckers'? Hal Brincker was here yesterday, but he didn't tell me you were staying there.'

Nora hesitated. 'No. The fact is, I have an old governess who lives at Ockham. I go and see her sometimes. And so I came on to Westover—' She paused, and Miss Aldis interrogated brightly: 'Yes?' as if prompting her in a lesson she was repeating.

'Because I saw Gladys Brincker the other day, and she told me that your brother was ill.'

'Oh.' Miss Aldis gave the syllable its full weight, and set a full stop after it. Her eyebrows went up, as if in a faint surprise. The silent room seemed to close in on the two speakers, listening. A resuscitated fly buzzed against the sunny window pane. 'Yes; he's ill,' she conceded at length.

'I'm so sorry; I . . . he has been . . . such a friend of ours . . . so long . . .'

'Yes; I've often heard him speak of you and Mr Frenway.' Another full stop sealed this announcement. ('No, she knows nothing,' Nora thought.) 'I remember his telling me that he thought a great deal of Mr Frenway's advice about moving trees. But then you see our soil is so different from yours. I suppose Mr Frenway has had your soil analyzed?'

'Yes; I think he has.'

'Christopher's always been a great gardener.'

'I hope he's not—not very ill? Gladys seemed to be afraid—'

'Illness is always something to be afraid of, isn't it?'

'But you're not—I mean, not anxious . . . not seriously?'

'It's so kind of you to ask. The doctors seem to think there's no particular change since yesterday.'

'And yesterday?'

'Well, yesterday they seemed to think there might be.'

'A change, you mean?'

'Well, yes.'

'A change—I hope for the better?'

'They said they weren't sure; they couldn't say.'

The fly's buzzing had become so insistent in the still room that it seemed to be going on inside of Nora's head, and in the confusion of sound she found it more and more difficult to regain a lead in the conversation. And the minutes were slipping by, and upstairs the man she loved was lying. It was absurd and lamentable to make a pretense of keeping up this twaddle. She would cut through it, no matter how.

'I suppose you've had—a consultation?'

'Oh, yes; Dr Knowlton's been down twice.'

'And what does he—'

'Well; he seems to agree with the others.'

There was another pause, and then Miss Aldis glanced out of the window. 'Why, who's that driving up?' she enquired. 'Oh, it's your taxi, I suppose, coming up the drive.'

'Yes. I got out at the gate.' She dared not add: 'For fear the noise might disturb him.'

'I hope you had no difficulty in finding a taxi at the Junction?'

'Oh, no; I had no difficulty.'

'I think it was so kind of you to come—not even knowing whether you'd find a carriage to bring you out all this way. And I know how busy you are. There's always so much going on in town, isn't there, even at this time of year?'

'Yes; I suppose so. But your brother—'

'Oh, of course my brother won't be up to any sort of gaiety; not for a long time.'

'A long time; no. But you do hope—'

'I think everybody about a sick bed ought to hope, don't you?'

'Yes; but I mean—'

Nora stood up suddenly, her brain whirling. Was it possible that she and that woman had sat thus facing each other for half an hour, piling up this conversational rubbish, while upstairs, out of sight, the truth, the meaning of their two lives hung on the frail thread of one man's intermittent pulse? She could not imagine why she felt so powerless and baffled. What had a woman who was young and handsome and beloved to fear from a dowdy and insignificant old maid? Why, the antagonism that these very graces and superiorities would create in the other's breast, especially if she knew they were all spent in charming the being on whom her life depended. Weak in herself, but powerful from her circumstances, she stood at bay on the ruins of all that Nora had ever loved. 'How she must hate me—and I never thought of it,' mused Nora, who had imagined that she had thought of everything where her relation to her lover was concerned. Well, it was too late now to remedy her omission; but at least she must assert herself, must say something to save the precious minutes that remained and break through the stifling web of platitudes which her enemy's tremulous hand was weaving around her.

'Miss Aldis—I must tell you—I came to see—'

'How he was? So very friendly of you. He would appreciate it, I know. Christopher is so devoted to his friends.'

'But you'll—you'll tell him that I—'

'Of course. That you came on purpose to ask about him. As soon as he's a little bit stronger.'

'But I mean—now?'

'Tell him now that you called to enquire? How good of you to think of that too! Perhaps tomorrow morning, if he's feeling a little bit brighter . . .'

Nora felt her lips drying as if a hot wind had parched them. They would hardly move. 'But now—now—today.' Her voice sank to a whisper as she added: 'Isn't he conscious?'

'Oh, yes; he's conscious; he's perfectly conscious.' Miss Aldis emphasized this with another of her long pauses. 'He shall certainly be told that you called.' Suddenly she too got up from her seat and moved toward the window. 'I must seem dreadfully inhospitable, not even offering you a cup of tea. But the fact is, perhaps I ought to tell you—if you're thinking of getting back to Ockham this afternoon there's only one train that stops at the Junction after three o'clock.' She pulled out an old-fashioned enamelled watch with a wreath of roses about the dial, and turned almost apologetically to Mrs Frenway. 'You ought to be at the station by four o'clock at the latest; and with one of those old Junction taxis . . . I'm so sorry; I know I must appear to be driving you away.' A wan smile drew up her pale lips.

Nora knew just how long the drive from Westover Junction had taken, and understood that she was being delicately dismissed. Dismissed from life—from hope—even from the dear anguish of filling her eyes for the last time with the face which was the one face in the world to her! ('But then she does know everything,' she thought.)

'I mustn't make you miss your train, you know.'

'Miss Aldis, is he—has he seen any one?' Nora hazarded in a painful whisper.

'Seen any one? Well, there've been all the doctors—five of them! And then the nurses. Oh, but you mean friends, of course. Naturally.' She seemed to reflect. 'Hal Brincker, yes; he saw our cousin Hal yesterday—but not for very long.'

Hal Brincker! Nora knew what Christopher thought of his Brincker cousins—blighting bores, one and all of them, he always said. And in the extremity of his illness the one person privileged to see him had been—Hal Brincker! Nora's eyes filled; she had to turn them away for a moment from Miss Aldis's timid inexorable face.

'But today?' she finally brought out.

'No. Today he hasn't seen any one; not yet.' The two women stood and looked at each other; then Miss Aldis glanced uncertainly about the room. 'But couldn't I— Yes, I ought at least to have asked you if you won't have a cup of tea. So stupid of me! There might still be time. I never take tea myself.' Once more she referred anxiously to her watch. 'The water is sure to be boiling, because the nurses' tea is just being taken up. If you'll excuse me a moment I'll go and see.'

'Oh, no; no!' Nora drew in a quick sob. 'How can you? . . . I mean, I don't want any. . .'

Miss Aldis looked relieved. 'Then I shall be quite sure that you won't reach the station too late.' She waited again, and then held out a long stony hand. 'So kind—I shall never forget your kindness. Coming all this way, when you might so easily have telephoned from town. Do please tell Mr Frenway how I appreciated it. You will remember to tell him, won't you? He sent me such an interesting collection of pamphlets about tree moving. I should like him to know how much I feel his kindness in letting you come.' She paused again, and pulled in her lips so that they became a narrow thread, a mere line drawn across her face by a ruler. 'But, no; I won't trouble you; I'll write to thank him myself.' Her hand ran out to an electric bell on the nearest table. It shrilled through the silence, and the parlour maid appeared with a stage-like promptness.

'The taxi, please? Mrs Frenway's taxi.'

The room became silent again. Nora thought: 'Yes; she knows everything.' Miss Aldis peeped for the third time at her watch, and then uttered a slight unmeaning laugh. The blue-bottle banged against the window and once more it seemed to Nora that its sonorities were reverberating inside her head. They were deafeningly mingled there with the explosion of the taxi's reluctant start-up and its convulsed halt at the front door. The driver sounded his horn as if to summon her.

'He's afraid too that you'll be late!' Miss Aldis smiled.

The smooth slippery floor of the hall seemed to Nora to extend away in front of her for miles. At its far end she saw a little tunnel of light, a miniature maid, a toy taxi. Somehow she managed to travel the distance that separated her from them, though her bones ached with weariness, and at every step she seemed to be lifting a leaden weight. The taxi was close to her now, its door was open, she was getting in. The same smell of damp hay and bad tobacco greeted her. She saw her hostess standing on the threshold. 'To the Junction, driver—back to the Junction,' she heard Miss Aldis say. The taxi began to roll toward the gate. As it moved away Nora heard Miss Aldis calling: 'I'll be sure to write and thank Mr Frenway.'

Kay Boyle

Natives Don't Cry

We went to Austria that summer. It was the time of year when hay-fever made father's eyes cry all day, and in the mountains there was no sign of dust, there was almost frost in the evenings, and if he saw any goldenrod growing he could take the long way round across the snow. We went to Austria, driving there from England, and Miss Henly came to us the night before we left. She was not very pleased to come, but it was only for the month, so she came as a gift to us. She did not believe she would like us because of the hotel where we were in London and because of the colour of mother's hair. She did not say these things in the same words to us, but she said them in other ways so that we knew. But the first night she came to us there was a Lord and Lady to dinner. They were an Irish Lord and Lady, brother and sister, twins. They were both sixteen. Miss Henly did not say much to them at table, but it was easy to see she was satisfied they were there.

The hotel belonged to Mrs Lewis, and she stood at the top of the stairway smoking cigarettes, knowing at once when you came in whether she'd like you or whether she wouldn't. There was a picture of the King, signed with his name, in her parlour, and she used to sit there talking to mother about the royalty. She said the Mother Queen wore a plaster mask on her face when she saw she was getting old; she couldn't bear the sight of her features falling to pieces in the glass. And Francis said:

'What did she do with the max when she had to laugh at something funny?' Mrs Lewis said: 'She never saw anything funny, never in all her life.'

She was always a little bit drunk when she received at Court, and one day they unveiled a statue for her, and the Mother Queen hiccoughed too much to speak the words she had to say, and they had to play the music.

'Ha, ha!' said Mrs Lewis after everything. 'What would your little girls like to see in London?'

'They'd like to see a Lord and a Lady,' mother said.

So Mrs Lewis invited the Lord and the Lady. Miss Henly came

in time to put Francis to bed and then she took us down to dinner. The Lord and Lady were waiting in the hall. The Lady wore a green dress, and she had long straight red hair, and because they both had freckles like our own we could scarcely look in their faces for sorrow.

'I don't believe they were a Lord and a Lady at all,' my sister said when we were in the room undressing.

'My dear child,' said Miss Henly, 'as you have doubtless never so much as laid eye on a titled Englishman, I daresay you have no reason to believe that these young people were impostors. I thought them very well-bred.'

'I know they couldn't have been a Lord and a Lady,' my sister said. 'They had freckles.'

'Nevertheless,' said Miss Henly, folding our dresses sharply into the open suitcase, 'I have no doubt they were, and I daresay I am a better judge of such things than a little girl who has always lived across the water.'

Miss Henly had a thin coat and a wide felt hat that almost escaped from her head when we drove. She had to hold it with her two hands, riding in the back between us. She was not dressed for driving, you could feel the bones in her legs shaking, but she was very vain of everything she had. Mother put a fur jacket in the back of the car at Southampton and said:

'If you feel the wind, just put this around you, Miss Henly.'

There was a ring of blue around Miss Henly's mouth and she had no gloves on her hands, but she said:

'Oh, I'm not accustomed to bundling up in season and out! In England we don't take our winter things out quite so early, you know. I would be very glad to know,' said Miss Henly, looking severely at mother, 'if it doesn't seem too presumptuous, where we may be going. It's on account of my mail, of course. I haven't anything else but my letters,' she said, and she looked at us all as if we were strangers to her. 'I have nothing else to live for now.'

We thought she was fifty because she had no colour in her face, and her hair was pinned back in a knot in her neck, and it was grey near the ears. Father took her passport on the French side, and when he came back to the car he said:

'I think you're much too young to be leaving home, Miss Henly.'

He had a soft voice, and whenever he smiled he seemed shy and uneasy to us.

'Miss Henly's almost as young as you girls,' said father, and we saw the colour run into her cheeks. 'She's only twenty-five!'

'How old did you think I was?' she said, and Francis said:

'A hundred.'

But he was so young there was nothing to say to him. It was just a number he had heard somewhere.

She had been born in Burma, she was a civil servant's daughter, and she had no patience for the ways of any children except the children she and her brothers had been. In the hotels at night she took their pictures from her bag and set them on the bureau. She spoke of them all, and of the places they had lived, as if these things were clearer seen than any others. And she spoke of them only a little at a time, and not too often, as if they were too good to be given quite away.

She did not say these things or anything like them to mother, but if mother was having her hair done over in Paris or Strasbourg or Munich, she said them to father and to us where we were having tea. She looked at mother in mirrors when mother was putting a dress on or changing her hat, but she never told her about Rudolpho although she wrote to him every day. She said to mother:

'Where would be a safe place to have mail sent to? I have to know about my letters.'

And mother would be looking at the side of her face through the hand-glass in the mirror, and she would say:

'Oh, I'm sure the American Express or Thomas Cook would do, don't you?'

But mother never said which city because she scarcely ever knew which country she was travelling in. She could not remember the capitals of Europe even. She could only remember people's faces and whether they liked Picasso. So Miss Henly did not say to her:

'When I was a little girl my father never could shave in the morning unless I was curled up on the table where his basin of water stood!' She gave such gasps and whispers of laughter while she spoke of herself to us that sometimes her words were lost for ever. Her cheeks squeezed up red and the tears of laughter seemed ready to fall from her eyes, and the glass with the cocktail in it shook in her hand. 'I always had to hold his brush for him, imagine!' she cried out. 'He used to make a moustache for me out of the lather—' She said more after this, but she laughed so wildly that we never made it out.

Her family was dead, even the brothers, so there was no one left to write to, but there was Rudolpho. He was a name written out very big across an envelope at night. Father said:

'If your young man likes to read so much, Miss Henly, I think he must be quite literary.'

Whenever we had tea with father, we had it beside the bar where he sat because he didn't like the drinks in other places. And after a week, Miss Henly forgot the tea. She sat at the table with us, but she had a cocktail and potato-chips instead.

'Oh, he's not exactly that!' said Miss Henly, laughing. 'He's foreign, of course, but so many people are these days that one gets accustomed to it. He's been ten years in London, too, so you'd scarcely know. I don't know what he's doing to cheer himself up, poor thing. He must feel like a duck out of water. He wanted me to go, of course, and he told me not to hurry back, but I know perfectly well what's going on inside him!'

'You'll probably have mail waiting in Salzburg,' said father. 'What about another cocktail?'

'Oh, I scarcely ever drink!' cried Miss Henly.

'But these are small,' said father.

'Yes,' said Miss Henly. 'That's quite true.' She saw mother coming in through the swinging-door and the smile went sharp on her lips, and she said:

'Do sit up, girls! Francis, take your spoon out of your cup! One would never think I'd been with you over a week now. I'd hoped to see much more improvement.'

'Well, anyway, they've learned to say lef-tenant,' father said.

Father went to the post office the first thing in Salzburg. He took the passports in his hand, and when he came back he was carrying a great many things. There were letters from America, and there was mother's picture playing golf in *The Tatler*, but there wasn't anything, there wasn't even a post card for Miss Henly. She did not say anything. She sat quite still on the terrace of the coffee-house on the Mozart Place, and the sun was shining for a change. She looked straight into the sun, past father, smiling at what he said. He had said:

'There wasn't anything for you today, Miss Henly. Better luck tomorrow.'

Mother opened her letters, and father opened his, and we did not look at Miss Henly. No one lifted their eyes, and no one felt easy in the silence at the table. Miss Henly sat with her cup of coffee and cream in front of her, and because she did not speak there was nothing for anyone to say. But Francis said:

'Maybe nobody likes you,' and mother said quickly:

'Would you like to wander around a bit by yourself this afternoon, Miss Henly? There's quite a lot to see here. I'll take the children out to the Grand Duke's palace to see Elizabeth Duncan. You might go and see Mozart's skull.'

'Mozart's skull!' cried Miss Henly. 'How disgusting!'

In the evening she was in the room still, she was sitting there in the half-darkness when we came home. She had been writing a letter by the window and she was putting the name on the envelope when we came in the door. Father came with us, and Miss Henly said:

'Where would the best place to change English money be?'

Miss Henly stood, very small and thin, with her hand holding to the back of the chair. She wore high black shoes, and a blouse, and a skirt that had no year or season, wide at the knees and dark. She had never worn anything else but this, no matter how the weather changed.

'Look here,' said father. 'If you'd like your salary in advance you just tell me. I can pay it now or whenever you want it just as you like.'

'Not at all,' said Miss Henly. 'I had no intention of asking for anything in advance. I just happened to find a few shillings in my pocket and thought I would change them here. I only want to buy a stamp,' she said.

She did not like the seeds in the bread, or the cream in the coffee. There wasn't a thing she could eat in the breweries, because of the thickness of the meat and the smell of beer in the place. The way of eating frankfurters in the fingers, and the linen suits the women wore were things she could never get over. She couldn't believe anyone could have so little care for the kind of figure they cut.

'Imagine going off on your honeymoon with your husband's head shaved like a convict's!' she said to father, having a drink in the Mirabell garden in the afternoon. 'I'll never forget these frightful heads if I live to be a hundred!'

'I'm afraid you favour the long-haired, artistic type,' said father. 'Let's try their Side-cars.'

'Oh, I never drink more than one, if that!' said Miss Henly. 'Of course, I've seen some of the funniest photographs of this young man in England I've spoken of before. When he was in the war, they got things, you know, things in their heads, if you can imagine it. They had to shave the entire regiment's heads! But he wouldn't let them touch his beard, and he did look too silly! He had a little bit of a beard, he was only twenty-one then—' Miss Henly's voice was lost in gasps of laughter, and father, although he had never seen the photographs, opened his mouth and laughed as well as he could. Miss Henly picked up the second cocktail, and suddenly she stopped laughing. 'I was wondering about something this morning,' she said. 'I was going to ask you, that is. The next time you do go to the post office, would you mind asking if there are any letters for Mary Gwendolyn, or for Gwendolyn Henly. My passport has my name down simply Mary Henly. But some of my friends were in the habit of calling me by my middle name, Gwendolyn. This friend I've mentioned to you before always called me that.'

At the end of the week we went away, we went up the valley into the mountains, and Miss Henly rode in the back with us. She held Francis on her lap, and she closed her eyes and told us of the places she had been. There were eight natives struck by lightning in the hills in Burma one night in the summer, and she had seen them in the morning when the others carried them down. Their bodies were burned as black as logs in the fire.

'What did you give them to make them stop crying?' Francis said.

'Natives don't cry,' said Miss Henly. 'They don't feel things the way other people do.'

It was cold climbing and father stopped the car for a glass of wine in a country tavern. We all went in and sat down by the stove, and mother and father and Miss Henly drank a pitcher of red, hot wine.

'How do you like Austria, Miss Henly?' mother said. 'This is Austria, isn't it?'

'Oh, it's very like the country in Burma, you know,' said Miss

Henly.'I was telling the children, I've a friend who has a little car of his own. He drives it all over England. I told him we would be driving around Salzburg. It would be a joke, wouldn't it, if he suddenly turned up on the road?'

'Perhaps he's going to surprise you by coming right over!' said father. Miss Henly's face squeezed up with laughter.

'It would be just like him to!' she said. 'I'll never forget the time we were asked to a fancy-dress party. He dressed up the same as two friends of his did, and I never knew until the party was over and everybody unmasked that I'd been dancing with somebody else all evening. He had got tired,' said Miss Henly, 'and gone home early.'

'That was a good joke,' said mother.

Father said: 'Have a little more wine.'

'Oh, I never take much,' said Miss Henly, watching him fill her glass up. 'If this friend I was speaking of did happen along the children would have a wonderful time with him. He's like a child himself,' she said, and she began to gasp with laughter. 'He'd be down on his hands and knees all the time playing with Francis if he were here.'

'Francis,' said mother, 'please get up off your hands and knees, darling.'

'If I get off my knees can I stay on my hands?' said Francis.

Day after day Miss Henly walked us slowly over the hillsides, in the rain even, with our thick boots on, and on cloudy windy days. Mother and father went up mountains together, escaping the goldenrod and the cut hay lying wet in the fields. Whenever we went back to the hotel, there would be letters on the table, but there would never be anything for Miss Henly.

'Nobody writes to you, Mrs Hen,' Francis said. He was proud because he had two cards one day from people we scarcely knew. He had a card with a cat's head on it, and when you pressed it the cat cried. And the other was of a man in a bathing suit, and when you undid the back of his trousers all the views of Venice opened out.

'My dear child,' said Miss Henly. '"Fools' names and fools' faces",' she said. 'As a matter of fact, Francis, if I wanted my letters sent here I could easily tell people to write to me here, couldn't I. So you see how silly you are.'

But we never saw her writing any more letters. She did not even speak of Rudolpho. She would sit reading books, that mother gave her, and she never found any of them very good, not so good as the books she had read somewhere else at some other time.

'Always the same old thing,' she said, and she gave them back to mother. 'Always love, love, love, and whether the beautiful girl will, or whether the handsome hero won't succumb! It's just a bit tiresome I think, you know.'

Mother and father put their feet out by the fire and mother said Miss Henly wasn't a good thing for the children even if she was leaving so soon. She said it was the worst thing to have this for every meal with you, this pall, this bitterness, this dead, unspoken sorrow. What could we give her to take away her silence, and her sharpness, and her grieving face? In a little while father said:

'What do you think if I should be Rudolpho? He's been an absolute skunk to her. I'd like to give him a piece of my mind. He probably took every penny she made from her, and now that she's down and out he's through with her. Anyway, I could write letters to her, I could typewrite them and sign them Rudolpho. I could tell her how much I miss her. They wouldn't have to be long.'

'How could you possibly get them mailed?' said mother putting the bright clear red on her fingernails.

'I could have them mailed from Innsbruck,' said father. 'I could tell her I couldn't stand England without her. I could tell her I'm going absolutely mad.'

'That much would be true anyway,' said mother.

In the morning, father and mother took us part way up a mountain. We were going to the first hut underneath the glacier, because anything else was too far. We left very early, while it was dark still, and we would be back late, in time for supper. Going up we would take it very easy, and we would not speak much, for you needed all the breath in your body for climbing. But coming down we could run as we liked and pick gentians and forget-me-nots all the way.

So we climbed quietly, very silent, my sister and I, listening to mother and father talking to each other ahead. It was growing light when we reached a plateau where the stream spread out and made soft, marshy ground, and at the far end of this we saw a herd of horses standing. They stood with their heads laid across each other's necks, a great many of them, dark and glossy in the early morning, with their long tails softly brushing across each other's flanks.

They did not move until we were near the centre of the field, and then they seemed to see us quickly, as if it were a game they were playing, and they broke apart and a few of them cried out in high clear voices. The largest horse had started towards us, her head down, her nostrils spread, her tail arched out behind. The others scattered across the end of the field, and then they wheeled and swung to the heels of their leader who was coming fast, pounding over a trail as if for water, following the smell of it hard to where we stood. Behind her came the others, younger and wilder, shouldering each other and rearing in their haste.

Mother said: 'Get behind me, girls. I never heard of such a thing. I never heard anything in my life about horses acting like this.'

Father waved his stick at them, but very gently, as if he would really do them no harm.

'Perhaps they've had an unfortunate experience with humans recently,' said father. 'They may be looking for someone in particular.'

Mother put her arms down about us and drew us off towards the tree that stood ahead, keeping us close beside her under her arms.

'I'm not in the least afraid of horses,' father said, waving his stick. 'I never have been. I've ridden all my life.'

'I know,' mother called back from where we were.

'Neither am I.'

But the horses knew very well what to do; when they were almost on us all, they drew their chins in close against their shining necks, as swans might floating on the water, and they swerved wildly and perfectly in their circle to the other side. First the leading horse drew in her head and made the curve, and then the others followed in the tumult of their advance. It might have been some kind of game they had made up out of their loneliness and their boredom on the mountainside. They went off over the deep marshy ground and near the edge they took their place again, their sides blowing fast, their heads shaking the hair on their necks from one side to the other, fitting again into their attitudes of rest.

We came home another way and we did not see them, and when we got to the hotel it was six o'clock and Miss Henly was giving

Francis his bath. There was a look of something else in her face, and whatever she said to us she couldn't keep from smiling.

'Did we get any mail?' said mother.

'Oh, all the mail was for me for a change today,' said Miss Henly.

'Oh, how nice!' said mother.

'It was quite a joke,' said Miss Henly, her face squeezed up with laughter. 'The porter came staggering up—three telegrams and seven letters! They'd never heard of such a thing here! You can imagine!'

'I hope your young man's well?' said father.

'Oh, he's awfully well, thank you,' said Miss Henly. 'He'd put the wrong address on all the letters and they were all returned to him. So that explains how it was, you see. He's awfully excited about the Lindberghs being in England. He's working on a newspaper now and he's been trying to find out where they are so as to get a peep at them and perhaps a word or two for a story.'

'Well, we'll get a good bottle of wine tonight,' said father, 'and we'll drink to Rudolpho!'

'Oh, that's so nice of you,' said Miss Henly, 'but you know how little I drink.' She stood up to put the bathtowel around Francis, and she said: 'The heat in here, you know, it really makes me a bit dizzy.'

It wasn't until after the bottle of wine had been drunk and Miss Henly had taken Francis to bed that father said anything about it. Then he said to mother at the table:

'There wasn't any mail at all today. The bus broke down on the main road and nothing ever came through. The porter told me when we came back this evening. The mailbag was still hanging there waiting in the hall.'

'I think the girls had better go up to bed,' said mother. 'They've been up a mountain and they're awfully tired.'

Henry Handel Richardson

Two Hanged Women

Hand in hand the youthful lovers sauntered along the esplanade. It was a night in midsummer; a wispy moon had set, and the stars glittered. The dark mass of the sea, at flood, lay tranquil, slothfully lapping the shingle.

'Come on, let's make for the usual,' said the boy.

But on nearing their favourite seat they found it occupied. In the velvety shade of the overhanging sea-wall, the outlines of two figures were visible.

'Oh, blast!' said the lad. 'That's torn it, What now, Baby?'

'Why, let's stop here, Pincher, right close up, till we frighten 'em off.'

And very soon loud, smacking kisses, amatory pinches and ticklings, and skittish squeals of pleasure did their work. Silently the intruders rose and moved away.

But the boy stood gaping after them, open-mouthed.

'Well, I'm *damned!* If it wasn't just two hanged women!'

Retreating before a salvo of derisive laughter, the elder of the girls said: 'We'll go out on the breakwater.' She was tall and thin, and walked with a long stride.

Her companion, shorter than she by a bobbed head of straight flaxen hair, was hard put to it to keep pace. As she pegged along she said doubtfully, as if in self-excuse: 'Though I really ought to go home. It's getting late. Mother will be angry.'

They walked with finger-tips lightly in contact; and at her words she felt what was like an attempt to get free, on the part of the fingers crooked in hers. But she was prepared for this, and held fast, gradually working her own up till she had a good half of the other hand in her grip.

For a moment neither spoke. Then, in a low muffled voice, came the question: 'Was she angry last night, too?'

The little fair girl's reply had an unlooked-for vehemence. 'You know she wasn't!' and mildly despairing: 'But you never *will* understand. Oh, what's the good of . . . of anything!'

And on sitting down she let the prisoned hand go, even putting it from her with a kind of push. There it lay, palm upwards, the fingers still curved from her hold, looking like a thing with a separate life of its own; but a life that was ebbing.

On this remote seat, with their backs turned on lovers, lights, the town, the two girls sat and gazed wordlessly at the dark sea, over which great Jupiter was flinging a thin gold line. There was no sound but the lapping, sucking, sighing, of the ripples at the edge of the breakwater, and the occasional screech of an owl in the tall trees on the hillside.

But after a time, having stolen more than one side-glance at her companion, the younger seemed to take heart of grace. With a childish toss of the head that set her loose hair swaying, she said, in a tone of meaning emphasis: 'I like Fred.'

The only answer was a faint, contemptuous shrug.

'I tell you, I *like* him!'

'Fred? Rats!'

'No it isn't . . . that's just where you're wrong, Betty. But you think you're so wise. Always.'

'I know what I know.'

'Or imagine you do! But it doesn't matter. Nothing you can say makes any difference. I like him, and always shall. In heaps of ways. He's so big and strong, for one thing: it gives you such a safe sort of feeling to be with him . . . as if nothing could happen while you were. Yes, it's . . . it's . . . well, I can't help it, Betty there's something *comfy* in having a boy to go about with—like other girls do. One they'd eat their hats to get, too! I can see it in their eyes when we pass; Fred with his great long legs and broad shoulders—I don't nearly come up to them—and his blue eyes with the black lashes, and his shiny black hair. And I like his tweeds, the Harris smell of them, and his dirty old pipe, and the way he shows his teeth—he's got *topping* teeth—when he laughs and says "ra-*ther!*" And other people, when they see us, look . . . well I don't quite know how to say it, but they look sort of pleased; and they make room for us and let us into the dark corner-seats at the pictures, just as if we'd a right to them. And they never laugh. (Oh, I can't *stick* being laughed at!—and that's the truth.) Yes, it's so comfy, Betty darling . . . such a warm cosy comfy feeling. Oh, *won't* you understand?'

'Gawd! why not make a song of it?' But a moment later, very

fiercely: 'And who is it's taught you to think all this? Who's hinted it and suggested it till you've come to believe it? . . . believe it's what you really feel.'

'She hasn't! Mother's never said a word . . . about Fred.'

'Words?—why waste words? . . . when she can do it with a cock of the eye. For your Fred, that!' and the girl called Betty held her fingers aloft and snapped them viciously. 'But your mother's a different proposition.'

'I think you're simply horrid.'

To this there was no reply.

'*Why* have you such a down on her? What's she ever done to you? . . . except not get ratty when I stay out late with Fred. And I don't see how you can expect . . . being what she is . . . and with nobody but me—after all she *is* my mother . . . you can't alter that. I know very well—and you know, too—I'm not *too* putrid-looking. But'—beseechingly—'I'm *nearly* twenty-five now, Betty. And other girls . . . well, she sees them every one of them, with a boy of their own, even though they're ugly or fat, or have legs like sausages—they've only got to ogle them a bit—the girls, I mean . . . and there they are. And Fred's a good sort—he is, really!—and he dances well, and doesn't drink, and so . . . so why *shouldn't* I like him? . . . and off my own bat . . . without it having to be all Mother's fault, and me nothing but a parrot, and without any will of my own?'

'Why? Because I know her too well, my child! I can read her as you'd never dare to . . . even if you could. She's sly, your mother is, so sly there's no coming to grips with her . . . one might as well try to fill one's hand with cobwebs. But she's got a hold on you, a stranglehold, that nothing'll loosen. Oh! mothers aren't fair—I mean it's not fair of nature to weigh us down with them and yet expect us to be our own true selves. The handicap's too great. All those months, when the same blood's running through two sets of veins—there's no getting away from that, ever after. Take yours. As I say, does she need to open her mouth? Not she! She's only got to let it hang at the corners, and you reek, you drip with guilt.'

Something in these words seemed to sting the younger girl. She hit back, 'I know what it is, you're jealous, that's what you are! . . . and you've no other way of letting it out. But I tell you this. If ever I marry—yes *marry!*—it'll be to please myself, and nobody else. Can you imagine me doing it to oblige her?'

Again silence.

'If I only think what it would be like to be fixed up and settled, and able to live in peace, without this eternal dragging two ways . . . just as if I was being torn in half. And see Mother smiling and happy again, like she used to be. Between the two of you I'm nothing but a punch-ball. Oh, I'm fed up with it! . . . fed up to the neck. As for you . . . And yet you can sit there as if you were made of stone! Why don't you *say* something? *Betty!* Why won't you speak?'

But no words came.

'I can *feel* you sneering. And when you sneer I hate you more than any one on earth. If only I'd never seen you!'

'Marry your Fred, and you'll never need to again.'

'I will, too! I'll marry him, and have a proper wedding like other girls, with a veil and bridesmaids and bushels of flowers. And I'll live in a house of my own, where I can do as I like, and be left in peace, and there'll be no one to badger and bully me—Fred wouldn't—ever! Besides, he'll be away all day. And when he came back at night, he'd . . . I'd . . . I mean I'd—' But here the flying words gave out; there came a stormy breath and a cry of: 'Oh, Betty, Betty! . . . I couldn't, no, I couldn't! It's when I think of *that* . . . Yes, it's quite true! I like him all right, I do indeed, but only as long as he doesn't come too near. If he even sits too close, I have to screw myself up to bear it'—and flinging herself down over her companion's lap, she hid her face. 'And if he tries to touch me, Betty, or even takes my arm or puts his round me . . . And then his face . . . when it looks like it does sometimes . . . all wrong . . . as if it had gone all wrong—oh! then I feel I shall have to scream—out loud. I'm afraid of him . . . when he looks like that. Once . . . when he kissed me . . . I could have died with the horror of it. His breath . . . his breath . . . and his mouth—like fruit pulp—and the black hairs on his wrists . . . and the way he looked—and . . . and everything! No, I can't, I can't . . . nothing will make me . . . I'd rather die twice over. But what am I to do? Mother'll *never* understand. Oh, why has it got to be like this? I want to be happy, too . . . and everything's all wrong. You tell me, Betty darling, you help me, you're older . . . you *know* . . . and you can help me, if you will . . . if you only will!' And locking her arms round her friend she drove her face deeper into the warmth and darkness, as if, from the very fervour of her clasp, she could draw the aid and strength she needed.

Betty had sat silent, unyielding, her sole movement being to loosen her own arms from her sides and point her elbows outwards, to hinder them touching the arms that lay round her. But at this last appeal, she melted; and gathering the young girl to her breast, she held her fast.—And so for long she continued to sit, her chin resting lightly on the fair hair, that was silky and downy as an infant's, and gazing with sombre eyes over the stealthily heaving sea.

ANTONIA WHITE

The House of Clouds

The night before, Helen had tried to drown herself. She did not know why, for she had been perfectly happy. The four of them, she and Robert and Dorothy and Louis, had been getting supper. Louis had been carrying on one of his interminable religious arguments, and she remembered trying to explain to him the difference between the Virgin Birth and the Immaculate Conception as she carried plates out of the kitchen. And then, suddenly, she had felt extraordinarily tired and had gone out into the little damp courtyard and out through the gate into the passage that led to the Thames. She wasn't very clear what happened next. She remembered that Robert had carried her back to Dorothy's room and had laid her on the bed and knelt beside her for a long time while neither of them spoke. And then they had gone back into the comfortable noise and warmth of Louis's studio next door, and the others had gone on getting supper exactly as if nothing had happened. Helen had sat by the fire, feeling a little sleepy and remote, but amazingly happy. She had not wanted any supper, only a little bread and salt. She was insistent about the salt, because salt keeps away evil spirits, and they had given it to her quietly without any fuss. They were gentle with her, almost reverent. She felt they understood that something wonderful was going to happen to her. She would let no one touch her, not Robert even. It was as if she were being charged with some force, fiery and beautiful, but so dangerous that a touch would explode it.

She did not remember how she got home. But today had been quite normal, till at dinner-time this strong impulse had come over her that she must go to Dorothy's, and here, after walking for miles in the fog, she was. She was lying in Dorothy's bed. There was a fire in the room, but it could not warm her. She kept getting up and wandering over to the door and looking out into the foggy courtyard. Over and over again, gently and patiently, as if she were a child, Dorothy had put her back to bed again. But she could not sleep. Sometimes she was in sharp pain; sometimes she was happy. She could hear herself singing over and over again, like an incantation:

O Deus, ego amo te
Nec amo te ut salves me
Nec quia non amantes te
Aeterno punis igne.

The priest who had married her appeared by her bed. She thought he was his own ghost come to give her the last sacraments and that he had died at that very moment in India. He twisted his rosary round her wrist. A doctor came too; the Irish doctor she hated. He tried to give her an injection, but she fought him wildly. She had promised someone (was it Robert?) that she would not let them give her drugs. Drugs would spoil the sharpness of this amazing experience that was just going to break into flower. But, in spite of her fighting, she felt the prick of the needle in her arm, and sobbing and struggling still, she felt the thick wave of the drug go over her. Was it morphia? Morphia, a word she loved to say, lengthening the first syllable that sounded like the note of a horn. 'Morphia, mo-orphia, put an "M" on my forehead,' she moaned in a man's voice.

Morning came. She felt sick and mortally tired. The doctor was there still; her father, in a brown habit, like a monk, sat talking to him. Her father came over to the bed to kiss her, but a real physical dislike of him choked her, and she pushed him away. She knew, without hearing, what he and the doctor had been talking about. They were going to take her away to use her as an experiment. Something about the war. She was willing to go; but when they lifted her out of bed she cried desperately, over and over again, for Robert.

She was in a cab, with her head on a nurse's shoulder. Her father and two other men were there. It seemed odd to be driving through South Kensington streets in broad daylight, dressed only in one of Dorothy's nightgowns and an old army overcoat of Robert's. They came to a tall house. Someone, Louis, perhaps, carried her up flights and flights of steps. Now she was in a perfectly ordinary bedroom. An old nurse with a face she liked sat by the fire; a young one, very pink and white and self-conscious, stood near her. Helen wandered over to the window and looked out. There went a red bus, normal and reassuring. Suddenly the young nurse was at her elbow, leading her away from the window.

'I shouldn't look out of the window if I were you, dear,' she said in a soft hateful voice. 'It's so ugly.' Helen let herself be led away. She was puzzled and frightened; she wanted to explain something; but she was tired and muddled; she could not speak. Presently she was in bed, alone but for the old nurse. The rosary was still on her wrist. She felt that her parents were downstairs, praying for her. Her throat was dry; a fearful weariness weighed her down. She was in her last agony. She must pray. As if the old nurse understood, she began the 'Our Father' and 'Hail Mary'. Helen answered. Decade after decade they recited in a mechanical rhythm. There were cold beads on Helen's forehead and all her limbs felt bruised. Her strength was going out of her in holy words. She was fighting the overpowering sleepiness that she knew was death. 'Holy Mary, Mother of God,' she forced out in beat after beat of sheer will-power. She lapsed at last. She was dead, but unable to leave the flesh. She waited, light, happy, disembodied.

Now she was a small child again and the nurse was the old Nanny at the house in Worcestershire. She lay very peacefully watching the nurse at her knitting under the green lamp. Pleasant thoughts went through her head of the red-walled kitchen garden, of the frost on the rosemary tufts, of the firelight dancing in the wintry panes before the curtains were drawn. Life would begin again here, a new life perfected day by day through a new childhood, safe and warm and orderly as this old house that smelt of pines and bees-wax. But the nightmares soon began. She was alone in a crypt watching by the coffin of a dead girl, an idiot who had died at school and who lay in a glass-topped coffin in her First Communion dress, with a gilt paper crown on her head. Helen woke up and screamed.

Another nurse was sitting by the green lamp.

'You must be quiet, dear,' said the nurse.

There were whispers and footsteps outside.

'I hear she is wonderful,' said a woman's voice.

'Yes,' said another, 'but all the conditions must be right, or it will be dangerous for her.'

'How?'

'You must all dress as nurses,' said the second voice, 'then she thinks she is in a hospital. She lives through it again, or rather, they do.'

'Who . . . the sons?'

'Yes. The House of Clouds is full of them.'

One by one, women wearing nurses' veils and aprons tiptoed in and sat beside her bed. She knew quite well that they were not nurses; she even recognized faces she had seen in picture papers. These were rich women whose sons had been killed, years ago, in the war. And each time a woman came in, Helen went through a new agony. She became the dead boy. She spoke with his voice. She felt the pain of amputated limbs, of blinded eyes. She coughed up blood from lungs torn to rags by shrapnel. Over and over again, in trenches, in field hospitals, in German camps, she died a lingering death. Between the bouts of torture, the mothers, in their nurses' veils, would kiss her hand and sob out their gratitude.

'She must never speak of the House of Clouds,' one said to another.

And the other answered:

'She will forget when she wakes up. She is going to marry a soldier.'

Months, perhaps years later, she woke up in a small, bare cell. The walls were whitewashed and dirty and she was lying on a mattress on the floor, without sheets, with only rough, red-striped blankets over her. She was wearing a linen gown, like an old-fashioned nightshirt, and she was bitterly cold. In front of her was the blank yellow face of a heavy door without a handle of any kind. Going over to the door, she tried frantically to push it open. It was locked. She began to call out in panic and to beat on the door till her hands were red and swollen. She had forgotten her name. She did not know whether she were very young or very old; a man or a woman. Had she died that night in Dorothy's studio? She could remember Dorothy and Robert, yet she knew that her memory of them was not quite right. Was this place a prison? If only, only her name would come back to her.

Suddenly the door opened. A young nurse was there, a nurse with a new face. As suddenly as the door had opened, Helen's own identity flashed up again. She called wildly, 'I know who I am. I'm Helen Ryder. You must ring up my father and tell him I'm here. I must have lost my memory. The number is Western 2159.'

The nurse did not answer, but she began to laugh. Slowly, mockingly, inch by inch, though Helen tried with all her strength to keep it open, she closed the door.

The darkness and the nightmare came back. She lost herself again; this time completely. For years she was not even a human being; she was a horse. Ridden almost to death, beaten till she fell, she lay at last on the straw in her stable and waited for death. They buried her as she lay on her side, with outstretched head and legs. A child came and sowed turquoises round the outline of her body in the ground, and she rose up again as a horse of magic with a golden mane, and galloped across the sky. Again she woke on the mattress in her cell. She looked and saw that she had human hands and feet again, but she knew that she was still a horse. Nurses came and dragged her, one on each side, to an enormous room filled with baths. They dipped her into bath after bath of boiling water. Each bath was smaller than the last, with gold taps that came off in her hands when she tried to clutch them. There was something slightly wrong about everything in this strange bathroom. All the mugs were chipped. The chairs had only three legs. There were plates lying about with letters round the brim, but the letters never read the same twice running. The nurses looked like human beings, but Helen knew quite well that they were wax dolls stuffed with hay.

They could torture her for all that. After the hot baths, they ducked her spluttering and choking, into an ice-cold one. A nurse took a bucket of cold water and splashed it over her, drenching her hair and half-blinding her. She screamed, and nurses, dozens of them, crowded round the bath to laugh at her, 'Oh, Nelly, you naughty, naughty girl,' they giggled. They took her out and dried her and rubbed something on her eyes and nostrils that stung like fire. She had human limbs, but she was not human; she was a horse or a stag being prepared for the hunt. On the wall was a looking-glass, dim with steam.

'Look, Nelly, look who's there,' said the nurses.

She looked and saw a face in the glass, the face of a fairy horse or stag, sometimes with antlers, sometimes with a wild, golden mane, but always with the same dark, stony eyes and nostrils red as blood. She threw up her head and neighed and made a dash for the door. The nurses caught and dragged her along a passage. The passage was like a long room; it had a shiny wooden floor with double iron tracks in it like the tracks of a model railway. The nurses held her painfully by the armpits so that her feet only brushed the floor. The passage was like a musty old museum.

There were wax flowers under cases and engravings of Queen Victoria and Balmoral. Suddenly the nurses opened a door in the wall, and there was her cell again. They threw her down on the mattress and went out, locking the door.

She went to sleep. She had a long nightmare about a girl who was lost in the dungeons under an old house on her wedding-day. Just as she was, in her white dress and wreath and veil, she fell into a trance and slept for thirty years. She woke up, thinking she had slept only a few hours, and found her way back to the house, and remembering her wedding, hurried to the chapel. There were lights and flowers and a young man standing at the altar. But as she walked up the aisle, people pushed her back, and she saw another bride going up before her. Up in her own room, she looked in the glass to see an old woman in a dirty satin dress with a dusty wreath on her head. And somehow, Helen herself was the girl who had slept thirty years, and they had shut her up here in the cell without a looking-glass so that she should not know how old she had grown.

And then again she was Robert, endlessly climbing up the steps of a dark tower by the sea, knowing that she herself was imprisoned at the top. She came out of this dream suddenly to find herself being tortured as a human being. She was lying on her back with two nurses holding her down. A young man with a signet ring on his finger was bending over her, holding a funnel with a long tube attached. He forced the tube down her nose and began to pour some liquid down her throat. There was a searing pain at the back of her nose; she choked and struggled, but they held her down ruthlessly. At last the man drew out the tube and dropped it coiling in a basin. The nurses released her, and all three went out and shut the door.

This horror came at intervals for days. She grew to dread the opening of the door, which was nearly always followed by the procession of nurses and the man with the basin and the funnel. Gradually she became a little more aware of her surroundings. She was no longer lying on the floor, but in a sort of wooden manger clamped to the ground in the middle of a cell. Now she had not even a blanket, only a kind of stiff canvas apron, like a piece of sail-cloth, stretched over her. And she was wearing, not a shirt, but a curious enveloping garment, very stiff and rough, that encased her legs and feet and came down over her hands. It had a leather collar, like an animal's, and a belt with a metal ring. Between the visitations of the funnel she dozed and dreamt. Or she would lie quietly, quite happy to watch, hour after hour, the play of pearly colours on the piece of sailcloth. Her name had irrevocably gone, but whole pieces of her past life, people, episodes, poems, remained embedded in her mind. She could remember the whole of 'The Mistress of Vision' and say it over to herself as she lay there. But if a word had gone, she could not suggest another to fill the gap, unless it was one of those odd, meaningless words that she found herself making up now and then.

One night there was a thunderstorm. She was frightened. The manger had become a little raft; when she put out her hand she could feel waves lapping right up to the brim. She had always been afraid of water in the dark. Now she began to pray. The door opened and a nurse, with a red face and pale hair and lashes, peered round the door, and called to her:

'Rosa Mystica.'

Helen called back.

'Turris Davidica.'

'Turris Eburnea,' called the nurse.

'Domus Aurea,' cried Helen.

And so, turn by turn, they recited the whole of the Litany of Our Lady.

One day she discovered that, by standing up in the manger, she could see through a high window, covered with close wire-netting, out into a garden. This discovery gave her great pleasure. In the garden women and nurses were walking; they did not look like real people, but oddly thin and bright, like figures cut out of coloured paper. And she could see birds flying across the sky, not real birds, but bird-shaped kites, lined with strips of white metal that flew on wires. Only the clouds had thickness and depth and looked as clouds had looked in the other world. The clouds spoke to her sometimes. They wrote messages in white smoke on the blue. They would take shape after shape to amuse her, shapes of swans, of feathers, of charming ladies with fluffy white muffs and toques, of soldiers in white busbies.

Once the door of her cell opened and there appeared, not a nurse, but a woman with short frizzy hair, who wore a purple jumper, a tweed skirt, and a great many amber beads. Helen at once decided that this woman's name was Stella. She had a friendly, silly face, and an upper lip covered with dark down.

'I've brought you a pencil,' she announced suddenly. 'I think you're so sweet. I've seen you from the garden, often. Shall we be friends?'

But before Helen could answer, the woman threw up her head, giggled, shot Helen an odd, sly look, and disappeared. With a sudden, sharp, quite normal horror, Helen thought, 'She's mad.'

She thought of the faces she had seen in the garden, with that same sly, shallow look. There must be other people in the place, then. For the first time, she was grateful for the locked door. She had a horror of mad people, of madness. Her own private horror had always been that she would go mad.

She was feeling quiet and reasonable that day. Her name had not come back to her, but she could piece together some shreds of herself. She recognized her hands; they were thinner and the nails were broken, but they were the hands she had had in the life with Dorothy and Robert and the others. She recognized a birthmark on her arm. She felt light and tired, as if she had recovered from a long illness, but sufficiently interested to ask the nurse who came in:

'What is this place?'

The nurse, who was young and pretty, with coppery hair and green eyes, looked at Helen with pity and contempt. She was kindly, with the ineffable stupid kindliness of nurses.

'I'm not supposed to tell you anything, you know.'

'I won't give you away,' promised Helen. 'What is it?'

'Well! it's a hospital, if you must know.'

'But what *kind* of a hospital?'

'Ah, that'd be telling.'

'What *kind* of a hospital?' persisted Helen.

'A hospital for girls who ask too many questions and have to give their brains a rest. Now go to sleep.'

She shook a playful finger and retreated.

It was difficult to know when the episode of the rubber room took place. Time and place were very uncertain, apt to remain stationary for months, and then to dissolve and fly in the most bewildering way. Sometimes it would take her a whole day to lift a spoon to her mouth; at other times she would live at such a pace that she could see the leaves of the ivy on the garden wall positively opening and growing before her eyes. The only thing she was sure of was that the rubber room came after she had been changed into a salmon and shut up in a little dry, waterless room behind a waterfall. She lay wriggling and gasping, scraping her scales on the stone floor, maddened by the water pouring just beyond the bars that she could not get through. Perhaps she died as a salmon as she had died as a horse, for the next thing she remembered was waking in a small six-sided room whose walls were all thick bulging panels of grey rubber. The door was rubber-padded too, with a small red window, shaped like an eye, deeply embedded in it. She was lying on the floor, and through the red, a face, stained red too, was watching her and laughing.

She knew without being told, that the rubber room was a compartment in a sinking ship, near the boiler room, which would burst at any minute and scald her to death. Somehow she must get out. She flung herself wildly against the rubber walls as if she could beat her way out by sheer force. The air was getting hotter. The rubber walls were already warm to touch. She was choking, suffocating; in a second her lungs would burst. At last the door opened. They were coming to rescue her. But it was only the procession of nurses and the funnel once more.

The fantasies were not always horrible. Once she was in a cell that was dusty and friendly, like an attic. There were spider-webs and an old ship's lamp on the ceiling. In the lamp was a face like a fox's mask, grinning down on her. She was sitting on a heap of straw, a child of eleven or so, with hair the colour of straw, and an old blue pinafore. Her name was Veronica. With crossed legs and folded arms she sat there patiently making a spell to bring her brother Nicholas safe home. He was flying back to her in a white aeroplane with a green propeller. She could see his face quite clearly as he sat between the wings. He wore a fur cap like a cossack's and a square green ring on his little finger. Enemies had put Veronica in prison, but Nicholas would come to rescue her as he had always come before. She and Nicholas loved each other with a love far deeper and more subtle than any love between husband and wife. She knew at once if he were in pain or danger, even if he were a thousand miles away.

Nicholas came to her window and carried her away. They flew to Russia, and landed on a plain covered with snow. Then they drove for miles in a sledge until they came to a dark pine forest.

They walked through the forest, hand in hand, Veronica held close in Nicholas's great fur cape. But at last she was tired, dazed by the silence and the endless trees, all exactly alike. She wanted to sit down in the snow, to sleep.

Nicholas shook her: 'Never go to sleep in the snow, Ronnie, or you will die.'

But she was too tired to listen, and she lay down in the snow that was soft and strangely warm, and fell into an exquisite dreamy torpor. And perhaps she did die in the snow as Nicholas had said, for the next thing she knew was that she was up in the clouds, following a beautiful Indian woman who sailed before her, and sifting snow down on the world through the holes in her pinafore.

Whenever things became too intolerable, the Indian woman would come with her three dark, beautiful sons, and comfort her. She would draw her sweet-smelling yellow veil over Helen and sing her songs that were like lullabies. Helen could never remember the songs, but she could often feel the Indian woman near, when she could not see her, and smell her sweet, musky scent.

She had a strange fantasy that she was Lord of the World. Whatever she ordered came about at once. The walls of the garden outside turned to blue ice that did not melt in the sun. All the doors of the house flew open and the passages were filled with children dressed in white and as lovely as dreams. She called up storms; she drove ships out of their courses; she held the whole world in a spell. Only herself she could not command. When the day came to an end she was tired out, but she could not sleep. She had forgotten the charm, or never known it, and there was no one powerful enough to say to her, 'Sleep.'

She raved, she prayed, but no sleep came. At last three women appeared.

'You cannot sleep unless you die,' they said.

She assented gladly. They took her to a beach and fettered her down on some stones, just under the bows of a huge ship that was about to be launched. One of the three gave a signal. Nothing could stop it now. On it came, grinding the pebbles to dust, deafening her with noise. It passed, slowly, right over her body. She felt every bone crack; felt the intolerable weight on her shoulders, felt her skull split like a shell. But she could sleep now.

She was free from the intolerable burden of having to will.

After this she was born and re-born with incredible swiftness as a woman, as an imp, as a dog, and finally as a flower. She was some nameless, tiny bell, growing in a stream, with a stalk as fine as hair and human voice. The water flowing through her flower throat made her sing all day a little monotonous song, 'Kulallah, Kulallah.' This happy flower-life did not last long. Soon there came a day when the place was filled with nurses who called her 'Helen'. She did not recognize the name as her own, but she began to answer it mechanically as a dog answers a familiar sound.

She began to put on ordinary clothes, clumsily and with difficulty, as if she had only just learned how, and to be taken for walks in a dreary yard; an asphalt-paved square with one sooty plane-tree and a broken bench in the middle. Wearily she would trail round and round between two nurses who polished their nails incessantly as they walked and talked about the dances they had been to. She began to recognize some of her companions in the yard. There was the woman with the beads, the Vitriol woman, and the terrible Caliban girl. The Caliban girl was called Micky. She was tall and rather handsome, but Helen never thought of her except as an animal or a monster, and was horrified when Micky tried to utter human words. Her face was half-beautiful, half-unspeakable, with Medusa curls and great eyes that looked as if they were carved out of green stone. Two long, yellow teeth, like tiger's fangs, grew right down over her lip. She had a queer passion for Helen, who hated and feared her. Whenever she could, Micky would break away from her nurses and try to fondle Helen. She would stroke her hair, muttering, 'Pretty, pretty,' with her deformed mouth. Micky's breath on her cheek was hot and sour like an animal's, her black hair was rough as wire. The reality of Micky was worse than any nightmare; she was shameful, obscene.

The Vitriol woman was far more horrible to look at, but far less repulsive. Helen had heard the nurses whispering how the woman's husband had thrown acid at her. Her face was one raw, red, shining burn, without lid or brow, almost without lips. She always wore a neat black hat and a neat, common blue coat with a fur collar. Everyone she met she addressed with the same agonized question: 'Have you seen Fred? Where's Fred? Take me to Fred!'

On one of the dirty walls someone had chalked up:

'Baby.'
'Blood.'
'Murder.'

And no one had bothered to wipe it out.

The yard was a horror that seemed to have no place in the world, yet from beyond the walls would come pleasant ordinary noises of motors passing, and people walking and bells ringing. Above the walls, Helen could see a rather beautiful, slender dome, pearl-coloured against the sky, and tipped with a gilt spear. It reminded her of some building she knew very well but whose name, like her own, she had forgotten.

One day, she was left almost alone in the yard. Sitting on the broken bench by the plane-tree was a young girl, weeping. Helen went up to her. She had a gentle, bewildered face; with loose, soft plaits falling round it. Helen went and sat by her and drew the girl's head on to her own shoulder. It seemed years since she had touched another person with affection. The girl nestled against her. Her neck was greenish-white, like privet; when Helen touched it curiously, its warmth and softness were so lovely that tears came into her eyes. The girl was so gentle and defenceless, like some small, confiding animal, that Helen felt a sudden love for her run through all her veins. There was a faint country smell about her hair, like clover.

'I love you,' murmured Helen, hardly knowing what she said.

But suddenly a flock of giggling nurses were upon them with a chatter of:

'Look at this, will you?' and,

'Break away there.'

She never saw the country girl again.

And so day after day went past, punctuated by dreary meals and drearier walks. She lived through each only because she knew that sooner or later Robert must come to fetch her away, and this hope carried her through each night. There were messages from him sometimes, half-glimpsed in the flight of birds, in the sound of a horn beyond the walls, in the fine lines ruled on a blade of grass. But he himself never came, and at last there came a day when she ceased to look for him. She gave up. She accepted everything. She was no longer Helen or Veronica, no longer even a fairy horse. She had become an Inmate.

EUDORA WELTY

Why I Live At The P.O.

I was getting along fine with Mama, Papa-Daddy and Uncle Rondo until my sister Stella-Rondo just separated from her husband and came back home again. Mr Whitaker! Of course I went with Mr Whitaker first, when he first appeared here in China Grove, taking 'Pose Yourself' photos, and Stella-Rondo broke us up. Told him I was one-sided. Bigger on one side than the other, which is a deliberate, calculated falsehood: I'm the same. Stella-Rondo is exactly twelve months to the day younger than I am and for that reason she's spoiled.

She's always had anything in the world she wanted and then she'd throw it away. Papa-Daddy gave her this gorgeous Add-a-Pearl necklace when she was eight years old and she threw it away playing baseball when she was nine, with only two pearls.

So as soon as she got married and moved away from home the first thing she did was separate! From Mr Whitaker! This photographer with the popeyes she said she trusted. Came home from one of those towns up in Illinois and to our complete surprise brought this child of two.

Mama said she like to made her drop dead for a second. 'Here you had this marvelous blonde child and never so much as wrote your mother a word about it,' says Mama. 'I'm thoroughly ashamed of you.' But of course she wasn't.

Stella-Rondo just calmly takes off this *hat*, I wish you could see it. She says, 'Why, Mama, Shirley-T's adopted, I can prove it.'

'How?' says Mama, but all I says was, 'H'm!' There I was over the hot stove, trying to stretch two chickens over five people and a completely unexpected child into the bargain, without one moment's notice.

'What do you mean—"H'm!"?' says Stella-Rondo, and Mama says, 'I heard that, Sister.'

I said that oh, I didn't mean a thing, only that whoever Shirley-T was, she was the spit-image of Papa-Daddy if he'd cut off his beard, which of course he'd never do in the world. Papa-Daddy's Mama's papa and sulks. Stella-Rondo got furious! She said,

'Sister, I don't need to tell you you got a lot of nerve and always did have and I'll thank you to make no future reference to my adopted child whatsoever.'

'Very well,' I said. 'Very well, very well. Of course I noticed at once she looks like Mr Whitaker's side too. That frown. She looks like a cross between Mr Whitaker and Papa-Daddy.'

'Well, all I can say is she isn't.'

'She looks exactly like Shirley Temple to me,' says Mama, but Shirley-T just ran away from her.

So the first thing Stella-Rondo did at the table was turn Papa-Daddy against me.

'Papa-Daddy,' she says. He was trying to cut up his meat. 'Papa-Daddy!' I was taken completely by surprise. Papa-Daddy is about a million years old and's got this long-long beard. 'Papa-Daddy, Sister says she fails to understand why you don't cut off your beard.'

So Papa-Daddy l-a-y-s down his knife and fork! He's real rich. Mama says he is, he says he isn't. So he says, 'Have I heard correctly? You don't understand why I don't cut off my beard?'

'Why,' I says, 'Papa-Daddy, of course I understand, I did not say any such of a thing, the idea!'

He says, 'Hussy!'

I says, 'Papa-Daddy, you know I wouldn't any more want you to cut off your beard than the man in the moon. It was the farthest thing from my mind! Stella-Rondo sat there and made that up while she was eating breast of chicken.'

But he says, 'So the postmistress fails to understand why I don't cut off my beard. Which job I got you through my influence with the government. "Bird's nest"—is that what you call it!'

Not that it isn't the next to smallest P.O. in the entire state of Mississippi.

I says, 'Oh, Papa-Daddy,' I says, 'I didn't say any such of a thing, I never dreamed it was a bird's nest, I have always been grateful though this is the next to smallest P.O. in the state of Mississippi, and I do not enjoy being referred to as a hussy by my own grandfather.'

But Stella-Rondo says, 'Yes, you did say it too. Anybody in the world could of heard you, that had ears.'

'Stop right there,' says Mama, looking at *me*.

So I pulled my napkin straight back through the napkin ring and left the table.

As soon as I was out of the room Mama says, 'Call her back, or she'll starve to death,' but Papa-Daddy says, 'This is the beard I started growing on the Coast when I was fifteen years old.' He would of gone on till nightfall if Shirley-T hadn't lost the Milky Way she ate in Cairo.

So Papa-Daddy says, 'I am going out and lie in the hammock, and you can all sit here and remember my words: I'll never cut off my beard as long as I live, even one inch, and I don't appreciate it in you at all.' Passed right by me in the hall and went straight out and got in the hammock.

It would be a holiday. It wasn't five minutes before Uncle Rondo suddenly appeared in the hall in one of Stella-Rondo's flesh-colored kimonos, all cut on the bias, like something Mr Whitaker probably thought was gorgeous.

'Uncle Rondo!' I says. 'I didn't know who that was! Where are you going?'

'Sister,' he says, 'get out of my way, I'm poisoned.'

'If you're poisoned stay away from Papa-Daddy,' I says. 'Keep out of the hammock. Papa-Daddy will certainly beat you on the head if you come within forty miles of him. He thinks I deliberately said he ought to cut off his beard after he got me the P.O., and I've told him and told him and told him, and he acts like he just don't hear me. Papa-Daddy must of gone stone deaf.'

'He picked a fine day to do it then,' says Uncle Rondo, and before you could say 'Jack Robinson' flew out in the yard.

What he'd really done, he'd drunk another bottle of that prescription. He does it every single Fourth of July as sure as shooting, and it's horribly expensive. Then he falls over in the hammock and snores. So he insisted on zigzagging right on out to the hammock, looking like a half-wit.

Papa-Daddy woke up with this horrible yell and right there without moving an inch he tried to turn Uncle Rondo against me. I heard every word he said. Oh, he told Uncle Rondo I didn't learn to read till I was eight years old and he didn't see how in the world I ever got the mail put up at the P.O., much less read it all, and he said if Uncle Rondo could only fathom the lengths he had gone to to get me that job! And he said on the other hand he thought Stella-Rondo had a brilliant mind and deserved credit for getting out of town. All the time he was just lying there swinging as pretty as you please and looping out his beard, and poor Uncle Rondo was *pleading* with him to slow down the hammock, it was making him as dizzy as a witch to watch it. But that's what Papa-Daddy likes about a hammock. So Uncle Rondo was too dizzy to get turned against me for the time being. He's Mama's only brother and is a good case of a one-track mind. Ask anybody. A certified pharmacist.

Just then I heard Stella-Rondo raising the upstairs window. While she was married she got this peculiar idea that it's cooler with the windows shut and locked. So she has to raise the window before she can make a soul hear her outdoors.

So she raises the window and says, *'Oh!'* You would have thought she was mortally wounded.

Uncle Rondo and Papa-Daddy didn't even look up, but kept right on with what they were doing. I had to laugh.

I flew up the stairs and threw the door open! I says, 'What in the wide world's the matter, Stella-Rondo? You mortally wounded?'

'No,' she says, 'I am not mortally wounded but I wish you would do me the favor of looking out that window there and telling me what you see.'

So I shade my eyes and look out the window.

'I see the front yard,' I says.

'Don't you see any human beings?' she says.

'I see Uncle Rondo trying to run Papa-Daddy out of the hammock,' I says. 'Nothing more. Naturally, it's so suffocating-hot in the house, with all the windows shut and locked, everybody who cares to stay in their right mind will have to go out and get in the hammock before the Fourth of July is over.'

'Don't you notice anything different about Uncle Rondo?' asks Stella-Rondo.

'Why, no, except he's got on some terrible-looking flesh-colored contraption I wouldn't be found dead in, is all I can see,' I says.

'Never mind, you won't be found dead in it; because it happens to be part of my trousseau, and Mr Whitaker took several dozen photographs of me in it,' says Stella-Rondo. 'What on earth could Uncle Rondo *mean* by wearing part of my trousseau out in the broad open daylight without saying so much as "Kiss my foot," *knowing* I only got home this morning after my separation and hung my negligee up on the bathroom door, just as nervous as I could be?'

'I'm sure I don't know, and what do you expect me to do about it?' I says. 'Jump out the window?'

'No, I expect nothing of the kind. I simply declare that Uncle Rondo looks like a fool in it, that's all,' she says. 'It makes me sick to my stomach.'

'Well, he looks as good as he can,' I says. 'As good as anybody in reason could.' I stood up for Uncle Rondo, please remember. And I said to Stella-Rondo, 'I think I would do well not to criticize so freely if I were you and came home with a two-year-old child I had never said a word about, and no explanation whatever about my separation.'

'I asked you the instant I entered this house not to refer one more time to my adopted child, and you gave me your word of honor you would not,' was all Stella-Rondo would say, and started pulling out every one of her eyebrows with some cheap Kress tweezers.

So I merely slammed the door behind me and went down and made some green-tomato pickle. Somebody had to do it. Of course Mama had turned both the Negroes loose; she always said no earthly power could hold one anyway on the Fourth of July, so she wouldn't even try. It turned out that Jaypan fell in the lake and came within a very narrow limit of drowning.

So Mama trots in. Lifts up the lid and says, 'H'm! Not very good for your Uncle Rondo in his precarious condition, I must say. Or poor little adopted Shirley-T. Shame on you!'

That made me tired. I says, 'Well, Stella-Rondo had better thank her lucky stars it was her instead of me came trotting in with that very peculiar-looking child. Now if it had been me that trotted in from Illinois and brought a peculiar-looking child of two, I shudder to think of the reception I'd of got, much less controlled the diet of an entire family.'

'But you must remember, Sister, that you were never married to Mr Whitaker in the first place and didn't go up to Illinois to live,' says Mama, shaking a spoon in my face. 'If you had I would of been just as overjoyed to see you and your little adopted girl as I was to see Stella-Rondo, when you wound up with your separation and came on back home.'

'You would not,' I says.

'Don't contradict me, I would,' says Mama.

But I said she couldn't convince me though she talked till she was blue in the face. Then I said, 'Besides, you know as well as I do that that child is not adopted.'

'She most certainly is adopted,' says Mama, stiff as a poker.

I says, 'Why Mama, Stella-Rondo had her just as sure as anything in this world, and just too stuck up to admit it.'

'Why, Sister,' said Mama. 'Here I thought we were going to have a pleasant Fourth of July, and you start right out not believing a word your own baby sister tells you!'

'Just like Cousin Annie Flo. Went to her grave denying the facts of life,' I remind Mama.

'I told you if you ever mentioned Annie Flo's name I'd slap your face,' says Mama, and slaps my face.

'All right, you wait and see,' I says.

'I,' says Mama, '*I* prefer to take my children's word for anything when it's humanly possible.' You ought to see Mama, she weighs two hundred pounds and has real tiny feet.

Just then something perfectly horrible occurred to me.

'Mama,' I says, 'can that child talk?' I simply had to whisper! 'Mama, I wonder if that child can be—you know—in any way? Do you realize,' I says, 'that she hasn't spoken one single, solitary word to a human being up to this minute? This is the way she looks,' I says, and I looked like this.

Well Mama and I just stood there and stared at each other. It was horrible!

'I remember well that Joe Whitaker frequently drank like a fish,' says Mama. 'I believed to my soul he drank *chemicals*.' And without another word she marches to the foot of the stairs and calls Stella-Rondo.

'Stella-Rondo? O-o-o-o-o! Stella-Rondo!'

'What?' says Stella-Rondo from upstairs. Not even the grace to get up off the bed.

'Can that child of yours talk?' asks Mama.

Stella-Rondo says, 'Can she what?'

'Talk! Talk!' says Mama. 'Burdyburdyburdyburdy!'

So Stella-Rondo yells back, 'Who says she can't talk?'

'Sister says so,' says Mama.

'You didn't have to tell me, I know whose word of honor don't mean a thing in this house,' says Stella-Rondo.

And in a minute the loudest Yankee voice I ever heard in my life yells out, 'OE'm Pop-OE the Sailor-r-r-r Ma-a-an!' and then somebody jumps up and down in the upstairs hall. In another second the house would of fallen down.

'Not only talks, she can tap-dance!' calls Stella-Rondo. 'Which is more than some people I won't name can do.'

'Why the little precious darling thing!' Mama says, so surprised. 'Just as smart as she can be!' Starts talking baby talk right there. Then she turns on me. 'Sister, you ought to be thoroughly ashamed! Run upstairs this instant and apologize to Stella-Rondo and Shirley-T.'

'Apologize for what?' I says. 'I merely wondered if the child was normal, that's all. Now that she's proved she is, why, I have nothing further to say.'

But Mama just turned on her heel and flew out, furious. She ran right upstairs and hugged the baby. She believed it was adopted. Stella-Rondo hadn't done a thing but turn her against me from upstairs while I stood there helpless over the hot stove. So that made Mama, Papa-Daddy and the baby all on Stella-Rondo's side.

Next, Uncle Rondo.

I must say that Uncle Rondo has been marvelous to me at various times in the past and I was completely unprepared to be made to jump out of my skin, the way it turned out. Once Stella-Rondo did something perfectly horrible to him—broke a chain letter from Flanders Field—and he took the radio back he had given her and gave it to me. Stella-Rondo was furious! For six months we all had to call her Stella instead of Stella-Rondo, or she wouldn't answer. I always thought Uncle Rondo had all the brains of the entire family. Another time he sent me to Mammoth Cave, with all expenses paid.

But this would be the day he was drinking that prescription, the Fourth of July.

So at supper Stella-Rondo speaks up and says she thinks Uncle Rondo ought to try to eat a little something. So finally Uncle Rondo said he would try a little cold biscuits and ketchup, but that was all. So *she* brought it to him.

'Do you think it wise to disport with ketchup in Stella-Rondo's flesh-coloured kimono?' I says. If Stella-Rondo couldn't watch out for her trousseau, somebody had to.

'Any objections?' asks Uncle Rondo, just about to pour out all the ketchup.

'Don't mind what she says, Uncle Rondo,' says Stella-Rondo. 'Sister has been devoting this solid afternoon to sneering out my bedroom window at the way you look.'

'What's that?' says Uncle Rondo. Uncle Rondo has got the most terrible temper in the world. Anything is liable to make him tear the house down if it comes at the wrong time.

So Stella-Rondo says, 'Sister says, "Uncle Rondo certainly does look like a fool in that pink kimono!"'

Do you remember who it was really said that?

Uncle Rondo spills out all the ketchup and jumps out of his chair and tears off the kimono and throws it down on the dirty floor and puts his foot on it. It had to be sent all the way to Jackson to the cleaners and re-pleated.

'So that's your opinion of your Uncle Rondo, is it?' he says. 'I look like a fool, do I? Well, that's the last straw. A whole day in this house with nothing to do, and then to hear you come out with a remark like that behind my back!'

'I didn't say any such of a thing, Uncle Rondo,' I says, 'and I'm not saying who did, either. Why, I think you look all right. Just try to take care of yourself and not talk and eat at the same time,' I says. 'I think you better go lie down.'

'Lie down my foot,' says Uncle Rondo. I ought to of known by that he was fixing to do something perfectly horrible.

So he didn't do anything that night in the precarious state he was in—just played Casino with Mama and Stella-Rondo and Shirley-T and gave Shirley-T a nickel with a head on both sides. It tickled her nearly to death, and she called him 'Papa.' But at 6:30 A.M. the next morning, he threw a whole five-cent package of some unsold one-inch firecrackers from the store as hard as he could into my bedroom and they every one went off. Not one bad in the string. Anybody else, there'd be one that wouldn't go off.

Well, I'm just terribly susceptible to noise of any kind, the doctor has always told me I was the most sensitive person he had ever seen in his whole life, and I was simply prostrated. I couldn't eat! People tell me they heard it as far as the cemetery, and old Aunt Jep Patterson, that had been holding her own so good, thought it was Judgment Day and she was going to meet her whole family. It's usually so quiet here.

And I'll tell you it didn't take me any longer than a minute to make up my mind what to do. There I was with the whole entire house on Stella-Rondo's side and turned against me. If I have anything at all I have pride.

So I just decided I'd go straight down to the P.O. There's plenty of room there in the back, I says to myself.

Well! I made no bones about letting the family catch on to what I was up to. I didn't try to conceal it.

The first thing they knew, I marched in where they were all playing Old Maid and pulled the electric oscillating fan out by the plug, and everything got real hot. Next I snatched the pillow I'd done the needlepoint on right off the davenport behind Papa-Daddy. He went 'Ugh!' I beat Stella-Rondo up the stairs and finally found my charm bracelet in her bureau drawer under a picture of Nelson Eddy.

'So that's the way the land lies,' says Uncle Rondo. There he was, piecing on the ham. 'Well, Sister, I'll be glad to donate my army cot if you got any place to set it up, providing you'll leave right this minute and let me get some peace.' Uncle Rondo was in France.

'Thank you kindly for the cot and "peace" is hardly the word I would select if I had to resort to firecrackers at 6:30 A.M. in a young girl's bedroom,' I says back to him. 'And as to where I intend to go, you seem to forget my position as postmistress of China Grove, Mississippi,' I says. 'I've always got the P.O.'

Well, that made them all sit up and take notice.

I went out front and started digging up some four-o'clocks to plant around the P.O.

'Ah-ah-ah!' says Mama, raising the window. 'Those happen to be my four-o'clocks. Everything planted in that star is mine. I've never known you to make anything grow in your life.'

'Very well,' I says. 'But I take the fern. Even you, Mama, can't stand there and deny that I'm the one watered that fern. And I happen to know where I can send in a box top and get a packet of one thousand mixed seeds, no two the same kind, free.'

'Oh, where?' Mama wants to know.

But I says, 'Too late. You 'tend to your house, and I'll 'tend to mine. You hear things like that all the time if you know how to listen to the radio. Perfectly marvelous offers. Get anything you want free.'

So I hope to tell you I marched in and got that radio, and they could of all bit a nail in two, especially Stella-Rondo, that it used to belong to, and she well knew she couldn't get it back, I'd sue for it like a shot. And I very politely took the sewing-machine motor I helped pay the most on to give Mama for Christmas back in 1929, and a good big calendar, with the first-aid remedies on it. The thermometer and the Hawaiian ukelele certainly were rightfully mine, and I stood on the step-ladder and got all my watermelon-rind preserves and every fruit and vegetable I'd put up, every jar. Then I began to pull the tacks out of the bluebird wall vases on the archway to the dining room.

'Who told you you could have those, Miss Priss?' says Mama, fanning as hard as she could.

'I bought 'em and I'll keep track of 'em,' I says. 'I'll tack 'em up one on each side the post-office window, and you can see 'em when you come to ask me for your mail, if you're so dead to see 'em.'

'Not I! I'll never darken the door to that post office again if I live to be a hundred,' Mama says. 'Ungrateful child! After all the money we spent on you at the Normal.'

'Me either,' says Stella-Rondo. 'You can just let my mail lie there and *rot*, for all I care. I'll never come and relieve you of a single, solitary piece.'

'I should worry,' I says. 'And who you think's going to sit down and write you all those big fat letters and postcards, by the way? Mr Whitaker? Just because he was the only man ever dropped down in China Grove and you got him—unfairly—is he going to sit down and write you a lengthy correspondence after you come home giving no rhyme nor reason whatsoever for your separation and no explanation for the presence of that child? I may not have your brilliant mind, but I fail to see it.'

So Mama says, 'Sister, I've told you a thousand times that Stella-Rondo simply got homesick, and this child is far too big to be hers,' and she says, 'Now, why don't you all just sit down and play Casino?'

Then Shirley-T sticks out her tongue at me in this perfectly horrible way. She has no more manners than the man in the moon. I told her she was going to cross her eyes like that some day and they'd stick.

'It's too late to stop me now,' I says. 'You should have tried that yesterday. I'm going to the P.O. and the only way you can possibly see me is to visit me there.'

So Papa-Daddy says, 'You'll never catch me setting foot in that post office, even if I should take a notion into my head to write a letter some place.' He says, 'I won't have you reachin' out of that little old window with a pair of shears and cuttin' off any beard of mine. I'm too smart for you!'

'We all are,' says Stella-Rondo.

But I said, 'If you're so smart, where's Mr Whitaker?'

So then Uncle Rondo says, 'I'll thank you from now on to stop reading all the orders I get on postcards and telling everybody in China Grove what you think is the matter with them,' but I says, 'I draw my own conclusions and will continue in the future to draw them.' I says, 'If people want to write their inmost secrets on penny postcards, there's nothing in the wide world you can do about it, Uncle Rondo.'

'And if you think we'll ever *write* another postcard you're sadly mistaken,' says Mama.

'Cutting off your nose to spite your face then,' I says. 'But if you're all determined to have no more to do with the U.S. mail, think of this: What will Stella-Rondo do now, if she wants to tell Mr Whitaker to come after her?'

'Wah!' says Stella-Rondo. I knew she'd cry. She had a conniption fit right there in the kitchen.

'It will be interesting to see how long she holds out,' I says. 'And now—I am leaving.'

'Goodbye,' says Uncle Rondo.

'Oh, I declare,' says Mama, 'to think that a family of mine should quarrel on the Fourth of July, or the day after, over Stella-Rondo leaving old Mr Whitaker and having the sweetest little adopted child! It looks like we'd all be glad!'

'Wah!' says Stella-Rondo, and has a fresh conniption fit.

'*He* left *her*—you mark my words,' I says. 'That's Mr Whitaker. I know Mr Whitaker. After all, I knew him first. I said from the beginning he'd up and leave her. I foretold every single thing that's happened.'

'Where did he go?' asks Mama.

'Probably to the North Pole, if he knows what's good for him,' I says.

But Stella-Rondo just bawled and wouldn't say another word.

She flew to her room and slammed the door.

'Now look what you've gone and done, Sister,' says Mama. 'You go apologize.'

'I haven't got time, I'm leaving,' I says.

'Well, what are you waiting around for?' asks Uncle Rondo.

So I just picked up the kitchen clock and marched off, without saying 'Kiss my foot' or anything, and never did tell Stella-Rondo goodbye.

There was a girl going along on a little wagon right in front.

'Girl,' I says, 'come help me haul these things down the hill, I'm going to live in the post office.'

Took her nine trips in her express wagon. Uncle Rondo came out on the porch and threw her a nickel.

And that's the last I've laid eyes on any of my family or my family laid eyes on me for five solid days and nights. Stella-Rondo may be telling the most horrible tales in the world about Mr Whitaker, but I haven't heard them. As I tell everybody, I draw my own conclusions.

But, oh, I like it here. It's ideal, as I've been saying. You see, I've got everything cater-cornered, the way I like it. Hear the radio? All the war news. Radio, sewing machine, book ends, ironing board and that great big piano lamp—peace, that's what I like. Butter-bean vines planted all along the front where the strings are.

Of course, there's not much mail. My family are naturally the main people in China Grove, and if they prefer to vanish from the face of the earth, for all the mail they get or the mail they write, why, I'm not going to open my mouth. Some of the folks here in town are taking up for me and some turned against me. I know which is which. There are always people who will quit buying stamps just to get on the right side of Papa-Daddy.

But here I am, and here I'll stay. I want the world to know I'm happy.

And if Stella-Rondo should come to me this minute, on bended knees, and *attempt* to explain the incidents of her life with Mr Whitaker, I'd simply put my fingers in both my ears and refuse to listen.

ELIZABETH BOWEN

The Happy Autumn Fields

The family walking party, though it comprised so many, did not deploy or straggle over the stubble but kept in a procession of threes and twos. Papa, who carried his Alpine stick, led, flanked by Constance and little Arthur. Robert and Cousin Theodore, locked in studious talk, had Emily attached but not quite abreast. Next came Digby and Lucius, taking, to left and right, imaginary aim at rooks. Henrietta and Sarah brought up the rear.

It was Sarah who saw the others ahead on the blond stubble, who knew them, knew what they were to each other, knew their names and knew her own. It was she who felt the stubble under her feet, and who heard it give beneath the tread of the others a continuous different more distant soft stiff scrunch. The field and all these outlying fields in view knew as Sarah knew that they were Papa's. The harvest had been good and was now in: he was satisfied—for this afternoon he had made the instinctive choice of his most womanly daughter, most nearly infant son. Arthur, whose hand Papa was holding, took an anxious hop, a skip and a jump to every stride of the great man's. As for Constance—Sarah could often see the flash of her hat-feather as she turned her head, the curve of her close bodice as she turned her torso. Constance gave Papa her attention but not her thoughts, for she had already been sought in marriage.

The landowner's daughters, from Constance down, walked with their beetle-green, mole or maroon skirts gathered up and carried clear of the ground, but for Henrietta, who was still ankle-free. They walked inside a continuous stuffy sound, but left silence behind them. Behind them, rooks that had risen and circled, sun striking blue from their blue-black wings, planed one by one to the earth and settled to peck again. Papa and the boys were dark-clad as the rooks but with no sheen, but for their white collars.

It was Sarah who located the thoughts of Constance, knew what a twisting prisoner was Arthur's hand, felt to the depths of Emily's pique at Cousin Theodore's inattention, rejoiced with Digby and Lucius at the imaginary fall of so many rooks. She fell back, however, as from a rocky range, from the converse of Robert and Cousin Theodore. Most she knew that she swam with love at the nearness of Henrietta's young and alert face and eyes which shone with the sky and queried the afternoon.

She recognized the colour of valediction, tasted sweet sadness, while from the cottage inside the screen of trees wood-smoke rose melting pungent and blue. This was the eve of the brothers' return to school. It was like a Sunday; Papa had kept the late afternoon free; all (all but one) encircling Robert, Digby and Lucius, they walked the estate the brothers would not see again for so long. Robert, it could be felt, was not unwilling to return to his books; next year he would go to college like Theodore; besides, to all this they saw he was not the heir. But in Digby and Lucius aiming and popping hid a bodily grief, the repugnance of victims, though these two were further from being heirs than Robert.

Sarah said to Henrietta: 'To think they will not be here tomorrow!'

'*Is* that what you are thinking about?' Henrietta asked, with her subtle taste for the truth.

'More, I was thinking that you and I will be back again by one another at table . . .'

'You know we are always sad when the boys are going, but we are never sad when the boys have gone.' The sweet reciprocal guilty smile that started on Henrietta's lips finished on those of Sarah. 'Also,' the young sister said, 'we know this is only something happening again. It happened last year, and it will happen next. But oh how should I feel, and how should you feel, if it were something that had not happened before?'

'For instance, when Constance goes to be married?'

'Oh, I don't mean *Constance*!' said Henrietta.

'So long,' said Sarah, considering, 'as, whatever it is, it happens to both of us?' She must never have to wake in the early morning except to the birdlike stirrings of Henrietta, or have her cheek brushed in the dark by the frill of another pillow in whose hollow did not repose Henrietta's cheek. Rather than they should cease to lie in the same bed she prayed they might lie in the same grave. 'You and I will stay as we are,' she said, 'then nothing can touch one without touching the other.'

'So you say; so I hear you say!' exclaimed Henrietta, who then, lips apart, sent Sarah her most tormenting look. 'But I cannot forget that you chose to be born without me; that you would not wait—' But here she broke off, laughed outright and said: 'Oh, *see*!'

Ahead of them there had been a dislocation. Emily took advantage of having gained the ridge to kneel down to tie her bootlace so abruptly that Digby all but fell over her, with an exclamation. Cousin Theodore had been civil enough to pause beside Emily, but Robert, lost to all but what he was saying, strode on, head down, only just not colliding into Papa and Constance, who had turned to look back. Papa, astounded, let go of Arthur's hand, whereupon Arthur fell flat on the stubble.

'Dear me,' said the affronted Constance to Robert.

Papa said, 'What is the matter there? May I ask, Robert, where you are going, sir? Digby, remember that is your sister Emily.'

'Cousin Emily is in trouble,' said Cousin Theodore.

Poor Emily, telescoped in her skirts and by now scarlet under her hatbrim, said in a muffled voice: 'It is just my bootlace, Papa.'

'Your bootlace, Emily?'

'I was just tying it.'

'Then you had better tie it—Am I to think,' said Papa, looking round them all, 'that you must all go down like a pack of ninepins because Emily has occasion to stoop?'

At this Henrietta uttered a little whoop, flung her arms round Sarah, buried her face in her sister and fairly suffered with laughter. She could contain this no longer; she shook all over. Papa, who found Henrietta so hopelessly out of order that he took no notice of her except at table, took no notice, simply giving the signal for the others to collect themselves and move on. Cousin Theodore, helping Emily to her feet, could be seen to see how her heightened colour became her, but she dispensed with his hand chillily, looked elsewhere, touched the brooch at her throat and said: 'Thank you, I have not sustained an accident.' Digby apologized to Emily, Robert to Papa and Constance. Constance righted Arthur, flicking his breeches over with her handkerchief. All fell into their different steps and resumed their way.

Sarah, with no idea how to console laughter, coaxed, 'Come, come, come,' into Henrietta's ear. Between the girls and the others the distance widened; it began to seem that they would be left alone.

'And why not?' said Henrietta, lifting her head in answer to Sarah's thought.

They looked around them with the same eyes. The shorn uplands seemed to float on the distance, which extended dazzling to tiny blue glassy hills. There was no end to the afternoon, whose light went on ripening now they had scythed the corn. Light filled the silence which, now Papa and the others were out of hearing, was complete. Only screens of trees intersected and knolls made islands in the vast fields. The mansion and the home farm had sunk for ever below them in the expanse of woods, so that hardly a ripple showed where the girls dwelled.

The shadow of the same rook circling passed over Sarah then over Henrietta, who in their turn cast one shadow across the stubble. 'But, Henrietta, we cannot stay here for ever.'

Henrietta immediately turned her eyes to the only lonely plume of smoke, from the cottage. 'Then let us go and visit the poor old man. He is dying and the others are happy. One day we shall pass and see no more smoke; then soon his roof will fall in, and we shall always be sorry we did not go today.'

'But he no longer remembers us any longer.'

'All the same, he will feel us there in the door.'

'But can we forget this is Robert's and Digby's and Lucius's goodbye walk? It would be heartless of both of us to neglect them.'

'Then how heartless Fitzgeorge is!' smiled Henrietta.

'Fitzgeorge is himself, the eldest and in the Army. Fitzgeorge I'm afraid is not an excuse for us.'

A resigned sigh, or perhaps the pretence of one, heaved up Henrietta's still narrow bosom. To delay matters for just a moment more she shaded her eyes with one hand, to search the distance like a sailor looking for a sail. She gazed with hope and zeal in every direction, but that in which she and Sarah were bound to go. Then—'Oh, but Sarah, here *they* are, coming—they are!' she cried. She brought out her handkerchief and began to fly it, drawing it to and fro through the windless air.

In the glass of the distance, two horsemen came into view, cantering on a grass track between the fields. When the track dropped into a hollow they dropped with it, but by now the drumming of hoofs was heard. The reverberation filled the land, the silence and Sarah's being; not watching for the riders to reappear she instead fixed her eyes on her sister's handkerchief which, let hang limp while its owner intently waited, showed a bitten corner as well as a damson stain. Again it became a flag, in furious motion—'Wave too, Sarah, wave too! Make your bracelet flash!'

'They must have seen us if they will ever see us,' said Sarah, standing still as a stone.

Henrietta's waving at once ceased. Facing her sister she crunched up her handkerchief, as though to stop it acting a lie. 'I can see you are shy,' she said in a dead voice. 'So shy you won't even wave to *Fitzgeorge*?'

Her way of not speaking the *other* name had a hundred meanings; she drove them all in by the way she did not look at Sarah's face. The impulsive breath she had caught stole silently out again, while her eyes—till now at their brightest, their most speaking—dulled with uncomprehending solitary alarm. The ordeal of awaiting Eugene's approach thus became for Sarah, from moment to moment, torture.

Fitzgeorge, Papa's heir, and his friend Eugene, the young neighbouring squire, struck off the track and rode up at a trot with their hats doffed. Sun striking low turned Fitzgeorge's flesh to coral and made Eugene blink his dark eyes. The young men reined in; the girls looked up at the horses. 'And my father, Constance, the others?' Fitzgeorge demanded, as though the stubble had swallowed them.

'Ahead, on the way to the quarry, the other side of the hill.'

'We heard you were all walking together,' Fitzgeorge said, seeming dissatisfied.

'We are following.'

'What, alone?' said Eugene, speaking for the first time.

'Forlorn!' glittered Henrietta, raising two mocking hands.

Fitzgeorge considered, said 'Good' severely, and signified to Eugene that they would ride on. But too late: Eugene had dismounted. Fitzgeorge saw, shrugged and flicked his horse to a trot; but Eugene led his slowly between the sisters. Or rather, Sarah walked on his left hand, the horse on his right and Henrietta the other side of the horse. Henrietta, acting like somebody quite alone, looked up at the sky, idly holding one of the empty stirrups. Sarah, however, looked at the ground with Eugene inclined as though to speak but not speaking. Enfolded, dizzied, blinded as though inside a wave, she could feel his features carved in brightness above her. Alongside the slender stepping of his horse,

Eugene matched his naturally long free step to hers. His elbow was through the reins; with his fingers he brushed back the lock that his bending to her had sent falling over his forehead. She recorded the sublime act and knew what smile shaped his lips. So each without looking trembled before an image, while slow colour burned up the curves of her cheeks. The consummation would be when their eyes met.

At the other side of the horse, Henrietta began to sing. At once her pain, like a scientific ray, passed through the horse and Eugene to penetrate Sarah's heart.

We surmount the skyline: the family come into our view, we into theirs. They are halted, waiting, on the decline to the quarry. The handsome statufied group in strong yellow sunshine, aligned by Papa and crowned by Fitzgeorge, turn their judging eyes on the laggards, waiting to close their ranks round Henrietta and Sarah and Eugene. One more moment and it will be too late; no further communication will be possible. Stop oh stop Henrietta's heart-breaking singing! Embrace her close again! Speak the only possible word! Say—oh, say what? Oh, the word is lost!

'*Henrietta . . .*'

A shock of striking pain in the knuckles of the outflung hand—Sarah's? The eyes, opening, saw that the hand had struck, not been struck: there was a corner of a table. Dust, whitish and gritty, lay on the top of the table and on the telephone. Dull but piercing white light filled the room and what was left of the ceiling; her first thought was that it must have snowed. If so, it was winter now.

Through the calico stretched and tacked over the window came the sound of a piano: someone was playing Tchaikowsky badly in a room without windows or doors. From somewhere else in the hollowness came a cascade of hammering. Close up, a voice: 'Oh, *awake*, Mary?' It came from the other side of the open door, which jutted out between herself and the speaker—he on the threshold, she lying on the uncovered mattress of a bed. The speaker added: 'I had been going away.'

Summoning words from somewhere she said: 'Why? I didn't know you were here.'

'Evidently—Say, who is "Henrietta"?'

Despairing tears filled her eyes. She drew back her hurt hand, began to suck at the knuckle and whimpered, 'I've hurt myself.'

A man she knew to be 'Travis', but failed to focus, came round the door saying: 'Really I don't wonder.' Sitting down on the edge of the mattress he drew her hand away from her lips and held it: the act, in itself gentle, was accompanied by an almost hostile stare of concern. 'Do listen, Mary,' he said. 'While you've slept I've been all over the house again, and I'm less than ever satisfied that it's safe. In your normal senses you'd never attempt to stay here. There've been alerts, and more than alerts, all day; one more bang anywhere near, which may happen at any moment, could bring the rest of this down. You keep telling me that you have things to see to—but do you know what chaos the rooms are in? Till they've gone ahead with more clearing, where can you hope to start? And if there *were* anything you could do, you couldn't do it. Your own nerves know that, if you don't: it was almost frightening, when I looked in just now to see the way you were sleeping—you've shut up shop.'

She lay staring over his shoulder at the calico window. He went on: 'You don't like it here. Your self doesn't like it. Your will keeps driving your self, but it can't be driven the whole way—it makes its own get-out: sleep. Well, I want you to sleep as much as you (really) do. But *not* here. So I've taken a room for you in a hotel; I'm going now for a taxi; you can practically make the move without waking up.'

'No, I can't get into a taxi without waking.'

'Do you realize you're the last soul left in the terrace?'

'Then who is that playing the piano?'

'Oh, one of the furniture-movers in Number Six. I didn't count the jaquerie; of course *they're* in possession—unsupervised, teeming, having a high old time. While I looked in on you in here ten minutes ago they were smashing out that conservatory at the other end. Glass being done in in cold blood—it was brutalizing. You never batted an eyelid: in fact, I thought you smiled.' He listened. 'Yes, the piano—they are highbrow all right. You know there's a workman downstairs lying on your blue sofa looking for pictures in one of your French books?'

'No,' she said. 'I've no idea who is there.'

'Obviously. With the lock blown off your front door anyone who likes can get in and out.'

'Including you.'

'Yes, I've had a word with a chap about getting that lock back before tonight. As for you, you don't know what is happening.'

'I did,' she said, locking her fingers before her eyes.

The unreality of this room and of Travis's presence preyed on her as figments of dreams that one knows to be dreams can do. This environment's being in semi-ruin struck her less than its being some sort of device or trap; and she rejoiced, if anything, in its decrepitude. As for Travis, he had his own part in the conspiracy to keep her from the beloved two. She felt he began to feel he was now unmeaning. She was struggling not to condemn him, scorn him for his ignorance of Henrietta, Eugene, her loss. His possessive angry fondness was part, of course, of the story of him and Mary, which like a book once read she remembered clearly but with indifference. Frantic at being delayed here, while the moment awaited her in the cornfield, she all but afforded a smile at the grotesqueries of being saddled with Mary's body and lover. Rearing up her head from the bare pillow, she looked, as far as the crossed feet, along the form inside which she found herself trapped: the irrelevant body of Mary, weighted down to the bed, wore a short black modern dress, flaked with plaster. The toes of the black suède shoes by their sickly whiteness showed Mary must have climbed over fallen ceilings; dirt engraved the fate-lines in Mary's palms.

This inspired her to say: 'But I've made a start; I've been pulling out things of value or things I want.'

For answer Travis turned to look down, expressively, at some object out of her sight, on the floor close by the bed. '*I* see,' he said, 'a musty old leather box gaping open with God knows what—junk, illegible letters, diaries, yellow photographs, chiefly plaster and dust. Of all things, Mary!—after a missing will?'

'Everything one unburies seems the same age.'

'Then what are these, where do they come from—family stuff?'

'No idea,' she yawned into Mary's hand. 'They may not even be mine. Having a house like this that had empty rooms must have made me store more than I knew, for years. I came on these, so I wondered. Look if you like.'

He bent and began to go through the box—it seemed to her, not unsuspiciously. While he blew grit off packets and fumbled with tapes she lay staring at the exposed laths of the ceiling, calculating. She then said: 'Sorry if I've been cranky, about the hotel and all. Go away just for two hours, then come back with a taxi, and I'll go quiet. Will that do?'

'Fine—except why not now?'

'*Travis . . .*'

'Sorry. It shall be as you say . . . You've got some good morbid stuff in this box, Mary—so far as I can see at a glance. The photographs seem more your sort of thing. Comic but lyrical. All of one set of people—a beard, a gun and a pot hat, a schoolboy with a moustache, a phaeton drawn up in front of mansion, a group on steps, a *carte de visite* of two young ladies hand-in-hand in front of a painted field—'

'*Give that to me*!'

She instinctively tried and failed, to unbutton the bosom of Mary's dress: it offered no hospitality to the photograph. So she could only fling herself over on the mattress, away from Travis, covering the two faces with her body. Racked by that oblique look of Henrietta's she recorded, too, a sort of personal shock at having seen Sarah for the first time.

Travis's hand came over her, and she shuddered. Wounded, he said: 'Mary . . .'

'Can't you leave *me* alone?'

She did not move or look till he had gone out saying: 'Then, in two hours.' She did not therefore see him pick up the dangerous box, which he took away under his arm, out of her reach.

They were back. Now the sun was setting behind the trees, but its rays passed dazzling between the branches into the beautiful warm red room. The tips of the ferns in the jardinière curled gold, and Sarah, standing by the jardinière, pinched at a leaf of scented geranium. The carpet had a great centre of pomegranates, on which no tables or chairs stood, and its whole circle was between herself and the others.

No fire was lit yet, but where they were grouped was a hearth. Henrietta sat on a low stool, resting her elbow above her head on the arm of Mamma's chair, looking away intently as though into a fire, idle. Mamma embroidered, her needle slowed down by her thoughts; the length of tatting with roses she had already done overflowed stiffly over her supple skirts. Stretched on the rug at Mamma's feet, Arthur looked through an album of Swiss views, not liking them but vowed to be very quiet. Sarah, from where she stood, saw fuming cataracts and null eternal snows as poor Arthur kept turning over the pages, which had tissue paper between.

Against the white marble mantelpiece stood Eugene. The dark red shadows gathering in the drawing-room as the trees drowned more and more of the sun would reach him last, perhaps never: it seemed to Sarah that a lamp was lighted behind his face. He was the only gentleman with the ladies: Fitzgeorge had gone to the stables, Papa to give an order; Cousin Theodore was consulting a dictionary; in the gunroom Robert, Lucius and Digby went through the sad rites, putting away their guns. All this was known to go on but none of it could be heard.

This particular hour of subtle light—not to be fixed by the clock, for it was early in winter and late in summer and in spring and autumn now, about Arthur's bed-time—had always, for Sarah, been Henrietta's. To be with her indoors or out, upstairs or down, was to share the same crepitation. Her spirit ran on past yours with a laughing shiver into an element of its own. Leaves and branches and mirrors in empty rooms became animate. The sisters rustled and scampered and concealed themselves where nobody else was in play that was full of fear, fear that was full of play. Till, by dint of making each other's hearts beat violently, Henrietta so wholly and Sarah so nearly lost all human reason that Mamma had been known to look at them searchingly as she sat instated for evening among the calm amber lamps.

But now Henrietta had locked the hour inside her breast. By spending it seated beside Mamma, in young imitation of Constance the Society daughter, she disclaimed for ever anything else. It had always been she who with one fierce act destroyed any toy that might be outgrown. Only by never looking at Sarah did she admit their eternal loss.

Eugene, not long returned from a foreign tour, spoke of travel, addressing himself to Mamma, who thought but did not speak of her wedding journey. But every now and then she had to ask Henrietta to pass the scissors or tray of carded wools, and Eugene seized every such moment to look at Sarah. Into eyes always brilliant with melancholy he dared begin to allow no other expression. But this in itself declared the conspiracy of still undeclared love. For her part she looked at him as though he, transfigured by the strange light, were indeed a picture, a picture who could not see her. The wallpaper now flamed scarlet behind his shoulder. Mamma, Henrietta, even unknowing Arthur were in no hurry to raise their heads.

Henrietta said 'If I were a man I should take my bride to Italy.'

'There are mules in Switzerland,' said Arthur.

'Sarah,' said Mamma, who turned in her chair mildly, 'where are you, my love; do you never mean to sit down?'

'To Naples,' said Henrietta.

'Are you not thinking of Venice?' asked Eugene.

'No,' returned Henrietta, 'why should I be? I should like to climb the volcano. But then I am not a man, and am still less likely ever to be a bride.'

'Arthur . . .' Mamma said.

'Mamma?'

'Look at the clock.'

Arthur sighed politely, got up and replaced the album on the circular table, balanced upon the rest. He offered his hand to Eugene, his cheek to Henrietta and to Mamma; then he started towards Sarah, who came to meet him. 'Tell me, Arthur,' she said, embracing him, 'what did you do today?'

Arthur only stared with his button blue eyes. 'You were there too; we went for a walk in the cornfield, with Fitzgeorge on his horse, and I fell down.' He pulled out of her arms and said: 'I must go back to my beetle.' He had difficulty, as always, in turning the handle of the mahogany door. Mamma waited till he had left the room, then said: 'Arthur is quite a man now; he no longer comes running to me when he has hurt himself. Why, I did not even know he had fallen down. Before we know, he will be going away to school too.' She sighed and lifted her eyes to Eugene. 'Tomorrow is to be a sad day.'

Eugene with a gesture signified his own sorrow. The sentiments of Mamma could have been uttered only here in the drawing-room, which for all its size and formality was lyrical and almost exotic. There was a look like velvet in darker parts of the air; sombre window draperies let out gushes of lace; the music on the piano-forte bore tender titles, and the harp though unplayed gleamed in a corner, beyond sofas, whatnots, armchairs, occasional tables that all stood on tottering little feet. At any moment a tinkle might have been struck from the lustres' drops of the brighter day, a vibration from the musical instruments, or a quiver from the fringes and ferns. But the towering vases upon the consoles, the albums piled on the tables, the shells and figurines on the flights of brackets, all had, like the alabaster Leaning Tower of Pisa, an equilibrium of their own. Nothing would fall or change. And everything in the drawing-room was muted, weighted, pivoted by Mamma. When she added: 'We shall not feel quite the same,' it was to be understood that she would not have spoken thus from her place at the opposite end of Papa's table.

'Sarah,' said Henrietta curiously, 'what made you ask Arthur what he had been doing? Surely you have not forgotten today?'

The sisters were seldom known to address or question one another in public; it was taken that they knew each other's minds. Mamma, though untroubled, looked from one to the other. Henrietta continued: 'No day, least of all today, is like any other—Surely that must be true?' she said to Eugene. 'You will never forget my waving my handkerchief?'

Before Eugene had composed an answer, she turned to Sarah: 'Or *you*, them riding across the fields?'

Eugene also slowly turned his eyes on Sarah, as though awaiting with something like dread her answer to the question he had not asked. She drew a light little gold chair into the middle of the wreath of the carpet, where no one ever sat, and sat down. She said: 'But since then I think I have been asleep.'

'Charles the First walked and talked half an hour after his head was cut off,' said Henrietta mockingly. Sarah in anguish pressed the palms of her hands together upon a shred of geranium leaf.

'How else,' she said, 'could I have had such a bad dream?'

'That must be the explanation!' said Henrietta.

'A trifle fanciful,' said Mamma.

However rash it might be to speak at all, Sarah wished she knew how to speak more clearly. The obscurity and loneliness of her trouble was not to be borne. How could she put into words the feeling of dislocation, the formless dread that had been with her since she found herself in the drawing-room? The source of both had been what she must call her dream. How could she tell the others with what vehemence she tried to attach her being to each second, not because each was singular in itself, each a drop condensed from the mist of love in the room, but because she apprehended that the seconds were numbered? Her hope was that the others at least half knew. Were Henrietta and Eugene able to understand how completely, how nearly for ever, she had been swept from them, would they not without fail each grasp one of her hands?—She went so far as to throw her hands out, as though alarmed by a wasp. The shred of geranium fell to the carpet.

Mamma, tracing this behaviour of Sarah's to only one cause, could not but think reproachfully of Eugene. Delightful as his conversation had been, he would have done better had he paid this call with the object of interviewing Papa. Turning to Henrietta she asked her to ring for the lamps, as the sun had set.

Eugene, no longer where he had stood, was able to make no gesture towards the bell-rope. His dark head was under the tide of dusk; for, down on one knee on the edge of the wreath, he was feeling over the carpet for what had fallen from Sarah's hand. In the inevitable silence rooks on the return from the fields could be heard streaming over the house; their sound filled the sky and even the room, and it appeared so useless to ring the bell that Henrietta stayed quivering by Mamma's chair. Eugene, rose, brought out his fine white handkerchief and, while they watched, enfolded carefully in it what he had just found, then returning the handkerchief to his breast pocket. This was done so deep in the reverie that accompanies any final act that Mamma instinctively murmured to Henrietta: 'But you will be my child when Arthur has gone.'

The door opened for Constance to appear on the threshold. Behind her queenly figure globes approached, swimming in their own light: these were the lamps for which Henrietta had not rung, but these first were put on the hall tables. 'Why, Mamma,' exclaimed Constance, 'I cannot see who is with you!'

'Eugene is with us,' said Henrietta, 'but on the point of asking if he may send for his horse.'

'Indeed?' said Constance to Eugene. 'Fitzgeorge has been asking for you, but I cannot tell where he is now.'

The figures of Emily, Lucius and Cousin Theodore criss-crossed the lamplight there in the hall, to mass behind Constance's in the drawing-room door. Emily, over her sister's shoulder, said: 'Mamma, Lucius wishes to ask you whether for once he may take his guitar to school.'—'One objection, however,' said Cousin Theodore, 'is that Lucius's trunk is already locked and strapped.' 'Since Robert is taking his box of inks,' said Lucius, 'I do not see why I should not take my guitar.'—'But Robert,' said Constance, 'will soon be going to college.'

Lucius squeezed past the others into the drawing-room in order to look anxiously at Mamma, who said: 'You have thought of this late; we must go and see.' The others parted to let Mamma, followed by Lucius, out. Then Constance, Emily and Cousin Theodore deployed and sat down in different parts of the drawing-room, to await the lamps.

'I am glad the rooks have done passing over,' said Emily, 'they make me nervous.'—'Why?' yawned Constance haughtily, 'what do you think could happen?' Robert and Digby silently came in.

Eugene said to Sarah: 'I shall be back tomorrow.'

'But, oh—' she began. She turned to cry: 'Henrietta!'

'Why, what is the matter?' said Henrietta, unseen at the back of the gold chair. 'What could be sooner than tomorrow?'

'But something terrible may be going to happen.'

'There cannot fail to be tomorrow,' said Eugene gravely.

'*I* will see that there is tomorrow,' said Henrietta.

'You will never let me out of your sight?'

Eugene, addressing himself to Henrietta, said: 'Yes, promise her what she asks.'

Henrietta cried: 'She *is* never out of my sight. Who are you to ask me that, you Eugene? Whatever tries to come between me and Sarah becomes nothing. Yes, come tomorrow, come sooner, come—when you like, but no one will ever be quite alone with Sarah. You do not even know what you are trying to do. It is *you* who are making something terrible happen.—Sarah, tell him that this is true! Sarah—'

The others, in the dark on the chairs and sofas, could be felt to turn their judging eyes upon Sarah, who, as once before, could not speak—

—The house rocked: simultaneously the calico window split and more ceiling fell, though not on the bed. The enormous dull sound of the explosion died, leaving a minor trickle of dissolution still to be heard in parts of the house. Until the choking, stinging plaster dust had had time to settle, she lay with lips pressed close, nostrils not breathing and eyes shut. Remembering the box, Mary wondered if it had been again buried. No, she found, looking over the edge of the bed: that had been unable to happen because the box was missing. Travis, who must have taken it, would when he came back no doubt explain why. She looked at her watch, which had stopped, which was not surprising; she did not remember winding it for the last two days, but then she could not remember much. Through the torn window appeared the timelessness of an impermeably clouded late summer afternoon.

There being nothing left, she wished he would come to take her to the hotel. The one way back to the fields was barred by Mary's surviving the fall of ceiling. Sarah was right in doubting that there would be tomorrow: Eugene, Henrietta were lost in time to the woman weeping there on the bed, no longer reckoning who she was.

At last she heard the taxi, then Travis hurrying up the littered stairs. 'Mary, you're all right, Mary—*another*?' Such a helpless white face came round the door that she could only hold out her arms and say: 'Yes, but where have *you* been?'

'You said two hours. But I wish—'

'I have missed you.'

'Have you? Do you know you are crying?'

'Yes. How are we to live without natures? We only know inconvenience now, not sorrow. Everything pulverizes so easily because it is rot-dry; one can only wonder that it makes so much noise. The source, the sap must have dried up, or the pulse must have stopped, before you and I were conceived. So much flowed through people; so little flows through us. All we can do is imitate love or sorrow.—Why did you take away my box?'

He only said: 'It is in my office.'

She continued: 'What has happened is cruel: I am left with a fragment torn out of a day, a day I don't even know where or when; and now how am I to help laying that like a pattern against the poor stuff of everything else?—Alternatively, I am a person drained by a dream. I cannot forget the climate of those hours. Or life at that pitch, eventful—not happy, no, but strung like a harp. I have had a sister called Henrietta.'

'And I have been looking inside your box. What else can you expect?—I have had to write off this day, from the work point of view, thanks to you. So could I sit and do nothing for the last two hours? I just glanced through this and that—still, I know the family.'

'You said it was morbid stuff.'

'Did I? I still say it gives off something.'

She said: 'And then there was Eugene.'

'Probably. I don't think I came on much of his except some notes he must have made for Fitzgeorge from some book on scientific farming. Well, there it is: I have sorted everything out and put it back again, all but a lock of hair that tumbled out of a letter I could not trace. So I've got the hair in my pocket.'

'What colour is it?'

'Ash-brown. Of course, it is a bit—desiccated. Do you want it?'

'No,' she said with a shudder. 'Really, Travis, what revenges you take!'

'I didn't look at it that way,' he said puzzled.

'Is the taxi waiting?' Mary got off the bed and, picking her way across the room, began to look about for things she ought to take with her, now and then stopping to brush her dress. She took the mirror out of her bag to see how dirty her face was. 'Travis—' she said suddenly.

'Mary?'

'Only, I—'

'That's all right. Don't let us imitate anything just at present.'

In the taxi, looking out of the window, she said: 'I suppose, then, that I am descended from Sarah?'

'No,' he said, 'that would be impossible. There must be some reason why you should have those papers, but that is not the one. From all negative evidence Sarah, like Henrietta, remained unmarried. I found no mention of either, after a certain date, in the letters of Constance, Robert or Emily, which makes it seem likely both died young. Fitzgeorge refers, in a letter to Robert written in his old age, to some friend of their youth who was thrown from his horse and killed, riding back after a visit to their home. The young man, whose name doesn't appear, was alone; and the evening, which was in autumn, was fine though late. Fitzgeorge wonders, and says he will always wonder, what made the horse shy in those empty fields.'

MARJORIE BARNARD

The Lottery

The first that Ted Bilborough knew of his wife's good fortune was when one of his friends, an elderly wag, shook his hand with mock gravity and murmured a few words of manly but inappropriate sympathy. Ted didn't know what to make of it. He had just stepped from the stairway on to the upper deck of the 6.15 p.m. ferry from town. Fred Lewis seemed to have been waiting for him, and as he looked about he got the impression of newspapers and grins and a little flutter of half derisive excitement, all focussed on himself. Everything seemed to bulge towards him. It must be some sort of leg pull. He felt his assurance threatened, and the corner of his mouth twitched uncomfortably in his fat cheek, as he tried to assume a hard boiled manner.

'Keep the change, laddie,' he said.

'He doesn't know, actually he doesn't know.'

'Your wife's won the lottery!'

'He won't believe you. Show him the paper. There it is as plain as my nose. Mrs. Grace Bilborough, 52 Cuthbert Street.' A thick, stained forefinger pointed to the words. 'First prize £5000 Last Hope Sydicate.'

'He's taking it very hard,' said Fred Lewis, shaking his head.

They began thumping him on the back. He had travelled on that ferry every week-day for the last ten years, barring a fortnight's holiday in January, and he knew nearly everyone. Even those he didn't know entered into the spirit of it. Ted filled his pipe nonchalantly but with unsteady fingers. He was keeping that odd unsteadyness, that seemed to begin somewhere deep in his chest, to himself. It was a wonder that fellows in the office hadn't got hold of this, but they had been busy today in the hot loft under the chromium pipes of the pneumatic system, sending down change and checking up on credit accounts. Sale time. Grace might have let him know. She could have rung up from Thompson's. Bill was always borrowing the lawn mower and the step ladder, so it would hardly be asking a favour in the circumstances. But that was Grace all over.

'If I can't have it myself, you're the man I like to see get it.'

They meant it too. Everyone liked Ted in a kind sort of way. He was a good fellow in both senses of the word. Not namby pamby, always ready for a joke but a good citizen too, a good husband and father. He wasn't the sort that refused to wheel the perambulator. He flourished the perambulator. His wife could hold up her head, they payed their bills weekly and he even put something away, not much but something, and that was a truimph the way things were, the ten per cent knocked off his salary in the depression not restored yet, and one thing and another. And always cheerful, with a joke for everyone. All this was vaguely present in Ted's mind. He'd always expected in a trusting sort of way to be rewarded, but not through Grace.

'What are you going to do with it, Ted?'

'You won't see him for a week, he's going on a jag.'

This was very funny because Ted never did, not even on Anzac Day.

A voice with a grievance said, not for the first time, 'I've had shares in a ticket every week since it started, and I've never won a cent.' No one was interested.

'You'll be going off for a trip somewhere?'

'They'll make you president of the Tennis Club and you'll have to donate a silver cup.'

They were flattering him underneath the jokes.

'I expect Mrs Bilborough will want to put some of it away for the children's future,' he said. It was almost as if he were giving an interview to the press, and he was pleased with himself for saying the right thing. He always referred to Grace in public as Mrs Bilborough. He had too nice a social sense to say 'the Missus.'

Ted let them talk, and looked out of the window. He wasn't interested in the news in the paper tonight. The little boat vibrated fussily, and left a long wake like moulded glass in the quiet river. The evening was drawing in. The sun was sinking into a bank of grey cloud, soft and formless as mist. The air was dusky, so that its light was closed into itself and it was easy to look at, a thick golden disc more like a moon rising through smoke than the sun. It threw a single column of orange light on the river, the ripples from the ferry fanned out into it, and their tiny shadows truncated it. The bank, rising steeply from the river and closing it in till it looked like a lake, was already bloomed with shadows. The shapes of two churches and a broken frieze of pine trees stood out against the gentle sky, not sharply, but with a soft arresting grace. The slopes, wooded and scattered with houses, were dim and sunk in idyllic peace. The river showed thinly bright against the dark lane. Ted could see that the smooth water was really a pale tawny gold with patches, roughened by the turning tide, of frosty blue. It was only when you stared at it and concentrated your attention that you realised the colours. Turning to look down stream away from the sunset, the water gleamed silvery grey with dark clear scrabblings upon it. There were two worlds, one looking towards the sunset with the dark land against it dreaming and still, and the other looking down stream over the silvery river to the other bank, on which all the light concentrated. Houses with windows of orange fire, black trees, a great silver gasometer, white oil tanks with the look of clumsy mushrooms, buildings serrating the sky, even a suggestion seen or imagined of red roofs, showing up miraculously in that airy light.

'Five thousand pounds,' he thought. 'Five thousand pounds.' Five thousand pounds at five per cent, five thousand pounds stewing gently away in its interest, making old age safe. He could do almost anything he could think of with five thousand pounds. It gave his mind a stretched sort of feeling, just thinking of it. It was hard to connect five thousand pounds with Grace. She might have let him know. And where had the five and threepence to buy the ticket come from? He couldn't help wondering about that. When you budgeted as carefully as they did there wasn't five and threepence over. If there had been, well, it wouldn't have been over at all, he would have put it in the bank. He hadn't noticed any difference in the housekeeping, and he prided himself he noticed everything. Surely she hadn't been running up bills to buy lottery tickets. His mind darted here and there suspiciously. There was something secretive in Grace, and he'd thought she told him everything. He'd taken it for granted, only, of course, in the ordinary run there was nothing to tell. He consciously relaxed the knot in his mind. After all, Grace had won the five thousand pounds. He remembered charitably that she had always been a good wife to him. As he thought that he had a vision of the patch on his shirt, his newly washed cream trousers laid out for tennis, the children's neatness, the tidy house. That was being a good wife. And he had been a good husband, always brought his money home and never looked at another woman. Theirs was a model home, everyone acknowledged it, but—well—somehow he found it easier to be cheerful in other people's homes than in his own. It was Grace's fault. She wasn't cheery and easy going. Something moody about her now. Woody. He'd worn better than Grace, anyone could see that, and yet it was he who had had the hard time. All she had to do was to stay at home and look after the house and the children. Nothing much in that. She always seemed to be working, but he couldn't see what there was to do that could take her so long. Just a touch of woman's perversity. It wasn't that Grace had aged. Ten years married and with two children, there was still something girlish about her—raw, hard girlishness that had never mellowed. Grace was—Grace, for better or for worse. Maybe she'd be a bit brighter now. He could not help wondering how she had managed the five and three. If she could shower five and threes about like that, he'd been giving her too much of the housekeeping. And why did she want to give it that damnfool name 'Last Hope.' That meant there had been others, didn't it? It probably didn't mean a thing, just a lucky tag.

A girl on the seat opposite was sewing lace on silkies for her trousseau, working intently in the bad light.

'Another one starting out,' Ted thought.

'What about it?' said the man beside him.

Ted hadn't been listening.

The ferry had tied up at his landing stage and Ted got off. He tried not to show in his walk that his wife had won £5000. He felt jaunty and tired at once. He walked up the hill with a bunch of other men, his neighbours. They were still teasing him about the money, they didn't know how to stop. It was a very still, warm evening. As the sun descended into the misty bank on the horizon it picked out the delicate shapes of clouds invisibly sunk in the mass, outlining them with a fine thread of gold.

One by one the men dropped out, turning into side streets or opening garden gates till Ted was alone with a single companion, a man who lived in a semi-detached cottage at the end of the street. They were suddenly very quiet and sober. Ted felt the ache round his mouth where he'd been smiling and smiling.

'I'm awfully glad you've had this bit of luck.'

'I'm sure you are, Eric,' Ted answered in a subdued voice.

'There's nobody I'd sooner see have it.'

'That's very decent of you.'

'I mean it.'

'Well, well, I wasn't looking for it.'

'We could do with a bit of luck like that in our house.'

'I bet you could.'

'There's an instalment on the house due next month, and Nellie's got to come home again. Seems as if we'd hardly done paying for the wedding.

'That's bad.'

'She's expecting, so I suppose Mum and Dad will be let in for all that too.'

'It seems only the other day Nellie was a kid getting round on a scooter.'

'They grow up,' Eric agreed. 'It's the instalment that's the rub. First of next month. They expect it on the nail too. If we hadn't that hanging over us it wouldn't matter about Nellie coming home. She's our girl, and it'll be nice to have her about the place again.'

'You'll be as proud as a cow with two tails when you're a grandpa.'

'I suppose so.'

They stood mutely by Eric's gate. An idea began to flicker in Ted's mind, and with it a feeling of sweetness and happiness and power such as he had never expected to feel.

'I won't see you stuck, old man,' he said.

'That's awfully decent of you.'

'I mean it.'

They shook hands as they parted. Ted had only a few steps more and he took them slowly. Very warm and dry, he thought. The garden will need watering. Now he was at his gate. There was no one in sight. He stood for a moment looking about him. It was as if he saw the house he had lived in for ten years, for the first time. He saw that it had a mean, narrow-chested appearance. The roof tiles were discoloured, the woodwork needed painting, the crazy pavement that he had laid with such zeal had an unpleasant flirtatious look. The revolutionary thought formed in his mind. 'We might leave here.' Measured against the possibilities that lay before him, it looked small and mean. Even the name, 'Emoh Ruo,' seemed wrong, pokey.

Ted was reluctant to go in. It was so long since anything of the least importance had happened between him and Grace, that it made him shy. He did not know how she would take it. Would she be all in a dither and no dinner ready? He hoped so but feared not.

He went into the hall, hung up his hat and shouted in a big bluff voice. 'Well, well, well, and where's my rich wife?'

Grace was in the kitchen dishing dinner.

'You're late,' she said. 'The dinner's spoiling.'

The children were quiet but restless, anxious to leave the table and go out to play. 'I got rid of the reporters,' Grace said in a flat voice. Grace had character, trust her to handle a couple of cub reporters. She didn't seem to want to talk about it to her husband either. He felt himself, his voice, his stature dwindling. He looked at her with hard eyes. 'Where did she get the money,' he wondered again, but more sharply.

Presently they were alone. There was a pause. Grace began to clear the table. Ted felt that he must do something. He took her awkwardly into his arms. 'Grace, aren't you pleased?'

She stared at him a second then her face seemed to fall together, a sort of spasm, something worse than tears. But she twitched away from him. 'Yes,' she said, picking up a pile of crockery and making for the kitchen. He followed her.

'You're a dark horse, never telling me a word about it.'

'She's like a Red Indian,' he thought. She moved about the kitchen with quick nervous movements. After a moment she answered what was in his mind:

'I sold my mother's ring and chain. A man came to the door buying old gold. I bought a ticket every week till the money was gone.'

'Oh,' he said. Grace had sold her mother's wedding ring to buy a lottery ticket.

'It was my money.'

'I didn't say it wasn't.'

'No, you didn't.'

The plates clattered in her hands. She was evidently feeling something, and feeling it strongly. But Ted didn't know what. He couldn't make her out.

She came and stood in front of him, her back to the littered table, her whole body taut. 'I suppose you're wondering what I am going to do? I'll tell you. I'm going away. By myself. Before it's too late. I'm going tomorrow.'

He didn't seem to be taking it in.

'Beattie will come and look after you and the children. She'll be glad to. It won't cost you a penny more than it does now,' she added.

He stood staring at her, his flaccid hands hanging down, his face sagging.

'Then you meant what you said in the paper. "Last Hope?" ' he said.

'Yes,' she answered.

ANNA KAVAN

An Unpleasant Reminder

Last summer, or perhaps it was only the other day—I find it so difficult to keep count of time now—I had a very disagreeable experience.

The day was ill-omened from the beginning; one of those unlucky days when every little detail seems to go wrong and one finds oneself engaged in a perpetual and infuriating strife with inanimate objects. How truly fiendish the sub-human world can be on these occasions! How every atom, every cell, every molecule, seems to be leagued in a maddening conspiracy against the unfortunate being who has incurred its obscure displeasure! This time, to make matters worse, the weather itself had decided to join in the fray. The sky was covered with a dull gray lid of cloud, the mountains had turned sour prussian blue, swarms of mosquitoes infested the shores of the lake. It was one of those sunless days that are infinitely more depressing than the bleakest winter weather; days when the whole atmosphere seems stale, and the world feels like a dustbin full of cold battered tins and fish scales and decayed cabbage stalks.

Of course, I was behindhand with everything all day long. I had to race through my changing for the game of tennis I had arranged to play in the afternoon, and as it was I was about ten minutes late. The other players had arrived and were having some practice shots as they waited for me. I was annoyed to see that they had chosen the middle court which is the one I like least of the three available for our use. When I asked why they had not taken the upper one, which is far the best, they replied that it had already been reserved for some official people. Then I suggested going to the lower court; but they grumbled and said that it was damp on account of the over-hanging trees. As there was no sun, I could not advance the principal objection to the middle court, which is that it lies the wrong way for the afternoon light. There was nothing for it but to begin playing.

The next irritating occurrence was that instead of keeping to my usual partner, David Post, it was for some reason decided that I should play with a man named Müller whom I hardly knew and who turned out to be a very inferior player. He was a bad loser as well, for as soon as it became clear that our opponents were too strong for us, he lost all interest in the game and behaved in a thoroughly unsporting manner. He was continually nodding and smiling to the people who stopped to watch us, paying far more attention to the onlookers than to the game. At other times, while the rest of us were collecting the balls or I was receiving the service, he would move away and stare at the main road which runs near, watching the cars as if he expected the arrival of someone he knew. In the end it became almost impossible to keep him on the court at all; he was always wandering off and having to be recalled by our indignant shouts. It seemed futile to continue the game in these circumstances, and at the end of the first set we abandoned play by mutual consent.

You can imagine that I was not in a particularly good mood when I got back to my room. Besides being in a state of nervous irritation I was hot and tired, and my chief object was to have a bath and change into fresh clothes as soon as possible. So I was not at all pleased to find a complete stranger waiting for me to whom I should have to attend before I did anything else.

She was a young woman of about my own age, quite attractive in a rather hard way, and neatly dressed in a tan linen suit, white shoes, and a hat with a white feather. She spoke well, but with a slight accent that I couldn't quite place: afterwards I came to the conclusion that she was a colonial of some sort.

As politely as I could I invited her to sit down and asked what I could do for her. She refused the chair, and, instead of giving a straightforward answer, spoke evasively, touching the racket which I still held in my hand, and making some inquiry about the strings. It seemed quite preposterous to me in the state I was in then to find myself involved with an unknown woman in an aimless discussion of the merits of different makes of rackets, and I'm afraid I closed the subject rather abruptly and asked her point-blank to state her business.

But then she looked at me in such a peculiar way, saying in quite a different voice, 'You know, I'm really sorry I have to give you this,' and I saw that she was holding out a box towards me, just an ordinary small, round, black pillbox that might have come from any druggist. And all at once I felt frightened and wished we could return to the conversation about the tennis rackets. But there was no going back.

I'm not sure now whether she told me in so many words or whether I simply deduced that the judgment which I had awaited so long had at last been passed upon me and that this was the end. I remember—of all things!—feeling a little aggrieved because the sentence was conveyed to me in such a casual, unostentatious way, almost as if it were a commonplace event. I opened the box and saw the four white pellets inside.

'Now?' I asked. And I found that I was looking at my visitor with altered eyes, seeing her as an official messenger whose words had acquired a fatal portentousness.

She nodded without speaking. There was a pause. 'The sooner the better,' she said. I could feel the perspiration, still damp on me from the game, turning cold as ice.

'But at least I must have a bath first!' I cried out in a frantic way, clutching the clammy neck of my tennis shirt. 'I can't stay like this—it's indecent—undignified!'

She told me that would be allowed as a special concession.

Into the bathroom I went like a doomed person, and turned on the taps. I don't remember anything about the bath; I suppose I must have washed and dried myself mechanically and put on my mauve silk dressing gown with the blue sash. Perhaps I even combed my hair and powdered my face. All I remember is the little black box confronting me all the time from the shelf over the basin where I had put it down.

At last I brought myself to the point of opening it and holding the four pills in the palm of my hand; I lifted them to my mouth. And then the most ridiculous contretemps occurred—there was no drinking glass in the bathroom. It must have got broken: or else the maid must have taken it away and forgotten to bring it back. What was I to do? I couldn't swallow even four such small pellets without a drink, and I couldn't endure any further delay. In despair I filled the soapdish with water and swallowed them down somehow. I hadn't even waited to wash out the slimy layer of soap at the bottom and the taste nearly made me sick. For several times I stood retching and choking and clinging to the edge of the basin. Then I sat down on the stool. I waited with my heart beating as violently as a hammer in my throat. I waited; and nothing happened; absolutely nothing whatever. I didn't even feel drowsy or faint.

But it was not till I got back to the other room and found my visitor gone that I realized that the whole episode had been a cruel hoax, just a reminder of what is in store for me.

CAROLINE GORDON

The Petrified Woman

We were sitting on the porch at the Fork—it is where two creeks meet—after supper, talking about our family reunion. It was to be held at a place called Arthur's Cave that year (it has the largest entrance in the world, though it is not so famous as Mammoth), and there was to be a big picnic dinner, and we expected all our kin and connections to come, some of them from as far off as California.

Hilda and I had been playing in the creek all afternoon and hadn't had time to wash our legs before we came in to supper, so we sat on the bottom step where it was dark. Cousin Eleanor was in the porch swing with Cousin Tom. She had on a long white dress. It brushed the floor a little every time the swing moved. But you had to listen hard to hear it, under the noise the creek made. Wherever you were in that house you could hear the creek running over the rocks. Hilda and I used to play in it all day long. I liked to stay at her house better than at any of my other cousins'. But they never let me stay there long at a time. That was because she didn't have any mother, just her old mammy, Aunt Rachel—till that spring, when her father, Cousin Tom, married a lady from Birmingham named Cousin Eleanor.

A mockingbird started up in the juniper tree. It was the same one sang all night long that summer; we called him Sunny Jim. Cousin Eleanor got up and went to the end of the porch to try to see him.

'Do they always sing when there's a full moon?' she asked.

'They're worse in August,' Cousin Tom said. 'Got their crops laid by and don't give a damn if they do stay up all night.'

'And in August the Fayerlees repair to Arthur's Cave,' she said. 'Five hundred people repairing *en masse* to the womb—what a sight it must be.'

Cousin Tom went over and put his arm about her waist. 'Do they look any worse than other folks, taking them by and large?' he asked.

The mockingbird burst out as if he was the one who would

answer, and I heard Cousin Eleanor's dress brushing the floor again as she walked back to the swing. She had on tiny diamond earrings that night and a diamond cross that she said her father had given her. My grandmother said that she didn't like her mouth. I thought that she was the prettiest person ever lived.

'I'd rather not take them by and large,' she said. 'Do we *have* to go, Tom?'

'Hell!' he said. 'I'm contributing three carcasses to the dinner. I'm going, to get my money's worth.'

'One thing, I'm not going to let Cousin Edward Barker kiss me tomorrow,' Hilda said. 'He's got tobacco juice on his mustaches.'

Cousin Tom hadn't sat down in the swing when Cousin Eleanor did. He came and stood on the step above us. 'I'm going to shave off my mustache,' he said, 'and then the women won't have any excuse.'

'Which one will you start with?'

'Marjorie Wrenn. She's the prettiest girl in Gloversville. No, she isn't. I'm going to start with Sally. She's living in town now. . . . Sally, you ever been kissed?'

'She's going to kiss me good night right this minute,' Cousin Eleanor said and got up from the swing and came over and bent down and put her hand on each of our shoulders and kissed us, French fashion, she said, first on one cheek and then on the other. We said good night and started for the door. Cousin Tom was there. He put his arm about our waists and bumped our heads together and kissed Hilda first, on the mouth, and then he kissed me and he said, 'What about Joe Larrabee now?'

After we got in bed Hilda wanted to talk about Joe Larrabee. He was nineteen years old and the best dancer in town. That was the summer we used to take picnic suppers to the cave, and after supper the band would play and the young people would dance. Once, when we were sitting there watching, Joe Larrabee stopped and asked Hilda to dance, and after that she always wanted to sit on that same bench and when he went past, with Marjorie Wrenn or somebody, she would squeeze my hand tight, and I knew that she thought that maybe he would stop and ask her again. But I didn't think he ever would, and anyway I didn't feel like talking about him that night, so I told her I had to go to sleep.

I dreamed a funny dream. I was at the family reunion at the cave. There were a lot of other people there, but when I'd look into their faces it would be somebody I didn't know and I kept thinking that maybe I'd gone to the wrong picnic, when I saw Cousin Tom. He saw me too, and he stood still till I got to where he was and he said, 'Sally, this is Tom.' He didn't say Cousin Tom, just Tom. I was about to say something but somebody came in between us, and then I was in another place that wasn't like the cave and I was wondering how I'd ever get back when I heard a *knock, knock, knock*, and Hilda said, 'Come on, let's get up.'

The knocking was still going on. It took me a minute to know what it was: the old biscuit block was on the downstairs back porch right under our room, and Jason, Aunt Rachel's grandson, was pounding the dough for the beaten biscuits that we were going to take on the picnic.

We got to the cave around eleven o'clock. They don't start setting the dinner out till noon, so we went on down into the hollow, where Uncle Jack Dudley and Richard were tending the fires in the barbecue pits. A funny-looking wagon was standing over by the spring, but we didn't know what was in it, then, so we didn't pay any attention, just watched them barbecuing. Thirteen carcasses were roasting over the pits that day. It was the largest family reunion we ever had. There was a cousin named Robert Dale Owen Fayerlee who had gone off to St. Louis and got rich and he hadn't seen any of his kin in a long time and wanted everybody to have a good time, so he had chartered the cave and donated five cases of whisky. There was plenty of whisky for the Negroes too. Every now and then Uncle Jack would go off into the bushes and come back with tin cups that he would pass around. I like to be around Negroes, and so does Hilda. We were just sitting there watching them and not doing a thing, when Cousin Tom came up.

There are three or four Cousin Toms. They keep them straight by their middle names, usually, but they call him Wild Tom. He is not awfully old and has curly brown hair. I don't think his eyes would look so light if his face wasn't so red. He is out in the sun a lot.

He didn't see us at first. He went up to Uncle Jack and asked, 'Jack, how you fixed?' Uncle Jack said, 'Mister Tom, I ain't fooling you. I done already fixed.' 'I ain't going to fool with you, then,' Cousin Tom said, and he was pulling a bottle out of his pocket when he saw us. He is a man that is particular about little girls. He said, 'Hilda, what are you doing here?' and when we said we weren't doing a thing he said, 'You go right on up the hill.'

The first person I saw up there was my father. I hadn't expected to see him because before I left home I heard him say, 'All those mediocre people, getting together to congratulate themselves on their mediocrity! I ain't going a step.' But I reckon he didn't want to stay home by himself and, besides, he likes to watch them making fools of themselves.

My father is not connected. He is Professor Aleck Maury and he had a boys' school in Gloversville then. There was a girls' school there too, Miss Robinson's, but he said that I wouldn't learn anything if I went there till I was blue in the face, so I had to go to school with the boys. Sometimes I think that that is what makes me so peculiar.

It takes them a long time to set out the dinner. We sat down on a top rail of one of the benches with Susie McIntyre and watched the young people dance. Joe Larrabee was dancing with Marjorie Wrenn. She had on a tan coat-suit, with buttons made out of brown braid. Her hat was brown straw, with a tan ribbon. She held it in her hand, and it flopped up and down when she danced. It wasn't twelve o'clock but Joe Larrabee already had whisky on his breath. I smelled it when they went past.

Susie said for us to go out there and dance too. She asked me first, and I started to, and then I remembered last year when I got off on the wrong foot and Cousin Edward Barker came along and stepped on me, and I thought it was better not to try than to fail, so I let Hilda go with Susie.

I was still sitting there on top of the bench when Cousin Tom came along. He didn't seem to remember that he was mad at us. He said, 'Hello, Bumps.' I am not Bumps. Hilda is Bumps, so I said, 'I'm just waiting for Hilda . . . want me to get her?'

He waved his hand and I smelled whisky on his breath. 'Well, hello, anyhow,' he said, and I thought for a minute that he was going to kiss me. He is a man that you don't so much mind having him kiss you, even when he has whisky on his breath. But he went on to where Cousin Eleanor was helping Aunt Rachel set out the dinner. On the way he knocked into a lady and when he stepped back he ran into another one, so after he asked them to excuse him he went off on tiptoe. But he lifted his feet too high and put one of them down in a basket of pies. Aunt Rachel hollered out before she thought, 'Lord God, he done ruint my pies!'

Cousin Eleanor just stood there and looked at him. When he got almost up to her and she still didn't say anything, he stopped and looked at her a minute and then he said, 'All right!' and went off down the hill.

Susie and Hilda came back and they rang a big bell and Cousin Sidney Grassdale (they call them by the names of their places when there are too many of the same name) said a long prayer, and they all went in.

My father got his plate helped first and then he turned around to a man behind him and said, 'You stick to me and you can't go wrong. I know the ropes.'

The man was short and fat and had on a cream-colored Palm Beach suit and smiled a lot. I knew he was Cousin Robert Dale Owen Fayerlee, the one that gave all the whisky.

I didn't fool with any of the barbecue, just ate ham and chicken. And then I had some chicken salad, and Susie wanted me to try some potato salad, so I tried that too, and then we had a good many hot rolls and some stuffed eggs and some pickles and some cocoanut cake and some chocolate cake. I had been saving myself up for Aunt Rachel's chess pies and put three on my plate when I started out, but by the time I got to them I wasn't really hungry and I let Susie eat one of mine.

After we got through, Hilda said she had a pain in her stomach and we sat down on a bench till it went away. My grandmother and Aunt Maria came and sat down too. They had on white shirtwaists and black skirts and they both had their palm-leaf fans.

Cousin Robert D. Owen got up and made a speech. It was mostly about his father. He said that he was one of nature's noblemen. My grandmother and Aunt Maria held their fans up before their faces when he said that, and Aunt Maria said, 'Chh! *Jim* Fayerlee!' and my grandmother said that all that branch of the family was boastful.

Cousin Robert D. Owen got through with his father and started on back. He said that the Fayerlees were descended from Edward the Confessor and *Philippe le Bel* of France and the grandfather of George Washington.

My father was sitting two seats down, with Cousin Edward Barker. 'Now ain't that tooting?' he said.

Cousin Edward Barker hit himself on the knee. 'I be damn if I don't write to the *Tobacco Leaf* about that,' he said. 'The Fayerlees have been plain, honest countrymen since 1600. Don't that fool know anything about his own family?'

Susie touched me and Hilda on the shoulder, and we got up and squeezed past my grandmother and Aunt Maria. 'Where you going?' my grandmother asked.

'We're just going to take a walk, Cousin Sally,' Susie said.

We went out to the gate. The cave is at the foot of a hill. There are some long wooden steps leading up to the top of the hill, and right by the gate that keeps people out if they haven't paid is a refreshment stand. I thought that it would be nice to have some orange pop, but Susie said, 'No, let's go to the carnival.'

'There isn't any carnival,' Hilda said.

'There is, too,' Susie said, 'but it costs a quarter.'

'I haven't got but fifteen cents,' Hilda said.

'Here comes Giles Allard,' Susie said. 'Make out you don't see him.'

Cousin Giles Allard is a member of our family connection who is not quite right in the head. He doesn't have any special place to live, just roams around. Sometimes he will come and stay two or three weeks with you and sometimes he will come on the place and not come up to the house, but stay down in the cabin with some darky that he likes. He is a little, warped-looking man with pale blue eyes. I reckon that before a family reunion somebody give him one of their old suits. He had on a nice gray suit that day and looked just about like the rest of them.

He came up to us and said, 'You all having a good time?' and we said, 'Fine,' and thought he would go on, but he stood and looked at us. 'My name is Giles Allard,' he said.

We couldn't think of anything to say to that. He pointed his finger at me. 'You're named for your grandmother,' he said, 'but your name ain't Fayerlee.'

'I'm Sally Maury,' I said, 'Professor Maury's daughter.' My father being no kin to us, they always call me and my brother Sally Maury and Frank Maury, instead of plain Sally and Frank, the way they would if our blood was pure.

'Let's get away from him,' Susie whispered and she said out loud, 'We've got to go down on the spring, Cousin Giles,' and we hurried on as fast as we could. We didn't realize at first that

Cousin Giles was coming with us.

'There comes Papa,' Hilda said.

'He looks to me like he's drunk,' Susie said.

Cousin Tom stood still till we got up to him, just as he did in my dream. He smiled at us then and put his hand on Hilda's head and said, 'How are you, baby?' Hilda said, 'I'm all right,' and he said, 'You are three, sweet, pretty little girls. I'm going to give each one of you fifty cents,' and he stuck his hand in his pocket and took out two dollar bills, and when Hilda asked how we were going to get the change out, he said, 'Keep the change.'

'Whoopee!' Susie said. 'Now we can go to the carnival. You come too, Cousin Tom,' and we all started out toward the hollow.

The Negroes were gone, but there were still coals in the barbecue pits. That fat man was kneeling over one, cooking something.

'What you cooking for, fellow?' Cousin Tom asked. 'Don't you know this is the day everybody eats free?'

The fat man turned around and smiled at us.

'Can we see the carnival?' Susie asked.

The fat man jumped up. 'Yes, *ma'am*,' he said, 'you sure can see the carnival,' and he left his cooking and we went over to the wagon.

On the way the fat man kept talking, kind of singsong: 'You folks are in luck. . . . Wouldn't be here now but for a broken wheel . . . but one man's loss is another man's gain . . . I've got the greatest attraction in the world . . . yes, sir. Behind them draperies of pure silk lies the world's greatest attraction.'

'Well, what is it?' Cousin Tom asked.

The fat man stopped and looked at us and then he began shouting:

> 'Stell-a, Stell-a, the One and Only Stella!
> Not flesh, not bone,
> But calkypyrate stone,
> Sweet Sixteen a Hundred Years Ago
> And Sweet Sixteen Today!'

A woman sitting on a chair in front of the wagon got up and ducked around behind it. When she came out again she had on a red satin dress, with ostrich feathers on the skirt, and a red satin hat. She walked up to us and smiled and said, 'Will the ladies be seated?' and the man got some little stools down, quick, from where they were hooked onto the end of the wagon, and we all sat down, except Cousin Giles Allard, and he squatted in the grass.

The wagon had green curtains draped at each end of it. Gold birds were on the sides. The man bent down and pushed a spring or something, and one side of the wagon folded back, and there, lying on a pink satin couch, was a girl.

She had on a white satin dress. It was cut so low that you could see her bosom. Her head was propped on a satin pillow. Her eyes were shut. The lashes were long and black, with a little gold on them. Her face was dark and shone a little. But her hair was gold. It waved down on each side of her face and out over the green pillow. *The pillow had gold fringe on it! . . . lightly prest . . . in palace chambers . . . far apart. . . . The fragrant tresses are not stirred . . . that lie upon her charmèd heart. . . .*

The woman went around to the other side of the wagon. The man was still shouting:

'Stell-a, Stell-a,
The One and Only Stell-a!'

Cousin Giles Allard squeaked like a rabbit. The girl's eyes had opened. Her bosom was moving up and down.

Hilda got hold of my hand and held it tight. I could feel myself breathing. . . . But *her* breathing *is not heard . . . in palace chambers, far apart*. Her eyes were no color you could name. There was a veil over them.

The man was still shouting:

'You see her now
As she was then,
Sweet Sixteen a Hundred Years Ago,
And Sweet Sixteen Today!'

'How come her bubbies move if she's been dead so long?' Cousin Giles Allard asked.

Cousin Tom stood up, quick. 'She's a pretty woman,' he said, 'I don't know when I've seen a prettier woman . . . lies, quiet, too. . . . Well, thank you, my friend,' and he gave the man two or three dollars and started off across the field.

I could tell that Susie wanted to stay and watch the girl some more, and it did look like we could, after he had paid all that money, but he was walking straight off across the field and we had to go after him. Once, before we caught up with him, he put his hand into his pocket, and I saw the bottle flash in the sun as he tilted it, but he had it back in his pocket by the time we caught up with him.

'You reckon she is sort of mummied, Cousin Tom, or is she just turned to pure rock?' Susie asked.

He didn't answer her. He was frowning. All of a sudden he opened his eyes wide, as if he had just seen something he hadn't expected to see. But there wasn't anybody around or anything to look at, except that purple weed that grows all over the field. He turned around. He hollered, the way he hollers at the hands on the place: 'You come on here, Giles Allard!' and Cousin Giles came running. Once he tried to turn back, but Cousin Tom wouldn't let him go till we were halfway up to the cave. He let him slip into the bushes then.

The sun was in all our eyes. Hilda borrowed Susie's handkerchief and wiped her face. 'What made you keep Cousin Giles with us Papa?' she asked. 'I'd just as soon not have him along.'

Cousin Tom sat down on a rock. The sun's fiery glare was full on his face. You could see the pulse in his temple beat. A little red vein was spreading over one of his eyeballs. He pulled the bottle out of his pocket. 'I don't want him snooping around Stella,' he said.

'How could he hurt her, Papa, if she's already dead?' Hilda asked.

Cousin Tom held the bottle up and moved it so that it caught the sun. 'Maybe she isn't dead,' he said.

Susie laughed out.

Cousin Tom winked his red eye at Susie and shook the bottle. 'Maybe she isn't dead,' he said again. 'Maybe she's just resting.'

Hilda stamped her foot on the ground. '*Papa!* I believe you've had too much to drink.'

He drank all there was in the bottle and let it fall to the ground. He stood up. He put his hand out, as if he could push the sun away. 'And what business is that of yours?' he asked.

'I just wondered if you were going back to the cave, where everybody is,' Hilda said.

He was faced toward the cave then, but he shook his head. 'No,' he said. 'I'm not going up to the cave,' and he turned around and walked off down the hill.

We stood there a minute and watched him. 'Well, anyhow, he isn't going up there where everybody is,' Susie said.

'Where Mama is,' Hilda said, 'It just drives her crazy when he drinks.'

'She better get used to it,' Susie said. 'All the Fayerlee men drink.'

The reunion was about over when we got up to the cave. I thought I had to go back to my grandmother's—I was spending the summer there—but Hilda came and said I was to spend the night at the Fork.

'But you got to behave yourselves,' Aunt Rachel said. 'Big doings tonight.'

We rode back in the spring wagon with her and Richard and the ice-cream freezers and what was left of the dinner. Cousin Robert D. Owen and his wife, Cousin Marie, were going to spend the night at the Fork too, and they had gone on ahead in the car with the others.

Hilda and I had long-waisted dimity dresses made just alike that summer. I had a pink sash and she had a blue one. We were so excited while we were dressing for supper that night that we couldn't get our sashes tied right. 'Let's get Mama to do it,' Hilda said, and we went in to Cousin Eleanor's room. She was sitting at her dressing table, putting rouge on her lips. Cousin Marie was in there, too, sitting on the edge of the bed. Cousin Eleanor tied our sashes—she had to do mine twice before she got it right—and then gave me a little spank and said, 'Now! You'll be the belles of the ball.'

They hadn't told us to go out, so we sat down on the edge of the bed too. 'Mama, where is Papa?' Hilda asked.

'I have *no* idea, darling,' Cousin Eleanor said. 'Tom is a law unto himself.' She said that to Cousin Marie. I saw her looking at her in the mirror.

Cousin Marie had bright black eyes. She didn't need to use any rouge, her face was so pink. She had a dimple in one cheek. She said, 'It's a *world* unto itself. Bob's been telling me about it ever since we were married, but I didn't believe him, till I came and saw for myself . . . These little girls, now, how are they related?'

'In about eight different ways,' Cousin Eleanor said.

Cousin Marie gave a kind of little yip. 'It's just like an English novel,' she said.

'They are mostly Scottish people,' Cousin Eleanor said, 'descended from Edward the Confessor and *Philippe le Bel* of France . . .'

'And the grandfather of George Washington!' Cousin Marie said, and rolled back on the bed in her good dress and giggled. 'Isn't Bob priceless? But it *is* just like a book.'

'I never was a great reader,' Cousin Eleanor said. 'I'm an outdoor girl.'

She stood up. I never will forget the dress she had on that night. It was black but thin and it had a rose-colored bow right on the hip. She sort of dusted the bow off, though there wasn't a thing on it, and looked around the room as if she never had been there before. 'I was, too,' she said. 'I was city champion for three years.'

'Well, my dear, you could have a golf course here,' Cousin Marie said. 'Heaven knows there's all the room in creation.'

'And draw off to swing, and a mule comes along and eats your golf ball up!' Cousin Eleanor said. 'No, thank you, I'm through with all that.'

They went down to supper. On the stairs Cousin Marie put her arm around Cousin Eleanor's waist, and I heard her say, 'Wine for dinner. We don't need it.' But Cousin Eleanor kept her face straight ahead. 'There's no use for us to deny ourselves just because Tom can't control himself,' she said.

Cousin Tom was already at the table when we got into the dining room. He had on a clean white suit. His eyes were bloodshot, and you could still see that vein beating in his temple. He sat at the head of the table, and Cousin Eleanor and Cousin Marie sat on each side of him. Cousin Sidney Grassdale and his daughter, Molly, were there. Cousin Sidney sat next to Cousin Marie, and Molly sat next to Cousin Eleanor. They had to do it that way on account of the overseer, Mr. Turner. He sat at the foot of the table, and Hilda and I sat on each side of him.

We usually played a game when we were at the table. It was keeping something going through a whole meal, without the grown folks knowing what it was. Nobody knew we did it except Aunt Rachel, and sometimes when she was passing things she would give us a dig in the ribs, to keep us quiet.

That night we were playing Petrified Woman. With everything

we said we put in something from the fat man's song; like Hilda would say, 'You want some butter?' and I would come back with, 'No, thank you, calkypyrate bone.'

Cousin Marie was asking who the lady with the white hair in the blue flowered dress was.

'That is Cousin Olivia Bradshaw,' Cousin Eleanor said.

'She has a pretty daughter,' Cousin Robert D. Owen said.

'*Mater pulcher, filia pulchrior*,' Cousin Sidney Grassdale said.

'And they live at Summer Hill?' Cousin Marie asked.

Cousin Tom laid his fork down. 'I never could stand those Summer Hill folks,' he said. 'Pretentious.'

'But the daughter has a great deal of charm,' Cousin Marie said.

'Sweet Sixteen a Hundred Years Ago,' Hilda said. 'Give me the salt.'

'And Sweet Sixteen Today,' I said. 'It'll thin your blood.'

Cousin Tom must have heard us. He raised his head. His bloodshot eyes stared around the table. He shut his eyes. I knew that he was trying to remember.

'I saw a woman today that had real charm,' he said.

Cousin Eleanor heard his voice and turned around. She looked him straight in the face and smiled, slowly. 'In what did her charm consist, Tom?'

'She was petrified,' Cousin Tom said.

I looked at her and then I wished I hadn't. She had blue eyes. I always thought that they were like violets. She had a way of opening them wide whenever she looked at you.

'Some women are just petrified in spots,' Cousin Tom said. 'She was petrified all over.'

It was like the violets were freezing, there in her eyes. We all saw it. Molly Grassdale said something, and Cousin Eleanor's lips smiled and she half bent toward her and then her head gave a little shake and she straightened up so that she faced him. She was still smiling.

'In that case, how did she exert her charm?'

I thought, 'Her eyes, they will freeze him, too.' But he seemed to like her to look at him like that. He was smiling, too.

'She just lay there and looked sweet,' he said. 'I like a woman to look sweet. . . . Hell, they ain't got anything else to do!'

Cousin Sidney's nose was working up and down, like a squirrel I had once, named Adji-Daumo. He said, 'Harry Crenfew seems to be very much in love with Lucy Bradshaw.'

'*I'm* in love!' Cousin Tom shouted. 'I'm in love with a petrified woman.'

She was still looking at him. I never saw anything as cold as her eyes.

'What is her name, Tom?'

'Stell-a!' he shouted. 'The One and Only Stell-a!' He pushed his chair back and stood up, still shouting. 'I'm going down to Arthur's Cave and take her away from that fellow.'

He must have got his foot tangled-up in Cousin Marie's dress, for she shrieked and stood up, too, and he went down on the floor, with his wineglass in his hand. Somebody noticed us after a minute and sent us out of the room. He was still lying there when we left, his arms flung out and blood on his forehead from the broken glass. . . . I never did even see him get up off the floor.

We moved away that year and so we never went to another family reunion. And I never went to the Fork again. It burned down that fall. They said that Cousin Tom set it on fire, roaming around at night, with a lighted lamp in his hand. That was after he and Cousin Eleanor got divorced. I heard that they both got married again but I never knew who it was they married. I hardly ever think of them any more. If I do, they are still there in that house. The mockingbird has just stopped singing. Cousin Eleanor, in her long white dress, is walking over to the window, where, on moonlight nights, we used to sit, to watch the water glint on the rocks . . . But Cousin Tom is still lying there on the floor. . . .

STEVIE SMITH

Sunday At Home

Ivor was a gigantic man; forty, yellow-haired, gray of face. He had been wounded in a bomb experiment, he was a brilliant scientist.

Often he felt himself to be a lost man. Fishing the home water with his favourite fly Coronal, he would say to himself, 'I am a lost man.'

But he had an excellent sardonic wit, and in company knew very well how to present himself as a man perfectly at home in the world.

He was spending this Sunday morning sitting in his bedroom reading Colonel Wanlip's 'Can Fish Think?' letter in ANGLING. '. . . the fallacious theory known as Behaviourism.'

As the doodle bomb came sailing overhead, he stepped into the airing cupboard and sighed heavily. He could hear his wife's voice from the sitting room, a childish, unhappy voice, strained (as usual) to the point of tears.

'All I ask' sang out Ivor, 'is a little peace and quiet; an agreeable wife, a wife who is pleasant to my friends; one who occasionally has the room swept, the breakfast prepared, and the expensive bric-a-brac of our cultivated landlord—*dusted*. I am after all a fairly easy fellow.'

'I can't go on' roared Glory. She waved her arms in the air and paced the sitting room table round and round.

Crump, crump, went the doodle bomb, getting nearer.

'Then why,' inquired Ivor from the cupboard (where he sat because the doodle bombs reminded him of the experiment) 'did you come back to me?'

Glory's arms at shoulder height dropped to her side. There was in this hopeless and graceful gesture something of the classic Helen, pacing the walls of Troy, high above the frozen blood and stench of Scamander Plain. Ten years of futile war. Heavens, how much longer.

She ran to the cupboard and beat with her fists upon the door. 'You ask that, you . . . you . . . you . . .'

'Why yes, dear girl, I do. Indeed I do ask just that. Why did you come back to me?'

'Yesterday in the fish queue . . . ' began Glory. But it was no use. No use to tell Ivor what Friedl had said to her in the fish queue . . . before all those people . . . the harsh, cruel words. No, it was no use.

The doodle bomb now cut out. Glory burst into tears and finished lamely, 'I never thought it was going to be like this.'

Crash. Now it was down. Three streets away perhaps. There was a clatter of glass as the gold-fish bowl fell off the mantlepiece. Weeping bitterly Glory knelt to scoop the fish into a half-full saucepan of water that was standing in the fender.

'They are freshwater fish' said Ivor, stepping from the cupboard.

Glory went into the kitchen and sat down in front of the cooking stove. How terrible it all was. Her fine brown hair fell over her eyes and sadly the tears fell down.

She picked up the french beans and began to slice them. Now it would have to be lunch very soon. And then some more washing up. And Mrs Dip never turned up on Friday. And the stove was covered with grease.

From the sitting room came the sound of the typewriter. 'Oh God' cried Glory, and buried her head in her arms, 'Oh God.'

Humming a little tune to himself, Ivor worked quickly upon a theme he was finishing. 'Soh, me, doh, soh, me. How happy, how happy to be wrapped in science from the worst that fate and females could do.'

'If only I had science to wrap myself up in' said poor Glory, and fell to thinking what she would wish, if she could wish one thing to have it granted. 'I should wish' she said, 'that I had science to wrap myself up in. But I have nothing. I love Ivor, I never see him, never have him, never talk to him, but that the science is wrapping him round. And the educated conversation of the clever girls. Oh God.'

Glory was not an educated girl, in the way that the Research Persons Baba and Friedl, were educated girls. They could talk in the informed light manner that Ivor loved (in spite of Friedl's awful accent.) But she could not. her feelings were too much for her; indeed too much.

'I do not believe in your specialist new world, where everybody is so intelligent and everybody is so equal and everybody works and the progress goes on getting more and more progressive,' said Glory crossly to Friedl one day. She shook her head and added darkly, 'There must be sin and suffering, you'll see.'

'Good God, Glory,' said Ivor, 'you sound like the Pythoness. Sin and suffering, ottotottoi; the old bundle at the cross roads. Dreams, dreams. And now I suppose we shall have the waterworks again.'

'Too true,' said Friedl, as again Glory fled weeping.

'Sin and suffering,' she cried now to herself, counting the grease drips down the white front of the stove. 'Sin, pain, death, hell; despair and die. The brassy new world, the brassy hard-voiced young women. And underneath, the cold cold stone.'

Why only the other day, coming from her Aunt's at Tetbury, there in the carriage was a group of superior schoolgirls all of the age of about sixteen. But what sixteen-year-olds, God, what terrible children. They were talking about their exams. 'Oh, Delia darling, it was brilliant of you to think of that. Wasn't it brilliant of Delia, Lois? But then I always say Delia is the seventeenth century, if-you-see-what-I-mean. And what fun for dear old Bolt that you actually remembered to quote her own foul poem on Strafford. No, not boring a bit, darling, but sweet and clever of you—especially sweet.'

At the memory of this atrocious conversation between the false and terrible children, Glory's sobs rose to a roar, so that Ivor, at pause in his theme, heard her and came storming into the kitchen.

'You are a lazy, slovenly, uncontrolled female,' he said, 'You are a barbarian. I am going out.'

'Round to Friedl's, round to Friedl's, round to Friedl's,' sang out Glory.

'Friedl is a civilised woman. I appreciate civilised conversation.' Ivor stood over Glory and laughed. 'I shall be out to lunch.'

He took his hat and went out.

'The beans,' yelled Glory, 'all those french beans.' But it was no good, he was gone.

Glory went to the telephone and rang up Greta.

Greta was lying in bed and thinking about hell and crying and thinking that hell is the continuation of policy. She thought about the times and the wars and the 'scientific use of force' that was the enemy's practique. She thought that evil was indivisible and growing fast. She thought that every trifling evil thing she did was but another drop of sustenance for the evil to lap up and grow fat on. Oh, how fat it was growing.

'Zing,' went the telephone, and downstairs padded Greta, mopping at her nose with a chiffon scarf which by a fortunate chance was in the pocket of her dressing gown. The thought of the evil was upon her, and the thought that death itself is no escape from it.

'Oh yes, Glory, oh yes.' (She would go to lunch with Glory.)

The meat was overcooked and the beans were undercooked. The two friends brought their plates of food into the sitting room and turned the gas fire up. Two of the asbestos props were broken, the room felt cold and damp.

'It is cold,' said Greta. 'Glory,' she said, 'I like your dressing gown with the burn down the front and the grease spots, somehow that is right, and the beastly dark room is right, and the dust upon the antique rare ornaments; the dust, and the saucepan with the goldfish in it, and the overcooked meat and the undercooked beans, it is right; it is an abandonment. It is what the world deserves.'

'Let us have some cocoa afterwards,' said Glory.

'Yes, cocoa, that is right too.'

They began to laugh. Cocoa *was* the thing.

'When you rang up,' said Greta, 'I was thinking, I said, Hell is the continuation of policy. And I was thinking that even death is not the end of it. You know, Glory, there is something frightening about the Christian idea, sometimes it is frightening.' She combed her hair through her fingers.

'I don't know,' said Glory, 'I never think about it.'

'The plodding on and on,' went on Greta, 'the de-moting and the up-grading; the marks and the punishments and the smugness.'

'Like school?' said Glory, waking up a bit to the idea.

'Yes, like school. And no freedom so that a person might stretch himself out. Never, never, never; not even in death; oh most of all not then.'

'I believe in mortality,' said Glory flippantly, 'I shall have on my tombstone, "In the confident hope of Mortality". If death is not the end,' she said, an uneasy note in her voice, 'then indeed there is nowhere to look.'

'When I was studying the Coptics,' said Greta, 'do you know what I found?'

'No, Greta, what was that?'

'It was the Angels and the Red Clay. The angels came one by one to the Red Clay and coaxed it saying that it should stand up and be Man, and that if the Red Clay would do this it should have the ups and downs, and the good fortune and the bad fortune, and all falling haphazard, so that no one might say when it should be this and when that, but no matter, for this the Red Clay should stand up at once and be Man. But, No, said the Red Clay, No, it was not good enough.'

Glory's attention moved off from the Coptics and fastened again upon the problem of Ivor and herself. Oh dear, oh dear. And sadly the tears fell down.

Greta glanced at her severely. 'You should divorce Ivor,' she said.

'I've no grounds,' wailed Glory, 'not since I came back to him.'

'Then you should provoke him to strangle you,' said Greta, who wished to get on with her story. 'That should not be difficult,' she said, 'And then you can divorce him for cruelty.'

'But I love Ivor,' said Glory, 'I don't want to divorce him.'

'Well, make up your mind. As I was saying,' said Greta, '..... so then came the Third Angel. "And what have you got to say for yourself?" said the Angel, "and death is the end." So at this up and jumps the Red Clay at once and becomes Man.'

'Oh Glory,' said Greta, when she had finished this recital, and paused a moment while the long tide of evil swept in again upon her, 'Oh Glory, I cannot bear the evil, and the cruelty, and the scientific use of force, and the evil.' She screwed her napkin into a twist, and wrung the hem of it, that was already torn, quite off. 'I do not feel that I can go on.'

At these grand familiar words Glory began to cry afresh, and Greta was crying too. For there lay the slop on the carpet where the goldfish had been, and there stood the saucepan with the fish resting languid upon the bottom, and there too was the dust and the dirt, now the plates also, with the congealed mutton fat close upon them.

'Oh do put some more water in the fish pan,' sobbed Greta.

Glory picked up the pan and ran across the room with it to take it to the kitchen tap. But now the front door, that was apt to jam, opened with a burst, and Ivor fell into the room.

'They were both out,' he said. 'I suppose you have eaten all the lunch? Oh, hello Greta.'

'Listen,' said Glory, 'there's another bomb coming.'

Ivor went into the cupboard.

'Do you know Ivor,' screamed Greta through the closed door, 'I had a dream and when I woke up I was saying, "Hell is the continuation of policy".'

'You girls fill your heads with a lot of bosh.'

Glory said, 'There's some bread and cheese in the kitchen, we are keeping the cocoa hot. Greta' she said, 'was telling me about the Coptics.'

'Eh?' said Ivor.

'Oh do take those fish out and give them some more water,' said Greta.

'The story about the Angels and the Red Clay.'

'Spurious,' yelled Ivor, 'all bosh. But how on earth did you get hold of the manuscript, Greta, it's very rare.'

'I don't think there's much in it,' said Glory, 'nothing to make you cry. Come, cheer up Greta. I say Ivor, the doodle has gone off towards the town, you can come out now.'

Ivor came out looking very cheerful. 'I tell you what, Greta,' he said, 'I'll show you my new plastic bait.' He took the brightly coloured monsters out of their tin and brought them to her on a plate. 'I use these for pike,' he said.

There was now in the room a feeling of loving kindness and peace. Greta fetched the cheese and bread from the kitchen and Glory poured the hot cocoa. 'There is nothing like industry, control, affection and discipline,' said Greta.

The sun came round to the french windows and struck through the glass pane at the straw stuffing that was hanging down from the belly of the sofa.

'Oh, look,' said Glory, pointing to the patch of sunlight underneath, 'there is the button you lost.'

Silence fell upon them in the sun-spiked room. Silently, happily, they went on with their lunch. The only sound now in the room was the faint sizzle of the cocoa against the side of the jug (that was set too close to the fire and soon must crack) and the far off bark of the dog Sultan, happy with his rats.

Mavis Gallant

The Ice Wagon Going Down The Street

Now that they are out of world affairs and back where they started, Peter Frazier's wife says, 'Everybody else did well in the international thing except us.'

'You have to be crooked,' he tells her.

'Or smart. Pity we weren't.'

It is Sunday morning. They sit in the kitchen, drinking their coffee, slowly, remembering the past. They say the names of people as if they were magic. Peter thinks, *Agnes Brusen*, but there are hundreds of other names. As a private married joke, Peter and Sheilah wear the silk dressing gowns they bought in Hong Kong. Each thinks the other a peacock, rather splendid, but they pretend the dressing gowns are silly and worn in fun.

Peter and Sheilah and their two daughters, Sandra and Jennifer, are visiting Peter's unmarried sister, Lucille. They have been Lucille's guests seventeen weeks, ever since they returned to Toronto from the Far East. Their big old steamer trunk blocks a corner of the kitchen, making a problem of the refrigerator door; but even Lucille says the trunk may as well stay where it is, for the present. The Fraziers' future is so unsettled; everything is still in the air.

Lucille has given her bedroom to her two nieces, and sleeps on a camp cot in the hall. The parents have the living-room divan. They have no privileges here; they sleep after Lucille has seen the last television show that interests her. In the hall closet their clothes are crushed by winter overcoats. They know they are being judged for the first time. Sandra and Jennifer are waiting for Sheilah and Peter to decide. They are waiting to learn where these exotic parents will fly to next. What sort of climate will Sheilah consider? What job will Peter consent to accept? When the parents are ready, the children will make a decision of their own. It is just possible that Sandra and Jennifer will choose to stay with their aunt.

The peacock parents are watched by wrens. Lucille and her nieces are much the same—sandy-colored, proudly plain. Neither of the girls has the father's insouciance or the mother's appearance—her height, her carriage, her thick hair, and sky-blue eyes. The children are more cautious than their parents; more Canadian. When they saw their aunt's apartment they had been away from Canada nine years, ever since they were two and four; and Jennifer, the elder, said, 'Well, now we're home.' Her voice is nasal and flat. Where did she learn that voice? And why should this be home? Peter's answer to anything about his mystifying children is, 'It must be in the blood.'

On Sunday morning Lucille takes her nieces to church. It seems to be the only condition she imposes on her relations: the children must be decent. The girls go willingly, with their new hats and purses and gloves and coral bracelets and strings of pearls. The parents, ramshackle, sleepy, dim in the brain because it is Sunday, sit down to their coffee and privacy and talk of the past.

'We weren't crooked,' says Peter. 'We weren't even smart.'

Sheilah's head bobs up; she is no drowner. It is wrong to say they have nothing to show for time. Sheilah has the Balenciaga. It is a black afternoon dress, stiff and boned at the waist; long for the fashions of now, but neither Sheilah nor Peter would change a thread. The Balenciaga is their talisman, their treasure; and after they remember it they touch hands and think that the years are not behind them but hazy and marvellous and still to be lived.

The first place they went to was Paris. In the early fifties the pick of the international jobs was there. Peter had inherited the last scrap of money he knew he was ever likely to see, and it was enough to get them over: Sheilah and Peter and the babies and the steamer trunk. To their joy and astonishment they had money in the bank. They said to each other, 'It should last a year.' Peter was fastidious about the new job; he hadn't come all this distance to accept just anything. In Paris he met Hugh Taylor, who was earning enough smuggling gasoline to keep his wife in Paris and a girl in Rome. That impressed Peter, because he remembered Taylor as a sour scholarship student without the slightest talent for life. Taylor had a job, of course. He hadn't said to himself, I'll go over to Europe and smuggle gasoline. It gave Peter an idea; he saw the shape of things. First you catch your fish. Later, at an international party, he met Johnny Hertzberg, who told him Germany was the place. Hertzberg said that anyone who came out of Germany broke now was too stupid to be here, and deserved to be back home at a desk. Peter nodded, as if he had already thought of that. He began to think about Germany. Paris was fine for a holiday, but it had been picked clean. Yes, Germany. His money was running low. He thought about Germany quite a lot.

That winter was moist and delicate; so fragile that they daren't speak of it now. There seemed to be plenty of everything and plenty of time. They were living the dream of a marriage, the fabric uncut, nothing slashed or spoiled. All winter they spent their money, and went to parties, and talked about Peter's future job. It lasted four months. They spent their money, lived in the future, and were never as happy again.

After four months they were suddenly moved away from Paris, but not to Germany—to Geneva. Peter thinks it was because of the incident at the Trudeau wedding at the Ritz. Paul Trudeau was a French Canadian Peter had known at school and in the Navy. Trudeau had turned into a snob, proud of his career and his Paris connections. He tried to make the difference felt, but Peter thought the difference was only for strangers. At the wedding reception Peter lay down on the floor and said he was dead. He held a white azalea in a brass pot on his chest, and sang, 'Oh, hear us when we cry to Thee for those in peril on the sea.' Sheilah bent over him and said, 'Pete, darling, get up. Pete, listen, every single person who can do something for you is in this room. If you love me, you'll get up.'

'I do love you,' he said, ready to engage in a serious conversation. 'She's so beautiful,' he told a second face. 'She's nearly as tall as I am. She was a model in London. I met her over in London in the war. I met her there in the war.' He lay on his back with the azalea on his chest, explaining their history. A waiter took the brass pot away, and after Peter had been hauled to his feet he knocked the waiter down. Trudeau's bride, who was freshly out of an Ursuline convent, became hysterical; and even though Paul Trudeau and Peter were old acquaintances, Trudeau never spoke to him again. Peter says now that French Canadians always have that bit of spite. He says Trudeau asked the Embassy to interfere. Luckily, back home there were still a few people to whom the name 'Frazier' meant something, and it was to these people that Peter appealed. He wrote letters saying that a French-Canadian combine was preventing his getting a decent job, and could anything be done? No one answered directly, but it was clear that what they settled for was exile to Geneva: a season of meditation and remorse, as he explained to Sheilah, and it was managed tactfully, through Lucille. Lucille wrote that a friend of hers, May Fergus, now a secretary in Geneva, had heard about a job. The job was filing pictures in the information service of an international agency in the Palais des Nations. The pay was so-so, but Lucille thought Peter must be getting fed up doing nothing.

Peter often asks his sister now who put her up to it—what important person told her to write that letter suggesting Peter go to Geneva?

'Nobody,' says Lucille, 'I mean, nobody in the way *you* mean. I really did have this girl friend working there,and I knew you must be running through your money pretty fast in Paris.'

'It must have been somebody pretty high up,' Peter says. He looks at his sister admiringly, as he has often looked at his wife.

Peter's wife had loved him in Paris. Whatever she wanted in marriage she found that winter, there. In Geneva, where Peter was a file clerk and they lived in a furnished flat, she pretended they were in Paris and life was still the same. Often, when the children were at supper, she changed as though she and Peter were dining out. She wore the Balenciaga, and put candles on the card table where she and Peter ate their meal. The neckline of the dress was soiled with make-up. Peter remembers her dabbing on the make-up with a wet sponge. He remembers her in the kitchen, in the soiled Balenciaga, patting on the make-up with a filthy sponge. Behind her, at the kitchen table, Sandra and Jennifer, in buttonless pajamas and bunny slippers, ate their supper of marmalade sandwiches and milk. When the children were asleep, the parents dined solemnly, ritually, Sheilah sitting straight as a queen.

It was a mysterious period of exile, and he had to wait for signs, or signals, to know when he was free to leave. He never saw the job any other way. He forgot he had applied for it. He thought he had been sent to Geneva because of a misdemeanor and had to wait to be released. Nobody pressed him at work. His immediate boss had resigned, and he was alone for months in a room with two desks. He read the *Herald-Tribune*, and tried to discover how things were here—how the others ran their lives on the pay they were officially getting. But it was a closed conspiracy. He was not dealing with adventurers now but civil servants waiting for pension day. No one ever answered his questions. They pretended to think his questions were a form of wit. His only solace in exile was the few happy weekends he had in the late spring and early summer. He had met another old acquaintance, Mike Burleigh. Mike was a serious liberal who had married a serious heiress. The Burleighs had two guest lists. The first was composed of stuffy people they felt obliged to entertain, while the second was made up of their real friends, the friends they wanted. The real friends strove hard to become stuffy and dull and thus achieve the first guest list, but few succeeded. Peter went on the first list straight away. Possibly Mike didn't understand, at the beginning, why Peter was pretending to be a file clerk. Peter had such an air—he might have been sent by a universal inspector to see how things in Geneva were being run.

Every Friday in May and June and part of July, the Fraziers rented a sky-blue Fiat and drove forty miles east of Geneva to the Burleighs' summer house. They brought the children, a suitcase, the children's tattered picture books, and a token bottle of gin. This, in memory, is a period of water and water birds, swans, roses, and singing birds. The children were small and still belonged to them. If they remember too much, their mouths water, their stomachs hurt. Peter says, 'It was fine while it lasted.' Enough. While it lasted Sheilah and Madge Burleigh were close. They abandoned their husbands and spent long summer afternoons comparing their mothers and praising each other's skin and hair. To Madge, and not to Peter, Sheilah opened her Liverpool childhood with the words 'rat poor.' Peter heard about it later, from Mike. The women's friendship seemed to Peter a bad beginning. He trusted women but not with each other. It lasted ten weeks. One Sunday, Madge said she needed the two bedrooms the Fraziers usually occupied for a party of sociologists from Pakistan, and that was the end. In November, the Fraziers heard that the summer house had been closed, and that the Burleighs were in Geneva, in their winter flat; they gave no sign. There was no help for it, and no appeal.

Now Peter began firing letters to anyone who had ever known his late father. He was living in a mild yellow autumn. Why does he remember the streets of the city dark, and the windows everywhere black with rain? He remembers being with Sheilah and the children as if they clung together while just outside their small shelter it rained and rained. The children slept in the bedroom of the flat because the window gave on the street and they could breathe air. Peter and Sheilah had the living-room couch. Their window was not a real window but a square on a well of cement. The flat seemed damp as a cave. Peter remembers steam in the kitchen, pools under the sink, sweat on the pipes. Water streamed on him, from the children's clothes, washed and dripping overhead. The trunk, upended in the children's room, was not quite unpacked. Sheilah had not signed her name to this life; she had not given in. Once Peter heard her drop her aitches. 'You kids are lucky,' she said to the girls. 'I never 'ad so much as a sit-down meal. I ate chips out of a paper or I 'ad a butty out on the stairs.' He never asked her what a butty was. He thinks it means bread and cheese.

The day he heard 'You kids are lucky' he understood they were becoming in fact something they had only *appeared* to be until now—the shabby civil servant and his brood. If he had been European he would have ridden to work on a bicycle, in the uniform of his class and condition. He would have worn a tight coat, a turned collar, and a dirty tie. He wondered then if coming here had been a mistake, and if he should not, after all, still be in a place where his name meant something. Surely Peter Frazier should live where 'Frazier' counts? In Ontario even now when he says 'Frazier' an absent look comes over his hearer's face, as if its owner were consulting an interior guide. What is Frazier? What does it mean? Oil? Power? Politics? Wheat? Real estate? The creditors had the house sealed when Peter's father died. His aunt collapsed with a heart attack in somebody's bachelor apartment, leaving three sons and a widower to surmise they had never known her. Her will was a disappointment. None of that generation left enough. One made it: the granite Presbyterian immigrants from Scotland. Their children, a generation of daunted women and maiden men, held still. Peter's father's crowd spent: they were not afraid of their fathers, and their grandfathers were old. Peter and his sister and his cousins lived on the remains. They were left the rinds of income, of notions, and the memories of ideas rather than ideas intact. If Peter can choose his reincarnation, let him be the oppressed son of a Scottish parson. Let Peter grow up on cuffs and iron principles. Let him make the fortune! Let him flee the manse! When he was small his patrimony was squandered under his nose. He remembers people dancing in his father's house. He remembers seeing and nearly understanding adultery in a guest room, among a pile of wraps. He thought he had seen a murder; he never told. He remembers licking glasses wherever he found them—on window sills, on stairs, in the pantry. In his room he listened while Lucille read Beatrix Potter. The bad rabbit stole the carrot from the good rabbit without saying please, and downstairs was the noise of the party—the roar of the crouched lion. When his father died he saw the chairs upside down and the bailiff's chalk marks. Then the doors were sealed.

He has often tried to tell Sheilah why he cannot be defeated. He remembers his father saying, 'Nothing can touch us,' and Peter believed it and still does. It has prevented his taking his troubles too seriously. 'Nothing can be as bad as this,' he will tell himself. 'It is happening to me.' Even in Geneva, where his status was file clerk, where he sank and stopped on the level of the men who never emigrated, the men on the bicycles—even there he had a manner of strolling to work as if his office were a pastime, and his real life a secret so splendid he could share it with no one except himself.

In Geneva Peter worked for a woman—a girl. She was a Norwegian from a small town in Saskatchewan. He supposed they had been put together because they were Canadians; but they were as strange to each other as if 'Canadian' meant any number of things, or had no real meaning. Soon after Agnes Brusen came to the office she hung her framed university degree on the wall. It was one of the gritty, prideful gestures that stand for push, toil, and family sacrifice. He thought, then, that she must be one of a family of immigrants for whom education is everything. Hugh Taylor had told him that in some families the older children never marry until the youngest have finished school. Sometimes every second child is sacrificed and made to work for the education of the next born. Those who finish college spend years paying back. They are white-hot Protestants, and they live with a load of work and debt and obligation. Peter placed his new colleague on scraps of information. He had never been in the West.

She came to the office on a Monday morning in October. The office was overheated and painted cream. It contained two desks, the filing cabinets, a map of the world as it had been in 19 the Charter of the United Nations left behind by Agnes l predecessor. (She took down the Charter without asking he minded, with the impudence of gesture you find in women who wouldn't say boo to a goose; and then she hung her college degree on the nail where the Charter had been.) Three people brought her in—a whole committee. One of them said, 'Agnes, this is Peter Frazier. Pete, Agnes Brusen, Pete's Canadian, too, Agnes. He knows all about the office, so ask him anything.'

Of course he knew all about the office: he knew the exact spot where the cord of the venetian blind was frayed, obliging one to give an extra tug to the right.

The girl might have been twenty-three: no more. She wore a brown tweed suit with bone buttons, and a new silk scarf and new shoes. She clutched an unscratched brown purse. She seemed dressed in going-away presents. She said, 'Oh, I never smoke,' with a convulsive movement of her hand, when Peter offered his case. He was courteous, hiding his disappointment. The people he worked with had told him a Scandinavian girl was arriving, and he had expected a stunner. Agnes was a mole: she was small and brown, and round-shouldered as if she had always carried parcels or younger children in her arms. A mole's profile was turned when she said goodbye to her committee. If she had been foreign, ill-favored though she was, he might have flirted a little, just to show that he was friendly; but their being Canadian, and suddenly left together, was a sexual damper. He sat down and lit his own cigarette. She smiled at him, questioningly, he thought, and sat as if she had never seen a chair before. He wondered if his smoking was annoying her. He wondered if she was fidgety about drafts, or allergic to anything, and whether she would want the blind up or down. His social compass was out of order because the others couldn't tell Peter and Agnes apart. There was a world of difference between them, yet it was she who had been brought in to sit at the larger of the two desks.

While he was thinking this she got up and walked around the office, almost on tiptoe, opening the doors of closets and pulling out the filing trays. She looked inside everything except the drawers of Peter's desk. (In any case, Peter's desk was locked. His desk is locked wherever he works. In Geneva he went into Personnel one morning, early, and pinched his application form.

He had stated on the form that he had seven years' experience in public relations and could speak French, German, Spanish, and Italian. He has always collected anything important about himself—anything useful. But he can never get on with the final act, which is getting rid of the information. He has kept papers about for years, a constant source of worry.)

'I know this looks funny, Mr Ferris,' said the girl. 'I'm not really snooping or anything. I just can't feel easy in a new place unless I know where everything is. In a new place everything seems so hidden.'

If she had called him 'Ferris' and pretended not to know he was Frazier, it could only be because they had sent her here to spy on him and see if he had repented and was fit for a better place in life. 'You'll be all right here,' he said. 'Nothing's hidden. Most of us haven't got brains enough to have secrets. This is Rainbow Valley.' Depressed by the thought that they were having him watched now, he passed his hand over his hair and looked outside to the lawn and the parking lot and the peacocks someone gave the Palais des Nations years ago. The peacocks love no one. They wander about the parked cars looking elderly, bad-tempered, mournful, and lost.

Agnes had settled down again. She folded her silk scarf and placed it just so, with her gloves beside it. She opened her new purse and took out a notebook and a shiny gold pencil. She may have written

Duster for desk
Kleenex
Glass jar for flowers
Air-Wick because he smokes
Paper for lining drawers

because the next day she brought each of these articles to work. She also brought a large black Bible, which she unwrapped lovingly and placed on the left-hand corner of her desk. The flower vase—empty—stood in the middle, and the Kleenex made a counterpoise for the Bible on the right.

When he saw the Bible he knew she had not been sent to spy on his work. The conspiracy was deeper. She might have been dispatched by ghosts. He knew everything about her, all in a moment: he saw the ambition, the terror, the dry pride. She was the true heir of the men from Scotland; she was at the start. She had been sent to tell him. 'You can begin, but not begin again.' She never opened the Bible, but she dusted it as she dusted her desk, her chair, and any surface the cleaning staff had overlooked. And Peter, the first days, watching her timid movements, her insignificant little face, felt, as you feel the approach of a storm, the charge of moral certainty round her, the belief in work, the faith in undertakings, the bread of the Black Sunday. He recognized and tasted all of it: ashes in the mouth.

After five days their working relations were settled. Of course, there was the Bible and all that went with it, but his tongue had never held the taste of ashes long. She was an inferior girl of poor quality. She had nothing in her favor except the degree on the wall. In the real world, he would not have invited her to his house except to mind the children. That was what he said to Sheilah. He said that Agnes was a mole, and a virgin, and that her tics and mannerisms were sending him round the bend. She had an infuriating habit of covering her mouth when she talked. Even at the telephone she put up her hand as if afraid of losing anything, even a word. Her voice was nasal and flat. She had two working costumes, both dull as the wall. One was the brown suit, the other a navy-blue dress with changeable collars. She dressed for no one; she dressed for her desk, her jar of flowers, her Bible, and her box of Kleenex. One day she crossed the space between the two desks and stood over Peter, who was reading a newspaper. She could have spoken to him from her desk, but she may have felt that being on her feet gave her authority. She had plenty of courage, but authority was something else.

'I thought—I mean, they told me you were the person. . . ' She got on with it bravely: 'If you don't want to do the filing or any work, all right, Mr Frazier. I'm not saying anything about that. You might have poor health or your personal reasons. But it's got to be done, so if you'll kindly show me about the filing I'll do it. I've worked in Information before, but it was a different office, and every office is different.'

'My dear girl,' said Peter. He pushed back his chair and looked at her, astonished. 'You've been sitting there fretting, worrying. How insensitive of me. How trying for you. Usually I file on the last Wednesday of the month, so you see, you just haven't been around long enough to see a last Wednesday. Not another word, please. And let us not waste another minute.' He emptied the heaped baskets of photographs so swiftly, pushing 'Iran—Smallpox Control' into 'Irish Red Cross' (close enough), that the girl looked frightened, as if she had raised a whirlwind. She said slowly, 'If you'll only show me, Mr Frazier, instead of doing it so fast, I'll gladly look after it, because you might want to be doing other things, and I feel the filing should be done every day.' But Peter was too busy to answer, and so she sat down, holding the edge of her desk.

'There,' he said, beaming. 'All done.' His smile, his sunburst, was wasted, for the girl was staring round the room as if she feared she had not inspected everything the first day after all; some drawer, some cupboard, hid a monster. That evening Peter unlocked one of the drawers of his desk and took away the application form he had stolen from Personnel. The girl had not finished her search.

'How could you *not* know?' wailed Sheilah. 'You sit looking at her every day. You must talk about *something*. She must have told you.'

'She did tell me,' said Peter, 'and I've just told you.'

It was this: Agnes Brusen was on the Burleighs' guest list. How had the Burleighs met her? What did they see in her? Peter could not reply. He knew that Agnes lived in a bed-sitting room with a Swiss family and had her meals with them. She had been in Geneva three months, but no one had ever seen her outside the office. 'You *should* know,' said Sheilah. 'She must have something, more than you can see. Is she pretty? Is she brilliant? What is it?'

'We don't really talk,' Peter said. They talked in a way: Peter teased her and she took no notice. Agnes was not a sulker. She had taken her defeat like a sport. She did her work and a good deal of his. She sat behind her Bible, her flowers, and her Kleenex, and answered when Peter spoke. That was how he learned about the Burleighs—just by teasing and being bored. It was a January afternoon. He said, '*Miss* Brusen. Talk to me. Tell me everything. Pretend we have perfect rapport. Do you like Geneva?'

'It's a nice clean town,' she said. He can see to this day the red and blue anemones in the glass jar, and her bent head, and her small untended hands.

'Are you learning beautiful French with your Swiss family?'

'They speak English.'

'Why don't you take an apartment of your own?' he said. Peter was not usually impertinent. He was bored. 'You'd be independent then.'

'I am independent,' she said. 'I earn my living. I don't think it proves anything if you live by yourself. Mrs Burleigh wants me to live alone, too. She's looking for something for me. It mustn't be dear. I send money home.'

Here was the extraordinary thing about Agnes Brusen: she refused the use of Christian names and never spoke to Peter unless he spoke first, but she would tell anything, as if to say, 'Don't waste time fishing. Here it is.'

He learned all in one minute that she sent her salary home, and that she was a friend of the Burleighs. The first he had expected; the second knocked him flat.

'She's got to come to dinner,' Sheilah said. 'We should have had her right from the beginning. If only I'd known! But *you* were the one. You said she looked like—oh, I don't even remember. A Norwegian mole.'

She came to dinner one Saturday night in January, in her navy-blue dress, to which she had pinned an organdy gardenia. She sat upright on the edge of the sofa. Sheilah had ordered the meal from a restaurant. There was lobster, good wine, and a *pièce-montée* full of kirsch and cream. Agnes refused the lobster; she had never eaten anything from the sea unless it had been sterilized and tinned, and said so. She was afraid of skin poisoning. Someone in her family had skin poisoning after having eaten oysters. She touched her cheeks and neck to show where the poisoning had erupted. She sniffed her wine and put the glass down without tasting it. She could not eat the cake because of the alcohol it contained. She ate an egg, bread and butter, a sliced tomato, and drank a glass of ginger ale. She seemed unaware she was creating disaster and pain. She did not help clear away the dinner plates. She sat, adequately nourished, decently dressed, and waited to learn why she had been invited here—that was the feeling Peter had. He folded the card table on which they had dined, and opened the window to air the room.

'It's not the same cold as Canada, but you feel it more,' he said, for something to say.

'Your blood has gotten thin,' said Agnes.

Sheilah returned from the kitchen and let herself fall into an armchair. With her eyes closed she held out her hand for a cigarette. She was performing the haughty-lady act that was a family joke. She flung her head back and looked at Agnes through half-closed lids; then she suddenly brought her head forward, widening her eyes.

'Are you skiing madly?' she said.

'Well, in the first place there hasn't been any snow,' said Agnes, 'So nobody's doing any skiing so far as I know. All I hear is people complaining because there's no snow. Personally, I don't ski. There isn't much skiing in the part of Canada I come from. Besides, my family never had that kind of leisure.'

'Heavens,' said Sheilah, as if her family had every kind.

I'll bet they had, thought Peter. On the dole.

Sheilah was wasting her act. He had a suspicion that Agnes knew it was an act but did not know it was also a joke. If so, it made Sheilah seem a fool, and he loved Sheilah too much to enjoy it.

'The Burleighs have been wonderful to me,' said Agnes. She seemed to have divined why she was here, and decided to give them all the information they wanted, so that she could put on her coat and go home to bed. 'They had me out to their place on the lake every weekend until the weather got cold and they moved back to town. They've rented a chalet for the winter, and they want me to come there, too. But I don't know if I will or not. I don't ski, and, oh, I don't know—I don't drink, either, and I don't always see the point. Their friends are too rich and I'm too Canadian.'

She had delivered everything Sheilah wanted and more: Agnes was on the first guest list and didn't care. No, Peter corrected; doesn't know. Doesn't care and doesn't know.

'I thought with you Norwegians it was in the blood, skiing. And drinking,' Sheilah murmured.

'Drinking, maybe,' said Agnes. She covered her mouth and said behind her spread fingers, 'In our family we were religious. We didn't drink or smoke. My brother was in Norway in the war. He saw some cousins. Oh,' she said, unexpectedly loud, 'Harry said it was just terrible. They were so poor. They had flies in their kitchen. They gave him something to eat a fly had been on. They didn't have a real toilet, and they'd been in the same house about two hundred years. We've only recently built our own home, and we have a bathroom and two toilets. I'm from Saskatchewan,' she said. 'I'm not from any other place.'

Surely one winter here had been punishment enough? In the spring they would remember him and free him. He wrote Lucille, who said he was lucky to have a job at all. The Burleighs had sent the Fraziers a second-guest-list Christmas card. It showed a Moslem refugee child weeping outside a tent. They treasured the card and left it standing long after the others had been given the children to cut up. Peter had discovered by now what had gone wrong in the friendship—Sheilah had charged a skirt at a dressmaker to Madge's account. Madge had told her she might, and then changed her mind. Poor Sheilah! She was new to this part of it—to the changing humors of independent friends. Paris was already a year in the past. At Mardi Gras, the Burleighs gave their annual party. They invited everyone, the damned and the dropped, with the prodigality of a child at prayers. The invitation said 'in costume,' but the Fraziers were too happy to wear a disguise. They might not be recognized. Like many of the guests they expected to meet at the party, they had been disgraced, forgotten, and rehabilitated. They would be anxious to see one another as they were.

On the night of the party, the Fraziers rented a car they had never seen before and drove through the first snowstorm of the year. Peter had not driven since last summer's blissful trips in the Fiat. He could not find the switch for the windshield wiper in this car. He leaned over the wheel. 'Can you see on your side?' he asked. 'Can I make a left turn here? Does it look like a one-way?'

'I can't imagine why you took a car with a right-hand drive,' said Sheilah.

He had trouble finding a place to park; they crawled up and down unknown streets whose curbs were packed with snow-covered cars. When they stood at last on the pavement, safe and sound, Peter said, 'This is the first snow.'

'I can see that,' said Sheilah. 'Hurry, darling. My hair.'

'It's the first snow.'

'You're repeating yourself,' she said. 'Please hurry, darling. Think of my poor shoes. My *hair*.'

She was born in an ugly city, and so was Peter, but they have this difference: she does not know the importance of the first snow—the first clean thing in a dirty year. He would have told her then that this storm, which was wetting her feet and destroying her hair, was like the first day of the English spring, but she made a frightened gesture, trying to shield her head. The gesture told him he did not understand her beauty.

'Let me,' she said. He was fumbling with the key, trying to lock the car. She took the key without impatience and locked the door on the driver's side; and then, to show Peter she treasured him and was not afraid of wasting her life or her beauty, she took his arm and they walked in the snow down a street and around a corner to the apartment house where the Burleighs lived. They were, and are, a united couple. They were afraid of the party, and each of them knew it. When they walk together, holding arms, they give each other whatever each can spare.

Only six people had arrived in costume. Madge Burleigh was disguised as Manet's 'Lola de Valence,' which everyone mistook for Carmen. Mike was an Impressionist-painter, with a straw hat and a glued-on beard. 'I am all of them,' he said. He would rather have dressed as a dentist, he said, welcoming the Fraziers as if he had parted from them the day before, but Madge wanted him to look as if he had created her. 'You know?' he said.

'Perfectly,' said Sheilah. Her shoes were stained and the snow had softened her lacquered hair. She was not wasted; she was the most beautiful woman here.

About an hour after their arrival, Peter found himself with no one to talk to. He had told about the Trudeau wedding in Paris and the pot of azaleas, and after he mislaid his audience he began to look round for Sheilah. She was on a window seat, partly concealed by a green velvet curtain. Facing her, so that their profiles were neat and perfect against the night, was a man. Their conversation was private and enclosed, as if they had in minutes covered leagues of time and arrived at the place where everything was implied, understood. Peter began working his way across the room, toward his wife, when he saw Agnes. He was granted the sight of her drowning face. She had dressed with comic intention, obviously with care, and now she was a ragged hobo, half tramp, half clown. Her hair was tucked up under a bowler hat. The six costumed guests who had made the same mistake—the ghost, the gypsy, the Athenian maiden, the geisha, the Martian, and the apache—were delighted to find a seventh; but Agnes was not amused; she was gasping for life. When a waiter passed with a crowded tray, she took a glass without seeing it; then a wave of the party took her away.

Sheilah's new friend was named Simpson. After Simpson said he thought perhaps he'd better circulate, Peter sat down where he had been. 'Now look, Sheilah,' he began. Their most intimate conversations have taken place at parties. Once at a party she told him she was leaving him; she didn't, of course. Smiling, blue-eyed, she gazed lovingly at Peter and said rapidly, 'Peter, shut up and listen. That man. The man you scared away. He's a big wheel in a company out in India or someplace like that. It's gorgeous out there. Pete, the *servants*. And it's warm. It never never snows. He says there's heaps of jobs. You pick them off the trees like . . . orchids. He says it's even easier now than when we owned all those places, because now the poor pets can't run anything and they'll pay *fortunes*. Pete, he says it's warm, it's heaven, and Pete, they pay.'

A few minutes later, Peter was alone again and Sheilah part of a closed, laughing group. Holding her elbow was the man from the place where jobs grew like orchids. Peter edged into the group and laughed at a story he hadn't heard. He heard only the last line, which was, 'Here comes another tunnel.' Looking out from the tight laughing ring, he saw Agnes again, and he thought, I'd be like Agnes if I didn't have Sheilah. Agnes put her glass down on a table and lurched toward the doorway, head forward. Madge Burleigh, who never stopped moving around the room and smiling, was still smiling when she paused and said in Peter's ear, 'Go with Agnes, Pete. See that she gets home. People will notice if Mike leaves.'

'She probably just wants to walk around the block,' said Peter. 'She'll be back.'

'Oh, stop thinking about yourself, for once, and see that that poor girl gets home,' said Madge. 'You've still got your Fiat, haven't you?'

He turned away as if he had been pushed. Any command is a release, in a way. He may not want to go in that particular direction, but at least he is going somewhere. And now Sheilah, who had moved inches nearer to hear what Madge and Peter were murmuring, said, 'Yes, go, darling,' as if he were leaving the gates of Troy.

Peter was to find Agnes and see that she reached home: this he repeated to himself as he stood on the landing, outside the Burleighs' flat ringing for the elevator. Bored with waiting for it, he ran down the stairs, four flights, and saw that Agnes had stalled the lift by leaving the door open. She was crouched on the floor, propped on her fingertips. Her eyes were closed.

'Agnes,' said Peter, '*Miss* Brusen, I mean. That's no way to leave a party. Don't you know you're supposed to curtsey and say thanks? My God, Agnes, anybody going by here just now might have seen you! Come on, be a good girl. Time to go home.'

She got up without his help and, moving between invisible crevasses, shut the elevator door. Then she left the building and Peter followed, remembering he was to see that she got home. They walked along the snowy pavement, Peter a few steps behind her. When she turned right for no reason, he turned, too. He had no clear idea where they were going. Perhaps she lived close by. He had forgotten where the hired car was parked, or what it looked like; he could not remember its make or its color. In any case, Sheilah had the key. Agnes walked on steadily, as if she knew their destination, and he thought, Agnes Brusen is drunk in the street in Geneva and dressed like a tramp. He wanted to say, 'This is the best thing that ever happened to you, Agnes; it will help you understand how things are for some of the rest of us.' But she stopped and turned and, leaning over a low hedge, retched on a frozen lawn. He held her clammy forehead and rested his hand on her arched back, on muscles as tight as a fist. She straightened up and drew a breath but the cold air made her cough. 'Don't breathe too deeply,' he said. 'It's the worst thing you can do. Have you got a handkerchief?' He passed his own handkerchief over her wet weeping face, upturned like the face of one of his little girls. 'I'm out without a coat,' he said, noticing it. 'We're a pair.'

'I never drink,' said Agnes. 'I'm just not used to it.' Her voice was sweet and quiet. He had never seen her so peaceful, so composed. He thought she must surely be all right, now, and perhaps he might leave her here. The trust in her tilted face had perplexed him. He wanted to get back to Sheilah and have her explain something. He had forgotten what it was, but Sheilah would know. 'Do you live around here?' he said. As he spoke, she let herself fall. He had wiped her face and now she trusted him to pick her up, set her on her feet, take her wherever she ought to be. He pulled her up and she stood, wordless, humble, as he brushed the snow from her tramp's clothes. Snow horizontally crossed the lamplight. The street was silent. Agnes had lost her hat. Snow, which he tasted, melted on her hands. His gesture of licking snow from her hands was formal as a handshake. He tasted snow on her hands and then they walked on.

'I never drink,' she said. They stood on the edge of a broad avenue. The wrong turning now could lead them anywhere; it was the changeable avenue at the edge of towns that loses its houses and becomes a highway. She held his arm and spoke in a gentle voice. She said, 'In our house we didn't smoke or drink. My mother was ambitious for me, more than for Harry and the others.' She said, 'I've never been alone before. When I was a kid I would get up in the summer before the others, and I'd see the ice wagon going down the street. I'm alone now. Mrs Burleigh's found me an apartment. It's only one room. She likes it because it's in the old part of town. I don't like old houses. Old houses are dirty. You don't know who was there before.'

'I should have a car somewhere,' Peter said. 'I'm not sure where we are.'

He remembers that on this avenue they climbed into a taxi, but nothing about the drive. Perhaps he fell asleep. He does remember that when he paid the driver Agnes clutched his arm, trying to stop him. She pressed extra coins into the driver's palm. The driver was paid twice.

'I'll tell you one thing about us,' said Peter. 'We pay everything twice.' This was part of a much longer theory concerning North American behavior, and it was not Peter's own. Mike Burleigh had held forth about it on summer afternoons.

Agnes pushed open a door between a stationer's shop and a grocery, and led the way up a narrow inside stair. They climbed one flight, frightening beetles. She had to search every pocket for the latchkey. She was shaking with cold. Her apartment seemed little warmer than the street. Without speaking to Peter she turned on all the lights. She looked inside the kitchen and bathroom and then got down on her hands and knees and looked under the sofa. The room was neat and belonged to no one. She left him standing in this unclaimed room—she had forgotten him—and closed a door behind her. He looked for something to do—some useful action he could repeat to Madge. He turned on the electric radiator in the fireplace. Perhaps Agnes wouldn't thank him for it; perhaps she would rather undress in the cold. 'I'll be on my way,' he called to the bathroom door.

She had taken off the tramp's clothes and put on a dressing gown of orphanage wool. She came out of the bathroom and straight toward him. She pressed her face and rubbed her cheek on his shoulder as if hoping the contact would leave a scar. He saw her back and her profile and his own face in the mirror over the fireplace. He thought, This is how disasters happen. He saw floods of sea water moving with perfect punitive justice over reclaimed land; he saw lava covering vineyards and overtaking dogs and stragglers. A bridge over an abyss snapped in two and the long express train, suddenly V-shaped, floated like snow. He thought amiably of every kind of disaster and thought, This is how they occur.

Her eyes were closed. She said: 'I shouldn't be over here. In my family we didn't drink or smoke. My mother wanted a lot from me, more than from Harry and the others.' But he knew all that; he had known from the day of the Bible, and because once, at the beginning, she had made him afraid. He was not afraid of her now.

She said, 'It's no use staying here, is it?'

'If you mean what I think, no.'

'It wouldn't be better anywhere.'

She let him see full on her blotched face. He was not expected to do anything. He was not required to pick her up when she fell or wipe her tears. She was poor quality, really—he remembered having thought that once. She left him and went quietly into the bathroom and locked the door. He heard taps running and supposed it was a hot bath. He was pretty certain there would be no more tears. He looked at his watch: Sheilah must be home, now, wondering what had become of him. He descended the beetles' staircase and for forty minutes crossed the city under a windless fall of snow.

The neighbor's child who had stayed with Peter's children was asleep on the living-room sofa. Peter woke her and sent her, sleepwalking, to her own door. He sat down, wet to the bone, thinking, I'll call the Burleighs. In half an hour I'll call the police. He heard a car stop and the engine running and a confusion of two voices laughing and calling goodnight. Presently Sheilah let herself in, rosy-faced, smiling. She carried his trenchcoat over her arm. She said: 'How's Agnes?'

'Where were you?' he said. 'Whose car was that?'

Sheilah had gone into the children's room. He heard her shutting their window. She returned, undoing her dress, and said, 'Was Agnes all right?'

'Agnes is all right. Sheilah, this is about the worst . . .'

She stepped out of the Balenciaga and threw it over a chair. She stopped and looked at him, and said, 'Poor old Pete, are you in love with Agnes?' And then, as if the answer were of so little importance she hadn't time for it, she locked her arms around him and said, 'My love, we're going to Ceylon.'

Two days later, when Peter strolled into his office, Agnes was at her desk. She wore the blue dress, with a spotless collar. White and yellow freesias were symmetrically arranged in the glass jar. The room was hot, and the spring snow, glued for a second when it touched the window, blurred the view of parked cars.

'Quite a party,' Peter said.

She did not look up. He sighed, sat down and thought if the snow held he would be skiing at the Burleighs' very soon. Impressed by his kindness to Agnes, Madge had invited the family for the first possible weekend.

Presently Agnes said, 'I'll never drink again or go to a house where people are drinking. And I'll never bother anyone the way I bothered you.'

'You didn't bother me,' he said. 'I took you home. You were alone and it was late. It's normal.'

'Normal for you, maybe, but I'm used to getting home by myself. Please never tell what happened.'

He stared at her. He can still remember the freesias and the Bible and the heat in the room. She looked as if the elements had no power. She felt neither heat nor cold. 'Nothing happened,' he said.

'I behaved in a silly way. I had no right to. I led you to think I might do something wrong.'

'I might have tried something,' he said gallantly. 'But that would be my fault and not yours.'

She put her knuckle to her mouth and he could scarcely hear. 'It was because of you. I was afraid you might be blamed, or else you'd blame yourself.'

'There's no question of any blame,' he said. 'Nothing happened. We'd both had a lot to drink. Forget about it. Nothing *happened*. You'd remember if it had.'

She put down her hand. There was an expression on her face. Now she sees me, he thought. She had never looked at him after the first day. (He has since tried to put a name to the look on her face; but how can he, now, after so many voyages, after Ceylon, and Hong Kong, and Sheilah's nearly leaving him, and all their difficulties—the money owed, the rows with hotel managers, the lost and found steamer trunk, the children throwing up the foreign food?) She sees me now, he thought. What does she see?

She said: 'I'm from a big family. I'm not used to being alone. I'm not a suicidal person, but I could have done something after that party, just not to see any more, or think or listen or expect anything. What can I think when I see these people? All my life I heard, Educated people don't do this, educated people don't do that. And now I'm here, and you're all educated people, and you're nothing but pigs. You're educated and you drink and do everything wrong and you know what you're doing, and that makes you worse than pigs. My family worked to make me an educated person, but they didn't know you. But what if I didn't see and hear and expect anything any more? It couldn't change anything. You'd all be still the same. Only *you* might have thought it was your fault. You might have thought you were to blame. It could worry you all your life. It would have been wrong for me to worry you.'

He remembered that the rented car was still along a snowy curb somewhere in Geneva. He wondered if Sheilah had the key in her purse and if she remembered where they'd parked.

'I told you about the ice wagon,' Agnes said. 'I don't remember everything, so you're wrong about remembering. But I remember telling you that. That was the best. It's the best you can hope to have. In a big family, if you want to be alone, you have to get up before the rest of them. You get up early in the morning in the summer and it's you, you, once in your life alone in the universe. You think you know everything that can happen . . . Nothing is ever like that again.'

He looked at the smeared window and wondered if this day could end without disaster. In his mind he saw her falling in the snow wearing a tramp's costume, and he saw her coming to him in the orphanage dressing gown. He saw her drowning face at the party. He was afraid for himself. The story was still unfinished. It had to come to a climax, something threatening to him. But there was no climax. They talked that day, and afterward nothing else was said. They went on in the same office for a short time, until Peter left for Ceylon; until somebody read the right letter, passed it on for the right initials, and the Fraziers began the Oriental tour that should have made their fortune. Agnes and Peter were too tired to speak after that morning. They were like a married couple in danger, taking care.

But what were they talking about that day, so quietly, such old friends? They talked about dying, about being ambitious, about being religious, about different kinds of love. What did she see when she looked at him—taking her knuckle slowly away from her mouth, bringing her hand down to the desk, letting it rest there? They were both Canadians, so they had this much together—the knowledge of the little you dare admit. Death, near-death, the best thing, the wrong thing—God knows what they were telling each other. Anyway, nothing happened.

When, on Sunday mornings, Sheilah and Peter talk about those times, they take on the glamor of something still to come. It is then he remembers Agnes Brusen. He never says her name. Sheilah wouldn't remember Agnes. Agnes is the only secret Peter has from his wife, the only puzzle he pieces together without her help. He thinks about families in the West as they were fifteen, twenty years ago—the iron-cold ambition, and every member pushing the next one on. He thinks of his father's parties. When he thinks of his father he imagines him with Sheilah, in a crowd. Actually, Sheilah and Peter's father never met, but they might have liked each other. His father admired good-looking women. Peter wonders what they were doing over there in Geneva—not Sheilah and Peter, *Agnes* and Peter. It is almost as if they had once run away together, silly as children, irresponsible as lovers. Peter and Sheilah are back where they started. While they were out in world affairs picking up microbes and debts, always on the fringe of disaster, the fringe of a fortune, Agnes went on and did—what?

They lost each other. He thinks of the ice wagon going down the street. He sees something he has never seen in his life—a Western town that belongs to Agnes. Here is Agnes—small, mole-faced, round-shouldered because she has always carried a younger child. She watches the ice wagon and the trail of ice water in a morning invented for her: hers. He sees the weak prairie trees and the shadows on the sidewalk. Nothing moves except the shadows and the ice wagon and the changing amber of the child's eyes. The child is Peter. He has seen the grain of the cement sidewalk and the grass in the cracks, and the dust, and the dandelions at the edge of the road. He is there. He has taken the morning that belongs to Agnes, he is up before the others, and he knows everything. There is nothing he doesn't know. He could keep the morning, if he wanted to, but what can Peter do with the start of a summer day? Sheilah is here, it is a true Sunday morning, with its dimness and headache and remorse and regrets, and this is life. He says, 'We have the Balenciaga.' He touches Sheilah's hand. The children have their aunt now, and he and Sheilah have each other. Everything works out, somehow or other. Let Agnes have the start of the day. Let Agnes think it was invented for her. Who wants to be alone in the universe? No, begin at the beginning: Peter lost Agnes. Agnes says to herself somewhere, Peter is lost.

FLANNERY O'CONNOR

Everything That Rises Must Converge

Her doctor had told Julian's mother that she must lose twenty pounds on account of her blood pressure, so on Wednesday nights Julian had to take her downtown on the bus for a reducing class at the Y. The reducing class was designed for working girls over fifty, who weighed from 165 to 200 pounds. His mother was one of the slimmer ones, but she said ladies did not tell their age or weight. She would not ride the buses by herself at night since they had been integrated, and because the reducing class was one of her few pleasures, necessary for her health, and *free*, she said Julian could at least put himself out to take her, considering all she did for him. Julian did not like to consider all she did for him, but every Wednesday night he braced himself and took her.

She was almost ready to go, standing before the hall mirror, putting on her hat, while he, his hands behind him, appeared pinned to the door frame, waiting like Saint Sebastian for the arrows to begin piercing him. The hat was new and had cost her seven dollars and a half. She kept saying, 'Maybe I shouldn't have paid that for it. No, I shouldn't have. I'll take it off and return it tomorrow. I shouldn't have bought it.'

Julian raised his eyes to heaven. 'Yes, you should have bought it,' he said. 'Put it on and let's go.' It was a hideous hat. A purple velvet flap came down on one side of it and stood up on the other; the rest of it was green and looked like a cushion with the stuffing out. He decided it was less comical than jaunty and pathetic. Everything that gave her pleasure was small and depressed him.

She lifted the hat one more time and set it down slowly on top of her head. Two wings of gray hair protruded on either side of her florid face, but her eyes, sky-blue, were as innocent and untouched by experience as they must have been when she was ten. Were it not that she was a widow who had struggled fiercely to feed and clothe and put him through school and who was supporting him still, 'until he got on his feet,' she might have been a little girl that he had to take to town.

'It's all right, it's all right,' he said. 'Let's go.' He opened the door himself and started down the walk to get her going. The sky was a dying violet and the houses stood out darkly against it, bulbous liver-colored monstrosities of a uniform ugliness though no two were alike. Since this had been a fashionable neighborhood forty years ago, his mother persisted in thinking they did well to have an apartment in it. Each house had a narrow collar of dirt around it in which sat, usually, a grubby child. Julian walked with his hands in his pockets, his head down and thrust forward and his eyes glazed with the determination to make himself completely numb during the time he would be sacrificed to her pleasure.

The door closed and he turned to find the dumpy figure, surmounted by the atrocious hat, coming toward him. 'Well,' she said, 'you only live once and paying a little more for it, I at least won't meet myself coming and going.'

'Some day I'll start making money,' Julian said gloomily—he knew he never would—'and you can have one of those jokes whenever you take the fit.' But first they would move. He visualized a place where the nearest neighbors would be three miles away on either side.

'I think you're doing fine,' she said, drawing on her gloves. 'You've only been out of school a year. Rome wasn't built in a day.'

She was one of the few members of the Y reducing class who arrived in hat and gloves and who had a son who had been to college. 'It takes time,' she said, 'and the world is in such a mess. This hat looked better on me than any of the others, though when she brought it out I said, "Take that thing back. I wouldn't have it on my head," and she said, "Now wait till you see it on," and when she put it on me, I said, "We-ull" and she said, "If you ask me, that hat does something for you and you do something for the hat, and besides," she said, "with that hat, you won't meet yourself coming and going."'

Julian thought he could have stood his lot better if she had been selfish, if she had been an old hag who drank and screamed at him. He walked along, saturated in depression, as if in the midst of his martyrdom he had lost his faith. Catching sight of his long, hopeless, irritated face, she stopped suddenly with a grief-stricken look, and pulled back on his arm. 'Wait on me,' she said, 'I'm going back to the house and take this thing off and tomorrow I'm going to return it. I was out of my head. I can pay the gas bill with the seven-fifty.'

He caught her arm in a vicious grip. 'You are not going to take it back,' he said. 'I like it.'

'Well,' she said, 'I don't think I ought . . .'

'Shut up and enjoy it,' he muttered, more depressed than ever.

'With the world in the mess it's in,' she said, 'it's a wonder we can enjoy anything. I tell you, the bottom rail is on the top.'

Julian sighed.

'Of course,' she said,'if you know who you are, you can go anywhere.' She said this every time he took her to the reducing class. 'Most of them in it are not our kind of people,' she said, 'but I can be gracious to anybody. I know who I am.'

'They don't give a damn for your graciousness,' Julian said savagely. 'Knowing who you are is good for one generation only. You haven't the foggiest idea where you stand now or who you are.'

She stopped and allowed her eyes to flash at him. 'I most certainly do know who I am,' she said, 'and if you don't know who you are, I'm ashamed of you.'

'Oh hell,' Julian said.

'Your great-grandfather was a former governor of this state,' she said. 'Your grandfather was a prosperous landowner. Your grand-mother was a Godhigh.'

'Will you look around you,' he said tensely, 'and see where you are now?' and he swept his arm jerkily out to indicate the neighborhood which the growing darkness at least made less dingy.

'You remain what you are,' she said. 'Your great-grandfather had a plantation and two hundred slaves.'

'There are no more slaves,' he said irritably.

'They were better off when they were,' she said. He groaned to see that she was off on that topic. She rolled onto it every few days like a train on an open track. He knew every stop, every junction, every swamp along the way, and knew the exact point at which her conclusion would roll majestically into the station: 'It's ridiculous. It's simply not realistic. They should rise, yes, but on their own side of the fence.'

'Let's skip it,' Julian said.

'The ones I feel sorry for,' she said, 'are the ones that are half white. They're tragic.'

'Will you skip it?'

'Suppose we were half white. We would certainly have mixed feelings.'

'I have mixed feelings now,' he groaned.

'Well let's talk about something pleasant,' she said. 'I remember going to Grandpa's when I was a little girl. Then the house had double stairways that went up to what was really the second floor—all the cooking was done on the first. I used to like to stay down in the kitchen on account of the way the walls smelled. I would sit with my nose pressed against the plaster and take deep breaths. Actually the place belonged to the Godhighs but your grandfather Chestny paid the mortgage and saved it for them. They were in reduced circumstances,' she said, 'but reduced or not, they never forgot who they were.'

'Doubtless that decayed mansion reminded them,' Julian muttered. He never spoke of it without contempt or thought of it without longing. He had seen it once when he was a child before it had been sold. The double stairways had rotted and been torn down. Negroes were living in it. But it remained in his mind as his mother had known it. It appeared in his dreams regularly. He would stand on the wide porch, listening to the rustle of oak leaves, then wander through the high-ceilinged hall into the parlor that opened onto it and gaze at the worn rugs and faded draperies. It occurred to him that it was he, not she, who could have appreciated it. He preferred its threadbare elegance to anything he could name and it was because of it that all the neighborhoods they had lived in had been a torment to him—whereas she had hardly known the difference. She called her insensitivity, 'being adjustable.'

'And I remember the old darky who was my nurse, Caroline. There was no better person in the world. I've always had a great respect for my colored friends,' she said. 'I'd do anything in the world for them and they'd . . .'

'Will you for God's sake get off that subject?' Julian said. When he got on a bus by himself, he made it a point to sit down beside a Negro, in reparation as it were for his mother's sins.

'You're mighty touchy tonight,' she said. 'Do you feel all right?'

'Yes I feel all right,' he said. 'Now lay off.'

She pursed her lips. 'Well, you certainly are in a vile humor,' she observed. 'I just won't speak to you at all.'

They had reached the bus stop. There was no bus in sight and Julian, his hands still jammed in his pockets and his head thrust forward, scowled down the empty street. The frustration of having to wait on the bus as well as ride on it began to creep up his neck like a hot hand. The presence of his mother was borne in upon him as she gave a pained sigh. He looked at her bleakly. She was holding herself very erect under the preposterous hat, wearing it like a banner of her imaginary dignity. There was in him an evil urge to break her spirit. He suddenly unloosened his tie and pulled it off and put it in his pocket.

She stiffened. 'Why must you look like *that* when you take me to town?' she said. 'Why must you deliberately embarrass me?'

'If you'll never learn where you are,' he said, 'you can at least learn where I am.'

'You look like a—thug,' she said.

'Then I must be one,' he murmured.

'I'll just go home,' she said. 'I will not bother you. If you can't do a little thing like that for me . . .'

Rolling his eyes upward, he put his tie back on. 'Restored to my class,' he muttered. He thrust his face toward her and hissed, 'True culture is in the mind, the *mind*,' he said, and tapped his head, 'the mind.'

'It's in the heart,' she said, 'and in how you do things and how you do things is because of who you *are*.'

'Nobody in the damn bus cares who you are.'

'I care who I am,' she said icily.

The lighted bus appeared on top of the next hill and as it approached, they moved into the street to meet it. He put his hand under her elbow and hoisted her up on the creaking step. She entered with a little smile, as if she were going into a drawing room where everyone had been waiting for her. While he put in the tokens, she sat down on one of the broad front seats for three which faced the aisle. A thin woman with protruding teeth and long yellow hair was sitting on the end of it. His mother moved up beside her and left room for Julian beside herself. He sat down and looked at the floor across the aisle where a pair of thin feet in red and white canvas sandals were planted.

His mother immediately began a general conversation meant to attract anyone who felt like talking. 'Can it get any hotter?' she said and removed from her purse a folding fan, black with a Japanese scene on it, which she began to flutter before her.

'I reckon it might could,' the woman with the protruding teeth said, 'but I know for a fact my apartment couldn't get no hotter.'

'It must get the afternoon sun,' his mother said. She sat forward and looked up and down the bus. It was half filled. Everybody was white. 'I see we have the bus to ourselves,' she said. Julian cringed.

'For a change', said the woman across the aisle, the owner of the red and white canvas sandals. 'I come on one the other day and they were thick as fleas—up front and all through.'

'The world is in a mess everywhere,' his mother said. 'I don't know how we've let it get in this fix.'

'What gets my goat is all those boys from good families stealing automobile tires,' the woman with the protruding teeth said. 'I told my boy, I said you may not be rich but you been raised right and if I ever catch you in any such mess, they can send you on to the reformatory. Be exactly where you belong.'

'Training tells,' his mother said. 'Is your boy in high school?'

'Ninth grade,' the woman said.

'My son just finished college last year. He wants to write but he's selling typewriters until he gets started,' his mother said.

The woman leaned forward and peered at Julian. He threw her such a malevolent look that she subsided against the seat. On the floor across the aisle there was an abandoned newspaper. He got up and got it and opened it out in front of him. His mother discreetly continued the conversation in a lower tone but the woman across the aisle said in a loud voice, 'Well that's nice. Selling typewriters is close to writing. He can go right from one to the other.'

'I tell him,' his mother said, 'that Rome wasn't built in a day.'

Behind the newspaper Julian was withdrawing into the inner compartment of his mind where he spent most of his time. This was a kind of mental bubble in which he established himself when he could not bear to be a part of what was going on around him. From it he could see out and judge but in it he was safe from any kind of penetration from without. It was the only place where he felt free of the general idiocy of his fellows. His mother had never entered it but from it he could see her with absolute clarity.

The old lady was clever enough and he thought that if she had started from any of the right premises, more might have been expected of her.She lived according to the laws of her own fantasy world, outside of which he had never seen her set foot. The law of it was to sacrifice herself to him after she had first created the necessity to do so by making a mess of things. If he had permitted her sacrifices, it was only because her lack of foresight had made them necessary. All of her life had been a struggle to act like a Chestny without the Chestny goods, and to give him everything she thought a Chestny ought to have; but since, said she, it was fun to struggle, why complain? And when you had won, as she had won, what fun to look back on the hard times! He could not forgive her that she had enjoyed the struggle and that she thought *she* had won.

What she meant when she said she had won was that she had brought him up successfully and had sent him to college and that he had turned out so well—good looking (her teeth had gone unfilled so that his could be straightened), intelligent (he realized he was too intelligent to be a success) and with a future ahead of him (there was of course no future ahead of him). She excused his gloominess on the grounds that he was still growing up and his radical ideas on his lack of practical experience. She said he didn't yet know a thing about 'life,' that he hadn't even entered the real world—when already he was as disenchanted with it as a man of fifty.

The further irony of all this was that in spite of her, he had turned out so well. In spite of going to only a third-rate college, he had, on his own initiative, come out with a first-rate education; in spite of growing up dominated by a small mind, he had ended up with a large one; in spite of all her foolish views, he was free of prejudice and unafraid to face facts. Most miraculous of all, instead of being blinded by love for her as she was for him, he had cut himself emotionally free of her and could see her with complete objectivity. He was not dominated by his mother.

The bus stopped with a sudden jerk and shook him from his meditation. A woman from the back lurched forward with little steps and barely escaped falling in his newspaper as she righted herself. She got off and a large Negro got on. Julian kept his paper lowered to watch. It gave him a certain satisfaction to see injustice in daily operation. It confirmed his view that with a few exceptions there was no one worth knowing within a radius of three hundred miles. The Negro was well dressed and carried a briefcase. He looked around and then sat down on the other end of the seat where the woman with the red and white canvas sandals was sitting. He immediately unfolded a newspaper and obscured himself behind it. Julian's mother's elbow at once prodded insistently into his ribs. 'Now you see why I won't ride on these buses by myself,' she whispered.

The woman with the red and white canvas sandals had risen at the same time the Negro sat down and had gone further back in the bus and taken the seat of the woman who had got off. His mother leaned forward and cast her an approving look.

Julian rose, crossed the aisle, and sat down in the place of the woman with the canvas sandals. From this position, he looked serenely across at his mother. Her face had turned an angry red. He stared at her, making his eyes the eyes of a stranger. He felt his tension suddenly lift as if he had openly declared war on her.

He would have liked to get in conversation with the Negro and to talk with him about art or politics or any subject that would be above the comprehension of those around him, but the man remained entrenched behind his paper. He was either ignoring the change of seating or had never noticed it. There was no way for Julian to convey his sympathy.

His mother kept her eyes fixed reproachfully on his face. The woman with the protruding teeth was looking at him avidly as if he were a type of monster new to her.

'Do you have a light?' he asked the Negro.

Without looking away from his paper, the man reached in his pocket and handed him a packet of matches.

'Thanks,' Julian said. For a moment he held the matches foolishly. A NO SMOKING sign looked down upon him from over the door. This alone would not have deterred him; he had no cigarettes. He had quit smoking some months before because he could not afford it. 'Sorry,' he muttered and handed back the matches. The Negro lowered the paper and gave him an annoyed look. He took the matches and raised the paper again.

His mother continued to gaze at him but she did not take advantage of his momentary discomfort. Her eyes retained their battered look. Her face seemed to be unnaturally red, as if her blood pressure had risen. Julian allowed no glimmer of sympathy to show on his face. Having got the advantage, he wanted desperately to keep it and carry it through. He would have liked to teach her a lesson that would last her a while, but there seemed no way to continue the point. The Negro refused to come out from behind his paper.

Julian folded his arms and looked stolidly before him, facing her but as if he did not see her, as if he had ceased to recognize her existence. He visualized a scene in which, the bus having reached their stop, he would remain in his seat and when she said, 'Aren't you going to get off?' he would look at her as at a stranger who had rashly addressed him. The corner they got off on was usually deserted, but it was well lighted and it would not hurt her to walk by herself the four blocks to the Y. He decided to wait until the time came and then decide whether or not he would let her get off by herself. He would have to be at the Y at ten to bring her back, but he could leave her wondering if he was going to show up. There was no reason for her to think she could always depend on him.

He retired again into the high-ceilinged room sparsely settled with large piece of antique furniture. His soul expanded momentarily but then he became aware of his mother across from him and the vision shriveled. He studied her coldly. Her feet in little pumps dangled like a child's and did not quite reach the floor. She was training on him an exaggerated look of reproach. He felt completely detached from her. At that moment he could with pleasure have slapped her as he would have slapped a particularly obnoxious child in his charge.

He began to imagine various unlikely ways by which he could teach her a lesson. He might make friends with some distinguished Negro professor or lawyer and bring him home to spend the evening. He would be entirely justified but her blood pressure would rise to 300. He could not push her to the extent of making her have a stroke, and moreover, he had never been successful at making any Negro friends. He had tried to strike up an acquaintance on the bus with some of the better types, with ones that looked like professors or ministers or lawyers. One morning he had sat down next to a distinguished-looking dark brown man who had answered his questions with a sonorous solemnity but who turned out to be an undertaker. Another day he had sat down beside a cigar-smoking Negro with a diamond ring on his finger, but after a few stilted pleasantries, the Negro had rung the buzzer and risen, slipping two lottery tickets into Julian's hand as he climbed over him to leave.

He imagined his mother lying desperately ill and his being able to secure only a Negro doctor for her. He toyed with that idea for a few minutes and then dropped it for a momentary vision of himself participating as a sympathizer in a sit-in demonstration. This was possible but he did not linger with it. Instead, he approached the ultimate horror. He brought home a beautiful suspiciously Negroid woman. Prepare yourself, he said. There is nothing you can do about it. This is the woman I've chosen. She's intelligent, dignified, even good, and she's suffered and she hasn't thought it *fun*. Now persecute us, go ahead and persecute us. Drive her out of here, but remember, you're driving me too. His eyes were narrowed and through the indignation he had generated, he saw his mother across the aisle, purple-faced, shrunken to the dwarf-like proportions of her moral nature, sitting like a mummy beneath the ridiculous banner of her hat.

He was tilted out of his fantasy again as the bus stopped. The door opened with a sucking hiss and out of the dark a large, gaily dressed, sullen-looking colored woman got on with a little boy. The child, who might have been four, had on a short plaid suit and a Tyrolean hat with a blue feather in it. Julian hoped that he would sit down beside him and that the woman would push in beside his mother. He could think of no better arrangement.

As she waited for her tokens, the woman was surveying the seating possibilities—he hoped with the idea of sitting where she was least wanted. There was something familiar-looking about her but Julian could not place what it was. She was a giant of a woman. Her face was set not only to meet opposition but to seek it out. The downward tilt of her large lower lip was like a warning sign: DON'T TAMPER WITH ME. Her bulging figure was encased in a green crepe dress and her feet overflowed in red shoes. She had on a hideous hat. A purple velvet flap came down on one side of it and stood up on the other; the rest of it was green and looked like a cushion with the stuffing out. She carried a mammoth red pocketbook that bulged throughout as if it were stuffed with rocks.

To Julian's disappointment, the little boy climbed up on the empty seat beside his mother. His mother lumped all children, black and white, into the common category, 'cute,' and she thought little Negroes were on the whole cuter than little white children. She smiled at the little boy as he climbed on the seat.

Meanwhile the woman was bearing down upon the empty seat beside Julian. To his annoyance, she squeezed herself into it. He saw his mother's face change as the woman settled herself next to him and he realized with satisfaction that this was more objectionable to her than it was to him. Her face seemed almost gray and there was a look of dull recognition in her eyes, as if suddenly she had sickened at some awful confrontation. Julian saw that it was because she and the woman had, in a sense, swapped sons. Though his mother would not realize the symbolic significance of this, she would feel it. His amusement showed plainly on his face.

The woman next to him muttered something unintelligible to herself. He was conscious of a kind of bristling next to him, muted growling like that of an angry cat. He could not see anything but the red pocketbook upright on the bulging green thighs. He visualized the woman as she had stood waiting for her tokens—the ponderous figure, rising from the red shoes upward over the solid hips, the mammoth bosom, the haughty face, to the green and purple hat.

His eyes widened.

The vision of the two hats, identical, broke upon him with the radiance of a brilliant sunrise. His face was suddenly lit with joy. He could not believe that Fate had thrust upon his mother such a lesson. He gave a loud chuckle so that she would look at him and see that he saw. She turned her eyes on him slowly. The blue in them seemed to have turned a bruised purple. For a moment he had an uncomfortable sense of her innocence, but it lasted only a second before principle rescued him. Justice entitled him to laugh. His grin hardened until it said to her as plainly as if he were saying aloud: Your punishment exactly fits your pettiness. This should teach you a permanent lesson.

Her eyes shifted to the woman. She seemed unable to bear looking at him and to find the woman preferable. He became conscious again of the bristling presence at his side. The woman was rumbling like a volcano about to become active. His mother's mouth began to twitch slightly at one corner. With a sinking heart, he saw incipient signs of recovery on her face and realized that this was going to strike her suddenly as funny and was going to be no lesson at all. She kept her eyes on the woman and an amused smile came over her face as if the woman were a monkey that had stolen her hat. The little Negro was looking up at her with large fascinated eyes. He had been trying to attract her attention for some time.

'Carver!' the woman said suddenly. 'Come heah!'

When he saw that the spotlight was on him at last, Carver drew his feet up and turned himself toward Julian's mother and giggled.

'Carver!' the woman said. 'You heah me? Come heah!'

Carver slid down from the seat but remained squatting with his back against the base of it, his head turned slyly around toward Julian's mother, who was smiling at him. The woman reached a hand across the aisle and snatched him to her. He righted himself and hung backwards on her knees, grinning at Julian's mother. 'Isn't he cute?' Julian's mother said to the woman with the protruding teeth.

'I reckon he is,' the woman said without conviction.

The Negress yanked him upright but he eased out of her grip and shot across the aisle and scrambled, giggling wildly, onto the seat beside his love.

'I think he likes me,' Julian's mother said, and smiled at the woman. It was the smile she used when she was being particulaly gracious to an inferior. Julian saw everything lost. The lesson had rolled off her like rain on a roof.

The woman stood up and yanked the little boy off the seat as if she were snatching him from contagion. Julian could feel the rage in her at having no weapon like his mother's smile. She gave the child a sharp slap across his leg. He howled once and then thrust his head into her stomach and kicked his feet against her shins. 'Behave,' she said vehemently.

The bus stopped and the Negro who had been reading the newspaper got off. The woman moved over and set the little boy down with a thump between herself and Julian. She held him firmly by the knee. In a moment he put his hands in front of his face and peeped at Julian's mother through his fingers.

'I see yoooooooo!' she said and put her hand in front of her face and peeped at him.

The woman slapped his hand down. 'Quit yo' foolishness,' she said, 'before I knock the living Jesus out of you!'

Julian was thankful that the next stop was theirs. He reached up and pulled the cord. The woman reached up and pulled it at the same time. Oh my God, he thought. He had the terrible intuition that when they got off the bus together, his mother would open her purse and give the little boy a nickel. The gesture would be as natural to her as breathing. The bus stopped and the woman got up and lunged to the front, dragging the child, who wished to stay on, after her. Julian and his mother got up and followed. As they neared the door, Julian tried to relieve her of her pocketbook.

'No,' she murmured, 'I want to give the little boy a nickel.'

'No!' Julian hissed. 'No!'

She smiled down at the child and opened her bag. The bus door opened and the woman picked him up by the arm and descended with him, hanging at her hip. Once in the street she set him down and shook him.

Julian's mother had to close her purse while she got down the bus step but as soon as her feet were on the ground, she opened it again and began to rummage inside. 'I can't find but a penny,' she whispered, 'but it looks like a new one.'

'Don't do it!' Julian said fiercely between his teeth. There was a streetlight on the corner and she hurried to get under it so that she could better see into her pocketbook. The woman was heading off rapidly down the street with the child still hanging backward on her hand.

'Oh little boy!' Julian's mother called and took a few quick steps and caught up with them just beyond the lamppost. 'Here's a bright new penny for you,' and she held out the coin, which shone bronze in the dim light.

The huge woman turned and for a moment stood, her shoulders lifted and her face frozen with frustrated rage, and stared at Julian's mother. Then all at once she seemed to explode like a piece of machinery that had been given one ounce of pressure too much. Julian saw the black fist swing out with the red pocketbook. He shut his eyes and cringed as he heard the woman shout, 'He don't take nobody's pennies!' When he opened his eyes, the woman was disappearing down the street with the little boy staring wide-eyed over her shoulder. Julian's mother was sitting on the sidewalk.

'I told you not to do that,' Julian said angrily. 'I told you not to do that!'

He stood over her for a minute, gritting his teeth. Her legs were stretched out in front of her and her hat was on her lap. He squatted down and looked her in the face. It was totally expressionless. 'You got exactly what you deserved,' he said. 'Now get up.'

He picked up her pocketbook and put what had fallen out back in it. He picked the hat up off her lap. The penny caught his eye on the sidewalk and he picked that up and let it drop before her eyes into the purse. Then he stood up and leaned over and held his hands out to pull her up. She remained immobile. He sighed. Rising above them on either side were black apartment buildings, marked with irregular rectangles of light. At the end of the block a man came out of a door and walked off in the opposite direction. 'All right,' he said, 'suppose somebody happens by and wants to know why you're sitting on the sidewalk?'

She took the hand and, breathing hard, pulled heavily up on it and then stood for a moment, swaying slightly as if the spots of light in the darkness were circling around her. Her eyes, shadowed and confused, finally settled on his face. He did not try to conceal his irritation. 'I hope this teaches you a lesson,' he said. She leaned forward and her eyes raked his face. She seemed trying to determine his identity. Then, as if she found nothing familiar about him, she started off with a headlong movement in the wrong direction.

'Aren't you going on to the Y?' he asked.

'Home,' she muttered.

'Well, are we walking?'

For answer she kept going. Julian followed along, his hands behind him. He saw no reason to let the lesson she had had go without backing it up with an explanation of its meaning. She might as well be made to understand what had happened to her. 'Don't think that was just an uppity Negro woman,' he said. 'That was the whole colored race which will no longer take your condescending pennies. That was your black double. She can wear the same hat as you, and to be sure,' he added gratuitously (because he thought it was funny), 'it looked better on her than it did on you. What all this means,' he said, 'is that the old world is gone. The old manners are obsolete and your graciousness is not worth a damn.' He thought bitterly of the house that had been lost for him. 'You aren't who you think you are,' he said.

She continued to plow ahead, paying no attention to him. Her hair had come undone on one side. She dropped her pocketbook and took no notice. He stooped and picked it up and handed it to her but she did not take it.

'You needn't act as if the world had come to an end,' he said, 'because it hasn't. From now on you've got to live in a new world and face a few realities for a change. Buck up,' he said, 'it won't kill you.'

She was breathing fast.

'Let's wait on the bus,' he said.

'Home,' she said thickly.

'I hate to see you behave like this,' he said. 'Just like a child. I should be able to expect more of you.' He decided to stop where he was and make her stop and wait for a bus. 'I'm not going any farther,' he said, stopping. 'We're going on the bus.'

She continued to go on as if she had not heard him. He took a few steps and caught her arm and stopped her. He looked into her face and caught his breath. He was looking into a face he had never seen before. 'Tell Grandpa to come get me,' she said.

He stared, stricken.

'Tell Caroline to come get me,' she said.

Stunned, he let her go and she lurched forward again, walking as if one leg were shorter than the other. A tide of darkness seemed to be sweeping her from him. 'Mother!' he cried. 'Darling, sweetheart, wait!' Crumpling, she fell to the pavement. He dashed forward and fell at her side, crying, 'Mamma, Mamma!' He turned her over. Her face was fiercely distorted. One eye, large and staring, moved slightly to the left as if it had become unmoored. The other remained fixed on him, raked his face again, found nothing and closed.

'Wait here, wait here!' he cried and jumped up and began to run for help toward a cluster of lights he saw in the distance ahead of him. 'Help, help!' he shouted, but his voice was thin, scarcely a thread of sound. The lights drifted farther away the faster he ran and his feet moved numbly as if they carried him nowhere. The tide of darkness seemed to sweep him back to her, postponing from moment to moment his entry into the world of guilt and sorrow.

ELIZABETH SPENCER

The Adult Holiday

That day there was a holiday for the college where he taught, but none for the schools, she was alone all day with her husband, and he was angry with her. She had really never seen him so angry. A flush of rage had come over him soon after breakfast, and going into his office, just off the kitchen, she ran straight into it at the door, like a fiery wall, though his back was turned, his long hand sorting through some letters. 'Oh,' she thought, and 'Oh,' and 'Oh,' and 'Oh . . .' even her thought fading, dissolving out to nothing, and then he turned and let her have it—a white lash of words during which she could only stand, try to catch her breath, try not to turn away, try to last it out, try in the end simply to survive.

Then it was over. It was the kind of thing she had never before experienced, something there was no apologizing for. If she had gone straight upstairs and packed a suitcase to go and get a job someplace, or to go back to her family and call a lawyer for a divorce, there was nothing he could have said to stop her, except possibly 'I must be insane, and will go to a psychiatrist immediately.' And he was not going to do that at all.

She clung about the house in corners all morning long, and finally fell to dusting the pictures. It had rained in the night, and the big maple on the back lawn stood pale green, enlarging itself in the new season. What did I do to start it, she wondered, as though by thinking of it in a small way, as just like any other quarrel, she might reduce it to being small. Had it been something about his mother? She knew that men were supposed to have deeply hidden sensibilities about their mothers. But all she said at breakfast was something mild about that lady's handwriting's getting worse—a fact they had often remarked upon before. Besides, he had always seemed more deeply aware of things about his father. Had she so much as alluded to his father? She did not think so. Had some chance association brought his father up? Had that arrogant face, ten years gone, intruded above her shoulder at breakfast to let her husband's vision cut through for once upon her, come straight into clear focus on the terrible creature that, for all she knew, she might really be? And had he not been able to bear that?

She didn't know . . . she didn't know. She turned herself all the way into a maid, and got out the silver to polish it. She did not wear her gloves and thought that now her hands would be splotched, which he didn't like but as he had let no stone of herself remain upon another in the general destruction, she felt that lamenting her hands would be like mourning the death of a kitten after the funeral of a child. She turned out a closet and straightened it, taking care to make no noise at all. She could not compose a grocery list, though she tried, and once she peeked down through a crack in the floor abovestairs and saw him eating lunch—he managed well enough alone. She fell to admiring how calmly he could assemble and digest everything. He had not forgotten the butter, nor the two kinds of bread—one for the salad, one for the meat and cheese—nor his favorite pepper mill. She lay hugged to the floor, thinking she would never eat again, but nonetheless admiring him, as a girl in the scullery might admire the lord of the castle. If she stayed on here, she would eventually have to speak to him; a word would have to crack through the voluminous stillness he had created in both their lives. She wondered what it would be. Eeny, meeny, miney, mo: 'Did you mail the check for the gas?' 'Let's go to the movies tonight.' 'My dearest wish was only that . . .'

But still she did not cross his path; she did not even cry until their little girl (the youngest, hence the earliest) came home from school and showed her the cutouts. Then her tears rolled down like rain.

'Why are you crying, Mother?'

'Well, I used to make cutouts at school, too,' she said, sobbing.

The cutouts—witches, gingerbread men, clowns, and princesses—got smeared and wet in this torrent, which the child did not like, but grew cautious about. She went in to her father, having gathered up the stack of them. 'Mother's crying,' she said. 'Do you know why?'

'She feels sad because it's my forty-fifth birthday,' he said.

'But your birthday is not till tomorrow,' said the child.

'I know that,' he said, 'but she was thinking of it.'

There was a long silence. Soon she would have to come alive, to walk on her two numb legs back into his presence and thus concede that the thing had happened indeed and that she could and would go on living there, that dinner would somehow appear for them as usual. She heard the child and her husband building a fire.

'Listen, Daddy,' said the child, 'how do you feel about getting so old?'

'I don't like it,' he said. 'I thought that's why they were giving us the holiday, but of course it wasn't.'

'The holiday is for Founder's Day.'

'That's right, but I didn't go to the ceremony.'

'Why didn't you?'

'Because I don't like being forty-five.'

The child was silent, thinking all this over. He had a nice way with children—just whimsical enough without exactly trying to fool them; he let them know they were being made to think instead of being made fun of. He was also good at making a child aware of the joins and turns of an adult conversation.

'Does Mother really care *that* much if you're forty-five?' asked the child, and, listening, the mother could all but see just how the child looked when she said that—the downward look of thinking, the crinkle of the brow when she turned up her face. Those sobs had been incongruous with both the reasons given for them; the child would have felt that clearly all along.

He had not answered, but she knew by the crackling sound and the smell of woodsmoke that he had lighted the fire. 'Anyway,' said the child, to whom the problem still was a dense one, 'she's just about thirty-seven herself.'

'She should have gone away soon after I met her,' he said, in his light, persistent way. 'Then I wouldn't be here now.'

'But where would you be?'

'Somewhere. Not here.'

'Where would it be?' cried the child, gathering a sort of anxious interest, as if he had drawn her into a game.

'Wherever it is, it's not where you are the day before your forty-fifth birthday,' he said. 'It never is.'

'Then where is it, Daddy?'

'If I knew, I'd go there.'

'Would you take me?'

'Why would I take you? Of course not.' He paused. 'To be there

I would have had to start going there the day your mother should have gone away.'

Caught in a tangle of syntax almost like an enchantment, the child laughed uneasily, and tried to repeat: 'To be there you . . . what now?'

'Try it,' he said.

In the silence of the study, not called for by either of them, she remembered the very day he meant, a quite different spring from this one. He had come down to the office where she worked and waited in the gritty hallway outside for her to finish, had followed her all the way home, talking eagerly about his work, and she knew that he was in love with her, this studious, brilliant, earnest young man who (they said) had the world before him. All the things other people said faded, not mattering, and the two of them, walking together, passed every which way through a world of streams, muddy paths, and flowers, through short cuts that lengthened the way endlessly before them.

It was the deliberate association of that day with this that crushed in upon her, listening, and so all but made up, she felt, the final sum of her life. She put aside the sewing basket—she must have done a month's mending, very skillfully and accurately, in spite of the fact that her glasses were smeared with drying tears and she couldn't see anything. The child was attempting, as with a riddle, to get the syntax right, repeating, 'For you to be there now you would have had . . . Wait. For you to be there now you would have had to start going there the day . . . Let me start over. For you to be there now . . .'

In another minute, she thought, the child would not only get it right but understand it, and then they all could vanish. She replaced her cleaned glasses and came to the living room door—a journey into the void. 'I didn't leave that day because I didn't want to leave.'

He at once said, trembling, 'Darling, you didn't leave because I didn't want you to.'

The child, greedy for happiness, looked up and smiled at them. Strung between them on a mended web of what they said, she abandoned the puzzle of her father's words forever.

Toni Cade Bambara

The Lesson

Back in the days when everyone was old and stupid or young and foolish and me and Sugar were the only ones just right, this lady moved on our block with nappy hair and proper speech and no makeup. And quite naturally we laughed at her, laughed the way we did at the junk man who went about his business like he was some big-time president and his sorry-ass horse his secretary. And we kinda hated her too, hated the way we did the winos who cluttered up our parks, and pissed on our handball walls and stank up our hallways and stairs so you couldn't halfway play hide-and-seek without a goddamn gas mask. Miss Moore was her name. The only woman on the block with no first name. And she was black as hell, cept for her feet, which were fish-white and spooky. And she was always planning these boring-ass things for us to do, us being my cousin, mostly, who lived on the block cause we all moved North the same time and to the same apartment then spread out gradual to breathe. And our parents would yank our heads into some kinda shape and crisp up our clothes so we'd be presentable for travel with Miss Moore, who always looked like she was going to church, though she never did. Which is just one of things the grown-ups talked about when they talked behind her back like a dog. But when she came calling with some sachet she'd sewed up or some gingerbread she'd made or some book, why then they'd all be too embarrassed to turn her down and we'd get handed over all spruced up. She'd been to college and said it was only right that she should take responsibility for the young ones' education, and she not even related by marriage or blood. So they'd go for it. Specially Aunt Gretchen. She was the main gofer in the family. You got some ole dumb shit foolishness you want somebody to go for, you send for Aunt Gretchen. She been screwed into the go-along for so long, it's a blood-deep natural thing with her. Which is how she got saddled with me and Sugar and Junior in the first place while our mothers were in a la-de-da apartment up the block having a good ole time.

So this one day Miss Moore rounds us all up at the mailbox and it's puredee hot and she's knockin herself out about arithmetic. And school suppose to let up in summer I heard, but she don't never let up. And the starch in my pinafore scratching the shit outta me and I'm really hating this nappy-head bitch and her goddamn college degree. I'd much rather go to the pool or to the show where it's cool. So me and Sugar leaning on the mailbox being surly, which is a Miss Moore word. And Flyboy checking out what everybody brought for lunch. And Fat Butt already wasting his peanut-butter-and-jelly sandwich like the pig he is. And Junebug punchin on Q.T.'s arm for potato chips. And Rosie Giraffe shifting from one hip to the other waiting for somebody to step on her foot or ask her if she from Georgia so she can kick ass, preferably Mercedes'. And Miss Moore asking us do we know what money is, like we a bunch of retards. I mean real money, she say, like it's only poker chips or monopoly papers we lay on the grocer. So right away I'm tired of this and say so. And would much rather snatch Sugar and go to the Sunset and terrorize the West Indian kids and take their hair ribbons and their money too. And Miss Moore files that remark away for next week's lesson on brotherhood, I can tell. And finally I say we oughta get to the subway cause it's cooler and besides we might meet some cute boys. Sugar done swiped her mama's lipstick, so we ready.

So we heading down the street and she's boring us silly about what things cost and what our parents make and how much goes for rent and how money ain't divided up right in this country. And then she gets to the part about we all poor and live in the slums, which I don't feature. And I'm ready to speak on that, but she steps out in the street and hails two cabs just like that. Then she hustles half the crew in with her and hands me a five-dollar bill and tells me to calculate 10 percent tip for the driver. And we're off. Me and Sugar and Junebug and Flyboy hangin out the window and hollering to everybody, putting lipstick on each other cause Flyboy a faggot anyway, and making farts with our sweaty armpits. But I'm mostly trying to figure how to spend this money. But they all fascinated with the meter ticking and Junebug starts laying bets as to how much it'll read when Flyboy can't hold his breath no more. Then Sugar lays bets as to how much it'll be when we get there. So I'm stuck. Don't nobody want to go for my plan, which is to jump out at the next light and run off to the first bar-b-que we can find. Then the driver tells us to get the hell out cause we there already. And the meter reads eighty-five cents. And I'm stalling to figure out the tip and Sugar say give him a dime. And I decide he don't need it bad as I do, so later for him. But then he tries to take off with Junebug foot still in the door so we talk about his mama something ferocious. Then we check out that we on Fifth Avenue and everybody dressed up in stockings. One lady in a fur coat, hot as it is. White folks crazy.

'This is the place,' Miss Moore say, presenting it to us in the voice she uses at the museum. 'Let's look in the windows before we go in.'

'Can we steal?' Sugar asks very serious like she's getting the ground rules squared away before she plays. 'I beg your pardon,' says Miss Moore, and we fall out. So she leads us around the windows of the toy store and me and Sugar screamin, 'This is mine, that's mine, I gotta have that, that was made for me, I was born for that,' till Big Butt drowns us out.

'Hey, I'm goin to buy that there.'

'That there?' You don't even know what it is, stupid.'

'I do so,' he say punchin on Rosie Giraffe. 'It's a microscope.'

'Whatcha gonna do with a microscope, fool?'

'Look at things.'

'Like what, Ronald?' ask Miss Moore. And Big Butt ain't got the first notion. So here go Miss Moore gabbing about the thousands of bacteria in a drop of water and the somethinorother in a speck of blood and the million and one living things in the air around us is invisible to the naked eye. And what she say that for? Junebug go to town on that 'naked' and we rolling. Then Miss Moore ask what it cost. So we all jam into the window smudgin it up and the price tag say $300. So then she ask how long'd take for Big Butt and Junebug to save up their allowances. 'Too long,' I say. 'Yeh,' adds Sugar, 'outgrown it by that time.' And Miss Moore say no, you never outgrow learning instruments. 'Why, even medical students and interns and,' blah, blah, blah. And we ready to choke Big Butt for bringing it up in the first damn place.

'This here costs four hundred eighty dollars,' say Rosie Giraffe. So we pile up all over her to see what she pointin out. My eyes tell me it's a chunk of glass cracked with something heavy, and different-color inks dripped into the splits, then the whole thing put into a oven or something. But for $480 it don't make sense.

'That's a paperweight made of semi-precious stones fused

together under tremendous pressure,' she explains slowly, with her hands doing the mining and all the factory work.

'So what's a paperweight?' asks Rosie Giraffe.

'To weigh paper with, dumbbell,' say Flyboy, the wise man from the East.

'Not exactly,' say Miss Moore, which is what she say when you warm or way off too. 'It's to weigh paper down so it won't scatter and make your desk untidy.' So right away me and Sugar curtsey to each other and then to Mercedes who is more the tidy type.

'We don't keep paper on top of the desk in my class,' say Junebug, figuring Miss Moore crazy or lyin one.

'At home, then,' she say. 'Don't you have a calendar and a pencil case and a blotter and a letter-opener on your desk at home where you do your homework?' And she know damn well what our homes look like cause she nosys around in them every chance she gets.

'I don't even have a desk,' say Junebug. 'Do we?'

'No. And I don't get no homework neither,' says Big Butt.

'And I don't even have a home,' say Flyboy like he do at school to keep the white folks off his back and sorry for him. Send this poor kid to camp posters, is his specialty.

'I do,' says Mercedes. 'I have a box of stationery on my desk and a picture of my cat. My godmother bought the stationery and the desk. There's a big rose on each sheet and the envelopes smell like roses.'

'Who wants to know about your smelly-ass stationery,' says Rosie Giraffe fore I can get my two cents in.

'It's important to have a work area all your own so that . . .'

'Will you look at this sailboat, please,' say Flyboy, cuttin her off and pointin to the thing like it was his. So once again we tumble all over each other to gaze at this magnificent thing in the toy store which is just big enough to maybe sail two kittens across the pond if you strap them to the posts tight. We all start reciting the price tag like we in assembly. 'Handcrafted sailboat of fibreglass at one thousand one hundred ninety-five dollars.'

'Unbelievable,' I hear myself say and am really stunned. I read it again for myself just in case the group recitation put me in a trance. Same thing. For some reason this pisses me off. We look at Miss Moore and she lookin at us, waiting for I dunno what.

'Who'd pay all that when you can buy a sailboat set for a

quarter at Pop's, a tube of glue for a dime, and a ball of string for eight cents?' It must have a motor and a whole lot else besides,' I say. 'My sailboat cost me about fifty cents.'

'But will it take water?' say Mercedes with her smart ass.

'Took mine to Alley Pond Park once,' say Flyboy. 'String broke. Lost it. Pity.'

'Sailed mine in Central Park and it keeled over and sank. Had to ask my father for another dollar.'

'And you got the strap,' laugh Big Butt. 'The jerk didn't even have a string on it. My old man wailed on his behind.'

Little Q.T. was staring hard at the sailboat and you could see he wanted it bad. But he too little and somebody'd just take it from him. So what the hell. 'This boat for kids, Miss Moore?'

'Parents silly to buy something like that just to get all broke up,' say Rosie Giraffe.

'That much money it should last forever,' I figure.

'My father'd buy it for me if I wanted it.'

'Your father, my ass,' say Rosie Giraffe getting a chance to finally push Mercedes.

'Must be rich people shop here,' say Q.T.

'You are a very bright boy,' say Flyboy. 'What was your first clue?' And he rap him on the head with the back of his knuckles, since Q.T. the only one he could get away with. Though Q.T. liable to come up behind you years later and get his licks in when you half expect it.

'What I want to know is,' I says to Miss Moore though I never talk to her, I wouldn't give the bitch that satisfaction, 'is how much a real boat costs? I figure a thousand'd get you a yacht any day.'

'Why don't you check that out,' she says, 'and report back to the group?' Which really pains my ass. If you gonna mess up a perfectly good swim day least you could do is have some answers. 'Let's go in,' she say like she got something up her sleeve. Only she don't lead the way. So me and Sugar turn the corner to where the entrance is, but when we get there I kinda hang back. Not that I'm scared, what's there to be afraid of, just a toy store. But I feel funny, shame. But what I got to be shamed about? Got as much right to go in as anybody. But somehow I can't seem to get hold of the door, so I step away for Sugar to lead. But she hangs back too. And I look at her and she looks at me and this is ridiculous. I mean, damn, I have never ever been shy about doing nothing or going nowhere. But then Mercedes steps up and then Rosie Giraffe and Big Butt crowd in behind and shove, and next thing we all stuffed into the doorway with only Mercedes squeezing past us, smoothing out her jumper and walking right down the aisle. Then the rest of us tumble in like a glued-together jigsaw done all wrong. And people lookin at us. And it's like the time me and Sugar crashed into the Catholic church on a dare. But once we got in there and everything so hushed and holy and the candles and the bow-in and the handkerchiefs on all the drooping heads, I just couldn't go through with the plan. Which was for me to run up to the altar and do a tap dance while Sugar played the nose flute and messed around in the holy water. And Sugar kept givin me the elbow. Then later teased me so bad I tied her up in the shower and turned it on and locked her in. And she'd be there till this day if Aunt Gretchen hadn't finally figured I was lyin about the boarder takin a shower.

Same thing in the store. We all walkin on tiptoe and hardly touchin the games and puzzles and things. And I watched Miss Moore who is steady watchin us like she waitin for a sign. Like Mama Drewery watches the sky and sniffs the air and takes note of just how much slant is in the bird formation. Then me and Sugar bump smack into each other, so busy gazing at the toys, 'specially the sailboat. But we don't laugh and go into our fat-lady bump-stomach routine. We just stare at that price tag. Then Sugar run a finger over the whole boat. And I'm jealous and want to hit her. Maybe not her, but I sure want to punch somebody in the mouth.

'Watcha bring us here for, Miss Moore?'

'You sound angry, Sylvia. Are you mad about something?' Givin me one of them grins like she tellin a grown-up joke that never turns out to be funny. And she's lookin very closely at me like maybe she plannin to do my portrait from memory. I'm mad, but I won't give her that satisfaction. So I slouch around the store being very bored and say, 'Let's go.'

Me and Sugar at the back of the train watchin the tracks whizzin by large then small then gettin gobbled up in the dark. I'm thinkin about this tricky toy I saw in the store. A clown that somersaults on a bar then does chin-ups just cause you yank lightly at his leg. Cost $35. I could see me askin my mother for a

$35 birthday clown. 'You wanna who that costs what?' she'd say, cocking her head to the side to get a better view of the hole in my head. Thirty-five dollars could buy new bunk beds for Junior and Gretchen's boy. Thirty-five dollars and the whole household could go visit Granddaddy Nelson in the country. Thirty-five dollars would pay for the rent and the piano bill too. Who are these people that spend that much for performing clowns and $1,000 for toy sailboats? What kinda work they do and how they live and how come we ain't in on it? Where we are is who we are, Miss Moore always pointin out. But it don't necessarily have to be that way, she always adds then waits for somebody to say that poor people have to wake up and demand their share of the pie and don't none of us know what kind of pie she talkin about in the first damn place. But she ain't so smart cause I still got her four dollars from the taxi and she sure ain't gettin it. Messin up my day with this shit. Sugar nudges me in my pocket and winks.

Miss Moore lines us up in front of the mailbox where we started from, seem like years ago, and I got a headache for thinkin so hard. And we lean all over each other so we can hold up under the draggy-ass lecture she always finishes us off with at the end before we thank her for borin us to tears. But she just looks at us like she readin tea leaves. Finally she say, 'Well, what did you think of F.A.O. Schwartz?'

Rosie Giraffe mumbles, 'White folks crazy.'

'I'd like to go there again when I get my birthday money,' says Mercedes, and we shove her out the pack so she has to lean on the mailbox by herself.

'I'd like a shower. Tiring day,' say Flyboy.

Then Sugar surprises me by sayin, 'You know, Miss Moore, I don't think all of us here put together eat in a year what that sailboat costs.' And Miss Moore lights up like somebody goosed her. 'And?' she say, urging Sugar on. Only I'm standin on her foot so she don't continue.

'Imagine for a minute what kind of society it is in which some people can spend on a toy what it would cost to feed a family of six or seven. What do you think?'

'I think,' say Sugar pushing me off her feet like she never done before, cause I whip her ass in a minute, 'that this is not much of a democracy if you ask me. Equal chance to pursue happiness means an equal crack at the dough, don't it?' Miss Moore is besides herself and I am disgusted with Sugar's treachery. So I stand on her foot one more time to see if she'll shove me. She shuts up, and Miss Moore looks at me, sorrowfully I'm thinkin. And somethin weird is goin on, I can feel it in my chest.

'Anybody else learn anything today?' lookin dead at me. I walk away and Sugar has to run to catch up and don't even seem to notice when I shrug her arm off my shoulder.

'Well, we got four dollars anyway,' she says.

'Uh hunh.'

'We could go to Hascombs and get half a chocolate layer and then go to the Sunset and still have plenty money for potato chips and ice-cream sodas.'

'Uh hunh.'

'Race you to Hascombs,' she say.

We start down the block and she gets ahead which is O.K. by me cause I'm goin to the West End and then over to the Drive to think this day through. She can run if she want to and even run faster. But ain't nobody gonna beat me at nuthin.

Patricia Highsmith

One for the Islands

The voyage wasn't to be much longer.

Most people were bound for the mainland, which was not far at all now. Others were bound for the islands to the west, some of which were very far indeed.

Dan was bound for a certain island that he believed probably farther than any of the others the ship would touch at. He supposed that he would be about the last passenger to disembark.

On the sixth day of the smooth, uneventful voyage, he was in excellent spirits. He enjoyed the company of his fellow-passengers, had joined them a few times in the games that were always in progress on the top deck forward, but mostly he strolled the deck with his pipe in his mouth and a book under his arm, the pipe unlighted and the book forgotten, gazing serenely at the horizon and thinking of the island to which he was going. It would be the finest island of them all, Dan imagined. For some months now, he had devoted much of his time to imagining its terrain. There was no doubt, he decided finally, that he knew more about his island than any man alive, a fact which made him smile whenever he thought of it. No, no one would ever know a hundredth of what he knew about his island, though he had never seen it. But then, perhaps no one else had ever seen it, either.

Dan was happiest when strolling the deck, alone, letting his eyes drift from soft cloud to horizon, from sun to sea, thinking always that his island might come into view before the mainland. He would know its outline at once, he was sure of that. Strangely, it would be like a place he had always known, but secretly, telling no one. And there he would finally be alone.

It startled him sometimes, unpleasantly, too, suddenly to encounter, face to face, a passenger coming round a corner. He found it disturbing to bump into a hurrying steward in one of the twisting, turning corridors of D-deck, which being third class was more like a catacomb than the rest, and which was the deck where Dan had his cabin. Then there had been the time, the second day of the voyage, when for an instant he saw very close to his eyes the ridged floor of the corridor, with a cigarette butt between two ridges, a chewing-gum wrapper, and a few discarded matches. That had been unpleasant, too.

'Are you for the mainland?' asked Mrs Gibson-Leyden, one of the first-class passengers, as they stood at the rail one evening.

Dan smiled a little and shook his head. 'No, the island,' he said pleasantly, rather surprised that Mrs Gibson-Leyden didn't know by now. But on the other hand, there had been little talk among the passengers as to where each was going. 'You're for the mainland, I take it?' He spoke to be friendly knowing quite well that Mrs Gibson-Leyden was for the mainland.

'Oh, yes,' Mrs Gibson-Leyden said. 'My husband had some idea of going to an island, but I said, not for me!'

She laughed with an air of satisfaction, and Dan nodded. He liked Mrs Gibson-Leyden because she was cheerful. It was more than could be said for most of the first-class passengers. Now he leant his forearms on the rail and looked out at the wake of moonlight on the sea that shimmered like the back of a gigantic sea dragon with silver scales. Dan couldn't imagine that anyone would go to the mainland when there were islands in abundance, but then he had never been able to understand such things, and with a person like Mrs Gibson-Leyden, there was no use in trying to discuss them and to understand. Dan drew gently on his empty pipe. He could smell a fragrance of lavender Cologne from Mrs Gibson-Leyden's direction. It reminded him of a girl he had once known, and he was amused now that he could feel drawn to Mrs Gibson-Leyden, certainly old enough to have been his mother, because she wore a familiar scent.

'Well, I'm supposed to meet my husband back in the game room,' Mrs Gibson-Leyden said, moving away. 'He went down to get a sweater.'

Dan nodded, awkwardly now. Her departure made him feel abandoned, absurdly lonely, and immediately he reproached himself for not having made more of an effort at communication with her. He smiled, straightened, and peered into the darkness over his left shoulder, where the mainland would appear before dawn, then his island, later.

Two people, a man and a woman, walked slowly down the deck, side by side, their figures quite black in the darkness. Dan was conscious of their separateness from each other. Another isolated figure, short and fat, moved into the light of the windows in the superstructure: Dr Eubanks, Dan recognized. Forward, Dan saw a group of people standing on deck and at the rails, all isolated, too. He had a vision of stewards and stewardesses below, eating their solitary meals at tiny tables in the corridors, hurrying about with towels, trays, menus. They were all alone, too. There was nobody who touched anybody, he thought, no man who held his wife's hand, no lovers whose lips met—at least he hadn't seen any so far on this voyage.

Dan straightened still taller. An overwhelming sense of aloneness, of his own isolation, had taken possession of him, and because his impulse was to shrink within himself, he unconsciously stood as tall as he could. But he could not look at the ship any longer, and turned back to the sea.

It seemed to him that only the moon spread its arms, laid its web protectively, lovingly, over the sea's body. He stared at the veils of moonlight as hard as he could, for as long as he could—which was perhaps twenty-five seconds—then went below to his cabin and to sleep.

He was awakened by the sound of running feet on the deck, and a murmur of excited voices.

The mainland, he thought at once, and threw off his bedcovers. He did want a good look at the mainland. Then as his head cleared of sleep, he realized that the excitement on deck must be about something else. There was more running now, a woman's wondering 'Oh!' that was half a scream, half an exclamation of pleasure. Dan hurried into his clothes and ran out of his cabin.

His view from the A-deck companionway made him stop and draw in his breath. The ship was sailing *downward*, had been sailing downward on a long, broad path in the sea itself. Dan had never seen anything like it. No one else had either, apparently. No wonder everyone was so excited.

'When?' asked a man who was running after the hurrying captain. 'Did you see it? What happened?'

The captain had no time to answer him.

'It's all right. This is right,' said a petty officer, whose calm serious face contrasted strangely with the wide-eyed alertness of everyone else.

'One doesn't notice it below,' Dan said quickly to Mr Steyne, who was standing near him, and felt idiotic at once, because what did it matter whether one felt it below or not? The ship was sailing downward, the sea sloped downward at about a twenty degree angle with the horizon, and such a thing had never been heard of before, even in the Bible.

Dan ran to join the passengers who were crowding the forward deck. 'When did it start? I mean, where?' Dan asked the person nearest him.

The person shrugged, though his face was as excited, as anxious as the rest.

Dan strained to see what the water looked like at the side of the swath, for the slope did not seem more than two miles broad. But whatever was happening, whether the swath ended in a sharp edge or sloped up to the main body of the sea, he could not make out, because a fine mist obscured the sea on either side. Now he noticed the golden light that lay on everything around them, the swath, the atmosphere, the horizon before them. The light was no stronger on one side than on the other, so it could not have been the sun. Dan couldn't find the sun, in fact. But the rest of the sky and the higher body of the sea behind them was bright as morning.

'Has anybody seen the mainland?' Dan asked, interrupting the babble around him.

'No,' said a man.

'There's no mainland,' said the same unruffled petty officer.

Dan had a sudden feeling of having been duped.

'This is right,' the petty officer added laconically. He was winding a thin line around and round his arm, bracing it on palm and elbow.

'Right?' asked Dan.

'This is it,' said the petty officer.

'That's right, this is it,' a man at the rail confirmed, speaking over his shoulder.

'No islands, either?' asked Dan, alarmed.

'No,' said the petty officer, not unkindly, but in an abrupt way that hurt Dan in his breast.

'Well—what's all this talk about the mainland?' Dan asked.

'Talk,' said the petty officer, with a twinkle now.

'Isn't it won-derful!' said a woman's voice behind him, and Dan turned to see Mrs Gibson-Leyden—Mrs Gibson-Leyden who had been so eager for the mainland—gazing rapturously at the empty white and gold mist.

'Do you know about this? How much farther does it go?' asked Dan, but the petty officer was gone. Dan wished he could be as calm as everyone else—generally he was calmer—but how could he be calm about his vanished island? How could the rest just stand there at the rails, for the most part taking it all quite calmly, he could tell by the voices now and their casual postures.

Dan saw the petty officer again and ran after him. What happens?' he asked. 'What happens next?' His questions struck him as foolish, but they were as good as any.

'This is *it*,' said the petty officer with a smile. 'Good God, boy!'

Dan bit his lips.

'This is *it*!' repeated the petty officer, 'What did you expect?'

Dan hesitated. 'Land,' he said in a voice that made it almost a question.

The petty officer laughed silently and shook his head. 'You can get off any time you like.'

Dan gave a startled look around him. It was true, people were getting off at the port rail, stepping over the side with their suitcases. 'Onto what?' Dan asked, aghast.

The petty officer laughed again, and disdaining to answer him, walked slowly away with his coiled line.

Dan caught his arm. 'Get off here? Why?'

'As good a place as any. Whatever spot strikes your fancy.' The petty officer chuckled. 'It's all alike.'

'All sea?'

'There's no sea,' said the petty officer. 'But there's certainly no land.'

And there went Mr and Mrs Gibson-Leyden now, off the starboard rail.

'Hey!' Dan called to them, but they didn't turn.

Dan watched them disappear quickly. He blinked his eyes. They had not been holding hands, but they had been near each other, they had been together.

Suddenly Dan realized that if he got off the boat as they had done, he could still be alone, if he wanted to be. It was strange, of course, to think of stepping out into space. But the instant he was able to conceive it, barely conceive it, it became right to do it. He could feel it filling him with a gradual but overpowering certainty, that he only reluctantly yielded to. This was right, as the petty officer had said. And this was as good a place as any.

Dan looked around him. The boat was really almost empty now. He might as well be last, he thought. He'd meant to be last. He'd go down and get his suitcase packed. What a nuisance! The mainland passengers, of course, had been packed since the afternoon before.

Dan turned impatiently on the companionway where he had once nearly fallen, and he climbed up again. He didn't want his suitcase after all. He didn't want anything with him.

He put a foot up on the starboard rail and stepped off. He walked several yards on an invisible ground that was softer than grass. It wasn't what he had thought it would be like, yet now that he was here, it wasn't strange, either. In fact there was even that sense of recognition that he had imagined he would feel when he set foot on his island. He turned for a last look at the ship that was still on its downward course. Then suddenly, he was impatient with himself. Why look at a ship, he asked himself, and abruptly turned and went on.

Jane Gardam

The Weeping Child

'Well, I have seen a ghost,' said Mrs Ingham, 'and it was the ghost of someone who is still alive.'

Then she got up and left them, putting down her knitting on a cane chair and walking off rather bent forward and clenching her rheumaticky hands. She was a big old woman with a large jaw and determined mouth, white hair screwed back anyhow, but eyes quite gentle. She visited her daughter in Jamaica—a lawyer's wife—in their beautiful great house in the mountains above Kingston harbour every other year at the end of January after the marmalade. The late spring was impossible because of the spring-cleaning and seeds, the summer because of the watering and the autumn because of the fruit. She lived in Surrey, England, in a sensible modern house the far side of Guildford near the arboretum and had two acres of garden. She was a J.P., a speaker for the W.I. and had been a keen Girl Guide until nearly sixty. Her long and expensive bi-annual flight above the Atlantic Ocean, moving her ten miles further from Surrey every minute, yet one hour back in time every thousand miles, she passed very steadily. Pipes had been lagged, stop-cocks manipulated, Christmas thank-you letters all disposed of, the tree tidily burned in the bonfire place. Keys had been hung labelled at strategic points and her will left conspicuous in case of hi-jack or engine trouble. The dahlias were safe under straw and excellent arrangements had been made for the cat. On the aeroplane she spoke to no one, sometimes looked out of the window and often at her watch, and dropping down and down at last through the bright air to the coconuts and coral and the wonders of her daughter's house which stood in a spice plantation and smelled night and day of incense, she lost no time in measuring her grandchildren for knitted cotton vests which they never dreamed of wearing.

But, 'Yes, I have seen a ghost,' she said.

'Where's she gone?' asked her daughter's husband, turning round with the decanter.

Her daughter blinked. It was late in the evening. She was great with a fifth child. It was astonishingly hot for the time of the year and their dinner guests wouldn't go.

Also her mother tired her. Not physically. Mrs Ingham had never had any wish to be taken about or entertained or shown the tourist attractions. Most days they just sat on the verandah together, with the smaller children flopping around them, the newest baby under its net wailing now and then until a servant came silently up with its bottle. Mrs Ingham required less physical effort than most visitors.

It was her simple presence that was tiring—her endless, sensible, practical conversation—committee meetings, local elections, deep-freezes, the failure of cabbages, the success of jam, the looking at the watch and saying, 'Isn't it time we started on the school-run now, dear?' or, 'If dinner's at nine, you'll want to have the lamb in the oven by eight. I will see to the mint sauce.'

When the guests arrived Mrs Ingham sat back, never trying to hold the floor, never conspicuous. Sensibly she had taken great trouble from her first visit to find out about clothes. 'Never sleeveless!' the dressmaker in Guildford had said, looking at Mrs Ingham's sinewy arms. 'Oh yes—everyone,' Mrs Ingham had said, 'tailored and pure cotton and quite short. And always sleeveless.'

'But just imagine. In January.'

Mrs Ingham hadn't been able to imagine it either. Imagining was her rarest occupation. But as Miranda had said before her first visit that it would be hot, she had taken care to find out how hot, to look at books and brochures and magazines and Philip's Modern Atlas. She had a reverence for properly checked facts and had been for many years an examiner of Queen's Guides. Thus at her daughter's dreamy and romantic dinner parties she sat unselfconscious and correct.

Miranda said to her husband sometimes as they lay in their four-poster bed and listened to the tree-frogs in the night, 'I wish she'd go.'

'Why,' he said, 'I like your mother.'

'She wears me out.'

'Wears you out! She just sits on the verandah.'

'She wears me out with guilt. She makes me feel fifteen again—not helping with the weeding.'

'But there isn't any weeding.'

'She's so rational and busy.'

'Well you don't have to be rational and busy.'

'She makes me feel bored all over again.'

'Come on,' he said, dropping an arm over her, 'you've left home now.'

'One doesn't,' she said, 'ever. And anyway she bores other people.'

'Don't be horrible,' he said, 'you miss her like hell always, after she's gone.'

Miranda was right in one thing, though, for Mrs Ingham did bore people sometimes, especially when Miranda herself was self-conscious about her mother's ordinariness and fell silent too. 'I am weighted down,' she thought tonight. She ran her hand over the new baby beneath her long dress and sighed. They were all sitting after dinner on the lovely pale verandah with the long eighteenth-century drawing-room stretching behind it and the shadows of the servants here and there in the windows or on the lawns in the hot night under the stars. The guests were a heavy lot. The dinner hadn't been the best she'd ever offered. The lamb, having been put in at eight, had been over-cooked when they sat down at ten which was of course what nine meant in Jamaican. Stephen had asked some Fillings of extraordinary deadliness—friends of friends of friends in London and a handsome but silent barrister. And there was an English judge's wife, quite a nice looking woman but with little to say. The other couple—two of their Jamaican friends—were beautiful and fashionable and cheerful, usually very cheerful. Great drinkers and laughers when the four of them were together. Witty. Hilarious. Not tonight.

The conversation had reached the stage when people were saying that coffee smells better than it tastes and Miranda shut her eyes.

'Wasn't this a coffee plantation once?' asked Mrs Filling.

'Coffee and spices,' said Stephen. 'The coffee beans were spread out upon the square—the place that looks like a school yard over in front of the guest house.'

'Was the guest house . . . ?'

'Yes—slave quarters. They kept fifty slaves here once.'

'What, here? Just here?'

'That's it,' said Stephen. 'We keep the chains under the beds.'

'*Do* you?' gasped Mrs Filling.

'Is it haunted?' asked the judge's wife.

'Sure,' said Stephen. 'You hear the groans and screams all night. Lashings and floggings. It's good for getting rid of guests. Nobody stops long.'

'I'm sure *I've* never heard anything,' said Mrs Ingham, knitting away, and with a sinking heart Miranda heard the conversation turn to ghosts. 'In a minute,' she thought, 'someone will say, "Isn't it funny—you never meet anyone who's actually seen a ghost—always it's a friend." When they say that,' she thought, easing her heavy self about in the chair, 'I shall scream and scream and run round the house and take a machete out of a woodshed and come back and chop everybody's head off.'

'Isn't it odd,' said the judge's wife, 'you never meet anyone who's in fact seen a ghost. Always . . . '

'But everyone believes in them, you know. We all believe in them,' said someone—the barrister, Robert Shaw.

'I don't see why we shouldn't believe in them,' said the Jamaican lawyer. 'I just don't see why we're supposed to find them interesting.' Miranda smiled at him.

'Oh, I think they are. I think they are,' said Mrs Filling and then sank back in her chair and said no more for the rest of the evening. Mr Filling cleared his throat. Miranda thought, my God, a ghost story.

'The trouble with ghost stories,' she said, 'is they're so long. Who'd like more coffee?'

'And Lady Fletcher's right,' said Stephen, 'no one has ever seen a ghost himself. It's always the other feller's, too much of it and the mixture as before.'

It was then that Mrs Ingham said, 'I have seen a ghost,' and getting up to leave them said, 'it was the ghost of someone who is still alive.'

'I thought I heard the children,' she said coming back. She picked up her knitting and sat back in her chair. 'I was wrong. No. Now. It is a very short story and not I think usual. I saw the ghost of a weeping child. It was standing in the corner of a greenhouse in an old kitchen garden. It was a boy. Eight years old.'

'Oh, I'm sure this country is full of ghosts,' said the judge's wife comfortably.

'This was not Jamaica,' said Mrs Ingham, 'it was at home in

Surrey. It was just outside Reigate. Last summer.'

'Ma,' said Miranda, 'are you all right?'

'It was on August the twentieth—a Wednesday—at three o'clock in the afternoon. It was the house of people I don't know. I had been told that the woman might lend the house for a Red Cross function and I had gone over to see if it would be suitable. When I got there I was given a cup of tea and was shown round and saw at once that the place would be most *un*suitable. There were imitation daffodils in a Ming vase and an indoor swimming pool. Very vulgar. No windows open and a fur sofa! I saw only the housekeeper who was a slut and kept a television set going—with the sound turned down—the whole time I was with her. All the time I talked she looked at it. She could hardly find her mouth with her cigarette.

'When I got up to go she said, "They said you'd want to see the gardens."

'"No thank you," I said.

'Then, when I got into the drive again I saw that the gardens were very much the best things there, and round the corner of a rose garden—beautifully kept—I thought I saw a kitchen garden wall. Now I am very fond of kitchen gardens and I said that I thought I would change my mind. "I will have a quick look about," I said and there was no need for her to accompany me.

'Well, round the end of the rose garden things were not so promising. There was a stable block, very broken down. Empty loose boxes put to no use. But I walked on a little and found a gate in a red wall and through it a really excellent kitchen garden. An *excellent* place. Beautifully kept. Huge. I could see the gardener bending over some beans at the far end and the wall beyond him was covered in the most splendid peaches and the wall at right angles to it—to the peach wall—had one of the longest conservatories I have ever seen in a private house running along it. Long enough for—two or three hundred tomato plants, I dare say. But oh, very battered and unpainted, very broken. Inside there was an old stone path stretching away down it with moss in the cracks and a huge vine with a bulging trunk, running everywhere. Miles and miles of it. In all directions. Beautifully cared for. The numbers on the bunches had been pruned out marvellously. I walked the whole length of the greenhouse, looking up into the branches and the dozens and dozens of bunches—it was a little white grape—like so many lanterns. Glorious. It was hot and steamy and good manure on all the roots, and the smell of greenhouse—delicious—very strong.

'And so quiet. I was admiring the vine so much and it was so quiet and the air so heavy and still that I felt, well, really quite reverent. Like in a church. I walked all the way down the greenhouse and all the way back gazing up above my head.

'And then, when I was nearly back to the door again I heard a child crying and saw that there was a little boy standing near the tap in the corner. He was sobbing and weeping dreadfully. As if his heart was quite broken. I went up to him and talked to him and tried to stop and comfort him but he paid no attention. He was in leggings and a shirt and he had red hair. He had his fists in his eyes and just stood there beside the bright brass tap and the more I spoke to him the more he wept and turned away from me.

'So I went out and said to the gardener who was still down at the end of the gardens with the beans that there was a boy crying in the greenhouse and he said, "Oh aye. It's me."

'I begged his pardon.

'He said, "It's me, ma'am, I'm often there. People are often seeing me."

'But I said, this was a child. Not more than nine.

'He said, "Eight, ma'am. I was eight," and he got up off his haunches and eased his back and looked at me with that look Scotsmen have. A sandy, grizzly-haired man. Tall. Abrupt. He was about seventy years old. A straight sort of a man. And a bit of an old stick, I should say. He didn't mind whether I believed him or not.

'"I was wrongfully accused," he said, "for something I never did. I'm very often there." Then he got down on his haunches again and went on picking beans and flinging them in handfuls into a chip basket.

'I went off back to the greenhouse but the child was not there any more. The tap was there, perhaps not so bright—and the vine was just the same—the rough, pale, splintery trunk, the dark leaves above. The light seemed different, though, and it was not so quiet.'

'Go on,' said Stephen. 'Ma—do go on.'

'That is all,' said Mrs Ingham. 'That is the story.'

'But didn't you go back?' said Miranda. 'Go back and ask him more?'

'What more?'

'Well—what it was he'd done? Whether he'd done it?'

'Oh, he hadn't done it. I rather think he'd forgotten what it was all about. I had that feeling. He certainly hadn't done anything wrong.'

'How could you be sure?' asked Robert Shaw.

'Oh, the weeping,' she said, 'it was the weeping. It was not remorse or anger the weeping. It was—well, tremendous disappointment and bitterness and sorrow. A sort of'—she wrinkled her sensible forehead—'it was a sort of essence of sorrow. Like a scent. A smell. Something very heavy and thick in the air.'

In the silence that followed she said, nodding round brightly, 'We ought to be so *careful* when we advise children. It's quite frightening what we do.'

'You never told me,' said her daughter, 'why ever didn't you tell me about it?' and she felt the usual dismal guilt confronting her mother's open face and with it an unusual violence and resentment. Ridiculously—her Jamaican friends looked at her in surprise—she thumped the chair arms. 'You might have *told* me that story. I should have been *told*. Why didn't you *write it* to me?'

'D'you know, I just can't say.' Her mother wound up her knitting and stuck the needles through the ball of wool. 'In a way I just seem to have remembered it.' Her voice, cool and self-reliant and thoughtful, left Miranda excluded.

'You might have *told* me.'

'But, dear, it seemed so—well, so ordinary at the time. Whatever time, of course—' and she gave her most sensible Queen's Guide smile, 'whatever time of course it was.'

Bessie Head

Looking for a Rain God

It is lonely at the lands where the people go to plough. These lands are vast clearings in the bush, and the wild bush is lonely too. Nearly all the lands are within walking distance from the village. In some parts of the bush where the underground water is very near the surface, people made little rest camps for themselves and dug shallow wells to quench their thirst while on their journey to their own lands. They experienced all kinds of things once they left the village. They could rest at shady watering places full of lush, tangled trees with delicate pale-gold and purple wild flowers springing up between soft green moss and the children could hunt around for wild figs and any berries that might be in season. But from 1958, a seven-year drought fell upon the land and even the watering places began to look as dismal as the dry open thorn-bush country; the leaves of the trees curled up and withered; the moss became dry and hard and, under the shade of the tangled trees, the ground turned a powdery black and white, because there was no rain. People said rather humorously that if you tried to catch the rain in a cup it would only fill a teaspoon. Towards the beginning of the seventh year of drought, the summer had become an anguish to live through. The air was so dry and moisture-free that it burned the skin. No one knew what to do to escape the heat and tragedy was in the air. At the beginning of that summer, a number of men just went out of their homes and hung themselves to death from trees. The majority of the people had lived off crops, but for two years past they had all returned from the lands with only their rolled-up skin blankets and cooking utensils. Only the charlatans, incanters, and witch-doctors made a pile of money during this time because people were always turning to them in desperation for little talismans and herbs to rub on the plough for the crops to grow and the rain to fall.

The rains were late that year. They came in early November, with a promise of good rain. It wasn't the full, steady downpour of the years of good rain, but thin, scanty, misty rain. It softened the earth and a rich growth of green things sprang up everywhere for the animals to eat. People were called to the village kgotla to hear the proclamation of the beginning of the ploughing season; they stirred themselves and whole families began to move off to the lands to plough.

The family of the old man, Mokgobja, were among those who left early for the lands. They had a donkey cart and piled everything onto it, Mokgobja—who was over seventy years old; two little girls, Neo and Boseyong; their mother Tiro and an unmarried sister, Nesta; and the father and supporter of the family, Ramadi, who drove the donkey cart. In the rush of the first hope of rain, the man, Ramadi, and the two women, cleared the land of thorn-bush and then hedged their vast ploughing area with this same thorn-bush to protect the future crop from the goats they had brought along for milk. They cleared out and deepened the old well with its pool of muddy water and still in this light, misty rain, Ramadi inspanned two oxen and turned the earth over with a hand plough.

The land was ready and ploughed, waiting for the crops. At night, the earth was alive with insects singing and rustling about in search of food. But suddenly, by mid-November, the rain fled away; the rain-clouds fled away and left the sky bare. The sun danced dizzily in the sky, with a strange cruelty. Each day the land was covered in a haze of mist as the sun sucked up the last drop of moisture out of the earth. The family sat down in despair, waiting and waiting. Their hopes had run so high; the goats had started producing milk, which they had eagerly poured on their porridge, now they ate plain porridge with no milk. It was impossible to plant the corn, maize, pumpkin and water-melon seeds in the dry earth. They sat the whole day in the shadow of the huts and even stopped thinking, for the rain had fled away. Only the children, Neo and Boseyong, were quite happy in their little girl world. They carried on with their game of making house like their mother and chattered to each other in light, soft tones. They made children from sticks around which they tied rags, and scolded them severely in an exact imitation of their own mother. Their voices could be heard scolding the day long: 'You stupid thing, when I send you to draw water, why do you spill half of it out of the bucket!' 'You stupid thing! Can't you mind the porridge-pot without letting the porridge burn!' And then they would beat the rag-dolls on their bottoms with severe expressions.

The adults paid no attention to this; they did not even hear the funny chatter; they sat waiting for rain; their nerves were stretched to breaking-point willing the rain to fall out of the sky. Nothing was important, beyond that. All their animals had been sold during the bad years to purchase food, and of all their herd only two goats were left. It was the women of the family who finally broke down under the strain of waiting for rain. It was really the two women who caused the death of the little girls. Each night they started a weird, high-pitched wailing that began on a low, mournful note and whipped up to a frenzy. Then they would stamp their feet and shout as though they had lost their heads. The men sat quiet and self-controlled; it was important for men to maintain their self-control at all times but their nerve was breaking too. They knew the women were haunted by the starvation of the coming year.

Finally, an ancient memory stirred in the old man, Mokgobja. When he was very young and the customs of the ancestors still ruled the land, he had been witness to a rain-making ceremony. And he came alive a little, struggling to recall the details which had been buried by years and years of prayer in a Christian church. As soon as the mists cleared a little, he began consulting in whispers with his youngest son, Ramadi. There was, he said, a certain rain god who accepted only the sacrifice of the bodies of children. Then the rain would fall; then the crops would grow, he said. He explained the ritual and as he talked, his memory became a conviction and he began to talk with unshakable authority. Ramadi's nerves were smashed by the nightly wailing of the women and soon the two men began whispering with the two women. The children continued their game: 'You stupid thing! How could you have lost the money on the way to the shop! You must have been playing again!'

After it was all over and the bodies of the two little girls had been spread across the land, the rain did not fall. Instead, there was a deathly silence at night and the devouring heat of the sun by day. A terror, extreme and deep, overwhelmed the whole family. They packed, rolling up their skin blankets and pots, and fled back to the village.

People in the village soon noted the absence of the two little girls. They had died at the lands and were buried there, the family said. But people noted their ashen, terror-stricken faces and a murmur arose. What had killed the children, they wanted to know? And the family replied that they had just died. And people said amongst themselves that it was strange that the two deaths had occurred at the same time. And there was a feeling of great unease at the unnatural looks of the family. Soon the police came around. The family told them the same story of death and burial at the lands. They did not know what the children had died of. So the police asked to see the graves. At this, the mother of the children broke down and told everything.

Throughout the terrible summer the story of the children hung like a dark cloud of sorrow over the village, and the sorrow was not assuaged when the old man and Ramadi were sentenced to death for ritual murder. All they had on the statute books was that ritual murder was against the law and must be stamped out with the death penalty. The subtle story of strain and starvation and breakdown was inadmissable evidence at court; but all the people who lived off crops knew in their hearts that only a hair's breadth had saved them from sharing a fate similar to that of the Mokgobja family. They could have killed something to make the rain fall.

Julia O'Faolain

Diego

Diego? He hasn't been in touch? Well, but that's his way, isn't it? He can just drop out of sight, then come back later, bubbling with good humour and gifts. He's so good-natured one has to forgive him. Of course he trades on that. I did see him recently, as it happens. Mmm. About two weeks ago and a funny thing happened then – funny things do when one is with him, don't you find? Or maybe it's he who makes them seem funny because he enjoys a laugh so much. He was giving me a lift home to have dinner with his wife and Mercedes, the little girl. Yes, she's ten now and bright as a button, a bit spoilt I'm afraid. Well, you'd expect Diego to spoil a daughter, wouldn't you? Of course he's in love with her and I must say she is a lovely creature. What was I going to tell you? Oh, about the supermarket. Well, Marie had asked him to stop and pick up some mangoes—you've never met *her*, have you? Am I putting my foot in it? Sorry. I know you're much older friends of Diego's than I am—but that's just the trouble, isn't it? You belong to the days when he was with Michèle and he has never felt able to present friends from those years to Marie. It's his delicacy. Another husband wouldn't give a damn. Hard on old friends. But you know what he says: 'How can I tell my wife "Here are my friends, X and Y, whom I've known for ten years but never brought home until now"?' In a way you can see his point. He neglected Marie awfully during all that time. Excluded her from his social life. You'd be a reminder of his bad behaviour. It would be different if they'd gone through with the divorce. His good nature prevented that. He couldn't bring himself to leave her and now he can't bring himself to leave Michèle, and so someone's always getting the short end of the stick.

I was telling you about the mangoes. Well, we went into the market to get them and it was one of those places in the *banlieue* where they weren't used to selling exotic fruit. Nobody knew the price and a girl was sent off with the ones Diego had picked to try and find the manager. Then she got waylaid or went to the phone and didn't come back. The woman at the check-out shouted on the intercom, *'Où sont les mangues de Monsieur?'* At this, Diego began to fall about laughing and then everyone in the shop began to see the thing as a gag. They began shouting at each other: 'His what?'—'His mangoes!'—'Lost his mangoes, has he? Oh that must be painful!'—'What? Mangoes? Oh, unmentionable!' And so forth. It was pretty mindless and any other customer might have been annoyed, but not Diego. He was delighted. 'They come from my country,' he told the girl and when he did I noticed that he *looks* like a mango: reddish and yellowish and a touch wizened. 'I'm half Red Indian,' he told her and it was obvious that if his mangoes hadn't turned up just then in a great burst of hilarity, he would have started getting off with her. He has a great way with him and he knows how to take the French. He keeps just that little touch of foreignness while speaking very racy Parisian and knowing everything there is to know about life here. They love that. He loves their ways and that makes them able to feel they can love his.

When we got back into the car, he started telling me of how once, years ago, when he first met Michèle, he was walking through the old Halles market, with her on one arm and Marie on the other, on their way to dine at an oyster bar, and one of those hefty lorry-drivers who used to bring in loads of produce began pointing at tiny Diego walking between these two splendid, *plantureuses* women—they looked like assemblages of melons, according to Diego—and, pretending to wipe his brow, raised his cap and roared: 'What a constitution?' *Quelle santé!* It was like the mango joke. Diego attracts such comments. When he told me the story, I got the idea that *that* could have been what started off his affaire with Michèle.

Because dear old Diego *is* a bit of a *macho*, isn't he, in the nicest possible way? *'Moi, j'aime la femme,'* he says. Awfully Latin! It sounds impossible in English. I mean you can't say it really: 'I love woman' sounds absurd. And if you say 'women' in the plural it sounds cheap. But what he means is the essence of woman, something he sees in every woman, even in his mother and, of course, especially in little Mercedes, right from the moment she was born. 'She was a woman,' he'll tell you—well, he probably *has* told you. He talks about her all the time. 'From the moment she was born she was a woman, a coquette, a flirt.'

As I was saying, he has spoilt her a bit—I tell a lie, he has spoilt her a great deal. In fact something happened later that evening which pointed up the dangers of this and was really quite upsetting. I don't know whether Diego will draw the lesson from it.

You haven't met Mercedes either, have you? You'd really have to see her to understand. You see, in a way, Diego is right. She *is* remarkably bright and perfectly bilingual because of his having always spoken Spanish to her. She *is* like a coquettish little princess stepped out of a canvas by Goya or Velázquez. This is partly because of her clothes which come from boutiques on the Faubourg Saint Honoré. Ridiculous clothes: hand-tucked muslin, silk, embroidered suede. I don't know who they were intended for, but Diego buys them. He buys her exactly the same sort of thing as he used to buy Michèle, and there is Marie in her denims with a daughter wearing a mink jacket at the age of ten. I don't know whether she approves or not. Their relationship is odd. Well, most marriages seem that way to me. What do I know of yours, for instance? Married people always strike me as treating each other a bit like bonsai trees. They nip and clip and train each other into odd, accommodating shapes, then sometimes complain about the result. Or one partner can go to endless lengths of patience with the other and then be obdurate about some trifling thing. It's a mystery. I watch with interest. I think you're all a dying species but fun to watch—like some product of a very ancient, constricting, complex civilization. Perhaps that's why I'm a gossip? As a feminist, I am in the same position as the Jesuits who watched and noted down the ways of the old Amerindians while planning to destroy them.

Diego claims sometimes to be part Amerindian. Maybe he is. Some of them used to cut out their victims' hearts with stone knives, used they not? I'm not sure whether *he* may not have blood on his hands. Metaphorical blood. After all, he's a member of the oligarchy of that repressive regime. It's true that he has been twenty-five years in Paris, reads the left-wing press and has picked up a radical vocabulary—but where does his money come from? Well, one doesn't probe but one can't help wondering. Another complexity. The troubling thing about sexists and members of old, blood-sodden castes is that they can be so delicate in their sensibilities and this does throw one. I keep meeting people like that here in Paris. It seems to draw them as honey draws wasps.

Am I being the Protestant spinster now? Forthright and angular and killing the thing I love as I lean over it with my frosty breath? In delighted disapproval? In disapproving delight. I mustn't kill this little story which I'm working my way round to telling you. It's about Mercedes and Michèle's dog. Yes, but first, have you got the background clear in your minds? Diego is so jokey and jolly and often—to be frank—drunk, that you mightn't. *Your* dealings with him were always social, weren't they? You'd meet in some smart night club or restaurant and, I suppose, dance till dawn with money no object and champagne flowing. That's how I imagine it—how Diego's led me to imagine it. Am I wrong? No? Good. Well, but, you see, that's only one side of Diego: the Don Diego swaggering side. There's also the plainer homebody. Did you know that Diego is simply the Spanish for James? I didn't either. Think of him as 'Jim' or 'Jacques' coming home in the dishwater-dawn light from those evenings to the suburban house where he'd parked Marie and the child.

Marie's *my* friend, by the way. I knew her before I did him. She had gone back to university to study law and we met in a feminist student group. Well, what would you have her do all those years while he used the house as a launching pad for his flights of jollification? He brought home the minimum cash—just like any working-class male taking half the budget for his pleasures. She could have left. She didn't. *There's* an area of motives which one cannot hope to map. *He* could have left and didn't. There's one I *can* map for you. He met Michèle through Marie. In those days she had prettier friends. I do occasionally wonder whether *I* was chosen as being unthreatening? No, no need to protest. I'm trying for accuracy. I like to take hold of as many elements in a situation as I can and I've admitted that Diego/Jim fascinates me. He is the Male Chauvinist Pig or Phallocrate seen close up, as I rarely get a chance to see the beast, and I do see his charm. It is his weapon and, when I say I see it, I really mean that I feel him seeing the woman in me. Men don't, very often. That's what I mean about Diego's *amour pour la femme* being non-sexist or sexist in such an all-embracing way that it gets close to universal love. He loves half humanity, half the human race, regardless of age, looks or health. Of course he is *also* a sex-snob and wants to be seen with a girl who does him credit—Michèle. That's the social side of him. But he responds to femininity wherever he finds it: in his mother, an old beggar woman, me. He's inescapably kind.

Why didn't he divorce, you ask? Kindness again. Really. He had fallen in love with Michèle: a tempestuous passion, I gather. They were swept off by it simultaneously, like a pair of flint stones knocking sparks off each other, like two salamanders sizzling in unison—he tells me about it when Marie's in the kitchen. He has to tell someone. It was his big experience and he made a mess of it and is still shocked at himself, yet can't see how he could have done other than he did. What he did was this: he proposed marriage to Michèle, was accepted and, brimful of bliss, looked at poor, blissless Marie and thought how lonely she must be and that he must do something for her. Now here is the part that touches me. He didn't think in terms of money, as most men would have. He thought in terms of love. He wanted her to have someone to love when he had gone off with Michèle and decided that *he* had better be the one to provide her with a love-object. Can you guess the next move? He made her pregnant. The noble sexist wanted to leave her with a child. Imagine Michèle's fury. She thought that he had got cold feet about marrying *her* and had cooked up this pretext for backing out. He assured her that he did very much want to marry her but that now he must stay with Marie until the baby was born so that it should be legitimate.

The baby, of course, was Mercedes and he fell in love with *her* at first sight, at first sound, at first touch. He was totally potty about her, obsessed and *at the same time* he was painfully in love with an estranged and furious Michèle on whom he showered guilty, cajoling gifts, spoiling and courting her and putting up with every caprice in an effort to earn back the total love which he had forfeited—she kept telling him—by his sexual treachery.

Those were the years when you knew him—the champagne and dancing years. He and Michèle had not got married and so their relationship became one long, festive courtship and she, from what he says, responded as someone who's fussed over for years might well be tempted to respond: she became a bit of a bitch. She brought boys home to the flat where he kept her like a queen, stood him up, tormented him and then, between lovers, just often enough to keep him hot for her, becoming as loving and playful as they had been in the early days. She was his *princesse lointaine*, radiant with the gleam of loss and old hope and he was romantic about her and probably happier than he admits with the arrangement which kept his loins on fire and fixed his wandering attention on her in whom he was able to find all women: the wife she should have become, the fickle tormentor she had become, his wronged great love and familiar old friend, his Donna Elvira and his spendthrift, nightclub succubus. She was all women except one and that one, to be sure, was Mercedes, the little girl who was growing up in an empty, half-furnished suburban house with a mother who was busy getting her law degree and a father who swept in from time to time with presents from Hamleys and Fouquets and organdie dresses and teddy bears twice her size which made her cry. Every penny he had went on Michèle and Mercedes. I remember that house when it hadn't a lamp or a table because Marie was damned if she'd spend *her* money on it and he was so rarely there that he never noticed what it did or didn't have apart from the Aladdin's Cave nursery in which Mercedes was happy while she was small. Later, at the ages of six and seven and eight, as she began to invite in her friends, she began to colonize the rest of the house and, as she did, he began to furnish it for her. Michèle's share of his budget shrank as Mercedes's grew. Shares in his time fluctuated too. He spent more of it at home; friends like you began to see less of him and Michèle had to start finding herself new escorts, not from bitchery but from need. But he would never abandon her completely. He had wasted her marriageable years and now he felt towards her the guilt he had once felt towards Marie. But what can he do? He's not Christ. He cannot divide up and distribute his body and blood.

He was telling me all this that night on the drive out from Paris and he got so upset that at one stage he stopped the car and walked into a hotel where we had a drink. This made us late for dinner, but Marie, of course, never complains. Who did complain was Mercedes. It was past her bed-time and she was irritable and sleepy when we arrived. She had waited up because she wanted to have a mango and, besides, Diego had promised her some small present. Right away she started being whingey and angry with me whom she blamed for keeping her Daddy late. Diego was amused, as he is by all Mercedes's caprices, and kept saying, 'She's jealous, you know!' As though that were something to be proud of! 'She's very possessive.'

There was a dog in the house, Michèle's silver poodle—perhaps you know it?—Rinaldino, a rather highly-strung creature which

Marie and Mercedes had been told was mine. Michèle had asked Diego to keep it for her because she was going on a cruise and it pines if left in a kennel. Diego can never say 'no' to Michèle, and so a story was concocted about my flat being painted and how I had had to move to a hotel where I couldn't take my new dog. All this because of Diego's not wanting his wife to know that she was being asked to house his mistress's dog. Surprisingly, the plan had worked up to now and Rinaldino had been three weeks at Diego's. Mercedes was mad about him and everyone had been pleased about that. This evening, however, she suddenly announced that from now on the dog was hers. She wasn't giving him back. She just wasn't. So there. The dog loved her, she claimed and, besides, she had told her friends it was hers and didn't want to be made to look a liar. She said all this in her grown-up way: half playful, half testing and I couldn't help having the old-fashioned notion that what she really wanted, deep down, was to be told 'no'. That used to be said, remember, when *we* were children. It was thought that children needed to know the limits of their possibilities.

Anyway, she kept on and Diego wouldn't contradict her and neither did Marie. I kept my mouth shut. It's not my business if Diego spoils his daughter as he spoils his mistress so, even though the dog was supposed to be mine, I didn't react when Mercedes started clamouring for a promise that Dino, as she had re-christened Rinaldino, should never leave. She would not go to bed till she got it, she said. It was obvious that she was trying to provoke me, but I pretended not to notice. Poor child, it's not her fault if she is the way she is.

'Dino likes me better than he likes you,' she told me.

'Why wouldn't he like you?' I asked. 'You're a good girl, aren't you?'

'He likes me whether I'm good or not. He likes me even when I hurt him.'

I can't remember what I said to that and doubt if it mattered. She had taken against me and the next thing she did was to start twisting the dog's ears.

'See,' she said. 'Even when I do this, he likes me. He likes me because he's mine. I'm his Mummy.'

Then she began to cuddle the animal in that way that children do if they're not stopped. She tied a napkin under its chin, half choking it, and held it as if it were a baby, bending its spine and pretending to rock it to sleep.

'Mine, mine, mine,' she crooned.

I had an odd sensation as I watched. What struck me was that in a way the dog was *Michèle's* baby, her substitute for the family she might have had if Mercedes had not been born. And now, here was Mercedes trying to steal even that from her. I found myself wondering whether some instinct was making her do it. An intuition? The thought was absurd but I let myself play with it to keep my mind off what the brat was doing to little Rinaldino. The French *are* insensitive about animals and Marie seemed indifferent. She often goes into a sort of passive trance when Diego is around and he, of course, has no feeling for creatures at all. Maybe I was showing my discomfort in spite of myself? I can't be sure. Anyway, the little beast—I'm talking about Mercedes—began to pull Rinaldino's whiskers and it was all I could do to keep myself from slapping her. I was on the point of warning her that she might get bitten when she gave a shriek and threw the dog violently across the room. For a moment I thought she might have broken its back, but no, it got up and scuttled under the sofa. That, it turned out, was good canine thinking.

It had bitten her cheek. Not deeply, but it had drawn blood.

Well, the scene after that was beyond description, unbelievable. It literally took my breath away, hysteria, screams, foot-stamping, hand-wringing—all the things you think real people never do, they did. And no initiative at all. *I* had to take charge and clean the child's cheek and put disinfectant on it. You'd think I'd cut off her head from the way she carried on. Diego was crying. Marie was tight-lipped and kept clenching her fists as though she was about to explode.

'Look,' I told them, 'it's a scratch. It's nothing. She'd have got worse from a bramble bush. Just *look*,' I kept insisting.

But they wouldn't. Not really. They kept exclaiming and averting their faces and clapping their hands over their eyes. They wanted their drama and were working each other up, so that when Mercedes shouted, 'I want the dog killed. Right now. It doesn't like me. It doesn't love me. It must be killed!' I realized that the adults were half ready to go along with the idea. Diego was completely out of his mind.

'Supposing it has rabies?' he whispered to me.

'It's been inoculated,' I told him.

'Are you sure?'

'Of course I am. It's on its name tag. Look. With the date.'

'I want it killed now! Here. Now. It doesn't love me. It's a bad dog,' screamed Mercedes.

'It's my dog,' I told her. 'You can't kill my dog.'

She began to kick me then. Hard. I still have bruised shins. She carried on as if she had rabies herself and her mother had to pull her off me and take her to bed.

'I want it killed!' She was screaming and scratching and biting as they went through the door. Later, I heard her still at it in her bedroom.

Diego looked distraught. He said he had heard of dogs which were rabid in spite of having been inoculated. Was I *sure* it had been inoculated? What did a name tag prove after all? It struck me then that he had either forgotten the dog was not mine or was trying to persuade himself that it was. We were alone together now but he avoided mentioning Michèle's name. Maybe he felt that some sin of his was coming to the fore and demanding a blood sacrifice? He kept pouring whisky and drinking it down fast. At one point he went into the kitchen and looked at the rack of knives.

Well, you can never tell how much that sort of thing is theatre, can you? I mean that theatre can spill into life if people work themselves up enough. Maybe he was seeing himself as an Amerindian priest? I don't mind telling you that I began to get scared. The thing was taking on odd dimensions as he got drunker and guiltier and the screams ebbed and started up again in the bedroom. Rinaldino, very sensibly, stayed right where he was under the sofa and that affected me more than anything. After all, dogs do pick up bad vibrations, don't they? Anyway, the outcome was that when Diego went into the lavatory I phoned a taxi, took the dog and left. I was convinced that by now he wasn't seeing the dog as a dog at all and that if I hadn't got it out of the house he would have ended up killing it—or worse.

Marie wouldn't have interfered. Even if she'd been standing beside him she wouldn't. I'm sure of that. They're extraordinary that way. I keep thinking of them now. Each is so intelligent and kind and—I want to say 'ordinary', when they're on their own. Normal? But let a scene start and you'd think you were dealing with members of the House of Atreus. Marie's passivity has started to seem sinister to me. I've started dreaming of that evening and it's become deformed in my memory. Sometimes it seems to me that she was the silent puppet-mistress pulling the strings and that even I was one of the puppets. Even the dog. Well, certainly the dog. Maybe it's self-referential to bring myself in? But I've started worrying whether Marie as well as Mercedes sees me as an intrusive female. 'She's jealous,' Diego told me that evening and laughed. He could have meant his wife. Could he? I'm only his confidante but Marie might dislike that, mightn't she? It's very unhealthy on my part to dwell on the thing and it would be absurd for me to have a crush on a man like Diego and I hope nobody thinks this is the case. In my more sober moments I know that any bad feeling that came my way that evening was really directed through me at Michèle. I was her stand-in. After all, I'd pretended to own her dog. But somehow, emotion sticks. I feel a little as though mud had been thrown at me and that I can't quite clean it off.

Cynthia Ozick

Levitation

A pair of novelists, husband and wife, gave a party. The husband was also an editor; he made his living at it. But really he was a novelist. His manner was powerless; he did not seem like an editor at all. He had a nice plain pale face, likable. His name was Feingold.

For love, and also because he had always known he did not want a Jewish wife, he married a minister's daughter. Lucy too had hoped to marry out of her tradition. (These words were hers. 'Out of my tradition,' she said. The idea fevered him.) At the age of twelve she felt herself to belong to the people of the Bible. ('A Hebrew,' she said. His heart lurched, joy rocked him.) One night from the pulpit her father read a Psalm; all at once she saw how the Psalmist meant *her*; then and there she became an Ancient Hebrew.

She had huge, intent, sliding eyes, disconcertingly luminous, and copper hair, and a grave and timid way of saying honest things.

They were shy people, and rarely gave parties.

Each had published one novel. Hers was about domestic life; he wrote about Jews.

All the roil about the State of the Novel had passed them by. In the evening after the children had been put to bed, while the portable dishwasher rattled out its smell of burning motor oil, they sat down, she at her desk, he at his, and began to write. They wrote not without puzzlements and travail; nevertheless as naturally as birds. They were devoted to accuracy, psychological realism, and earnest truthfulness; also to virtue and even to wit. Neither one was troubled by what had happened to the novel: all those declarations about the end of Character and Story. They were serene. Sometimes, closing up their notebooks for the night, it seemed to them that they were literary friends and lovers, like George Eliot and George Henry Lewes.

In bed they would revel in quantity and murmur distrustingly of theory. 'Seven pages so far this week.' 'Nine-and-a-half, but I had to throw out four. A wrong tack.' 'Because you're doing first person. First person strangles. You can't get out of their skin.' And so on. The one principle they agreed on was the importance of never writing about writers. Your protagonist always has to be someone *real*, with real work-in-the-world—a bureaucrat, a banker, an architect (ah, they envied Conrad his shipmasters!)—otherwise you fall into solipsism, narcissism, tedium, lack of appeal-to-the-common-reader; who knew what other perils.

This difficulty—seizing on a concrete subject—was mainly Lucy's. Feingold's novel—the one he was writing now—was about Menachem ben Zerach, survivor of a massacre of Jews in the town of Estella in Spain in 1328. From morning to midnight he hid under a pile of corpses, until a 'compassionate knight' (this was the language of the history Feingold relied on) plucked him out and took him home to tend his wounds. Menachem was then twenty; his father and mother and four younger brothers had been cut down in the terror. Six thousand Jews died in a single day in March. Feingold wrote well about how the mild winds carried the salty fragrance of fresh blood, together with the ashes of Jewish houses, into the faces of the marauders. It was nevertheless a triumphant story: at the end Menachem ben Zerach becomes a renowned scholar.

'If you're going to tell about how after he gets to be a scholar he just sits there and *writes*,' Lucy protested, 'then you're doing the Forbidden Thing.' But Feingold said he meant to concentrate on the massacre, and especially on the life of the 'compassionate knight.' What had brought him to this compassion? What sort of education? What did he read? Feingold would invent a journal of the compassionate knight, and quote from it. Into this journal the compassionate knight would direct all his gifts, passions, and private opinions.

'Solipsism,' Lucy said. 'Your compassionate knight is only another writer. Narcissism. Tedium.'

They talked often about the Forbidden Thing. After a while they began to call it the Forbidden City, because not only were they (but Lucy especially) tempted to write—solipsistically, narcissistically, tediously, and without common appeal—about writers, but, more narrowly yet, about writers in New York.

'The compassionate knight,' Lucy said, 'lived on the Upper West Side of Estella. He lived on the Riverside Drive, the West

End Avenue, of Estella. He lived in Estella on Central Park West.'

The Feingolds lived on Central Park West.

In her novel—the published one, not the one she was writing now—Lucy had described, in the first person, where they lived:

> By now I have seen quite a few of those West Side apartments. They have mysterious layouts. Rooms with doors that go nowhere—turn the knob, open: a wall. Someone is snoring behind it, in another apartment. They have made two and three or even four and five flats out of these palaces. The toilet bowls have antique cracks that shimmer with moisture like old green rivers. Fluted columns and fireplaces. Artur Rubinstein once paid rent here. On a gilt piano he raced a sonata by Beethoven. The sounds went spinning like mercury. Breathings all lettered now. Editors. Critics. Books, old, old books, heavy as centuries. Shelves built into the cold fireplace; Freud on the grate, Marx on the hearth, Melville, Hawthorne, Emerson. Oh God, the weight, the weight.

Lucy felt herself to be a stylist; Feingold did not. He believed in putting one sentence after another. In his publishing house he had no influence. He was nervous about his decisions. He rejected most manuscripts because he was afraid of mistakes; every mistake lost money. It was a small house panting after profits; Feingold told Lucy that the only books his firm respected belonged to the accountants. Now and then he tried to smuggle in a novel after his own taste, and then he would be brutal to the writer. He knocked the paragraphs about until they were as sparse as his own. 'God knows what you would do to mine,' Lucy said; 'bald man, bald prose.' The horizon of Feingold's head shone. She never showed him her work. But they understood they were lucky in each other. They pitied every writer who was not married to a writer. Lucy said: 'At least we have the same premises.'

Volumes of Jewish history ran up and down their walls; they belonged to Feingold. Lucy read only one book—it was *Emma*—over and over again. Feingold did not have a 'philosophical' mind. What he liked was event. Lucy liked to speculate and ruminate. She was slightly more intelligent than Feingold. To strangers he seemed very mild. Lucy, when silent, was a tall copper statue.

They were both devoted to omniscience, but they were not acute enough to see what they meant by it. They thought of themselves as children with a puppet theater: they could make anything at all happen, speak all the lines, with gloved hands bring all the characters to shudders or leaps. They fancied themselves in love with what they called 'imagination.' It was not true. What they were addicted to was counterfeit pity, and this was because they were absorbed by power, and were powerless.

They lived on pity, and therefore on gossip: who had been childless for ten years, who had lost three successive jobs, who was in danger of being fired, which agent's prestige had fallen, who could not get his second novel published, who was *persona non grata* at this or that magazine, who was drinking seriously, who was a likely suicide, who was dreaming of divorce, who was secretly or flamboyantly sleeping with whom, who was being snubbed, who counted or did not count; and toward everyone in the least way victimized they appeared to feel the most immoderate tenderness. They were, besides, extremely 'psychological': kind listeners, helpful, lifting hot palms they would gladly put to anyone's anguished temples. They were attracted to bitter lives.

About their own lives they had a joke: they were 'secondary-level' people. Feingold had a secondary-level job with a secondary-level house. Lucy's own publisher was secondary-level; even the address was Second Avenue. The reviews of their books had been written by secondary-level reviewers. All their friends were secondary-level: not the presidents or partners of the respected firms, but copy editors and production assistants; not the glittering eagles of the intellectual organs, but the wearisome hacks of small Jewish journals; not the fiercely cold-hearted literary critics, but those wan and chattering daily reviewers of film. If they knew a playwright, he was off-off Broadway in ambition and had not yet been produced. If they knew a painter, he lived in a loft and had exhibited only once, against the wire fence in the outdoor show at Washington Square in the spring. And this struck them as mean and unfair; they liked their friends, but other people—why not they?—were drawn into the deeper caverns of New York, among the lions.

New York! They risked their necks if they ventured out to Broadway for a loaf of bread after dark; muggers hid behind the seesaws in the playgrounds, junkies with knives hung upside down in the jungle gym. Every apartment a lit fortress; you admired the lamps and the locks, the triple locks on the caged-in windows, the double locks and the police rods on the doors, the lamps with timers set to make burglars think you were always at home. Footsteps in the corridor, the elevator's midnight grind; caution's muffled gasps. Their parents lived in Cleveland and St Paul, and hardly ever dared to visit. All of this: grit and unsuitability (they might have owned a snowy lawn somewhere else); and no one said their names, no one had any curiosity about them, no one ever asked whether they were working on anything new. After half a year their books were remaindered for eighty-nine cents each. Anonymous mediocrities. They could not call themselves forgotten because they had never been noticed.

Lucy had a diagnosis: they were, both of them, sunk in a ghetto. Feingold persisted in his morbid investigations into Inquisitional autos-da-fé in this and that Iberian marketplace. She herself had supposed the inner life of a housebound woman—she cited *Emma*—to contain as much comedy as the cosmos. Jews and women! They were both beside the point. It was necessary to put aside pity; to look to the center; to abandon selflessness; to study power.

They drew up a list of luminaries. They invited Irving Howe, Susan Sontag, Alfred Kazin, and Leslie Fiedler. They invited Norman Podhoretz and Elizabeth Hardwick. They invited Philip Roth and Joyce Carol Oates and Norman Mailer and William Styron and Donald Barthelme and Jerzy Kosinski and Truman Capote. None of these came; all of them had unlisted numbers, or else machines that answered the telephone, or else were in Prague or Paris or out of town. Nevertheless the apartment filled up. It was a Saturday night in a chill November. Taxis whirled on patches of sleet. On the inside of the apartment door a mound of rainboots grew taller and taller. Two closets were packed tight with raincoats and fur coats; a heap of coats smelling of skunk and lamb fell tangled off a bed.

The party washed and turned like a sluggish tub; it lapped at all the walls of all the rooms. Lucy wore a long skirt, violet-colored, Feingold a lemon shirt and no tie. He looked paler than ever. The apartment had a wide center hall, itself the breadth of a room; the dining room opened off it to the left, the living room to the right. The three party-rooms shone like a triptych: it was as if you could fold them up and enclose everyone into darkness. The guests were free-standing figures in the niches of a cathedral; or else dressed-up cardboard dolls, with their drinks, and their costumes all meticulously hung with sashes and draped collars and little capes, the women's hair variously bound, the men's sprouting and spilling: fashion stalked, Feingold moped. He took in how it all flashed, manhattans and martinis, earrings and shoe-tips—he marveled, but knew it was a falsehood, even a figment. The great world was somewhere else. The conversation could fool you: how these people talked! From the conversation itself—grains of it, carried off, swallowed by new eddyings, swirl devouring swirl, every moment a permutation in the tableau of those free-standing figures or dolls, all of them afloat in a tub—from this or that hint or syllable you could imagine the whole universe in the process of ultimate comprehension. Human nature, the stars, history—the voices drummed and strummed. Lucy swam by blank-eyed, pushing a platter of mottled cheeses. Feingold seized her: 'It's a waste!' She gazed back. He said, 'No one's here!' Mournfully she rocked a stump of cheese; then he lost her.

He went into the living room: it was mainly empty, a few lumps on the sofa. The lumps wore business suits. The dining room was better. Something in formation: something around the big table: coffee cups shimmering to the brim, cake cut onto plates (the mock-Victorian rosebud plates from Boots's drug store in London: the year before their first boy was born Lucy and Feingold saw the Brontës' moors; Coleridge's house in Highgate; Lamb House, Rye, where Edith Wharton had tea with Henry James; Bloomsbury; the Cambridge stairs Forster had lived at the top of)—it seemed about to become a regular visit, with points of view, opinions; a discussion. The voices began to stumble; Feingold liked that, it was nearly human. But then, serving round the forks and paper napkins, he noticed the awful vivacity of their falsetto phrases: actors, theater chatter, who was directing whom, what was opening where; he hated actors. Shrill puppets. Brainless. A double row of faces around the table; gurgles of fools.

The center hall—swept clean. No one there but Lucy, lingering.

'Theater in the dining room,' he said. 'Junk.'

'Film. I heard film.'

'Film too,' he conceded. 'Junk. It's mobbed in there.'

'Because they've got the cake. They've got all the food. The living room's got nothing.'

'My God,' he said, like a man choking, 'do you realize *no one came?*'

The living room had—had once had—potato chips. The chips were gone, the carrot sticks eaten, of the celery sticks nothing left but threads. One olive in a dish; Feingold chopped it in two with vicious teeth. The business suits had disappeared. 'It's awfully early,' Lucy said; 'a lot of people had to leave.' 'It's a cocktail party, that's what happens,' Feingold said. 'It isn't *exactly* a cocktail party,' Lucy said. They sat down on the carpet in front of the fireless grate. 'Is that a real fireplace?' someone inquired. 'We never light it,' Lucy said. 'Do you light those candlesticks ever?' 'They belonged to Jimmy's grandmother,' Lucy said, 'we never light them.'

She crossed no-man's-land to the dining room. They were serious in there now. The subject was Chaplin's gestures.

In the living room Feingold despaired; no asked him, he began to tell about the compassionate knight. A problem of ego, he said: compassion being superconsciousness of one's own pride. Not that he believed this; he only thought it provocative to say something original, even if a little muddled. But no one responded. Feingold looked up. 'Can't you light that fire?' said a man. 'All right,' Feingold said. He rolled a paper log made of last Sunday's *Times* and laid a match on it. A flame as clear as a streetlight whitened the faces of the sofa-sitters. He recognized a friend of his from the Seminary—he had what Lucy called 'theological' friends—and then and there, really very suddenly, Feingold wanted to talk about God. Or, if not God, then certain historical atrocities, abominations: to wit, the crime of the French nobleman Draconet, a proud Crusader, who in the spring of the year 1247 arrested all the Jews of the province of Vienne, castrated the men, and tore off the breasts of women; some he did not mutilate, and only cut in two. It interested Feingold that Magna Carta and the Jewish badge of shame were issued in the same year, and that less than a century afterward all the Jews were driven out of England, even families who had been settled there seven or eight generations. He had a soft spot for Pope Clement IV, who absolved the Jews from responsibility for the Black Death. 'The plague takes the Jews themselves,' the Pope said. Feingold knew innumerable stories about forced conversions, he felt at home with these thoughts, comfortable, the chairs seemed dense with family. He wondered whether it would be appropriate —at a cocktail party, after all!—to inquire after the status of the Seminary friend's agnosticism: was it merely that God had stepped out of history, left the room for a moment, so to speak, without a pass, or was there no Creator to begin with, nothing has been created, the world was a chimera, a solipsist's delusion?

Lucy was uneasy with the friend from the Seminary; he was the one who had administered her conversion, and every encounter was like a new stage in a perpetual examination. She was glad there was no Jewish catechism. Was she a back-slider? Anyhow she felt tested. Sometimes she spoke of Jesus to the children. She looked around—her great eyes wheeled—and saw that everyone in the living room was a Jew.

There were Jews in the dining room too, but the unruffled, devil-may-care kind: the humorists, the painters, film reviewers who went off to studio showings of *Screw on Screen* on the eve of the Day of Atonement. Mostly there were Gentiles in the dining room. Nearly the whole cake was gone. She took the last piece, cubed it on a paper plate, and carried it back to the living room. She blamed Feingold, he was having one of his spasms of fanaticism. Everyone normal, everyone with sense—the humanists and humorists, for instance—would want to keep away. What was he now, after all, but one of those boring autodidacts who spew out everything they read? He was doing it for spite, because no one had come. There he was, telling about the blood-libel. Little Hugh of Lincoln. How in London, in 1279, Jews were torn to pieces by horses, on a charge of having crucified a Christian child. How in 1285, in Munich, a mob burned down a synagogue on the same pretext. At Eastertime in Mainz two years earlier. Three centuries of beatified child martyrs, some of them figments, all called 'Little Saints.' The Holy Niño of LaGuardia. Feingold was crazed by these tales, he drank them like a vampire. Lucy stuck a square of chocolate cake in his mouth to shut him up. Feingold was waiting for a voice. The friend from the Seminary, pragmatic, licked off his bit of cake hungrily. It was a cake sent from home, packed by his wife in a plastic bag, to make sure there was something to eat. It was a guaranteed no-lard cake. They were all ravenous. The fire crumpled out in big paper cinders.

The friend from the Seminary had brought a friend. Lucy

examined him: she knew how to give catechisms of her own, she was not a novelist for nothing. She catechized and catalogued: a refugee. Fingers like long wax candles, snuffed at the nails. Black sockets: was he blind? It was hard to tell where the eyes were under that ledge of skull. Skull for a head, but such a cushioned mouth, such lips, such orderly expressive teeth. Such a bone in such a dry wrist. A nose like a saint's. The face of Jesus. He whispered. Everyone leaned over to hear. He was Feingold's voice: the voice Feingold was waiting for.

'Come to modern times,' the voice urged. 'Come to yesterday.' Lucy was right: she could tell a refugee in an instant, even before she heard any accent. They all reminded her of her father. She put away this insight (the resemblance of Presbyterian ministers to Hitler refugees) to talk over with Feingold later: it was nicely analytical, it had enough mystery to satisfy. 'Yesterday,' the refugee said, 'the eyes of God were shut.' And Lucy saw him shut his hidden eyes in their tunnels. 'Shut,' he said, 'like iron doors'—a voice of such nobility that Lucy thought immediately of that eerie passage in Genesis where the voice of the Lord God walks in the Garden in the cool of the day and calls to Adam, 'Where are you?'

They all listened with a terrible intensity. Again Lucy looked around. It pained her how intense Jews could be, though she too was intense. But she was intense because her brain was roiling with ardor, she wooed mind-pictures, she was a novelist. *They* were intense all the time; she supposed the grocers among them were as intense as any novelist; was it because they had been Chosen, was it because they pitied themselves every breathing moment?

Pity and shock stood in all their faces.

The refugee was telling a story. 'I witnessed it,' he said. 'I am the witness.' Horror, sadism; corpses. As if—Lucky took the image from the elusive wind that was his voice in its whisper—as if hundreds and hundreds of Crucifixions were all happening at once. She visualized a hillside with multitudes of crosses, and bodies dropping down from big bloody nails. Every Jew was Jesus. That was the only way Lucy could get hold of it: otherwise it was only a movie. She had seen all the movies, the truth was she could feel nothing. That same bulldozer shoveling those same sticks of skeletons, that same little boy in a cap with twisted mouth and his hands in the air—if there had been a camera at the Crucifixion Christianity would collapse, no one would ever feel anything about it. Cruelty came out of the imagination, and had to be witnessed by the imagination.

All the same, she listened. What he told was exactly like the movies. A gray scene, a scrubby hill, a ravine. Germans in helmets, with shining tar-black belts, wearing gloves. A ragged bundle of Jews at the lip of the ravine—an old grandmother, a child or two, a couple in their forties. All the faces stained with grayness, the stubble on the ground stained gray, the clothes on them limp as shrouds but immobile, as if they were already under the dirt, shut off from breezes, as if they were already stone. The refugee's whisper carved them like sculptures—there they stood, a shadowy stone asterisk of Jews, you could see their nostrils, open as skulls, the stony round ears of the children, the grandmother's awful twig of a neck, the father and mother grasping the children but strangers to each other, not a touch between them, the grandmother cast out, claiming no one and not claimed, all prayerless stone gums. There they stood. For a long while the refugee's voice pinched them and held them, so that you had to look. His voice made Lucy look and look. He pierced the figures through with his whisper. Then he let the shots come. The figures never teetered, never shook: the stoniness broke all at once and they fell cleanly, like sacks, into the ravine. Immediately they were in a heap, with random limbs all tangled together. The refugee's voice like a camera brought a German boot to the edge of the ravine. The boot kicked sand. It kicked and kicked, the sand poured over the family of sacks.

Then Lucy saw the fingers of the listeners—all their fingers were stretched out.

The room began to lift. It ascended. It rose like an ark on waters. Lucy said inside her mind, 'This chamber of Jews.' It seemed to her that the room was levitating on the little grains of the refugee's whisper. She felt herself alone at the bottom, below the floorboards, while the room floated upward, carrying Jews. Why did it not take her too? Only Jesus could take her. They were being kidnapped, these Jews, by a messenger from the land of the dead. The man had a power. Already he was in the shadow of another tale: she promised herself she would not listen, only Jesus could make her listen. The room was ascending. Above her head it grew smaller and smaller, more and more remote, it fled deeper and deeper into upwardness.

She craned after it. Wouldn't it bump into the apartment upstairs? It was like watching the underside of an elevator, all dirty and hairy, with dust-roots wagging. The black floor moved higher and higher. It was getting free of her, into loftiness, lifting Jews.

The glory of their martyrdom.

Under the rising eave Lucy had an illumination: she saw herself with the children in a little city park. A Sunday afternoon early in May. Feingold has stayed home to nap, and Lucy and the children find seats on a bench and wait for the unusual music to begin. The room is still levitating, but inside Lucy's illumination the boys are chasing birds. They run away from Lucy, they return, they leave. They surround a pigeon. They do not touch the pigeon; Lucy has forbidden it. She has read that city pigeons carry meningitis. A little boy in Red Bank, New Jersey, contracted sleeping sickness from touching a pigeon; after six years, he is still asleep. In his sleep he has grown from a child to an adolescent; puberty has come on him in his sleep, his testicles have dropped down, a benign blond beard glints mildly on his cheeks. His parents weep and weep. He is still asleep. No instruments or players are visible. A woman steps out onto a platform. She is an anthropologist from the Smithsonian Institution in Washington, D.C. She explains that there will be no 'entertainment' in the usual sense; there will be no 'entertainers.' The players will not be artists; they will be 'real peasants.' They have been brought over from Messina, from Calabria. They are shepherds, goatherds. They will sing and dance and play just as they do when they come down from the hills to while away the evenings in the taverns. They will play the instruments that scare away the wolves from the flock. They will sing the songs that celebrate the Madonna of Love. A dozen men file onto the platform. They have heavy faces that do not smile. They have heavy dark skins, cratered and leathery. They have ears and noses that look like dried twisted clay. They have gold teeth. They have no teeth. Some are young; most are in their middle years. One is very old; he wears bells on his fingers. One has an instrument like a butter churn: he shoves a stick in and out of a hole in a wooden tub held under his arm, and a rattling screech spurts out of it. One blows on two slender pipes simultaneously.

One has a long strap, which he rubs. One has a frame of bicycle bells; a descendant of the bells the priests used to beat in the temple of Minerva.

The anthropologist is still explaining everything. She explains the 'male' instrument: three wooden knockers; the innermost one lunges up and down between the other two. The songs, she explains, are mainly erotic. The dances are suggestive.

The unusual music commences. The park has filled with Italians—greenhorns from Sicily, settled New Yorkers from Naples. An ancient people. They clap. The old man with the bells on his fingers points his dusty shoe-toes and slowly follows a circle of his own. His eyes are in trance, he squats, he ascends. The anthropologist explains that up-and-down dancing can also be found in parts of Africa. The singers wail like Arabs; the anthropologist notes that the Arab conquest covered the southernmost portion of the Italian boot for two hundred years. The whole chorus of peasants sings in a dialect of archaic Greek; the language has survived in the old songs, the anthropologist explains. The crowd is laughing and stamping. They click their fingers and sway. Lucy's boys are bored. They watch the man with the finger-bells; they watch the wooden male pump up and down. Everyone is clapping, stamping, clicking, swaying, thumping. The wailing goes on and on, faster and faster. The singers are dancers, the dancers are singers, they turn and turn, they are smiling the drugged smiles of dervishes. At home they grow flowers. They follow the sheep into the deep grass. They drink wine in the taverns at night. Calabria and Sicily in New York, sans wives, in sweat-blotched shirts and wrinkled dusty pants, gasping before strangers who have never smelled the sweetness of their village grasses!

Now the anthropologist from the Smithsonian has vanished out of Lucy's illumination. A pair of dancers seize each other. Leg winds over leg, belly into belly, each man hopping on a single free leg. Intertwined, they squat and rise, squat and rise. Old Hellenic syllables fly from them. They send out high elastic cries. They celebrate the Madonna, giver of fertility and fecundity. Lucy is glorified. She is exalted. She comprehends. Not that the musicians are peasants, not that their faces and feet and necks and wrists are blown grass and red earth. An enlightenment comes on her: she sees what is eternal: before Aphrodite, Astarte. The womb of the goddess is garden, lamb, and babe. She is the river and the waterfall. She causes grave men of business—goatherds are men of business—to cavort and to flash their gold teeth. She induces them to blow, beat, rub, shake and scrape objects so that music will drop out of them.

Inside Lucy's illumination the dancers are seething. They are writhing, for the sake of the goddess, for the sake of the womb of the goddess, they are turning into serpents. When they grow still they are earth. They are from always to always. Nature is their pulse. Lucy sees: she understands: the gods are God. How terrible to have given up Jesus, a man like these, made of earth like these, with a pulse like these, God entering nature to become God! Jesus, no more miraculous than an ordinary goatherd; is a goatherd miracle? Is a leaf? A nut, a pit, a core, a seed, a stone? Everything is miracle! Lucy sees how she has abandoned nature, how she has lost true religion on account of the God of the Jews. The boys are on their bellies on the ground, digging it up with sticks. They dig and dig: little holes with mounds beside them. They fill them with peach pits, cherry pits, cantaloupe rinds. The Sicilians and Neapolitans pick up their baskets and purses and shopping bags and leave. The benches smell of eaten fruit, running juices, insect-mobbed. The stage is clean.

The living room has escaped altogether. It is very high and extremely small, no wider than the moon on Lucy's thumbnail. It is still sailing upward, and the voices of those on board are so faint that Lucy almost loses them. But she knows which word it is they mainly use. How long can they go on about it? How long? A morbid cud-chewing. Death and death and death. The word is less a human word than an animal's cry; a crow's. Caw caw. It belongs to storms, floods, avalanches. Acts of God. 'Holocaust,' someone caws dimly from above; she knows it must be Feingold. He always says this word over and over and over. History is bad for him: how little it makes him seem! Lucy decides it is possible to become jaded by atrocity. She is bored by the shootings and the gas and the camps, she is not ashamed to admit this. They are as tiresome as prayer. Repetition diminishes conviction; she is thinking of her father leading the same hymns week after week. If you said the same prayer over and over again, wouldn't your brain turn out to be no better than a prayer wheel?

In the dining room all the springs were running down. It was stale in there, a failed party. They were drinking beer or Coke or whiskey-and-water and playing with the cake crumbs on the tablecloth. There was still some cheese left on a plate, and half a bowl of salted peanuts. 'The impact of Romantic Individualism,' one of the humanists objected. 'At the Frick?' 'I never saw that.' 'They certainly are deliberate, you have to say that for them.' Lucy, leaning abandoned against the door, tried to tune in. The relief of hearing atheists. A jacket designer who worked in Feingold's art department came in carrying a coat. Feingold had invited her because she was newly divorced; she was afraid to live alone. She was afraid of being ambushed in her basement while doing laundry. 'Where's Jimmy?' the jacket designer asked. 'In the other room.' 'Say goodbye for me, will you?' 'Goodbye,' Lucy said. The humanists—Lucy saw how they were all compassionate knights—stood up. A puddle from an overturned saucer was leaking onto the floor. 'Oh, I'll get that,' Lucy told the knights, 'don't think another thought about it.'

Overhead Feingold and the refugee are riding the living room. Their words are specks. All the Jews are in the air.

FAY WELDON

Weekend

By seven-thirty they were ready to go. Martha had everything packed into the car and the three children appropriately dressed and in the back seat, complete with educational games and wholewheat biscuits. When everything was ready in the car Martin would switch off the television, come downstairs, lock up the house, front and back, and take the wheel.

Weekend! Only two hours' drive down to the cottage on Friday evenings, three hours' drive back on Sunday nights. The pleasures of greenery and guests in between. They reckoned themselves fortunate, how fortunate!

On Fridays Martha would get home on the bus at six-twelve and prepare tea and sandwiches for the family: then she would strip four beds and put the sheets and quilt covers in the washing machine for Monday: take the country bedding from the airing basket, plus the books and games, plus the weekend food—acquired at intervals throughout the week, to lessen the load—plus her own folder of work from the office, plus Martin's drawing materials (she was a market researcher in an advertising agency, he a freelance designer) plus hairbrushes, jeans, spare T-shirts, Jolyon's antibiotics (he suffered from sore throats), Jenny's recorder, Jasper's cassette player and so on—ah, the so on!—and would pack them all, skilfully and quickly, into the boot. Very little could be left in the cottage during the week. ('An open invitation to burglars': Martin). Then Martha would run round the house tidying and wiping, doing this and that, finding the cat at one neighbour's and delivering it to another, while the others ate their tea; and would usually, proudly, have everything finished by the time they had eaten their fill. Martin would just catch the BBC2 news, while Martha cleared away the tea table, and the children tossed up for the best positions in the car. 'Martha,' said Martin, tonight, 'you ought to get Mrs Hodder to do more. She takes advantage of you.'

Mrs Hodder came in twice a week to clean. She was over seventy. She charged two pounds an hour. Martha paid her out of her own wages: well, the running of the house was Martha's concern. If Martha chose to go out to work—as was her perfect right, Martin allowed, even though it wasn't the best thing for the children, but that must be Martha's moral responsibility—Martha must surely pay her domestic stand-in. An evident truth, heard loud and clear and frequent in Martin's mouth and Martha's heart.

'I expect you're right,' said Martha. She did not want to argue. Martin had had a long hard week, and now had to drive. Martha couldn't. Martha's licence had been suspended four months back for drunken driving. Everyone agreed that the suspension was unfair: Martha seldom drank to excess: she was for one thing usually too busy pouring drinks for other people or washing other people's glasses to get much inside herself. But Martin had taken her out to dinner on her birthday, as was his custom, and exhaustion and excitement mixed had made her imprudent, and before she knew where she was, why there she was, in the dock, with a distorted lamp-post to pay for and a new bonnet for the car and six months' suspension.

So now Martin had to drive her car down to the cottage, and he was always tired on Fridays, and hot and sleepy on Sundays and every rattle and clank and bump in the engine she felt to be somehow her fault.

Martin had a little sports car for London and work: it could nip in and out of the traffic nicely: Martha's was an old estate car, with room for the children, picnic baskets, bedding, food, games, plants, drink, portable television and all the things required by the middle classes for weekends in the country. It lumbered rather than zipped and made Martin angry. He seldom spoke a harsh word, but Martha, after the fashion of wives, could detect his mood from what he did not say rather than what he did, and from the tilt of his head, and the way his crinkly, merry eyes seemed crinklier and merrier still—and of course from the way he addressed Martha's car.

'Come along, you old banger you! Can't you do better than that?

You're too old, that's your trouble. Stop complaining. Always complaining, it's only a hill. You're too wide about the hips. You'll never get through there.'

Martha worried about her age, her tendency to complain, and the width of her hips. She took the remarks personally. Was she right to do so? The children noticed nothing: it was just funny lively laughing Daddy being witty about Mummy's car. Mummy, done for drunken driving. Mummy, with the roots of melancholy somewhere deep beneath the bustling, busy, everyday self. Busy: ah so busy!

Martin would only laugh if she said anything about the way he spoke to her car and warn her against paranoia. 'Don't get like your mother, darling.' Martha's mother had, towards the end, thought that people were plotting against her. Martha's mother had led a secluded, suspicious life, and made Martha's childhood a chilly and a lonely time. Life now, by comparison, was wonderful for Martha. People, children, houses, conversations, food, drink, theatres—even, now, a career. Martin standing between her and the hostility of the world—popular, easy, funny Martin, beckoning the rest of the world into earshot.

Ah, she was grateful: little earnest Martha, with her shy ways and her penchant for passing boring exams—how her life had blossomed out! Three children too—Jasper, Jenny and Jolyon—all with Martin's broad brow and open looks, and the confidence born of her love and care, and the work she had put into them since the dawning of their days.

Martin drives. Martha, for once, drowses.

The right food, the right words, the right play. Doctors for the tonsils: dentists for the molars. Confiscate guns: censor television: encourage creativity. Paints and paper to hand: books on the shelves: meetings with teachers. Music teachers. Dancing lessons. Parties. Friends to tea. School plays. Open days. Junior orchestra.

Martha is jolted awake. Traffic lights. Martin doesn't like Martha to sleep while he drives.

Clothes. Oh, clothes! Can't wear this: must wear that. Dress shops. Piles of clothes in corners: duly washed, but waiting to be ironed, waiting to be put away.

Get the piles off the floor, into the laundry baskets. Martin doesn't like a mess.

Creativity arises out of order, not chaos. Five years off work while the children were small: back to work with seniority lost. What, did you think something was for nothing? If you have children, mother, that is your reward. It lies not in the world.

Have you taken enough food? Always hard to judge.

Food, Oh, food! Shop in the lunch-hour. Lug it all home. Cook for the freezer on Wednesday evenings while Martin is at his car-maintenance evening class, and isn't there to notice you being unrestful. Martin likes you to sit down in the evenings. Fruit, meat, vegetables, flour for home-made bread. Well, shop bread is full of pollutants. Frozen food, even your own, loses flavour. Martin often remarks on it. Condiments. Everyone loves mango chutney. But the expense!

London Airport to the left. Look, look, children! Concorde? No, idiot, of course it isn't Concorde.

Ah, to be all things to all people: children, husband, employer, friends! It can be done: yes, it can: super woman.

Drink. Home-made wine. Why not? Elderberries grown thick and rich in London: and at least you know what's in it. Store it in high cupboards: lots of room: up and down the step-ladder. Careful! Don't slip. Don't break anything.

No such thing as an accident. Accidents are Freudian slips: they are wilful, bad-tempered things.

Martin can't bear bad temper. Martin likes slim ladies. Diet. Martin rather likes his secretary. Diet. Martin admires slim legs and big bosoms. How to achieve them both? Impossible. But try, oh try, to be what you ought to be, not what you are. Inside and out.

Martin brings back flowers and chocolates: whisks Martha off for holiday weekends. Wonderful! The best husband in the world: look into his crinkly, merry, gentle eyes; see it there. So the mouth slopes away into something of a pout. Never mind. Gaze into the eyes. Love. It must be love. You married him. *You*. Surely *you* deserve true love?

Salisbury Plain. Stonehenge. Look, children, look! Mother, we've seen Stonehenge a hundred times. Go back to sleep.

Cook! Ah cook. People love to come to Martin and Martha's dinners. Work it out in your head in the lunch-hour. If you get in at six-twelve, you can seal the meat while you beat the egg white while you feed the cat while you lay the table while you string the beans while you set out the cheeses, goat's cheese, Martin loves goat's cheese, Martha tries to like goat's cheese—oh, bed, sleep, peace, quiet.

Sex! Ah sex. Orgasm, please. Martin requires it. Well, so do you. And you don't want his secretary providing a passion you neglected to develop. Do you? Quick, quick, the cosmic bond. Love. Married love.

Secretary! Probably a vulgar suspicion: nothing more. Probably a fit of paranoics, à la mother, now dead and gone.
At peace.
R.I.P.
Chilly, lonely mother, following her suspicions where they led.

Nearly there, children. Nearly in paradise, nearly at the cottage. Have another biscuit.

Real roses round the door.

Roses. Prune, weed, spray, feed, pick. Avoid thorns. One of Martin's few harsh words.

'Martha, you can't not want roses! What kind of person am I married to? An anti-rose personality?'

Green grass. Oh, God, grass. Grass must be mown. Restful lawns, daisies bobbing, buttercups glowing. Roses and grass and books. Books.

Please, Martin, do we have to have the two hundred books, mostly twenties' first editions, bought at Christie's book sale on one of your afternoons off? Books need dusting.

Roars of laughter from Martin, Jasper, Jenny and Jolyon. Mummy says we shouldn't have the books: books need dusting!

Roses, green grass, books and peace.

Martha woke up with a start when they got to the cottage, and gave a little shriek which made them all laugh. Mummy's waking shriek, they called it.

Then there was the car to unpack and the beds to make up, and the electricity to connect, and the supper to make, and the cobwebs to remove, while Martin made the fire. Then supper—pork chops in sweet and sour sauce ('Pork is such a *dull* meat if you don't cook it properly': Martin), green salad from the garden, or such green salad as the rabbits had left. ('Martha, did you really net them properly? Be honest, now!': Martin) and sauté potatoes. Mash is so stodgy and ordinary, and instant mash unthinkable. The children studied the night sky with the aid of their star map. Wonderful, rewarding children!

Then clear up the supper: set the dough to prove for the bread: Martin already in bed: exhausted by the drive and lighting the fire. ('Martha, we really ought to get the logs stacked properly. Get the children to do it, will you?': Martin) Sweep and tidy: get the TV aerial right. Turn up Jasper's jeans where he has trodden the hem undone. ('He can't go around like *that*, Martha. Not even Jasper': Martin)

Midnight. Good night. Weekend guests arriving in the morning.

Seven for lunch and dinner on Saturday. Seven for Sunday breakfast, nine for Sunday lunch. ('Don't fuss, darling. You always make such a fuss': Martin) Oh, God, forgotten the garlic squeezer. That means ten minutes with the back of a spoon and salt. Well, who wants *lumps* of garlic? No one. Not Martin's guests. Martin said so. Sleep.

Colin and Katie. Colin is Martin's oldest friend. Katie is his new young wife. Janet, Colin's other, earlier wife, was Martha's friend. Janet was rather like Martha, quieter and duller than her husband. A nag and a drag, Martin rather thought, and said, and of course she'd let herself go, everyone agreed. No one exactly excused Colin for walking out, but you could see the temptation.

Katie versus Janet.

Katie was languid, beautiful and elegant. She drawled when she spoke. Her hands were expressive: her feet were little and female. She had no children.

Janet plodded round on very flat, rather large feet. There was something wrong with them. They turned out slightly when she walked. She had two children. She was, frankly, boring. But Martha liked her: when Janet came down to the cottage she would wash up. Not in the way that most guests washed up—washing dutifully and setting everything out on the draining board, but actually drying and putting away too. And Janet would wash the bath and get the children all sat down, with chairs for everyone, even the littlest, and keep them quiet and satisfied so the grown-ups—well, the men—could get on with their conversation and their jokes and their love of country weekends, while Janet stared into space, as if grateful for the rest, quite happy.

Janet would garden, too. Weed the strawberries, while the men went for their walk; her great feet standing firm and square and sometimes crushing a plant or so, but never mind, oh never mind. Lovely Janet; who understood.

Now Janet was gone and here was Katie.

Katie talked with the men and went for walks for the men, and moved her ashtray rather impatiently when Martha tried to clear the drinks round it.

Dishes were boring, Katie implied by her manner, and domesticity was boring, and anyone who bothered with that kind of thing was a fool. Like Martha. Ash should be allowed to stay where it was, even if it was in the butter, and conversations should never be interrupted.

Knock, knock. Katie and Colin arrived at one-fifteen on Saturday morning, just after Martha had got to bed. 'You don't mind? It was the moonlight. We couldn't resist it. You should have seen Stonehenge! We didn't disturb you? Such early birds!'

Martha rustled up a quick meal of omelettes. Saturday nights' eggs ('Martha makes a lovely omelette': Martin) ('Honey, make one of your mushroom omelettes: cook the mushrooms, separately, remember, with lemon. Otherwise the water from the mushrooms gets into the eggs, and spoils everything.') Sunday supper mushrooms. But ungracious to say anything.

Martin had revived wonderfully at the sight of Colin and Katie. He brought out the whisky bottle. Glasses. Ice. Jug for water. Wait. Wash up another sinkful, when they're finished. 2 a.m.

'Don't do it tonight, darling.'
'It'll only take a sec.' Bright smile, not a hint of self-pity. Self-pity can spoil everyone's weekend.
Martha knows that if breakfast for seven is to be manageable the sink must be cleared of dishes. A tricky meal, breakfast. Especially if bacon, eggs and tomatoes must all be cooked in separate pans. ('Separate pans means separate flavours!': Martin)

She is running around in her nightie. Now if that had been Katie—but there's something so *practical* about Martha. Reassuring, mind; but the skimpy nightie and the broad rump and the thirty-eight years are all rather embarrassing. Martha can see it in Colin and Katie's eyes. Martin's too. Martha wishes she did not see so much in other people's eyes. Her mother did, too. Dear, dead mother. Did I misjudge you?

This was the second weekend Katie had been down with Colin but without Janet. Colin was a photographer: Katie had been his accessoriser. First Colin and Janet: then Colin, Janet and Katie: now Colin and Katie!

Katie weeded with rubber gloves on and pulled out pansies in mistake for weeds and laughed and laughed along with everyone when her mistake was pointed out to her, but the pansies died. Well, Colin had become with the years fairly rich and fairly famous, and what does a fairly rich and famous man want with a wife like Janet when Katie is at hand?

On the first of the Colin/Janet/Katie weekends Katie had appeared out of the bathroom. 'I say,' said Katie, holding out a damp towel with evident distaste. 'I can only find this. No hope of a dry one?' and Martha had run to fetch a dry towel and amazingly found one, and handed it to Katie who flashed her a brilliant smile and said, 'I can't bear damp towels. Anything in the world but damp towels,' as if speaking to a servant in a time of shortage of staff, and took all the water so there was none left for Martha to wash up.

The trouble, of course, was drying anything at all in the cottage. There were no facilities for doing so, and Martin had a horror of clothes lines which might spoil the view. He toiled and moiled all week in the city simply to get a country view at the weekend. Ridiculous to spoil it by draping it with wet towels! But now Martha had bought more towels, so perhaps everyone could be satisfied. She would take nine damp towels back on Sunday evenings in a plastic bag and see to them in London.

On this Saturday morning, straight after breakfast, Katie went out to the car—she and Colin had a new Lamborghini, hard to imagine Katie in anything duller—and came back waving a new Yves St Laurent towel. 'See! I brought my own, darlings.'

They'd brought nothing else. No fruit, no meat, no vegetables, not even bread, certainly not a box of chocolates. They'd gone off to bed with alacrity, the night before, and the spare room rocked and heaved: well, who'd want to do washing-up when you could do that, but what about the children? Would they get confused? First Colin and Janet, now Colin and Katie?

Martha murmured something of her thoughts to Martin, who looked quite shocked. 'Colin's my best friend. I don't expect him to bring anything,' and Martha felt mean. 'And good heavens, you can't protect the kids from sex for ever; don't be so prudish,' so that Martha felt stupid as well. Mean, complaining and stupid.

Janet had rung Martha during the week. The house had been sold over her head, and she and the children had been moved into a small flat. Katie was trying to persuade Colin to cut down on her allowance, Janet said.

'It does one no good to be materialistic,' Katie confided. 'I have nothing. No home, no family, no ties, no possessions. Look at me! Only me and a suitcase of clothes.' But Katie seemed highly satisfied with the me, and the clothes were stupendous. Katie drank a great deal and became funny. Everyone laughed, including Martha. Katie had been married twice. Martha marvelled at how someone could arrive in their mid-thirties with nothing at all to their name, neither husband, nor children, nor property and not mind.

Mind you, Martha could see the power of such helplessness. If Colin was all Katie had in the world, how could Colin abandon her? And to what? Where would she go? How would she live? Oh, clever Katie.

'My teacup's dirty,' said Katie, and Martha ran to clean it, apologising, and Martin raised his eyebrows, at Martha, not Katie.

'I wish *you'd* wear scent,' said Martin to Martha, reproachfully. Katie wore lots. Martha never seemed to have time to put any on, though Martin bought her bottle after bottle. Martha leaped out of bed each morning to meet some emergency—miaowing cat, coughing child, faulty alarm clock, postman's knock—when was

Martha to put on scent? It annoyed Martin all the same. She ought to do more to charm him.

Colin looked handsome and harrowed and younger than Martin, though they were much the same age. 'Youth's catching,' said Martin in bed that night. 'It's since he found Katie.' Found, like some treasure. Discovered; something exciting and wonderful, in the dreary world of established spouses.

On Saturday morning Jasper trod on a piece of wood ('Martha, why isn't he wearing shoes? It's too bad': Martin) and Martha took him into the hospital to have a nasty splinter removed. She left the cottage at ten and arrived back at one, and they were still sitting in the sun, drinking, empty bottles glinting in the long grass. The grass hadn't been cut. Don't forget the bottles. Broken glass means more mornings at the hospital. Oh, don't fuss. Enjoy yourself. Like other people. Try.

But no potatoes peeled, no breakfast cleared, nothing. Cigarette ends still amongst old toast, bacon rind and marmalade. 'You could have done the potatoes,' Martha burst out. Oh, bad temper! Prime sin. They looked at her in amazement and dislike. Martin too.

'Goodness,' said Katie, 'Are we doing the whole Sunday lunch bit on Saturday? Potatoes? Ages since I've eaten potatoes. Wonderful!'

'The children expect it,' said Martha.

So they did. Saturday and Sunday lunch shone like reassuring beacons in their lives. Saturday lunch: family lunch: fish and chips. ('So much better cooked at home than bought': Martin) Sunday. Usually roast beef, potatoes, peas, apple pie. Oh, of course. Yorkshire pudding. Always a problem with oven temperatures. When the beef's going slowly the Yorkshire should be going fast. How to achieve that? Like big bosom and little hips.

'Just relax,' said Martin. 'I'll cook dinner, all in good time. Splinters always work their own way out: no need to have taken him to hospital. Let life drift over you, my love. Flow with the waves, that's the way.'

And Martin flashed Martha a distant, spiritual smile. His hand lay on Katie's slim brown arm, with its many gold bands.

'Anyway, you do too much for the children,' said Martin. 'It isn't good for them. Have a drink.'

So Martha perched uneasily on the step and had a glass of cider, and wondered how, if lunch was going to be late, she would get cleared up and the meat out of the marinade for the rather formal dinner that would be expected that evening. The marinaded lamb ought to cook for at least four hours in a low oven; and you couldn't use that and the grill at the same time and Martin liked his fish grilled, not fried. Less cholesterol.

She didn't say as much. Domestic details like this were very boring, and any mild complaint was registered by Martin as a scene. And to make a scene was so ungrateful.

This was the life. Well, wasn't it? Smart friends in large cars and country living and drinks before lunch and roses and bird song—'Don't drink *too* much,' said Martin, and told them about Martha's suspended driving licence.

The children were hungry so Martha opened them a can of beans and sausages and heated them up. ('Martha, do they have to eat that crap? Can't they wait?': Martin)

Katie was hungry: she said so, to keep the children in face. She was lovely with children—most children. She did not particularly like Colin and Janet's children. She said so, and he accepted it. He only saw them once a month now, not once a week.

'Let me make lunch,' Katie said to Martha. 'You do so much, poor thing!'

And she pulled out of the fridge all the things Martha had put away for the next day's picnic lunch party—Camembert cheese and salad and salami and made a wonderful tomato salad in two minutes and opened the white wine—'not very cold, darling. Shouldn't it be chilling?'—and had it all on the table in five amazing competent minutes. 'That's all we need, darling,' said Martin. 'You are funny with your fish-and-chip Saturdays! What could be nicer than this? Or simpler?'

Nothing, except there was Sunday's buffet lunch for nine gone, in place of Saturday's fish for six, and would the fish stretch? No. Katie had had quite a lot to drink. She pecked Martha on the forehead. 'Funny little Martha,' she said. 'She reminds me of Janet. I really do like Janet.' Colin did not want to be reminded of Janet, and said so. 'Darling, Janet's a fact of life,' said Katie. 'If you'd only think about her more, you might manage to pay her less.' And she yawned and stretched her lean, childless body and smiled at Colin with her inviting, naughty little girl eyes, and Martin watched her in admiration.

Martha got up and left them and took a paint pot and put a coat of white gloss on the bathroom wall. The white surface pleased her. She was good at painting. She produced a smooth, even surface. Her legs throbbed. She feared she might be getting varicose veins.

Outside in the garden the children played badminton. They were bad-tempered, but relieved to be able to look up and see their mother working, as usual: making their lives for ever better and nicer: organising, planning, thinking ahead, side-stepping disaster, making preparations, like a mother hen, fussing and irritating: part of the natural boring scenery of the world.

On Saturday night Katie went to bed early: she rose from her chair and stretched and yawned and poked her head into the kitchen where Martha was washing saucepans. Colin had cleared the table and Katie had folded the napkins into pretty creases, while Martin blew at the fire, to make it bright. 'Good night,' said Katie.

Katie appeared three minutes later, reproachfully holding out her Yves St Laurent towel, sopping wet. 'Oh dear,' cried Martha. 'Jenny must have washed her hair!' And Martha was obliged to rout Jenny out of bed to rebuke her, publicly, if only to demonstrate that she knew what was right and proper. That meant Jenny would sulk all weekend, and that meant a treat or an outing mid-week, or else by the following week she'd be having an asthma attack. 'You fuss the children too much,' said Martin. 'That's why Jenny has asthma.' Jenny was pleasant enough to look at, but not stunning. Perhaps she was a disappointment to her father? Martin would never say so, but Martha feared he thought so.

An egg and an orange each child, each day. Then nothing too bad would go wrong. And it hadn't. The asthma was very mild. A calm, tranquil environment, the doctor said. Ah, smile, Martha smile. Domestic happiness depends on you. 21 × 52 oranges a year. Each one to be purchased, carried, peeled and washed up after. And what about potatoes. 12 × 52 pounds a year? Martin liked his potatoes carefully peeled. He couldn't bear to find little cores of black in the mouthful. ('Well, it isn't very nice, is it?': Martin)

Martha dreamt she was eating coal, by handfuls, and liking it.

Saturday night. Martin made love to Martha three times. Three times? How virile he was, and clearly turned on by the sounds from the spare room. Martin said he loved her. Martin always did. He was a courteous lover; he knew the importance of foreplay. So did Martha. Three times.

Ah, sleep. Jolyon had a nightmare. Jenny was woken by a moth. Martin slept through everything. Martha pottered about the house in the night. There was a moon. She sat at the window and stared out into the summer night for five minutes, and was at peace, and then went back to bed because she ought to be fresh for the morning.

But she wasn't. She slept late. The others went out for a walk. They'd left a note, a considerate note: 'Didn't wake you. You looked tired. Had a cold breakfast so as not to make too much mess. Leave everything 'til we get back.' But it was ten o'clock, and guests were coming at noon, so she cleared away the bread, the butter, the crumbs, the smears, the jam, the spoons, the spilt sugar, the cereal, the milk (sour by now) and the dirty plates, and swept the floors, and tidied up quickly, and grabbed a cup of coffee, and prepared to make a rice and fish dish, and a chocolate mousse and sat down in the middle to eat a lot of bread and jam herself. Broad hips. She remembered the office work in her file and knew she wouldn't be able to do it. Martin anyway thought it was ridiculous for her to bring work back at the weekends. 'It's your holiday,' he'd say. 'Why should they impose?' Martha loved her work. She didn't have to smile at it. She just did it.

Katie came back upset and crying. She sat in the kitchen while Martha worked and drank glass after glass of gin and bitter lemon. Katie liked ice and lemon in gin. Martha paid for all the drink out of her wages. It was part of the deal between her and Martin—the contract by which she went out to work. All things to cheer the spirit, otherwise depressed by a working wife and mother, were to be paid for by Martha. Drink, holidays, petrol, outings, puddings, electricity, heating: it was quite a joke between them. It didn't really make any difference: it was their joint money, after all. Amazing how Martha's wages were creeping up, almost to the level of Martin's. One day they would overtake. Then what?

Work, honestly, was a piece of cake.

Anyway, poor Katie was crying. Colin, she'd discovered, kept a photograph of Janet and the children in his wallet. 'He's not free of her. He pretends he is, but he isn't. She has him by a stranglehold. It's the kids. His bloody kids. Moaning Mary and that little creep Joanna. It's all he thinks about. I'm nobody.'

But Katie didn't believe it. She knew she was somebody all right. Colin came in, in a fury. He took out the photograph and set fire to it, bitterly, with a match. Up in smoke they went. Mary and Joanna and Janet. The ashes fell on the floor. (Martha swept them up when Colin and Katie had gone. It hardly seemed polite to do so when they were still there.) 'Go back to her,' Katie said. 'Go back to her. I don't care. Honestly, I'd rather be on my own. You're a nice old fashioned thing. Run along then. Do your thing, I'll do mine. Who cares?'

'Christ, Katie, the fuss! She only just happens to be in the photograph. She's not there on purpose to annoy. And I do feel bad about her. She's been having a hard time.'

'And haven't you, Colin? She twists a pretty knife, I can tell you. Don't you have rights too? Not to mention me. Is a little loyalty too much to expect?'

They were reconciled before lunch, up in the spare room. Harry and Beryl Elder arrived at twelve-thirty. Harry didn't like to hurry on Sundays; Beryl was flustered with apologies for their lateness. They'd brought artichokes from their garden. 'Wonderful,' cried Martin. 'Fruits of the earth? Let's have a wonderful soup! Don't fret, Martha. I'll do it.'

'Don't fret.' Martha clearly hadn't been smiling enough. She was in danger, Martin implied, of ruining everyone's weekend. There was an emergency in the garden very shortly—an elm tree which had probably got Dutch elm disease—and Martha finished the artichokes. The lid flew off the blender and there was artichoke purée everywhere. 'Let's have lunch outside,' said Colin. 'Less work for Martha.'

Martin frowned at Martha: he thought the appearance of martyrdom in the face of guests to be an unforgivable offence.

Everyone happily joined in taking the furniture out, but it was Martha's experience that nobody ever helped to bring it in again. Jolyon was stung by a wasp. Jasper sneezed and sneezed from hay fever and couldn't find the tissues and he wouldn't use loo paper. ('Surely you remembered the tissues, darling?': Martin)

Beryl Elder was nice. 'Wonderful to eat out,' she said, fetching the cream for her pudding, while Martha fished a fly from the liquefying Brie ('You shouldn't have bought it so ripe, Martha': Martin)—'except it's just some other woman has to do it. But at least it isn't *me*.' Beryl worked too, as a secretary, to send the boys to boarding school, where she'd rather they weren't. But her husband was from a rather grand family, and she'd been only a typist when he married her, so her life was a mass of amends, one way or another. Harry had lately opted out of the stockbroking rat race and become an artist, choosing integrity rather than money, but that choice was his alone and couldn't of course be inflicted on the boys.

Katie found the fish and rice dish rather strange, toyed at it with her fork, and talked about Italian restaurants she knew. Martin lay back soaking in the sun: crying, 'Oh, this is the life.' He made coffee, nobly, and the lid flew off the grinder and there were coffee beans all over the kitchen especially in amongst the row of cookery books which Martin gave Martha Christmas by Christmas. At least they didn't have to be brought back every weekend. ('The burglars won't have the sense to steal those': Martin)

Beryl fell asleep and Katie watched her, quizzically. Beryl's mouth was open and she had a lot of fillings, and her ankles were thick and her waist was going, and she didn't look after herself. 'I love women,' sighed Katie. 'They look so wonderful asleep. I wish I could be an earth mother.'

Beryl woke with a start and nagged her husband into going home, which he clearly didn't want to do, so didn't. Beryl thought she had to get back because his mother was coming round later. Nonsense! Then Beryl tried to stop Harry drinking more home-made wine and was laughed at by everyone. He was driving, Beryl couldn't, and he did have a nasty scar on his temple from a previous road accident. Never mind.

'She does come on strong, poor soul,' laughed Katie when they'd finally gone. 'I'm never going to get married,'—and Colin looked at her yearningly because he wanted to marry her more than anything in the world and Martha cleared the coffee cups.

'Oh don't *do* that,' said Katie, 'do just sit *down*, Martha, you make us all feel bad,' and Martin glared at Martha who sat down and Jenny called out for her and Martha went upstairs and Jenny had started her first period and Martha cried and cried and knew she must stop because this must be a joyous occasion for Jenny or her whole future would be blighted, but for once, Martha couldn't.

Her daughter Jenny: wife, mother, friend.

Rachel Ingalls

Third Time Lucky

Lily had married first when she was eighteen. He'd been killed in Vietnam. She'd married again when she was twenty-one. He too had died in Vietnam. She'd had proposals after that, but she'd refused without even considering the possibility of accepting. She was sure that if she said yes, he'd be killed just as the first two had been. It was like having a curse on you: she could feel it. Perhaps when she'd agreed to go to the Egyptian exhibition she'd been attracted by the knowledge that there was something called the Curse of The Pharaohs.

She'd forgotten all about that. She didn't remember it again until long after she'd heard the radio interview with the old woman who lived in Cairo.

Lily listened to the radio a lot. As a child she'd been introduced to literature through the soap operas; even at the age of seven, she'd realized that the stories were preposterous, but she loved them. She'd also liked the way they gave you only a little piece of each story every day, so that if you were lucky enough to get sick, or if school had been cancelled because of snow, you could hear the complete collection from morning to late afternoon—like eating a whole meal of Lifesavers, all in different flavours.

In her teens she'd watched television, mainly the late-night movies. And then later, when the most popular family show had been the war, she'd stopped. She'd gone back to the radio. Her favourite station broadcast its programmes from the other side of the ocean in British voices that sounded just like the people in the movies. She was charmed by their accents.

The woman who lived in Egypt had spoken in one of a number of interviews compiled by an English woman reporter. The programmes set out to make a study of British people who had lived in Egypt for a long time. All the broadcasters were women: that, apparently, was the point of the series. One of the speakers was a girl who'd married an Egyptian; she talked about what it was like to become part of the family, how it was different from life at home, and so on: she seemed to have a very happy marriage. She could also throw in foreign phrases as easily as she spoke her own language, her voice full of enthusiasm. She praised her mother-in-law. Lily was drawn across the room as she listened: she went and sat right next to the radio to make sure she didn't miss anything or that she could retune if the speech broke up in static—a thing that often happened during the international programmes.

She was fascinated by accounts of other people's marriages. She couldn't hear enough. It was like being told fairytales, and yet it was the real thing—real people her own age. Once she'd grown up, she'd started to prefer fact to fiction. That was what she thought, anyway.

Immediately after the young married woman came an archaeologist. And after her, the reporter introduced the old woman.

Her name was Sadie. She'd been born and brought up in London. When she was six years old her father had taken her to the British Museum to look at the exhibits. There she had seen a room full of Egyptian mummies and had been so impressed by them that she couldn't sleep. She'd said to her parents that her home was in the place where those people had lived, and that was where she wanted to go, because that was where she belonged. Her parents had told her not to be silly. When she persisted, they called in a friend who wasn't exactly a doctor, but who knew a lot. The friend succeeded in restoring Sadie's sleep by assuring her that strange as her story sounded to everyone else, there might be something to it. She would be free to test the truth of it as soon as she grew up. But to insist on instant transportation to a distant country wouldn't be fair to her parents while they were still trying to give her a good home and make sure she was well-fed and healthy.

Sensible man, Lily thought. That was the kind of doctor people should have—not like the ones who'd tried to deal with her and who'd probably primed her mother with a load of nonsense until the whole family was driving her crazy. It had been as if twice in her life she'd become a freak—like a woman who'd been struck by lightning and survived. It was almost like going through the sort of thing she'd read about in magazine stories: accounts of women who'd had to keep on living in a community when everyone there knew they'd been the victims of some shameful act of violence or humiliation.

Of course people felt sorry for you and they hoped to make you well again. They believed that you ought to recover. They tried to cheer you up and yet they wanted you to be suffering the correct amount for the occasion, otherwise they got nervous: there might be some extra grief around that wasn't being taken care of. She herself had sometimes thought: *Am I feeling the right things? Am I even feeling enough?* She didn't know. She thought she didn't know much of anything any more.

She started hanging around the museum in order to fill up her days. She'd gone back to work, but there were lunch hours when she didn't want to be eating her sandwiches with the rest of the girls, and the museum wasn't far from the job she'd had at the time.

She began by just walking around. That first day she saw Greek statues and Roman coins. The second time she went, she looked at Chinese jade and Japanese scroll paintings. On her third visit she got lost trying to find the Etruscans, and came upon ancient Egypt instead. It hadn't produced an instant, revelatory obsession like the one experienced by the six-year-old Sadie, but it had certainly done something extraordinary to her. She had felt magnetized by the appearance of everything: the colours, the style of drawing, the mysterious hieroglyphics—the whole look. The museum had several items that were rare and important: a black wooden panther surmounted by a golden god in a high hat; a painted mummy case that was covered in pictures of birds, animals and pictograph writing; a grey stone hawk that stood about four feet high; and a granite statue of a seated Pharaoh who had a face framed by a head-dress that merged with the shoulders, so that he too had the silhouette of a hawk.

She knew then, at her first sight of the sculpture and painting, that she wanted to find out more about the people who had made them. She picked up a leaflet at the main desk. It turned out that there were museum lectures you could attend in the mornings or afternoons. There were even some that took place during the lunch hour. She signed up in a hurry.

Her real conversion to the art of Egypt happened in semi-darkness, to the accompaniment of a low hum given off by the museum's slide projector. She studied temples, frescoes, jewellery, furniture, corpses thousands of years old. She felt that all these sights and objects were familiar to her in a way that her own life was not.

The Englishwoman named Sadie hadn't needed lectures. After the family friend had made her see reason, she'd struck a bargain with her parents: that she'd be good and do what they told her, as long as they realized that her one ambition was to go to Egypt, and that she actually did plan to go there as soon as she was grown up. It took several more years, and undoubtedly a certain amount of research, before she narrowed down the rather vague passion for Egyptology to a specific dedication: she found out through a dream that in a former life she'd been a priestess of Isis and many centuries ago she had lived in a particular house, where she'd had a wonderful garden full of flowers and herbs, and plants that possessed healing properties. It became her mission to return to the house, live there and replant her garden.

It had taken Sadie twelve years of work in London to raise the money for her fare. On her arrival in Egypt she attached herself to British archaeological societies, which allowed her to earn a little by helping them, although—because she'd had so little formal schooling—they discounted anything she had to say on their subject. It came as a surprise to the official bodies when she discovered the ruins of what she insisted was her house, and which, as it was excavated, proved to have contained at one time a plentifully stocked courtyard garden. It was surprising, but not in anyone else's opinion a matter of supernatural or preternatural knowledge, as Sadie claimed. In spite of the scepticism of the experts, she managed to present the urgency of her desire so convincingly that she was given permission to camp out in the ruins and eventually to try to reconstruct the house and garden.

When the woman reporter interviewed her, Sadie was eighty-two. She spoke of the quest for her true home with an assurance and simplicity that made Lily think what a good life it had been: to know so exactly, from such an early age, what you wanted and where you belonged. If she herself had had that kind of vision as a child, she might now feel that her life meant something, instead of thinking that it all just seemed to be dribbling away around her, never getting anywhere, always going wrong.

Egypt had begun to be important to her for about a year and a half, yet she didn't recall the circumstances of her breakdown until she'd been going to the lectures for five weeks. The memory came back as if it had fallen on top of her. While she was looking at slides of famous statues and wall paintings, she recognized certain things that she'd seen when the great Tutankhamun exhibition had come over to America. That was shortly after she was supposed to have recovered from her second widowing. Friends and relatives had thought it would be a nice idea, a treat, to take her to the show. She didn't care what she went to see. She'd said sure, OK.

It was too long a trip to make all in one day, so she'd stayed with her aunt, and even then it was a considerable drive by car from there. Her cousin, Charlie, and his girlfriend, Sue, drove in one car, while two of Sue's old schoolfriends went in the second one, together with some friends of theirs—a man who, Lily suspected, had been asked along because of her. That too had happened after her first husband had died: everybody had started trying to match her up with somebody.

The lines of sightseers waiting to get in to see the exhibition had been so long, and so often mentioned in the papers, that everyone had a different theory about what was the best time to go, when to avoid the school groups, the adult education classes, the old, the young, the tourists. They got into the line in the middle of the afternoon, and were fortunate—they had to wait for only an hour and a quarter.

Lily took out her wallet to pay, but Charlie and Sue insisted on buying her ticket. She put the ticket into the change compartment of the wallet, on the side where she kept her backdoor key and her lucky-piece—an old silver coin covered in patterns that might have been foreign writing; a great-uncle had brought it back from overseas. The coin had been in the safe with the rest of her grandmother's treasured and worthless ornaments. Her father had given it to her because she'd seemed to be so interested in the marking on it.

The line advanced slowly, even after they had paid. The guards were being careful to let in only a certain number at a time. Nobody wanted to have overcrowding or pushing. And, naturally, the people who were already inside would feel they were entitled to stay there a good long while, after having waited so long, paid so much, and at last come face to face with objects of such magnificence.

Lily wasn't expecting to be asked for her ticket when a hand was suddenly held out to her. She scrabbled around quickly in her bag and found the stub as the crowd moved forward into the darkness.

All at once everyone fell silent. People were afraid of tripping over themselves in the dark, or bumping into each other. She fumbled in her wallet, shut the change purse, zipped up her bag and held on to it tightly. She was looking at a set of floodlit glass boxes that sprang from the darkness like lighted boats crossing an ocean at night. In each glass case a single treasure was positioned. The lighting must have been controlled from above, although it was impossible to see how. The impression was definitely that all the illumination emanated from the golden deities and blue animals, painted birds and flowers.

Lily stared and lost track of the time. There was no doubt in her mind that the jars, tables, gods, faces, jewels and masks were gazing back, looking out from the repose of their long past and giving something to her as she passed by.

She stopped in front of an alabaster vase shaped like a lotus blossom on its stem. The crowd jostled her lightly, but no one was shoving. The atmosphere seemed churchlike: the worshippers in darkness, the sacred relics shining. She lingered for a long time in front of a beautiful face—yellow-white, with black lines painted on the eyebrows, around the eyes and outward at the sides. The face was framed in a head-dress like the one worn by the sphinx. And the whole thing, according to the description underneath, was part of a canopic jar. She'd forgotten what canopic meant.

She stepped aside, to let other people see. In front of the cases of jewellery, a young man had come to a standstill; he'd apparently been in the same place for a long while, because an official was trying to get him to move. The young man responded immediately, saying—in a very audible voice—that he'd paid his money and he had a right to look for as long as he wanted to. The official backed away, murmuring about being fair to the other people: he didn't want to start a fight in the middle of the crowd or to disrupt the discreet, artistic and historic hush brought about by the presence of so many tons of gold and lapis lazuli.

She took a good look herself at the young king in his blue-and-gold headcloth, which fell in stripes to his shoulders. And as she walked on, she realized that she'd worked her way around to the exit. The others were nearby. Sometimes people went through exhibits at such different rates that it made more sense to split up for a set period; but they'd all finished at about the same time.

They moved out into the shopping area where people were

selling books and postcards. Lily opened her bag and got out her wallet. She unsnapped the coin compartment and began to rummage inside it. She couldn't feel her lucky-piece. She couldn't see it. She shook the bag from side to side. Sue asked what was wrong. Charlie said, 'If you're looking for your wallet, you're already holding it in your hand.'

The next thing she knew, she was screaming. Everyone tried to calm her down but she let go completely, shrieking hysterically, 'I've lost it, oh God. It isn't anywhere.'

'Something important?' a voice said.

'The most important thing I've got,' she spluttered. 'It's my lucky-piece.' She wanted to go back into the exhibition rooms, to make the museum authorities turn up the lights and hold the crowds back, so that she could go over the whole floor.

They couldn't do that, everyone told her. They'd report the loss and hope the staff would pick up the coin at closing-time.

That wasn't good enough, she yelled.

Shock, embarrassment, distaste, were on people's faces. She didn't care. She could barely see them but she could hear the change in the sounds around her, and especially the difference in their voices as they let her know that everything she wanted was impossible and unreasonable. They thought her lucky-piece was insignificant; she was in the presence of Art and of the past, and of an entire civilization that had been lost. She even heard one of their own crowd whispering about her—though later on she wasn't sure if she might not have imagined it—saying, 'Don't know why she wants it back—it didn't do her much good, did it?' All she knew was that losing the coin seemed to her the final blow. She'd lost everything else: she couldn't lose that, too.

The lucky-piece had had little worth as silver and no real value to anyone but her. Nevertheless, despite the efforts of the museum authorities and their cleaning crew, the coin never turned up. And she finally learned to accept its loss, as well as to understand that she'd had some sort of collapse, and that maybe she had needed to express her grief in that way, in public. She also realized—many months after the event—what she must have forgotten at the time: that all those wonderful objects they'd been admiring had been the contents of a grave.

And, eventually, it seemed to her that the loss of the lucky-piece had been a sign; it had been intended to happen, so that she would have no doubt about the fact that there was a curse on her. She had married two men and both of them had died. She was certain that if she tried to find happiness again, the same thing would happen a third time.

She didn't say anything about the curse to the men who took her out, courted her, and wanted to marry her or just to sleep with her. She merely said no. When Don Parker asked her to be his wife, she said no for four months, said maybe for two, and in the end told him she would if he'd take her to Egypt for the honeymoon.

'You don't know how lucky you are,' her mother said to her one evening. 'The chances you've had. They aren't going to keep asking for ever, you know.'

From across the room Lily gave her newspaper a shake. Her mother sewed a button on the wristband of a blouse. They were waiting for Channel Two to show the play. That week it was a repeat of an old one—Ingrid Bergman and Trevor Howard in *Hedda Gabler*. Lily read in her paper about an African bird called a hoopoe that had been closed up inside a packing crate by mistake and been found at a German airport; the authorities had trapped it in an airline hangar and were just about to catch it with a net—in order to send it back to its own country—when it flew into one of the wire-strengthened glass panes up near the ceiling and broke its neck.

She turned the page. The paper crinkled noisily. She held it high, the way her father did at the breakfast table. She read about floods, fires, insurrections, massacres and robberies. She read about a chemist in Florida who believed that the building-blocks of ancient Egypt's pyramids could have been poured into moulds rather than quarried.

Everything she saw now reminded her of Egypt. It was like following the clues in a detective story. It was like being in love. Once you were aware of a thing, a name, or a word, you began to notice it everywhere. And once you had seen the truth of one cause of pain, you could recognize others. It was only after her breakdown in the museum that she understood how little her mother liked her—in fact, that her mother had never loved her. Perhaps she'd never loved Lily's sister, Ida, either. Ida was married and had two children; her husband had divorced her. And now Ida and her mother and the two children—both girls—were locked in an insatiable battle of wills that everyone except Lily would probably have called familial love. To Lily it seemed to be an unending struggle invented by her mother because otherwise life would have no meaning. Lily's father hadn't been enough of a challenge. And Lily herself had escaped into the protection of the two tragic events that had isolated her from other people.

'There's a man down in Florida,' Lily said, 'who thinks the pyramids were poured.'

'Oh?' her mother answered. She wasn't interested. She probably thought it meant they'd been poured through a funnel.

'It could be true, I guess. There's been a lot about Egypt recently. There was the woman who believed she was the priestess of Isis. I told you about her. She went to live there.'

'Just another nut. She's like that woman who says she's receiving spirit messages from Mozart and Beethoven, and then she plays those cheap little things.'

'That isn't a very good example. She's such a nut, she's made millions—on TV and everything. But in her case, you really wonder if she's a fraud.'

'Are you kidding? Of course she is. You think Beethoven—'

'You wonder if she's tricking people deliberately, instead of just deceiving herself. Now, this other woman—well, what you wonder about that, is: could there actually be some deep, biological, hereditary impulse directing her? Something we don't know about yet. See what I mean? I read an article a few years ago that talked all about people's sense of direction; it said they've found out that we've all got this magnetic centre in the brain.'

'Oh, boy.'

'Well, that's what it said.'

'What does Don say when you come out with these things?'

'He said yes. I told him I'd marry him if he took me to Egypt for the honeymoon, so he said he would. He's getting the tickets this week.'

Her mother's face came up from the buttons and thread. 'What are you talking about?'

'We're getting married after New Year's,' Lily announced. 'I just said so.' Her mother looked astounded. 'I told you,' Lily repeated. 'When I said we were going to Egypt.'

'I didn't take it in,' her mother said. She stared.

'Well, that's the end of the news.'

'That means . . . the wedding, the invitations, the catering. Why does it have to be so soon?'

'That's the best time to go.'

'Go? Where?'

'To Egypt,' Lily snapped. 'Are you feeling all right? We're planning a quiet wedding, in a registry office. His mother's going to take care of the reception at that house they've got down in the country.'

'You don't know how lucky you are,' her mother said again.

And you resent that, Lily thought.

'To have a boy like that.'

It doesn't matter how nice people are, if you don't love them. You love him more than I do. To me, he's unexciting. I've been at parties where girls were flirting with him, and I've said to myself: well, they just don't know how dull he is. I've even been in a shop where the tie salesman obviously thought he was the nearest thing to a classical statue he'd ever come across. But not for me.

'So good-looking.'

So boring, and actually sometimes irritating. I couldn't last out a lifetime of it. I should never have gotten myself into this mess. But it's nice to be admired like that; it's flattering. And I can't go on living this way.

Her mother said, 'I guess that extra-sensory, reincarnation stuff started back in the twenties, when they found the tomb.'

'No. It began before that. It was part of the Victorian interest in psychic phenomena. It all had to do with the disintegration of Christianity.'

'Is that right?'

'That's what they told us in school.'

Her mother went back to her sewing. They didn't talk again. They hardly ever talked, anyway. Ida had always taken the brunt of her mother's blame, inquisitiveness, disapproval, worry and desire to interfere. Lily used to think that that showed a difference in the quality of her mother's love, though recently it had occurred to her that maybe it was simply a matter of positioning: that she had been in the wrong place at the wrong time, so that the only mother-love she could remember had come from her father, her grandfather, one aunt, and a cousin who was of her grandmother's generation. She knew how lucky she was about that: some people didn't have anyone at all.

She and Don had the vaccinations they needed, got the passports ready, and rushed out invitations. Lily had no time to go to the museum any more, but she began to have the same dream at night, often several times in the week: she found herself standing in sunlight, under a blue sky, and looking up at a huge, almost endlessly high sandstone wall above her; it was a golden-tan colour and carved all over with strange writings like hieroglyphics. In the dream she stood and looked at the picture-writing and couldn't figure out what it said. She guessed that the lines on her lucky-piece had been the same—they'd meant something, but no one knew what. She liked the dream. Very few dreams in her life had ever repeated; the ones that did were all landscape-dreams: just special places she remembered, that were good spots for nice dreams to start from. She'd never had a repeating dream that was a puzzle, but it pleased her to be standing in the sun, under the hot sky that was so blue and far away, and examining the foreign shapes of an unknown language. In real life, outside the dream and outside her apartment, the air was bitter, there was deep snow on the ground and more blizzards had been forecast. She hoped that the airlines wouldn't have to ground their planes for long. She was impatient to leave.

Two days before they were due to fly, they read and heard about a sandstorm that had closed all the airports in Egypt. The storm was actually a giant cloud. The papers and television said it stretched from Cairo to Israel. Lily became agitated. She thought they might not be able to take off. Don patted her arm and smiled at her. Ever since she'd accepted his proposal he'd been smiling inanely; it made her so guilty and annoyed that she almost wanted to hurt him in some way. She could feel herself burning up, unable to get where she was going, or do what she wanted to do. She meant to reach Cairo even if she had to walk.

'These things usually blow themselves out within twenty-four hours,' he told her. 'We'll be OK.'

'I hope so,' she said. 'We wouldn't get any refunds. This is one of those things in the Act-of-God clause, isn't it?'

He sat up. 'Of course they'd refund us. They'd have to.'

'I bet they wouldn't. It isn't their fault there's a sandstorm.'

'Well, it isn't mine, either.'

'Tough,' she said.

He got on the phone about it and tried to force a response out of the travel company. No one would give him a straight answer because so far nothing had gone wrong; but they seemed to be saying that if things did go wrong, then it wouldn't be up to them to indemnify anybody. In a case of delay the agency might—as a gesture of goodwill—be able to offer a day in a different country, but not an extra day in Egypt once the plane got there. He hung up.

'Told you,' she said.

'I guess they could send us to the Riviera. That might be nice.'

'It's freezing there. This is the coldest January they've had in Europe since 1948 or something like that.'

He put his arm around her and said he didn't care where he was as long as he was with her.

She smiled back, feeling mean, unable to join him except by pretence. She knew already that she could never stay faithful to him. She'd been faithful to her first and second husbands, both when they were alive and after they'd died. But she could tell this was going to be different.

She honestly didn't love him, that was the trouble. And all at once she couldn't believe that she'd said yes, that she had the ring on her finger and was on her honeymoon. Why hadn't she just gone to bed with him and left it at that?

When they arrived, the air smelled hot and scorched, the sky was still laden with the aftermath of the storm: tiny particles that were invisible, but made it impossible to see clearly for very far. Lily didn't mind. She didn't mind anything, now that they were there.

Their hotel windows looked out on to two nineteenth-century villas set among palm trees. She was practically delirious with excitement. She didn't want to stay indoors and rest, or eat, or make love. She wanted to be outside, seeing everything.

He wasn't quite so enraptured. He hadn't realized it was going to be difficult to get his favourite brand of sourmash. And he said he thought the people were dark and dumpy.

'They're wonderful-looking,' she told him. 'Especially their faces. You aren't seeing them right. Why don't you like it here?'

'It doesn't seem all that romantic to me.'

'Wait till we get to the pyramids. We haven't even started.'

'I keep thinking what Ollie and Phil said about the

flies. Sandflies everywhere.'

'But that's later in the year, not now.'

'And how sick they were with that gut-rot they picked up.'

'You won't pick up anything if you dress right. That's what my book says: wear a heavy sweater.'

'Not in the sun.'

'All the time. Dress like the locals, and you'll be all right.'

They went through the markets, where he was disappointed once more, because they couldn't find any sheets that were a hundred per cent cotton. The only ones on sale were cotton mixed with polyester; the rest had been exported.

But he liked the fact that she had calmed down. She held his hand now as they walked, where back home she had always seemed to be slipping her hand out of his. She smiled at him, saying, 'I love it here.' He said, 'And I love you.'

They began the tours. Straight away they were put into the middle of the place where all the pictures came from: the sphinx, the pyramids, the vast space full of chairs for the *son-et-lumière* show. She was trembling with eagerness. She almost seemed to be a little crazed. He whispered, 'Are you OK?' and she nodded vigorously, while motioning him with her hand to be quiet.

Their guide was a thin, grey-haired Austrian woman who had a thick accent. The other members of the troop were all American. Lily could see, as the guide took them from one spot to the next, how most of the little parties of tourists had been grouped according to nationality, so that the guides wouldn't have to repeat the same information in different languages; she wondered why their guide, Lisabette, had been chosen for an English-speaking group. Lisabette was definitely good at her job and made her subject sound interesting, but some of the others said afterwards that they were having trouble understanding her. Don said he'd heard her stating that one of the ancient characters on their list had had to 'accept the inedible'.

There were two old people in their group: Selma and Orville Potts. Selma had something to do with a cultural club back home. Orville was retired from the bank. They enjoyed everything and asked a lot of questions. They had also read a lot, unlike Don or the couple called Darrell—John and Patsy—who had a nine-year-old child in tow. The child's name was Cindy; she was orange-haired, freckled, and had white eyelashes and pale eyes. Despite the weak eyes, she was a determined starer. Selma had tried to make friends with the child, failed, and commented to the mother, Patsy, that, 'I reckon it's real nice for little Cindy to get let off school to go on vacation with you.' Patsy said, 'Oh, Cindy's between schools at the moment.' At the same time, John said, 'They've closed her school for a couple of weeks to fix the pipes.'

'Well,' Selma said brightly, 'and are you having a good time?'

Cindy glared up at the old face peering down at her. Lily thought for a moment that the child was going to spit, but after a hesitation she muttered, 'Sure. It's OK.' Selma simpered. Cindy walked off, as if there were something a few feet away that she wanted to look at. Patsy and John seemed relieved.

Don and Lily moved ahead a few steps. They were followed by the other honeymoon couple, Ruth-Ann and Howie: she was tall, toothy and raucous; he was a tubby, high-voiced man. The idea of coming to Egypt had been his. Ruth-Ann didn't mind where she was, as long as they got away from the snow. She'd been thinking more of Hawaii, but this was fine. The only drawback was—

'No booze,' Howie complained.

'You're kidding,' Don said. 'You at some kind of Temperance hotel?'

'Oh, they've got a bar, but not like a real American bar. And no Jim Beam in the entire town, far as I can see.'

'You've got to bring it with you.'

'You're telling me,' Ruth-Ann said. 'We got so worried about rationing it for two whole weeks that we drank it all in the first three days. God, the hangovers we've had. It's like those stories about twenty people in a life-raft and only one canteen of water. What are you doing about it?'

'Well, we just got here,' Don said. 'I guess we'll measure it out in thimbles till the week is up, and then go on to wine. At least they still sell the stuff. I've heard they're thinking of making the whole country teetotal.'

Lily asked, 'Were you here for the sandstorm?'

'We sure were,' said Howie. 'We went to this hotel to meet a friend of Ruth-Ann's mother, and suddenly everything started to get dark, and then—Wham!—they pulled all the shutters down, and we were stuck inside.'

'It can kill you.' Ruth-Ann said.

Lisabette was looking at her watch. It was almost time to start the tour again. Ruth-Ann said, 'Doesn't she look like something off of one of those tombs?'

Lily turned her head. Lisabette, small and emaciated, was adjusting the shoulderstrap of her bag. She still had her walking stick clenched to her, which made the operation more cumbersome. But when she finally straightened up, she put a hand to the piece of cloth wound around her head from the front to below the tight, grey bun at the back; she changed the stick over to her right side, then stood still. And it was true—she resembled some sort of ancient court official bearing a ceremonial staff.

'And what's the story with the kid?' Ruth-Ann murmured. 'Jesus, what an argument for birth-control.'

Howie sniggered. Lisabette raised her stick a few inches and looked up. Her nine listeners grouped around her again.

At the next break, most people took photographs. Lily hadn't thought about bringing a camera. She'd said she'd rather have a good postcard. But Don had brought along a small, cheap, foolproof camera. He told her, 'What I want are pictures of you.' He took two of her, then they changed places. She clicked the button twice, closed the slide over the lens and handed the camera back. She looked past him at one of the pyramids. 'The eternal triangles,' she said, and laughed.

'They aren't triangles. They've got five surfaces and the base is a squ—'

'For heaven's sake. I know that.' She turned away abruptly. She'd been careful for so long about not showing her true thoughts, that she was afraid to let out even a little irritation. When the outburst came, she might just start screaming, 'Oh Christ, you're so boring,' for half an hour. She was turning herself inside-out to entertain him and knocking herself out in bed to please him, just because she didn't love him enough. And it wasn't his fault. He was a good, decent man; her mother was right. But it didn't make any difference. When she'd married before, both times, she'd been in love; she'd shared herself. Now she was only pretending. As a child, she'd loved playing make-believe. Now it wasn't for fun: now it was cheating.

She'd never be able to keep going. He'd be true to her—she was sure of him that way. And besides, he'd grown up in a family of ugly women who'd sat on him hard. The father had been the one with the looks, and had used them too, being unfaithful all over the place and finally leaving Don's mother. The mother and his two sisters looked like parodies of plain frontierswomen. They were also very concerned about all sorts of social, public and political issues that didn't interest Lily. They were the kind of women who would talk for hours about Vietnam at cocktail parties instead of getting married to somebody who'd die there. Don thought the way his sisters did, but he'd wanted to marry something different.

'What's wrong?' he said, hurrying up behind her.

'Nothing's wrong. I'm fine. She's going to start the spiel again, that's all.'

Lisabette raised her stick and brought it down on the ground. It made no noise, but the movement caught the attention of the rest of the group.

'You aren't mad at me, are you?' he said.

'Of course not.' She didn't take his arm or even look at him. She hated the way she was behaving.

'Egypt,' Lisabette said, 'is a marriage between the Nile and the desert.' She began to talk about the importance of the periods of inundation and about the special regard paid to the androgynous deity of the Nile, Hapy. Lily's glance moved across the other tourists; it stopped at nine-year-old Cindy, whose fixed stare was boring into the back of Orville Potts; she suddenly felt a horror of the child. Something was wrong with Cindy. The parents obviously knew it, too. The mother was a nervous wreck. And the father—it was hard to tell: he wouldn't have had to live with the worry, the way the mother would. He'd only have to hear about it in the evenings and say, 'Yes, dear.'

Don reached out for Lily. She jumped as he touched her. He was trying to slide his hand up under her folded arms. She let him, since other people were there. If they'd been alone, she'd have pushed him away and walked off. She tried to concentrate on what Lisabette was telling them. Lisabette actually looked less like a living monument to ancient Egypt than like someone who'd once been alive and was now mummified; 'Hathor,' she said. 'The cow-goddess.'

Cindy grinned. Her eyes began to rove to other people. Lily moved her head and looked somewhere else.

On their way back to the bus, Howie said, 'You know what really turned me on to all this stuff? It was that big show from

Tutankhamun's tomb.'

'Yes, I saw that, too,' Lily said.

Don pulled back on her hand. 'You did?' he asked. 'You never told me that.'

She shrugged. 'Me and about fifty million other people. Didn't you?'

'No, I missed it.'

'It was something,' Ruth-Ann told him. 'Talk about gorgeous —you can have all that Greek and Roman stuff.'

'Oh, I like that too,' Lily said. 'Only it never grabbed me the same way. It didn't have the philosophy.'

'The what?' Don asked.

'Haven't you been listening to what Lisabette's been saying?'

'Sure. All about the Nile god and the cow-goddess, and that kind of thing.'

'The first pyramids were built in steps, so the Pharaoh could go up there and into the sky and come back down again. After they died, they had their insides put into separate jars and they sailed across the sky in a boat. When they got to the other side, they went into the palace of death and answered all the questions about what kind of life they'd led. And if it was all right, then they started to sing chants to get back their stomach and brain and everything. The priest and the relatives of the dead person would help from back at the tomb. There were even little prayers for the heart, except that was the one thing they didn't take out. But I guess it had to be started up again. They called all the essential parts back into the body. And then the dead person would be whole in the other world.' She stopped, breathless.

'That isn't philosophy,' Don said.

'Hit him with your handbag,' Ruth-Ann told her.

'I'll hit him with the guidebook.'

'It still wouldn't make all that rigmarole philosophy.'

'Well, religion. I like the way they thought about people and animals and kings, and all the natural elements: all in one big lump.'

'They didn't think much of women, though,' Ruth-Ann said. 'You see these big statues of men, and way down near their feet is a tiny little figure of the wife—that's how unimportant they were.'

'No, it's just the opposite. The wife shouldn't be there at all. If you see one of those statues, it's really just supposed to represent the man, but he's specially asked to have his wife mentioned—for luck, or for sentiment. It's like nowadays, if a painter did a portrait of a businessman and the man insisted on taking a pose where he was holding a photograph of his wife. See? It's a gesture of affection. Nothing to do with despising anybody. They told us that in the museum lectures I went to.'

'There,' Howie said. 'They weren't so bad, after all.' He patted Ruth-Ann's behind lightly. She shooed him away. 'My wife's got this thing about victimized females.'

'My wife. He keeps saying it like that. I feel like I've lost my name all of a sudden.'

'I like the sound of it,' Howie said. 'I like trying it out. It's like driving around in a new car.'

Ruth-Ann climbed into the bus. 'Howie and his cars,' she said. Don followed. As Lisabette gave the driver the sign to start, he said to Lily, 'You should be hiring yourself out to one of these tourist outfits. I didn't realize you knew so much about the place.'

'I just went to all those lectures and I remember what they told us. You know how it is when you really like something.'

'Sure,' he said. 'I know how it is.' He put his arm around her again and she relaxed. She'd forgotten her irritation. She was glad to be with him and to have him holding her close to him.

That night she had a dream. It began like the dreams she'd had before leaving on the trip: she was standing under the blue sky, with the sun pouring down, and she was looking at the hieroglyphics on the wall. But this time as she scanned the carvings, they began to form a story. The picture-writings seemed to be changing shape, running into each other and reforming. And after that, they became images that moved across the wall. It was like watching a film. In the picture-story she saw her first husband. He was standing on the bank of the river. Two servants were wrapping him in a length of white cloth that left him naked from the waist up. The material had been wound up into a long skirt. Then they continued. He raised his arms a little, while the men circled him with the bolt of material; they wrapped him to the midpoint of his chest, made him fold his arms, and proceeded to wind the cloth so that the arms were taped down.

She started to feel anxious. The place she was watching from began to draw nearer to the riverbank but she was still too far away to reach him. The long, white banner went around his neck. She could see they were going to bandage his face, too. She tried to call out, to move forward, to do anything to stop the men: but nothing worked. They wrapped her husband up completely, as if he'd been inside a cocoon. Only his legs, under the skirt, were free to walk. She looked on miserably until the work was finished.

The two men turned her husband around and walked him forward—one on each side—to the river, where a boat was waiting for them. As she saw him going away from her like that—entirely enclosed in white, and because of that seeming to be blind all over—she grew frantic. She screamed, but no one paid any attention to her. Her husband stepped forward into the boat. The servants guided him to the central part of the vessel, where a curtain hung. He went behind the curtain and she couldn't see him any more.

She wanted to go with him. She tried to run forward. The boat floated off, carrying him away. She tried to call out again, and again no one took any notice. She woke up. Don was kissing her in the dark. They began to make love before she realized that they were in their hotel room and that it was in Egypt.

The tour took them to the Valley of the Kings and the Valley of the Queens, the Tombs of the Nobles. Lily held their guidebook in one hand and talked as fast as a racetrack reporter about deities, animals, heavenly bodies, cults. Strange-sounding names flowed easily from her. Sometimes it seemed that in her zeal she was getting everything mixed up—that she was repeating a lot of misinformation, jumbling thoughts, condensing centuries, forgetting who the real people were and who were the gods.

Ruth-Ann said that if she tried for ten years, she was never going to be able to pronounce the name. Hatshepsut. 'It's quite simple,' Lisabette told her. 'Hat-shep-sut. Repeat that.' Howie went off into a fit of giggles. Don said in a low voice that he found all of those names a little weird and couldn't remember any of them.

'That's because you didn't study them beforehand.' Lily said. 'If you don't know the names, how can you tell one god from another?'

'I can tell which one is supposed to be some animal. The cow-goddess and the jackal-god and the alligator-god.' He laughed.

'There's even a hippo-god, isn't there?'

'She's a goddess. She's a goddess of childbirth.'

'That figures. I guess they thought she had to be pregnant if she was so fat.'

'They didn't look at it that way.' She was beginning to get annoyed with him again. 'They thought that fat was a sign of abundance and good health.'

'And a high social standing.' Howie said. 'You can't stay overweight unless you keep up the food supply.'

'That's why the Nile was so important to them. They wouldn't have had any food without it.' The wind blew Lily's hair back, the sun was hot on her face. You could feel it was a genuine desert air. And now that all the dust had settled from the storm, the clarity—the light, was like nothing she'd ever imagined.

Ruth-Ann rejoined them. She said to Howie, 'Where's your sweater?'

'It's too hot.'

'You know what Lisabette told us: you'll pick up one of those bugs if you don't keep it on.'

'How could that help?'

'Well, she lives here. She ought to know.'

Lily teamed up with the Pottses, while Don got into a discussion with John Darrell. Orville and Selma—Selma especially—shared Lily's interest in Egyptian art and mythology. Ruth-Ann and Howie kept to themselves for a while, occasionally bursting into laughter. Once Lily heard Ruth Ann pronounce 'Hatshepsut' again in a loud voice.

Lisabette concentrated on her three best students. Behind her shoulder, off in the distance, Patsy Darrell talked earnestly to her daughter; she'd come all the way around the world to do something she could have done at home—unless, possibly, the child was demanding the discussion in order to make sure that her mother didn't have the time to enjoy herself.

'I wish we were going to Saqqarah too,' Selma said, 'but we just don't have the time.'

'Never mind,' Lisabette told her. 'You will be fully satisfied by Karnak, I can assure you.'

'And Abu Simbel,' Orville said. 'I'm very interested in how they moved it. That must have been a magnificent feat of engineering.'

'And of international cooperation. It shows what can be

accomplished when people work together in a spirit of peace.'

'And honesty,' Orville added. 'They tried to save Venice too. Pouring all that money into rescue funds—so now they've made about three people there into millionaires and the place is still sinking.'

'It's such a shame to have just one week,' Selma said. 'Well, a couple of days over a week.'

Lily agreed. She thought that she'd much rather go to Saqqarah than to Abu Simbel.

'It isn't on our tour,' Don told her. 'It's back where we came from.'

'We could change. Just go by ourselves one day.'

'If we took a whole day out, we might as well go to Alexandria.'

'But there isn't anything there.'

'There's a whole town.'

'There isn't anything old.'

'Lily, Abu Simbel's on the tour. You know it's going to be great. Haven't you seen the pictures?'

'Maybe we could stay on a little afterwards.'

'Our plane tickets—'

'Just a few days.'

'Maybe,' he said. 'We'll see.' He wouldn't say no outright. He didn't want to start an argument with her. She could see he was hoping that by the end of the week she'd have forgotten.

She walked back to the bus with Ruth-Ann, who told her, 'I was talking with Patsy back there. That's a real sick kid she's got. Jesus. She sets fire to things—I mean, like, houses. She isn't in school because—if you can believe it—she just burned it down. Honest to God. They keep moving all around. He's always got to find a new job, or get transferred.'

'Isn't there anything—doctors? Psychiatrists?'

'They're spending everything they've got on the doctors already. Her parents gave them the trip.'

Lily looked again at the Darrells, who were now standing near Lisabette. She wondered whether anything could help a child like Cindy. 'And they don't have any other children?' she said.

'I guess one was enough. A brat like that—I'm telling you: I'd sell her to the Arabs.'

'I don't know that the Arabs would like her any better than we do. I wonder if she was just born that way, or what?'

'You know what they say—some are born crazy, some become crazy and some have craziness thrust upon them. It all comes to the same thing in the long run.'

'Yes.'

'That's a real cute husband you've got there.'

Lily smiled. 'Want to trade?' she suggested.

Ruth-Ann shrieked with laughter. Howie came striding up to them, saying, 'What's she done—forgotten that name again?'

That night Lily had the dream again. She stood in front of the wall, stared at the writing, and it started to turn into pictures that told her a story. It was the same story, but this time the man being prepared for the ride in the boat was her second husband. She watched, as before: at the beginning surprised and touched to see him, and wanting to walk up and talk to him; then, when it was too late, desperate to be heard—trying to stop the others from taking him away. And she woke up again.

'What's wrong?' Don whispered.

'Dream,' she said.

'I thought you were in pain. You were making noises.'

'No, it's all right.'

'Maybe I'd better check everything, just to make sure. Does this feel all right?'

She put her arms around him and said that felt fine; and there, and that, too.

They went to Karnak. As Lily stepped into the ferry, she remembered her dream; but this was a modern craft, whereas the one in her dream had been like the ones on the frescoes, ancient.

They both loved Karnak. Don took a lot of photographs and Lily changed her mind about the camera. She became interested in trying to get pictures of the undersides of the overhead stone beams. The intensity of light around them was so great that it was thrown up, illuminating the colours on the surfaces high over their heads.

'This place is gigantic,' Don said. 'I've never seen anything like it.' He and Howie and Orville moved off together, leaving Ruth Ann with Lily. Selma wanted Lisabette to look at something in her guidebook. Patsy, as usual, stayed at a distance from the rest of them, keeping watch over Cindy. John started to walk towards the group of men.

'Those two,' Ruth-Ann said.

'Patsy and John?'

'Patsy and her child-arsonist.'

'Poor woman. What can she do? All of a sudden when they're five, you find out you've got a bum one—you can't take it back to the store. She's stuck with that, I guess.'

'And so's he.'

Lily looked at the men. She noticed that Howie was in his shirtsleeves. All the others had on sweaters or jackets. John was gesturing up at the columns. 'I don't know,' she said. 'He might walk out any time now. What do you think?'

'Oh? I guess it's possible. She can't have much time for him if she's got her hands full like that. Did you hear what happened when we were getting into the boat? Cindy said something to Selma.'

'What?'

'I didn't hear. But I've never seen such a reaction. Selma and Orville, too. Then the two of them started to say something to Patsy and she blew up. John tried to calm them all down. And that horrible, rat-faced kid just looked smug.'

'I wonder what it was.'

'Something mean, I bet.'

Later in the day, Selma came and sat next to Lily. They talked about the ruins. Lily admired the other guidebook, which was larger than her own, and full of coloured pictures. 'I'll give it to you when we leave,' Selma said. 'I bought two, because I knew the one I'd be carrying around was bound to get all tattered. Just tell me the name of your hotel in Cairo and I'll drop it off there. If you don't mind it in this condition.'

'I'd love it,' Lily told her.

'I'll tell you something, though: a lot of the information in it is different than we're being told. Sometimes the change is just very slight, and sometimes it really contradicts what the book says. Makes you wonder.'

'How?'

'Well, you know those two statues of the king on his throne? Here's the picture.'

'The husband and wife in their chairs. Sure. The ones that had the singing heads till the nineteenth-century restorers filled them up.'

'That's just it. That's so far from what the guidebook says that you could suspect she just made it up. First of all, both of those figures are the king: Amenhotep III. Then, it says here that one of them, the north one, was so badly damaged in the earthquake of 27BC that part of it cracked and fell. And that was the one that became famous for singing—because the sun used to heat up the cracks, or the wind got into it or something. But all that was way, way back. It was written about by the Romans. And the Romans restored the statue two hundred years or so after it was broken. So, Lisabette's story about how they were built that way in the first place—it just doesn't make sense. That's what she said, wasn't it—that they were part of the sunworship?'

They were, Lisabette had told them, embodiments of conjugal love; although the seated figures represented a great king and queen, who were the guardians of their people, they were also just like anyone else: a husband and wife. They too obeyed natural laws and worshipped the gods. When the sun-god reached the horizon in his boat and prepared to sail across the sky, they would welcome him, praising him with their voices.

'They sang,' Lisabette had said. 'They were constructed as musical instruments. A work of genius.' Their heads were hollow, carved inside with a system of intricately fluted trails and passageways. When the morning sun struck their foreheads, its heat activated the air within and made the stone sing—not singing according to a melody, but long, sustained notes that changed tone as the light grew stronger. In the last century, in order to preserve them, the statues were repaired, the heads filled with cement. And now they no longer made a sound. The two giant figures stared straight ahead, waiting for the sun, silent.

'Did you ask her about it?' Lily said.

'I told her my guidebook talked about reconstruction by Septimus Severus, and all that.'

'And?'

'And she said that a lot of these books used different sources.'

'That's probably true, isn't it?'

'But not that true. Not so you'd make a mistake like that. And anyway, you can certainly see they're both men—not a married couple.'

'I think I like her version better.'

'No, dear. Not if it's fictitious. The truth is always better.'

'If you can tell what it is.'

Selma sighed and said how strange it was to be in a modern country whose whole appearance was still dominated by the culture of its past. Cairo was a modern city, to be sure, but so much of Egypt seemed the same as in ancient days. Yet it wasn't the same, naturally. The only country left where you could say the past and present were still the same was India: she'd always wanted to go there, but Orville had this ridiculous feeling against it. He wouldn't go. 'All the methods of making things, the craftsmanship, is still the same there,' she said. 'They still wear the same clothes. But above all, what makes the real difference is that they still believe in and practise the same religions. And that's all gone here.'

Lily said yes, and thought again about the two statues. She looked up into the huge gatework of sunlit, painted stone, down at the canyoned pathways in shadow. 'You can still feel it, though,' she said. 'Especially in a place like this.'

'Yes, indeed. It's like the travel people said: you can almost imagine the gods walking here.'

Lily remembered the Englishwoman who lived in the house that was supposed to be dedicated to Isis. 'There's something I've got to ask Lisabette before I forget,' she said.

'Make sure you check it in a book afterwards. Unless it's something about herself. Now that's a tragic story. She told me her father was killed in the First World War, her first husband and her brother died in the Second World War and her son was killed in the June War.'

'I guess that's one of the things that last longer than religions,' Lily said. 'People killing each other.'

'I've never heard of one person having so much bad luck. Orville said how did I know she hadn't just concocted the story about her sad personal history—that's what he said: concocted. But I can't believe it. No. You can see she's had sorrows in her life. Maybe they've driven her to—you know, sort of invent things. Well, not really. They wouldn't hire somebody who did that. I expect she exaggerates a little, that's all.'

Lily got to her feet. She said the thing about bad luck was that no matter what kind it was, a little went a long way.

She found Lisabette standing in the shade, not far from Orville and Ruth-Ann. 'I wonder if you can help me,' she began.

Lisabette moved her head stiffly. 'Yes?'

'I've heard about an Englishwoman who lives in Egypt—I think maybe in Cairo—in a house she thinks used to belong to a priestess of Isis. I wondered if you'd know anything about her. Or even about the house.'

'No, I've never heard of this.'

'It was on the radio. She did excavation work on the house and found the garden, and that kind of thing.'

'I don't know of such a person.'

'Could you tell me where I could go to find out?'

'Possibly the embassy?'

Of *course*, Lily thought. She should have figured that out herself. The woman had been working with the British archaeological teams: the embassy would know how to get in touch with them.

'Isis?' Ruth-Ann said behind her shoulder. 'She's the one that cut off her husband's prick and grew him again from it. That's some trick, huh?'

'It's one of the great pagan myths,' Lisabette said curtly.

'And how.'

'Containing profound observations on the nature of death, sacrifice and regeneration, life after death, and the power of love.'

'And bereavement,' Lily said. Lisabette's eyes met hers. The old woman's face lost its lecture-look; it lapsed into a softer expression that made her appear even older and more exhausted. It reminded Lily of the way Don's small, ugly, buck-toothed mother had looked when she'd wished them both a happy marriage and added that her own wedding day had been the happiest day of her life.

'Just so,' Lisabette said.

On the way back from Karnak there was a quarrel among the other passengers, or perhaps a continuation of whatever had already started between the Darrells and the Pottses. In the stark, offended silence that followed, Howie's voice could be heard announcing that he didn't feel well; he was sure it was the restaurant they'd been to the night before: the lousy, contaminated food they served you in this country. Lisabette threw a lizardlike look over the back of her seat and told him without sympathy that he shouldn't have taken off his pullover while the wind was still blowing so strongly—it was no wonder he'd caught something.

'I really do feel pretty bad,' he said a few more times. By the end of the ride he looked almost green in the face. As they left the ferry, Ruth-Ann told Lily and Don that if Howie had to change their travel arrangements, this would be goodbye, but she wanted to say it had been nice to meet them. Everyone offered to help. Ruth-Ann shook her head. She'd ask the hotel, she said; they'd find her a doctor if Howie needed one.

Late that evening Lily said that she wanted to go to Abydos and Saqqarah. And they should be staying on the other bank anyway, in Luxor.

'I guess we'll have to leave them for another trip,' Don told her.

'When do you think we'd ever get back? It's such a long way from home. Doesn't it make more sense to go now, when we're here?'

'We just don't have the time, honey.'

'And at Luxor: the temple. We're right here on the spot.'

'We can't. We—'

She stood up and delivered a tirade about the importance of beauty to the development of a culture. He didn't know what she was talking about, and he didn't think she understood half of what she was saying, but in the end he agreed to change all their plans, so that they'd be able to get back to Luxor. Abydos was out, he declared. If she got Luxor, he'd be allowed Abu Simbel.

She then wanted to start telephoning the British embassy to find out where to get hold of the priestess of Isis. 'Later,' he told her: after they got back from the next day's sightseeing.

On their way out in the morning, the man at the desk handed Lily a package—a book wrapped in a piece of hotel writing paper that was held tightly by a rubber band. On the paper was a short note from Selma, saying that they too had changed plans and were going to visit a shrine somewhere out in the desert. The book was the guidebook she'd promised to let Lily keep.

Lily's pleasure in the book was the only sign that she still considered the world worth noticing. She read while standing, sitting or walking. She read the book all through the journey to Abu Simbel and parts of the actual tour. She was in such a bad mood that Don was almost frightened for her.

They had said goodbye to Lisabette and the Darrells. Now they were with a larger group, of sixteen people: Americans,

Australians, Britons and South Africans. Their guide was a young man named Franz, who came from a part of Switzerland that was mainly German-speaking. His accent was a good deal better than Lisabette's, but he had a rapid-fire delivery that left many of his hearers mystified, especially when he reeled off lists of ancient deities or rulers.

During one of the breaks when they were supposed to wander around by themselves or take their photographs, Don sat down next to Lily. He tried to coax the guidebook from her. She dodged away. He dropped something into her lap. 'What's that?' she asked.

'A lucky stone. It's got a ring around it.'

'Stones don't last long in the desert,' she said. 'They all turn to sand.' She picked the stone out of her lap and threw it away. It bounced off the side of a larger stone and fell into a heap of pebbles. The bright light made it indistinguishable from the other shapes around the place where it had landed.

'I ought to hit you,' he said.

'Go ahead. Go right ahead.'

'You won't take anything from me, will you?'

It was true. She wanted to scream with rage, or get up and start running, or hit him first. She'd never treated anyone so badly. She was ashamed of herself, but she couldn't quit. She even wondered if she'd married him because—believing that there was a curse on her—she'd been willing to let him die. She also realized that although she couldn't accept his love, she wanted him to keep on caring. Her resistance to him was like a lack of faith, an atheistic impulse; if there were suddenly nothing against which to fight, she might be completely lost.

'Christ, what I'd like to do to you,' he said.

She thought he really was going to hit her, but he turned and stormed off in the direction of the river. He stood looking out at the water, with his back to her.

She felt tears of stubborness and remorse rising in her eyes. Her throat ached. But she was also proud at the way he was standing up to her. If he could hold out like that, he might win her over and exorcize the curse. Or maybe it had nothing to do with him; it might be more important that she should talk with the priestess of Isis.

That night, as they were getting ready to go to bed, Lily said, 'I wonder where the others are now—if Howie's all right.'

'He'll be fine. People don't die of a stomach ache.'

'I wonder what the quarrel was about. The one between Selma and that horrible little girl.'

'What are any quarrels about?'

'Well, I guess each one's different.'

'Your mother warned me about you, you know.'

'Great,' she said. 'That's the kind of mother to have. OK, what did she say?'

'Oh, never mind.'

'You can't leave it there. If you don't tell me, I'll call her up long distance, right this minute.' Her mother; suddenly it was like having another person along on the honeymoon. Her mother envied her the two widowings. They were even more romantic and dramatic than Ida's divorce.

'She said you thought there was a curse on you.'

'Oh?'

'Well?'

'Well, I sometimes feel like that, yes.'

She got into the bed, taking the guidebook with her, but when he reached towards the lamp, she put the book on the night-table. He turned out the light. She waited in the darkness for him to go on with the conversation.

At last he said, 'You never talk about the others.'

'What others?' she whispered.

'The other two.'

She didn't answer.

'Your husbands,' he said.

There was a silence again, longer than the first one.

'What for?' she asked.

'It's something important in your life.'

She rolled to the side, to get near the edge of the bed. He put out his arm and pulled her back.

'It was a long time ago,' she said. 'They both were. I don't remember. And I don't want to. When people die, you get over it by moving forward.'

'And I guess some people never get over it.'

'I don't know.'

I don't know what other people remember, she thought, *but I remember everything—every room we were in, every place. Love does that; everything new, fun, easy to remember. It was the only time I felt I was living. I just can't talk about it, that's all.*

'If I died, you'd move forward?' he asked.

'That's a dumb thing to say. Besides, you had girlfriends before you met me.'

'I was never married.'

'It amounts to the same.'

'No, it doesn't. It's completely different.'

'I don't think so.'

He said, 'I used to have this idea that you were like one of those maidens in the fairytales, who had to have the spell broken.'

'And what do you think now?'

'I think maybe you don't love me very much.'

Here it comes, she thought. But no, he wouldn't really believe that. He'd just want her to say: *Of course I do.*

She said, 'You don't have any reason to think that. It's because I get into bad moods, isn't it?'

He stretched and shifted his weight, moving his arm an inch higher under her back. He said, 'Well, not exactly.'

His voice sounded faint and sad. Suddenly she was weeping uncontrollably. Of course I love you,' she sobbed. 'Of course I do.'

Their time was running out. They could go back to Cairo and enjoy the town for a day, or they could see one other site and hurry back. Lily held the guidebook tightly and said that she absolutely needed to see Abydos and Edfu and Bubastis and Saqqarah: and after that, they had to have a few days extra in Cairo so that she could find the priestess of Isis.

'Say all that again,' he told her.

'The sanctuary of Abydos and the sacred lake of—'

'No: the priestess part.'

She told him about the Englishwoman who lived in Cairo and believed herself to be the incarnation of an ancient priestess of Isis.

He said, 'Listen, you really want to see some old crone suffering from delusions? Didn't you notice, we've got plenty of those at home?'

'We don't have the temple of Isis or the house of the priestess.'

'Well, we can ask somebody, I guess.'

'I asked Lisabette. She hadn't heard of her.'

'That settles it.'

'She said I should try the embassy.'

'Oh?'

'I did. When you went to see about the tickets. But I don't think I got hold of the right people. Nobody knew. They gave me a lot of names of different people and they turned out to be away on trips. But all I need to do is wait. Lots of people must have heard of her if she was on the radio.'

'I'm not going to spend all the time we've got left, trying to track down some old woman. She's probably died by now, anyway. Why do you want to see her?'

Lily didn't know. There wasn't any reason, just the desire. She tried to think of something to tell him.

'I want to see her because she, um, lives in that place.'

'Where?'

'Well, it's an ancient Egyptian house, with a garden in it. And anyhow, she's the priestess of Isis. That's why I want to see her.'

'We just don't have the time.'

'I want to stay,' she said. 'To stay here longer.'

'Of course you can't stay. I've got to get back to the office.'

Now he'd be saying to himself: who's footing the bill for all this? *Well*, she thought, *he offered*. She took a firm grip on the guidebook and looked up into his eyes. 'You can get back to the office,' she suggested. 'And I could stay on here for a while.'

'No.' He said it so loudly that a cluster of other guests in the hotel lobby turned around to look.

'Just a few—'

'Don't push your luck, Lil,' he said. He stared at her so fiercely that he looked almost frightening, but also exciting. She leaned forward and put her hands on his arms, turned her face upward.

He grabbed hold of both her hands and began to pull her across the floor to the elevator. A group of people were standing in front of the doors. He started to drag her around the corner and up the stairs. 'What's wrong?' she said. 'Where are we going?'

'Upstairs,' he answered.

'What for?'

'It's the only place I can get any sense out of you.'

She tried to kiss him on the neck and sat down in the middle of the staircase. He piled on top of her, laughing. A woman's voice from below them called, 'Hello, hello, you two. Did you drop this?'

They turned their heads. Down at the bottom of the staircase stood a woman who was smiling broadly. She was holding the guidebook in her right hand and waving it back and forth.

By mid-morning they were on their way to the ruins. Don seemed to be dozing behind his sunglasses. Lily sat quietly, the book held primly in her lap as if it might have been a prayerbook. Their new touring companions included two burly, grey-haired men—one Dutch and the other Irish—who were travelling together; an old Canadian woman on her own; and an American family of five: father, mother, two well-developed teenaged daughters and a son of about twelve. The son was interested in the height, width, and exact measurements of all the parts of every building they saw. He told Franz, the group in general and then Don in particular, that he'd worked out a theory about pyramidology that explained just everything you'd ever want to know. His two sisters had their eyes on Franz; the younger one, called Tina, was dressed—foolishly, so her mother told her—in a white T-shirt and red shorts. 'They aren't shorts,' the girl objected. 'They're hot pants.' The older sister, Lucille, was more conservative; she had on a pair of long trousers and a matching jacket.

Lily moved away from Don early in the tour. She told him that she wanted to read up on a few things. She sat down and looked out into the distance. Behind her people were taking photographs. The older American girl came up to where Lily was sitting; her face still covered by the camera, she said, 'This is just great. Isn't it great?'

'Mm.'

'The lure of the ancient world—I was always nuts about that kind of thing.' She said that what had really convinced her parents had been her brother's insistence on his theory; he was going to make it his school topic for the coming term. She too had been thinking about Egypt for years, having been extremely impressed by an opera she'd once been taken to: Egyptian dress and scenery had figured prominently among the memorable aspects of the production. The name of the composer escaped her at the moment though she hummed a little of her favourite tune from it, which she said was called 'The Nuns' Chorus From Aida'.

Lily said that was nice; her own introduction had been through the museums.

Yes, the girl told her, they were OK, but you had to get outdoors to see what was left of the buildings: she liked the temples and things best. She liked, she said, as she moved away with the camera, the way they'd built everything on such a big scale.

Lily closed the guidebook. She felt that she wanted to stay where she was for a long time, just sitting and doing nothing. She remembered a day at home, a few years back, when she'd gone for a walk in the park. It had been an afternoon in the fall—the distances full of hazy sunshine, the leaves gold, brown, coppery. Two young mothers had been sitting on a bench in front of hers. Each of them had a baby carriage nearby. Sometimes nurses and babysitters came to the park but these girls, she'd felt sure, were the real mothers. And something about the scene, or the season, or maybe just the weather, had made her think what a waste it was that people had only one life, that the choices were always so few, that you couldn't lead several lives all at once or one after the other.

But now it seemed to her that what remained of the past was just as much where she belonged as was the present. In fact, you couldn't help living more lives than one. Thought took you into other times. And there was always going to be so much to see and learn: you could never reach the end of it.

Don came and sat down beside her. 'That kid's obsessed,' he said. 'Another one.'

'Numerology?'

'Everything except spacemen. He thinks they had astronomical observatories and balloon flight and just about everything.'

'I think the real facts are more interesting.'

'The reincarnation of priestesses—that kind of thing?'

'Like the fact that all the lower-class people had broken teeth from eating stone-ground bread. Everyone I've ever met who's had a thing about health-food bread has chipped a tooth at least once.'

'Is that in the guidebook?'

'That was in the lectures. They also told us: the men who worked in the mummifying business were divided into different classes, too. And the ones that handled all the poor people's trade considered it a privilege of the profession that they should be allowed to have sexual intercourse with the corpses.'

'You're kidding.'

'Apparently it's a well-known thing.'

'Of course they were completely dominated by the idea of death.'

'Most cultures are. Don't you like all this?'

'Sure. It's terrific. But I'm going to be glad to get back.'

'Snow and ice?'

'This is fine for a time. But you know what it is.'

'It's history.'

'It's a graveyard.'

'So's most of history. They lived a long time ago. And all that's left is what survived. This is here because it's stone. The houses where they lived were made out of wood and mud and plastery stuff. So, they're all gone. The tombs and temples—the religious side of life—they were built to last. It's not so different nowadays; most old churches are made out of stone.'

'Uh-huh.' He took the guidebook out of her lap and flipped through the pages. 'Franz says he's going on to Abydos with the group.'

'Good. That's one of the most sacred places.'

'It's too far away. It's got to be someplace nearer. We'd just have time to make Saqqarah, if you wanted to. I'd rather go straight back to Cairo and not have to rush so much.'

'OK,' she said. 'Saqqarah.' She breathed in and stood up, saying, 'It's so clean here. The light's so wonderful. And the air—you can understand why some people decide they want to go off into the desert and never come back.'

'Would you ever do that?'

'Not without a guidebook,' she said, taking it back from him.

They strolled towards the others. Don said, 'This is another funny bunch, though. We seem to end up with the oddballs.'

'The family's nice.'

'But a little weird.'

'I don't think so.'

'That boy?'

'That's just getting carried away by his ideas. And I liked the older girl. She loves everything about the place.'

'I think maybe her sister's the one that's going to get Franz.'

'Oh, no. If anybody's going to get Franz, I'd put my money on the mother.'

He laughed and took her free hand. They were in tune for the rest of the day: all during the trip back to their hotel, through the evening and night, for the next leg of their journey and on their arrival at the new hotel.

In the morning they started to quarrel. It happened so fast that before either one of them knew what had led to it, he was hissing at her, 'The minute you get out of bed, it's all gone. All I get is that silence. It's like you can't stand to be near me. You don't even look at me. You'd be that way in bed with anybody, wouldn't you?'

She wouldn't answer back. She just continued to put her clothes on, trying to keep out of his way in the small room.

He came up to her and turned her around. 'Tell me about them,' he said. 'Tell me about the other two.'

She plunged away, furious, and said, 'No.' If it was going to turn into a real fight, she was all set to pick up an ashtray or a lamp and throw it at him. She went on getting dressed.

They didn't speak to each other on the way to the site, or when they got there. They sat or stood side by side, enraged and indignant. No one noticed anything wrong because, for the first time, they were in a large group of tourists—nearly twenty people—who didn't seem to have been brought together before. There was no chatting among the crowd. The guide was an Egyptian woman of studious appearance, who might have been a teacher or lecturer on the off-season. Her voice was rather soft, which meant that her audience had to crowd up close, to be sure not to miss anything.

They saw the frescoes, heard about the cult of the bull, passed by one of the most famous pyramids. The ancient Egyptians, they were reminded, called every pyramid 'the house of eternity'; the king's statue would be seated inside, looking out on to the world through peepholes. If the statue was there, the king was there. The work of art had a purpose beyond mere decoration: it was a stand-in.

They walked in the direction of a huge mound of building rubble that looked like another, unfinished, pyramid. Lily had forgotten which places were ancient and which had been left by the excavators. Her strength began to recede as they neared the base of the structure. She thought how pointless her whole life had turned out to be. It was no use trying to fight bad luck; some people just had that deal from the deck. To consider marriage for a third time had been foolish beyond comprehending. She didn't feel that she could ever possibly get to know him, or that she'd want to; and she was suddenly so tired that she was ready to lie down in the sand and stay there.

He grabbed her hand. She looked back over her shoulder for the others; they'd gone somewhere else with the guide.

He started to tug her along the ground, yanking her hard by the arm. And he began to yell abuse at her. He was dragging her towards the pyramid-like hill—she couldn't imagine why. He said that she could damn well pull herself together and take an interest in their future and be a little nice to him sometimes and show that she appreciated it when he gave in to her—because that was what he was always having to do, all the time, and never getting any thanks for it, either.

When they came to the beginnings of stonework, he started to climb up, hauling her along with him. She had to follow. If she tried to sit down, she'd be cut and bruised. She called out for him to wait, but he wouldn't. 'You're hurting my arm,' she said. He climbed higher, taking her with him, until she thought her arm was going to twist out of her shoulder. And all at once he stopped, sweating, and faced her. He let go of her hand.

'You know what else your mother said?' he told her. 'She said maybe it was a blessing in disguise that your first two husbands died so soon, before they found out what a spoiled bitch you really are.'

She stepped back. She felt the sun shining on the top of her head, but she was cold. It was like the time when she'd lost her lucky-piece: the same terror. A few voices from below came up to her.

'Oh Jesus, Lily,' he said. 'I'm sorry.'

She took another step back. She still wasn't able to answer, though her eyes hadn't moved from his face.

'Look out,' he said suddenly.

She turned, knew that she was slipping and saw her foot skidding over the edge. She started to fall. He grabbed her by her skirt and slid past her. They tumbled downward for several yards and stopped a few feet apart. More voices came up from below them, shouting loudly.

Lily picked herself up carefully. Her knees and shins were

scraped, her left elbow and forearm were bleeding. Otherwise, she seemed to be all right. She crawled over to where Don had fallen. He was lying on his back, looking up at her. She sat down beside him.

He said, 'I didn't mean it.'

'It doesn't matter.'

'Are you all right?' he asked.

'I'm fine.'

He said, 'I can't move.'

She called down to the people standing below. She screamed for them to bring help. They said that they were coming; several of them started up the rock surface.

She touched his cheek with her fingers and took his hand in hers. He smiled a little. Soon after that, he died. She was still holding his hand, so she felt and saw the moment when it happened. She hadn't been able to be with her first two husbands when they'd died.

At the airport both mothers were waiting: hers and his. Her mother began to cry straight away, loudly announcing, 'Oh, poor Lily—I thought this time it had to be all right. But it wasn't meant to be.'

Lily gave her a brief hug, pushed her aside and walked on, to where Don's mother stood. Lily embraced her, finding it strange that the one who was the mother should be the small one. 'I was with him,' she said. 'He wasn't in pain at all.' Her mother-in-law nodded. Lily said, 'It was so quick. He asked me if I was all right. He was thinking of me, not of himself. And then he just went.' She started to cry. Her mother-in-law too, wept. And behind her, her mother sobbed noisily, still saying that she'd been so sure everything was going to work out this time; that she couldn't believe *it had happened again*.

The funeral was down in the country at his mother's place, where they'd had the wedding reception. As Lily walked out of the front door and over to the car, she remembered the other time: when she'd emerged with Don from the identical doorway, to get into the car that was to carry them to their future as husband and wife.

She asked her mother-in-law if she could stay with her for a while. The two of them took walks together in the snow. Lily began to see more of her sisters-in-law; it was a large family and a lot of them lived near enough to turn up for Sunday lunch.

She kept expecting to have the same dream about Don that she'd had about her other husbands: to see him being dressed in the winding-sheet and taken away in the boat. But she had stopped having dreams.

She was pregnant. She told her mother-in-law first. And she was thankful that her sister was planning to remarry near the end of September, so that her mother's attention would be deflected from her at the crucial time.

The child was born: a boy. She couldn't sleep. She couldn't concentrate on anything else. She forgot the pain and regret she had felt about not having been able to love her husband. The business of being a mother was harder than anyone had led her to believe. It was exhausting to the limit of her patience, and at times so far beyond that she didn't think she was going to get through it.

One day she looked at her son as he stood aside from a group of children he was playing with. He reminded her suddenly of a photograph she had that showed her grandfather at the same age; and also, she realised, of Don: the resemblance was so startling that it was almost like a reincarnation.

She confessed to her mother-in-law that she thought she hadn't loved Don enough—not as much as he'd deserved.

Her mother-in-law said, 'That's the way people always feel. But I know you loved him. Anyone can see what a good mother you are.'

She didn't think she was such a good mother. She thought she was slapdash and nervous, constantly fussing. The only thing she was sure of was that she loved her son. And she was delighted and extremely surprised that her father, who had always seemed hopeless as far as family matters were concerned, had fallen in love with the child: he'd turn up on the doorstep to take the boy for a ride, or to play outdoors somewhere, or to go on a trip to the zoo; they had private jokes together and stories that they told each other. She began to be fond of her father again, as she had been when she was young.

One day a reporter wanted to interview her. Her statements were to be included in a programme about war widows, which was going to be broadcast as a companion-piece to a documentary that dealt with veterans. The compilers planned to talk to children, too. They seemed irritated that Lily hadn't had any children by her first two husbands.

She told them that she was happy. It hadn't been easy, she said, and it had taken a long time, but she'd had a lot of help. She praised her mother-in-law.

Even if she'd been in the mood for it, she hardly had the time to dream. But she often remembered Egypt. One picture especially came back to her from the trip: of two immense statues made of stone—each out of a single piece—that were represented seated on chairs; the figures were sitting out in the middle of nowhere, side by side and both looking in the same direction: east, towards the sunrise. Sometimes she thought about them.

JAMAICA KINCAID

What I Have Been Doing Lately

What I have been doing lately: I was lying in bed and the doorbell rang. I ran downstairs. Quick. I opened the door. There was no one there. I stepped outside. Either it was drizzling or there was a lot of dust in the air and the dust was damp. I stuck out my tongue and the drizzle or the damp dust tasted like government school ink. I looked north. I looked south. I decided to start walking north. While walking north, I noticed that I was barefoot. While walking north, I looked up and saw the planet Venus. I said, 'It must be almost morning.' I saw a monkey in a tree. The tree had no leaves. I said, 'Ah, a monkey. Just look at that. A monkey.' I walked for I don't know how long before I came up to a big body of water. I wanted to get across it but I couldn't swim. I wanted to get across it but it would take me years to build a boat. I wanted to get across it but it would take me I didn't know how long to build a bridge. Years passed and then one day, feeling like it, I got into my boat and rowed across. When I got to the other side, it was noon and my shadow was small and fell beneath me. I set out on a path that stretched out straight ahead. I passed a house, and a dog was sitting on the verandah but it looked the other way when it saw me coming. I passed a boy tossing a ball in the air but the boy looked the other way when he saw me coming. I walked and I walked but I couldn't tell if I walked a long time because my feet didn't feel as if they would drop off. I turned around to see what I had left behind me but nothing was familiar. Instead of the straight path, I saw hills. Instead of the boy with his ball, I saw tall flowering trees. I looked up and the sky was without clouds and seemed near, as if it were the ceiling in my house and, if I stood on a chair, I could touch it with the tips of my fingers. I turned around and looked ahead of me again. A deep hole had opened up before me. I looked in. The hole was deep and dark and I couldn't see the bottom. I thought, What's down there?, so on purpose I fell in. I fell and I fell, over and over, as if I were an old suitcase. On the sides of the deep hole I could see things written, but perhaps it was in a foreign language because I couldn't read them.

Still I fell, for I don't know how long. As I fell I began to see that I didn't like the way falling made me feel. Falling made me feel sick and I missed all the people I had loved. I said, I don't want to fall anymore, and I reversed myself. I was standing again on the edge of the deep hole. I looked at the deep hole and I said, You can close up now, and it did. I walked some more without knowing distance. I only knew that I passed through days and nights, I only knew that I passed through rain and shine, light and darkness. I was never thirsty and I felt no pain. Looking at the horizon, I made a joke for myself: I said, 'The earth has thin lips,' and I laughed.

Looking at the horizon again, I saw a lone figure coming toward me, but I wasn't frightened because I was sure it was my mother. As I got closer to the figure, I could see that it wasn't my mother, but still I wasn't frightened because I could see that it was a woman.

When this woman got closer to me, she looked at me hard and then she threw up her hands. She must have seen me somewhere before because she said, 'It's you. Just look at that. It's you. And just what have you been doing lately?'

I could have said, 'I have been praying not to grow any taller.'

I could have said, 'I have been listening carefully to my mother's words, so as to make a good imitation of a dutiful daughter.'

I could have said, 'A pack of dogs, tired from chasing each other all over town, slept in the moonlight.'

Instead, I said, What I have been doing lately: I was lying in bed on my back, my hands drawn up, my fingers interlaced lightly at the nape of my neck. Someone rang the doorbell. I went downstairs and opened the door but there was no one there. I stepped outside. Either it was drizzling or there was a lot of dust in the air and the dust was damp. I stuck out my tongue and the drizzle or the damp dust tasted like government school ink. I looked north and I looked south. I started walking north. While walking north, I wanted to move fast, so I removed the shoes from my feet. While walking north, I looked up and saw the planet Venus and I said, 'If the sun went out, it would be eight minutes before I would know it.' I saw a monkey sitting in a tree that had no leaves and I said, 'A monkey. Just look at that. A monkey.' I picked up a stone and threw it at the monkey. The monkey, seeing the stone, quickly moved out of its way. Three times I threw a stone at the monkey and three times it moved away. The fourth time I threw the stone, the monkey caught it and threw it back at me. The stone struck me on my forehead over my right eye, making a deep gash. The gash healed immediately but now the skin on my forehead felt false to me. I walked for I don't know how long before I came to a big body of water. I wanted to get across, so when the boat came I paid my fare. When I got to the other side, I saw a lot of people sitting on the beach and they were having a picnic. They were the most beautiful people I had ever seen. Everything about them was black and shiny. Their skin was black and shiny. Their shoes were black and shiny. Their hair was black and shiny. The clothes they wore were black and shiny. I could hear them laughing and chatting and I said, I would like to be with these people, so I started to walk toward them, but when I got up close to them I saw that they weren't at a picnic and they weren't beautiful and they weren't chatting and laughing. All around me was black mud and the people all looked as if they had been made up out of the black mud. I looked up and saw that the sky seemed far away and nothing I could stand on would make me able to touch it with my fingertips. I thought, If only I could get out of this, so I started to walk. I must have walked for a long time because my feet hurt and felt as if they would drop off. I thought, If only just around the bend I would see my house and inside my house I would find my bed, freshly made at that, and in the kitchen I would find my mother or anyone else that I loved making me a custard. I thought, If only it was a Sunday and I was sitting in a church and I had just heard someone sing a psalm. I felt very sad so I sat down. I felt so sad that I rested my head on my own knees and smoothed my own head. I felt so sad I couldn't imagine feeling any other way again. I said, I don't like this. I don't want to do this anymore. And I went back to lying in bed, just before the doorbell rang.

Rose Tremain

My Wife Is a White Russian

I'm a financier. I have financial assets, world-wide. I'm in nickel and pig-iron and gold and diamonds. I like the sound of all these words. They have an edge, I think. The glitter of saying them sometimes gives me an erection.

I'm saying them now, in this French restaurant, where the tablecloths and the table napkins are blue linen, where they serve sea-food on platters of seaweed and crushed ice. It's noisy at lunchtime. It's May and the sun shines in London, through the open restaurant windows. Opposite me, the two young Australians blink as they wait (so damned courteous, and she has freckles like a child) for me to stutter out my hard-word list, to manipulate tongue and memory so that the sound inside me forms just behind my lips and explodes with extraordinary force above my oysters.

Diamonds!

But then I feel a soft, perfumed dabbing at my face. I turn away from the Australians and there she is. My wife. She is smiling as she wipes me. Her gold bracelets rattle. She is smiling at me. Her lips are astonishing, the colour of claret. I've been wanting to ask her for some time: 'Why are your lips this terrible dark colour these days? Is it a lipstick you put on?'

Still smiling at me, she's talking to the Australians with her odd accent: 'He's able to enjoy the pleasures of life once more, thank God. For a long time afterwards, I couldn't take him out. Terrible. We couldn't do one single thing, you know. But now . . . He enjoys his wine again.'

The dabbing stops. To the nurse I tried to say when I felt a movement begin: 'Teach me how to wipe my arse. I cannot let my wife do this because she doesn't love me. If she loved me, she probably wouldn't mind wiping my arse and I wouldn't mind her wiping my arse. But she doesn't love me.'

The Australian man is talking now. I let my hand go up and take hold of my big-bowled wine glass into which a waiter has poured the expensive Chablis my wife likes to drink when she eats fish. Slowly, I guide the glass across the deadweight distance between the table and my mouth. I say 'deadweight' because the spaces between all my limbs and the surfaces of tangible things have become mighty. To walk is to wade in waist-high water. And to lift this wine glass . . . 'Help me,' I want to say to her, 'just this once. Just this once.'

'Heck,' says the Australian man, 'we honestly thought he'd made a pretty positive recovery.' His wife, with blue eyes the colour of the napkins, is watching my struggles with the glass. She licks her fine line of a mouth, sensing, I suppose, my longing to taste the wine. The nurse used to stand behind me, guiding the feeding cup in my hand. I never explained to her that the weight of gravity had mysteriously increased. Yet often, as I drank from the feeding cup, I used to imagine myself prancing on the moon.

'Oh this is a very positive recovery,' says my wife. 'There's very little he can't do now. He enjoys the ballet, you know, and the opera. People at Covent Garden and the better kind of place are very considerate. We don't go to the cinema because there you have a very inconsiderate type of person. Don't you agree? So riff-raffy? Don't you agree?'

The Australian wife hadn't listened to a word. The Australian wife puts out a lean freckled arm and I watch it come towards me, astounded as usual these days by the speed with which other people can move parts of their bodies. But the arm, six inches from my hand holding the glass, suddenly stops. 'Don't help him!' snaps my wife. The napkin-blue eyes are lowered. The arm is folded away.

Heads turn in the restaurant. I suppose her voice has carried its inevitable echo round the room where we sit: 'Don't help him! Don't help him!' But now that I have an audience, the glass begins to jolt, the wine splashing up and down the sides of the bowl. I smile. My smile widens as I watch the Chablis begin to slop onto the starched blue cloth. *Waste!* She of all people understands the exquisite luxury of waste. Yet she snatches the glass out of my hand and sets it down by her own. She snaps her fingers and a young beanstick of a waiter arrives. He spreads out a fresh blue napkin where I have spilt my wine. My wife smiles her claret smile. She sucks an oyster into her dark mouth.

The Australian man is, I was told, the manager of the Toomin Valley Nickel Consortium. The Australian man is here to discuss expansion, supposedly with me, unaware until he met me this lunchtime that, despite the pleasing cadences of the words, I'm unable to say 'Toomin Valley Nickel Consortium'. I can say 'nickel'. My tongue lashes around in my throat to form the click that comes in the middle of the word. Then out it spills. Nickel! In my mind, oddly enough, the word 'nickel' is the exact greyish-white colour of any oyster. But 'consortium' is too difficult for me. I know my limitations.

My wife is talking again: 'I've always loved the ballet, you see. This is my only happy memory of Russia—the wonderful classical ballet. A little magic. Don't you think? I would never want to be without this kind of magic, would you? Do you have the first-rate ballet companies in Australia? You do? Well, that's good. *Giselle* of course. That's the best one. Don't you think? The dead girl. Don't you think? Wonderful.'

We met on a pavement. I believe it was in the Avenue Matignon but it could have been in the Avenue Montaigne. I often get these muddled. It was in Paris, anyway. Early summer, as it is now. Chestnut candle blooms blown along the gutters. I waited to get into the taxi she was leaving. But I didn't get into it. I followed her. In a bar, she told me she was very poor. Her father drove the taxi I had almost hired. She spoke no English then, only French with a heavy Russian accent. I was just starting to be a financier at that time, but already I was quite rich, rich by her standards—she who had been used to life in post-war Russia. My hotel room was rather grand. She said in her odd French: 'I'll fuck for money.'

I gave her fifty francs. I suppose it wasn't much, not as much as she'd hoped for, a poor rate of exchange for the white, white body that rode astride me, head thrown back, breasts bouncing. She sat at the dressing table in the hotel room. She smoked my American cigarettes. More than anything, I wanted to brush her gold hair, brush it smooth and hold it against my face. But I didn't ask her if I could do this. I believe I was afraid she would say: 'You can do it for money.'

The thin waiter is clearing away our oyster platters. I've eaten only three of my oysters, yet I let my plate go. She pretends not to notice how slow I've been with the oysters. And my glass of wine still stands by hers, untasted. Yet she's drinking quite fast. I hear her order a second bottle. The Australian man says: 'First-rate choice, if I may say. We like Chably.' I raise my left arm and touch her elbow, nodding at the wine. Without looking at me, she puts my glass down in front of me. The Australian wife stares at it. Neither she nor I dare to touch it.

My wife is explaining to the Australians what they are about to eat, as if they were children: 'I think you will like the turbot very much. *Turbot poché hollandaise*. They cook it very finely. And the hollandaise sauce, you know this of course? Very difficult to achieve, lightness of this sauce. But here they do it very well. And the scallops in saffron. Again a very light sauce. Excellent texture. Just a little cream added. And fresh scallops naturally. We never go to any restaurant where the food is frozen. So I think you will like these dishes you have chosen very much . . .'

We have separate rooms. Long before my illness, when I began to look (yet hardly to feel) old, she demanded her privacy. This was how she put it: she wanted to be private. The bedroom we used to share and which is now hers is very large. The walls are silk. She said: 'There's no sense in being rich and then cooped up together in one room.' Obediently, I moved out. She wouldn't let me have the guest room, which is also big. I have what we call 'the little room', which I always used to think of as a child's room. In her 'privacy' I expect she smiles: 'the child's room is completely right for him. He's a helpless baby!' Yet she's not a private person. She likes to go out four or five nights a week, returning at two or three in the morning, sometimes with friends, sitting and drinking brandy. Sometimes they play music. Elton John. She has a lover (I don't know his name) who sends her lilies.

I'm trying to remember the Toomin Valley. I believe it's an immense desert of a place, inhabited by no one and nothing except the mining machinery and the Nickel Consortium employees, whose clusters of houses I ordered to be whitewashed to hide the cheap grey building blocks. The windows of the houses are small, to keep out the sun. In the back yards are spindly eucalyptus trees, blown by the scorching winds. I want to ask the Australian wife: 'Did you have freckles before you went to live in the Toomin Valley, and does some wandering prima ballerina dance *Giselle* on the gritty escarpment above the mine?'

My scallops arrive, saffron yellow and orange in the blue and white dish—the colours of a childhood summer. The flesh of a scallop is firm yet soft, the texture of a woman's thigh (when she is young, of course; before the skin hardens and the flesh bags out).

A forkful of scallop is immeasurably easier to lift than the glass of wine, and the Australian wife (why don't I know either of their names?) smiles at me approvingly as I lift the succulent parcel of food to my mouth and chew it without dribbling. My wife, too, is watching, ready with the little scented handkerchief, yet talking as she eats, talking of Australia as the second bottle of Chablis arrives and she tastes it hurriedly, with a curt nod to the thin waiter. I exist only in the corner of her eye, at its inmost edge, where the vulnerable triangle of red flesh is startling.

'Of course I've often tried to tell Hubert' (she pronounces my name 'Eieu-bert', trying and failing with what she recognises as the upper class 'h') 'that it's very unfair to expect people like you to live in some out-of-the-way place. I was brought up in a village, you see, and I know that an out-of-the-way village is so dead. No culture. The same in Toomin, no? Absolutely no culture at all. Everybody dead.'

The Australian wife looks—seemingly for the first time—straight at my wife. 'We're outdoor people,' she says.

I remember now. A river used to flow through the Toomin Valley. Torrential in the rainy season, they said. It dried up in the early forties. One or two sparse willows remain, grey testimony to the long-ago existence of water-rich soil. I imagine the young Australian couple, brown as chestnuts, swimming in the Toomin River, resting on its gentle banks with their fingers touching, a little loving nest of bone. There is no river. Yet when they look at each other, almost furtively under my vacant gaze, I recognise the look. The look says: 'These moments with strangers are nothing. Into our private moments together—only there—is crammed all that we ask of a life.'

'Yes, we're outdoor folk.' The Australian man is smiling. 'You can play tennis most of the year round at Toomin. I'm President of the Tennis Club. And we have our own pool now.'

I don't remember these things: tennis courts and swimming pools.

'Well, of course you have the climate for this.' My wife is signalling our waiter to bring her Perrier water. 'And it's something to do, isn't it? Perhaps, when the new expansions of the company are made, a concert hall could be built for you, or a theatre?'

'A theatre!' The Australian wife's mouth opens to reveal

perfect, freshly peeled teeth and a laugh escapes. She blushes. My wife's dark lips are puckered into a sneer. But the Australian man is laughing too—a rich laugh you might easily remember on the other side of the world—and slapping his thigh. 'A theatre! What about that, ay!'

She wanted, she said as she smoked my American cigarettes, to see *Don Giovanni*. Since leaving Russia with her French mother and her Russian father, no one had ever taken her to the opera. She had seen the posters advertising *Don Giovanni* and asked her father to buy her a ticket. He had shouted to her: 'Remember whose child you are! Do you imagine taxi drivers can afford seats at the Opéra?'

'Take me to see *Don Giovanni*,' she said, 'and then I will fuck for nothing.'

I've never really appreciated the opera. The Don was fat. It was difficult imagining so many women wanting to lie with this fat man. Yet afterwards, she leant over and put her head on my shoulder and wept. Nothing, she told me, had ever moved her so much, nothing in her life had touched the core of her being as this had done, this production of *Don Giovanni*. 'If only,' she said, 'I had money as you have money, then I would go to hear music all the time and see the classical ballet and learn from these what is life.'

The scallops are good. She never learned what is life. I feel emboldened by the food. I put my hand to my glass, heavier than ever now because the waiter has filled it up. The sun shines on my wine and on my hand blotched (splattered, it seems) with the oddly repulsive stains of old age. For a second, I see my hand and the wine glass as a still-life. But then I lift the glass. The Australian wife lowers her eyes. My wife for a moment is silent. I drink. I smile at the Australian wife because I know she wants to applaud.

I'm talking. The words are like stones, weighing down my lower jaw. Nickel. I'm trying to tell the Australian man that I dream about the nickel mine. In my dreams, the Australian miners drag carts loaded with threepenny bits. I run my hands through the coins as through a sack of wheat, and the touch of them is pleasurable and perfect. I also want to say to the Australian man: 'I hope you're happy in your work. When I was in control, I visited all my mines and all my subsidiaries at least once a year. Even in South Africa, I made sure a living wage was paid. I said to the men underground, I hope you're happy in your work.'

But now I have a manager, a head manager to manage all the other managers, including this one from the Toomin Valley. I am trundled out in my chair to meet them when they come here to discuss redundancy or expansion. My wife and I give them lunch in a restaurant. They remind me that I still have an empire to rule, if I was capable, if my heart had not faltered, if indeed my life had been different since the night of *Don Giovanni*.

When I stopped paying her to sleep with me, her father came to see me. He held his cap in his hands. 'We're hoping for a marriage,' he said. And what more could I have given—what *less* to the body I had begun to need so terribly? The white and gold of her, I thought, will ornament my life.

Yet now I never touch her. The white and the gold of her lies only in the lilies they send, the unknown lovers she finds in the night, while I lie in the child's room and dream of the nickel mines. My heart is scorched dry like the dry hills of the Toomin Valley. I am punished for my need of her while her life stalks my silence: the white of her, the gold of her—the white of Dior, the gold of Cartier. Why did she never love me? In my dreams, too, the answer comes from deep underground: it's the hardness of my words.

SUNITI NAMJOSHI

Three Feminist Fables

The Giantess

Thousands of years ago in far away India, which is so far away that anything is possible, before the advent of the inevitable Aryans, a giantess was in charge of a little kingdom. It was small by her standards, but perhaps not by our own. Three oceans converged on its triangular tip, and in the north there were mountains, the tallest in the world, which would perhaps account for this singular kingdom. It was not a kingdom, but the word has been lost and I could find no other. There wasn't any king. The giantess governed and there were no other women. The men were innocent and happy and carefree. If they were hurt, they were quickly consoled. For the giantess was kind, and would set them on her knee and tell them they were brave and strong and noble. And if they were hungry, the giantess would feed them. The milk from her breasts was sweeter than honey and more nutritious than mangoes. If they grew fractious, the giantess would sing, and they would clamber up her leg and onto her lap and sleep unruffled. They were a happy people and things might have gone on in this way forever, were it not for the fact that the giantess grew tired. Her knees felt more bony, her voice rasped, and on one or two occasions she showed irritation. They were greatly distressed. 'We love you,' they said to the tired giantess, 'Why won't you sing? Are you angry with us? What have we done?' 'You are dear little children,' the giantess replied, 'but I have grown very tired and it's time for me to go.' 'Don't you love us anymore? We'll do what you want. We will make you happy. Only please don't go.' 'Do you know what I want?' the giantess asked. They were silent for a bit, then one of them said, 'We'll make you our queen.' And another one said, 'We'll write you a poem.' And the third one shouted (while turning cartwheels), 'We'll bring you many gifts of oysters and pearls and pebbles and stones.' 'No,' said the giantess, 'No.' She turned her back and crossed the mountains.

Of Cats and Bells

'Who will bell the cat?' 'Not I,' said the Brown Mouse, 'I have too many babies, and a hundred things to do, and a long shopping list.' 'Not I,' said the Blue Mouse, 'I hate silly fights and I believe in peace.' 'Not I,' said the Little Mouse, 'I am too little, and the bell is too heavy.' 'Nor I,' said the Big Mouse, 'I do not understand the nature of bells, and moreover, they bore me.' 'Well, I'll bell the cat,' said the Lunatic Mouse, 'I'll do it for a lark. It's really quite funny.' 'No, I'll bell the cat,' said the Heroic Mouse, 'I want the glory.' 'If we wait long enough,' said the Clever Mouse, 'the cat will die, and then we needn't worry.' 'Yes,' said the mice, 'let us forget it;' and some didn't and some did.

Svayamvara

Once upon a time there was a little princess who was good at whistling. 'Don't whistle,' said her mother. 'Don't whistle,' said her father, but the child was good at it and went on whistling. Years went by and she became a woman. By this time she whistled beautifully. Her parents grieved. 'What man will marry a whistling woman?' said her mother dolefully. 'Well,' said her father, 'we will have to make the best of it. I will offer half my kingdom and the princess in marriage to any man who can beat her at whistling.' The king's offer was duly proclaimed, and soon the palace was jammed with suitors whistling. It was very noisy. Most were terrible and a few were good, but the princess was better and beat them easily. The king was displeased, but the princess said, 'Never mind, father. Now let me set a test and perhaps some good will come of it.' Then she turned to the suitors, 'Do you acknowledge that you were beaten fairly?' 'No,' they all roared, all except one, 'we think it was magic or some sort of trick.' But one said, 'Yes.' 'Yes,' he said, 'I was beaten fairly.' The princess smiled and turning to her father she pointed to this man. 'If he will have me,' she said, 'I will marry him.'

Svayamvarah—the choosing of a husband by the bride herself (Sanskrit Dictionary).

K. Arnold Price

The White Doll

The sergeant had been a long time with my father. It was early in the day for a policeman's visit, not ten o'clock yet and a Saturday too.

Because it was Saturday I had come down a bit late for breakfast. Colin had already gone but my mother was still sitting at the table with a bit of toast on her plate, pretending very nicely that she was still eating and so assuring me that I was not really very late. Colin was different from my mother about this; he was reasonable and understanding about nearly everything, but he had a silly idea that one should be punctual for eating.

When I had finished I went out and hung about near the front steps, so that when the sergeant left I could ask Colin if there was anything he wanted me to do. Quite often on a Saturday morning we did some job together if the weather was good.

I hoped that the sergeant hadn't come about the travelling people. Colin had given them permission to camp at the end of our bottoms and their ponies were grazing there. They were nearer to the village than to us, and someone, the postmistress, for instance, might have made a complaint about them. The postmistress was very good at complaining. Mrs Mandy wouldn't complain because she and my father were friends, and Ignatius Keogh wasn't the sort of man to complain about anything. There was the new pub we didn't know anything about, but a man that was still a stranger in the village wouldn't be such a fool as to complain about anything.

The sergeant might have come about poachers. Colin was very odd about poaching. He got very furious regularly about poachers on the river but when we had roast pheasant for dinner, he never asked where it came from. 'A very good bird,' he would say, and that was all.

My mother and Anastasia had a private arrangement with Tim to bring a pheasant to the back door late in the evening when my father would have settled down to reading and would hear and notice nothing. My mother didn't mind at all buying birds from a poacher; maybe it was because she had grown up in Connemara, and I suppose there are no pheasants there because there are no trees.

Then I saw the policeman coming down the hall. My father strolled out after him and stood on the steps while he picked up his bicycle, mounted it and rode slowly off down the drive. My father said nothing as he went off. He was never hearty in his manner, he was quiet and leisurely, as if there was all the time in the world, and really, at Ballygullion there usually was.

All the same, I thought there was something queer about the silence; the sergeant didn't say anything as he was going and Colin stood quite still, staring at nothing.

I went up to the steps and stopped.

'Was it the tinkers?' I said.

Colin glanced at me and looked away again.

'No, no,' he said, quite impatiently, as if I had asked a silly question.

He looked down and scuffed a couple of dead leaves off the step.

A kind of alarm went prickling through me. Was there something wrong? Really wrong? Could it be about us? There seemed to be an awfully long pause before he spoke again.

'Mr Dowland has trouble,' he said.

'Trouble?'

'His wife is dead.'

I relaxed. I nearly said, *Is that all? For it wasn't us!*—and we didn't know Mrs Dowland at all; she was Mr Dowland's wife, but then we scarcely knew Mr Dowland.

'Mother said she was delicate,' I said.

'Yes,' said Colin, looking down at the dead leaves. It sounded like no.

Then he suddenly raised his head and looked at me quite disagreeably.

'Now, mind,' he said, 'there's to be no shouting or whistling, you understand, we're very near—'

'Of course not,' I said, offended.

'It's easy to forget,' said Colin. He turned and went indoors.

My father was a calm, mild-mannered man. Something had annoyed or disturbed him. Even when I was a small boy he had not given me orders; and now I was out of childhood and going to boarding school next year. It was something the sergeant had told him; but it really couldn't have been the news that Mrs Dowland had died!

Mr Dowland was our nearest neighbour; his outhouses almost touched the boundary wall of our back avenue. I believe his name was Paul, but everyone called him Mr Dowland and he looked like a mister. He had a small brown beard and he always wore a collar and tie. You never saw him coming home in the evening astride a horse and leading another. Maybe he hadn't any horses; or maybe he grazed and stabled them over the hill on his second farm where he had more outhouses and a big yard where the threshing was done. Even on the days of the threshing no sound of it reached us because the hill field came between.

Mr Dowland was a small man. He held his head on one side and spoke rather carefully in a soft voice. He smiled a great deal but he was not an interesting man. If he happened to overtake me on the road he always asked me a lot of questions that I found boring. One day he even asked me if I worked hard and got good marks! He didn't go to the pubs, and he didn't come to my father's ballad parties; really, we only saw him now and then on the road. The farm house was a good two-storey house, and he kept it and the outhouses in good repair. The front door got a coat of paint sometimes, but it didn't look as if it was ever opened. In fact, it was a dull house and I thought Dowland a dull sort of man, but I had never said that to my parents or to anyone else. For several years I had learned to keep my views of life and people to myself, and to go along with whatever other people said when I was with them. As long as you are a baby you can say anything; when you are a child you may still say what you like and be scolded and forgiven for it; after that you must learn to be a hypocrite and remain one for the rest of your life.

I was feeling peaceful and a bit sleepy, as I always did on Saturday, and I strolled up to the orchard and picked up a few slug-eaten windfalls and brought them back for Jenny; I was feeding them to her when Colin came looking for me. He wanted me to come with him and Letitia to the station, and drive Jenny back, and come to meet them on the five-forty train, as it was Saturday and the men would be gone.

So I went with them to the station, and my mother gave me a list of things to buy in the village on the way back. It was nearly twelve o'clock when I drove into the stable yard. Pakey appeared, and we unharnessed Jenny and left the trap resting on its shafts ready for the afternoon. I was already hungry but it was too early for lunch. I lagged after Pakey into the harness room.

'Did you hear Mrs Dowland was dead?' I said, for something to say.

'Aye,' said Pakey, who was slinging the harness over the high hooks.

'We didn't even know she was ill.'

'She wasn't ill,' said Pakey. He was stooping and peering at the floor at the shadowy end of the harness room, as if he had dropped something.

'Did she have an accident?'

'I wouldn't say that,' said Pakey. He straightened up, took his coat off a hook and came into the light, putting it on.

'She hanged herself,' he said.

I stared at Pakey. His face was red, perhaps from stooping, and his black hair tousled. I had known Pakey since I was four years old and yet he looked unknown, a stranger, possibly because what he said was so strange, so unbelievable.

'Hanged herself . . .?

'Hanged herself in the end outhouse this morning,' said Pakey. He gave a hitch to his trousers, began to button his coat and went on:

'When your man came down this morning he found her hanging in the end house and he went straight up for Doctor O'Dwyer and then the police. That must have been before eight o'clock for the postman had it. It was all over the village, no doubt, within the hour.'

I had nothing to say; but I asked faintly: '*Why*, Pakey?'

'Indeed, you may ask,' said Pakey.

We were standing close together in the doorway. I watched his big hands moving as he buttoned his coat, looked up at his strong face with the rough black eyebrows and thick black hair. There was power in him, the power of a man; something I didn't know yet. I was thinking this confusedly even while I spoke. He looked up at the sky as he moved out.

'Do you think it will keep up?' he said.

'I think it will.'

'Well, so long.'

'So long.'

He crossed the stable yard, moving heavily, but fast, his feet making a dull sound on the cobbles. I had just heard something extraordinary, and yet my mind flew away from it; I began thinking about Pakey; he was really, if only partly, a son of the house. He had come straight from school as a servant boy, sleeping over the stable and taking his meals in the kitchen. He must, in eight years, have learned a fair lot about horses, though my father never kept more than two. He was now mainly a groom, though he still did a number of odd jobs, sometimes telling Colin what jobs needed doing. My father had taught me to ride, but it was Pakey who first put me on a horse's back (that is, a very small pony) and walked us up and down the avenue, keeping his arm round me. He was a very thin boy then, and I remembered him as having a pale bony face. He was now a tough young man, looking as strong as a bullock, and I hadn't noticed when he had changed. When I saw him walking away from me across the yard, I knew that he was walking away into his own life, a life that had nothing to do with Ballygullion.

I came out of the stable yard and opened the glass door into the house. I walked slowly down the corridor into the hall and heard the grandfather clock on the landing halfway up the stairs saying slowly *hanged* . . . her*self* . . . *hanged* . . . her*self* . . .

I opened the door of the morning room and saw that my lunch was already laid, with a glass of milk standing by my plate and a bowl of apples and pears on the table. Across the table I could see a red fire burning quietly. Because it was a dark day and the light in the room was dim I noticed small gleams all over the room—a gleam on the table from the forks and the salt-cellar, another from something brass on the mantelpiece, a sparkle from a glass bowl on a small table.

Everything was really the same as it had been at breakfast-time but everything looked different because my mother was not there and because Mrs Dowland had hanged herself.

I sat down and took up my knife and fork. Of course I had read scores of stories about murder and suicide, torture and garrotting . . . but they had been in Chicago or Paris, Japan or Mexico . . . this was in Ballygullion.

As I ate lunch I began to be sure of three things: one, that there would be an inquest, and very soon; two, that my parents would never speak of it, at least in my presence; three, that I would never ask them anything about it.

I knew already that my mother never talked about anything she found unpleasant; if, as a small boy, I told her how *much* my knee had bled when I fell down, she would say, laughing: 'Oh, *please!* Not at table!'

The house and grounds seemed absolutely still and silent; only the fire behind me made soft sounds as it sank. When I got up from the table I looked around me, for I was very seldom there without Colin and Letitia; without them it was just a room. I had always thought our house small and very simple, for I went to parties at much grander ones; looking round now I saw that every surface that could be polished was polished; that opposite me was a tall cabinet with my mother's collection of glass; on a small table there was an enormous jar of chrysanthemums that she must have cut and arranged before she went out. It seemed to me a room in which people couldn't have trouble, couldn't be unhappy; I tried to think of the house next door, but I had never seen it; Mr Dowland was in trouble; my mind said the words, *Poor Mr Dowland*, but they didn't mean anything. In less than an hour I had got over any feeling of horror; I only felt curiosity. I was shocked at myself and went quickly out of doors. I found that rain was beginning to fall and the sky was overcast. I came indoors and went up to my room. Now that my tutor kept me busy from Monday morning to Friday afternoon, I sometimes spent Saturday afternoon reading in my room, although when it was fine I always went out. Now I was not going to read. I lay down on my bed, first taking off my shoes and removing the counterpane as I did not want to get into trouble with Anastasia. Then I lay with my feet crossed and my hands behind my head. I could only see the sky and a branch of an old ornamental cherry tree. The tree was very old and had lost its beauty; every autumn Colin talked about having it cut down; but it was still there. It produced very little blossom and some branches had broken in storms, so that it was now lop-sided. The branch that stretched across my window pane looked deformed; a few colourless leaves still hung from it. I was so used to it that it was just part of the view. Now I looked at the poor thing, its scragginess and ragged leaves, quite peacefully. I intended to think in a systematic way about the extraordinary case of Mrs Dowland. I had very little data—only what Pakey had said—but it was probably as much as anyone knew so far. I carefully repeated in my mind: *When your man came down he found her hanging in the end house . . . went straight up for Dr O'Dwyer and then the police . . .*

Without any examination, I was checked at once: *went straight up . . .*

Straight up. Why *straight* up? Why? Just left her hanging and went off? She was dead, of course. But she was his wife; wouldn't he first, unreasonably and in despair, cut her down, loosen the noose, try to pretend she botched it, that she would revive?

What would I do if I found Anastasia hanging in an outhouse? Impossible to see or imagine, but still I think I would shout *Anastasia!* and put a table, or a barrel, my shoulders even, under her feet.

The doctor . . . the doctor when he came would have given the probable time when death had occurred; but Dr O'Dwyer . . . no one would pay much attention to what he said.

. . . hanging in the end house . . .

Why the *end* house? Why not the nearest to the dwelling house? Well, it might be full of junk, or it might be the henhouse, or maybe the sheepdog slept there. There must have been some such reason, otherwise why should a woman who wanted to hang herself patter out over mud and stones to the end—and then I discovered something; while thinking of Mrs Dowland I had been seeing a small figure like a doll hanging in a white nightdress with bare feet dangling . . . that was too absurd. No, she must have got up early and dressed herself . . . how odd to dress yourself knowing that in a few minutes you are going to be dead; when she put on her shoes she must have thought: *Shoes, you are going only one way; you are not coming back.*

Did she get up very quietly so as not to disturb her husband and dress in the dark? Perhaps she didn't sleep with him. Colin and my mother didn't sleep together but the country people mostly did. But she was delicate, my mother had said; so perhaps she slept in a different room . . .

Dressing in the dark . . . just as if she had to catch the 7.45 train . . . and creeping down the stairs that creaked—all stairs creak at night—and did not her husband hear her and come downstairs too? No, of course he didn't, for if he had—no, she got down to the kitchen, where there would be a lantern hanging on a nail or maybe standing on a shelf, and she lit the lantern and went out to the end outhouse—and there I stuck, for again I saw the white doll figure dangling, feet bare.

I knew there was something wrong about all this; I had forgotten or overlooked something; I couldn't remember a situation like this in any of the stories I had read. For the time being I gave it up.

I fell asleep without meaning to and only woke barely in time to go out to the stable yard and get Jenny harnessed and drive to the station to meet my parents. As it was I arrived just as the train was running in. The next week passed very quickly; I heard nothing about the Dowland affair and had no time or inclination to think of anything outside my own life. I was hunting twice a week and on the other days a tutor came in the morning and stayed till half past three or four o'clock to give me coaching in preparation for boarding school next year. However, on Saturday morning I drove into the village with a long shopping list from my mother. I stopped in front of Mrs Mandy's, and as I got out and looked at the wide peaceful street I remembered Pakey's words: *it was all over the village within the hour*.

Sitting up on a high stool beside the pub counter, I said chattily to Mrs Mandy: 'Have you seen Mr Dowland since . . .?' She took her time about answering. She was studying my mother's list.

'I don't see Mr Dowland,' she said at last.

'I know he doesn't drink,' I said. 'He told me he took the pledge as a child; but he might want a pair of socks, or a new bucket, or paraffin—'

I had been visiting Mrs Mandy from the age of four, and knew that she sold everything that the dwellers in the village and the townland might need.

'He might,' said Mrs Mandy, 'but he doesn't get them from me.'

I considered Mrs Mandy had a beautiful voice; it was usually mild and slow, with a touch of depth in it, though she could bring out a couple of high notes if she wanted to. But now she nearly scratched me with it.

'Did you know Mrs Dowland?' I went on.

'Know her?' said Mrs Mandy walking away from the counter. I waited.

'Nobody knew Mrs Dowland,' said her voice from the storeroom.

'She was never seen out,' she said, coming back with a packet of oatmeal. She laid it on the counter and went on studying the list. 'No one laid eyes on her.'

'She was a sort of cripple?' I suggested as a half-question.

Mrs Mandy looked at me very sharply.

'Not at all!' she said. 'Who told you that?'

'I'm not sure,' I said; and at that moment I was not sure of anything. What had made me say that Mrs Dowland was a cripple?

But Mrs Mandy had gone to the back of the shop and was taking down a biscuit tin from a shelf. She brought it back to the counter, took off the lid and tilted the tin towards me. 'It's a new assortment,' she said.

I selected two biscuits and began to munch while Mrs Mandy went noiselessly to and fro. She was fat and moved almost silently. The tradition of eating biscuits while she made up the order dated from the days when Jimmy brought me in and put me sitting on the counter and biscuits were doled out to keep me quiet. It struck me that she wanted to keep me quiet now, too. I was sure she did not care much whether the Dowlands had dealt with her or not. Mrs Mandy was said to be 'very comfortable'; some said she was rich.

Very soon the groceries were packed into a box and we carried it out to the trap.

In the weeks and months that followed I never heard the name Dowland mentioned; it was as if both were dead. But I did find, first of all with annoyance, and then with alarm, that frequently when I half-woke in the night and turned over there came before me an absurd dangling figure, barefoot and featureless, clear and small against a dark background. I began to get a bit nervous about this doll image of a woman I had never seen; was it going to stay with me? I tried telling it to go away, and it seemed to me that it did for a week or more; but then one night I came quietly awake and found I was watching a man walk along a dry track in darkness; I could not see his face nor recognise his background, but I knew it was Mr Dowland coming out of his back door and walking along the track to the end outhouse. I felt no fear or surprise; I thought, *He sees the dangling doll too; he's going along to see if she's still there.* Lying in bed, awake, but only just, this seemed to me quite reasonable. He would, of course, sleeping or waking, be drawn to the end house.

Every time I walked down the back avenue, I looked up at the gable of the Dowlands' end outhouse; they were stone outhouses, as solidly built as the dwelling house. The gable almost touched the boundary wall between our avenue and their land. I had a stupid but very strong desire to see the inside of the end house, although there was probably nothing there that would tell me anything; nevertheless the desire stayed with me and I knew that one day I would scramble between the wire palings on top of the low wall and walk in. Avoiding Dowland would be simple enough; every afternoon he went over the hill for the milking on the second farm. My parents very often went visiting in the afternoon and then would be away for a few hours. But I must not be caught by Anastasia wandering down the back avenue in her free time to visit her pals, nor indeed by anyone coming up. The itch to go and see for myself gave me no peace, and one afternoon, after watching Downland go up the hill field and disappear over the top, I did creep through the palings and walked to the door of the end outhouse. What I saw checked me; or rather, what I didn't see.

The outhouse was completely empty; the floor was clean and dry.

I turned round in the doorway and looked cautiously up the hill and back into the avenue. There was not a sound or a movement. And yet my mouth was quite dry as I walked in. I paused in the middle and looked up. There, indeed, was a beam; it seemed very high up. I knew my own height; about four feet ten inches. It seemed to me, staring up in the dusky light and moving a little from one side to the other, that the beam was about twice my height from the ground; that is, nearly ten feet from the floor. What had she stood on? It wasn't a case of standing on a box . . . and kicking it away. A step-ladder? I stopped looking up and stood trying to think it out. I couldn't. *Of course* Mr Dowland would have cleared everything out of that house, everything that she had used and that would remind him . . . I went quickly out and darted into the second house. There was an old wardrobe standing opposite the door. A broken dining-room chair stood beside it. In one corner there was a small kitchen table. I went over and lifted it slightly, and one leg fell against the wall as I did so. I set it down, propping it against the wall. I looked all around.

There were shelves with paint pots and bottles on them. There was nothing else. I ran out and went to the door of the third house, which was next to the dwelling house. Here the hens were already beginning to settle down for the night. I walked quickly back to the wall, slid between the wires, jumped down and stood for a moment looking both ways. The avenue was empty. I began to saunter back to the house, hanging my head and thinking. I was trying to consider the practical problem of hanging oneself. In all the stories I had read I couldn't remember one case. By the time I had got as far as the side door I had only got as far as deciding by very simple arithmetic that Mrs Dowland, even if she had been a tall woman, must have stood on something at least four feet high.

I went up to my room, took my ruler and measured the height of my bedside table and my study table under the window. Tables, it seemed, were about two feet six inches high. I threw down the ruler. Well. It must have been a step ladder. What had she done? Stood on the top step to throw the rope over the beam and to settle the noose round her neck . . . and then taken a little hop off the ladder, into the air, into her death?

I felt frustrated and suddenly tired. I went down to the morning room where there was a good fire and the two dogs on the hearthrug. I lay down beside them, trying to comfort myself against their bodies; but they were twitchy and restless, sitting up suddenly and listening to some sound they had heard which they hoped, as I did, was the sound of Colin and Letitia returning.

Hours later, when I went up to bed, I saw the ruler lying on my bedside table and the mood of irritation, frustration and suspicion came back. I hadn't solved anything. I didn't know what else to do. There was Dr O'Dwyer: he would know; or, at least, he should know how she did it, for he had been the first to arrive. Mr Dowland had gone straight up to him, before going to the police . . . gone straight up to him . . . how did we know? Well, Mr Dowland had said so . . .

Dr O'Dwyer was very popular with everyone. His cheeks were purple, his eyes bulged and hs hands shook, nevertheless he was a dead shot, a good host and kept good whiskey. In the long, long past he had had a wife, but now he had dogs and a housekeeper. If the country people became ill it was usually consumption and as there was no cure for it you couldn't tell whether he was a good doctor or not.

And then, suddenly, I stopped thinking about the Dowland case, forgot it completely, the way one forgets an indoor game that is played every day during a spell of bad weather, and then abandoned when the sun shines again. I found that after a day's hunting I could scarcely keep my eyes open after dinner; pride kept me struggling with drowsiness for at least an hour before I felt I could say good-night and escape to my bedroom. There I fell asleep at once and was waked by my father at a quarter to eight next morning. My tutor, alas, arrived very punctually at ten minutes to nine.

The week as well as the winter's day had become very short.

The name of Dowland was never mentioned and the farmhouse next door remained, as it had always been, silent and private.

One Saturday afternoon I had to drive over to Clonmore to fetch my mother from a horticultural show she had gone to. When I arrived she was already waiting in the porch of the hall where the show was held, and beside her was a large woman whom I recognised as Mrs Toomey, a small farmer's wife from the far side of Ballygullion. She had one arm round a big marrow and the other round a pot of chrysanthemums. My mother was giving her a lift home. The trap sunk almost to the ground as she clambered in and the shafts rose up. When we reached our gate my mother got out and told me to lead Mrs Toomey home.

As I walked Jenny up the short hill beyond our gate Mrs Toomey looked across at Mr Dowland's house.

'Do you see that poor man at all?' she asked without mentioning his name.

'We haven't seen him lately.' And then I added, to keep the conversation going: 'He has his tillage mostly on the second farm; he's probably been getting his potatoes out.'

'Well, he'll have a bit of peace now,' said Mrs Toomey. 'He had a long pull with that one.'

'He'll have to get his own meals—do all his own cooking now,' I said.

'Indeed, I'm sure he's been doing that for a long time,' said Mrs Toomey. 'She wouldn't be much use to him in the house.'

'I think I heard my mother say that she was delicate,' I said, looking straight ahead.

'*Delicate*,' said Mrs Toomey. There was a pause.

'Well, I suppose you might call it that,' she said. 'There was very little she could manage. She was simple, you know.'

At the stone stile Mrs Toomey said she would get down and take the path across the field home. She got herself out of the trap, the shafts returned to the horizontal and I turned Jenny's head for home.

Simple: what exactly did that mean? Did it mean anything *exactly at all*? I had to find out. It was two days before I had an opportunity to say to my mother in a tone of innocent enquiry: 'When the country people say someone is "simple", what do they mean?'

'Oh,' said my mother, pausing for a moment in her work of filling a jar with autumn boughs. '*Well* . . .' said she, very reluctantly, 'I suppose it means . . . that there is some mental weakness . . .'

'Would you say mental deficiency?'

'That may be too strong,' said my poor mother unhappily. 'It might mean that a child's mind did not develop as the body grew . . . there are some adults can't take responsibility, for example. It's not the same as being stupid.'

I did not want to press her further; and I thought I had enough. I had to make up my mind about something; it was a burden; it frightened me; but at the same time I felt a thrilling, a really shocking elation.

'Delicate,' my mother had said; 'simple,' Mrs Toomey had said. Could I find a word that had a meaning halfway between the two? I decided there wasn't one. But supposing both ladies were mistaken? Then, I knew nothing. But, I reflected, Mrs Toomey lived only a short mile away from the Dowlands; her husband and Mr Dowland were both farmers; would she not *sometimes* have been in the Dowlands' house and have observed for herself what Mrs Dowland could and could not do? But perhaps the Dowlands didn't ever have visitors, didn't ever want them; but didn't they go to parties even when they were young? Was that because Mrs Dowland was 'simple'? And had Mr Dowland, that neat, soft-spoken man, had he married a 'simple' girl, *knowing* she was 'simple'? There were questions, but no answers.

Next morning there was work until lunch; but because my mother had gone out to lunch, the three of us ate more quickly than usual, and my tutor brought up his cup of coffee to my room and we started work again at twenty to two; I saw him off with great joy at a quarter to three. I turned back from the front steps and, with no conscious plan in my head, I went rambling about, looking at nothing, thinking of nothing; yet in a minute or two I had come to Colin's carpentry shed and saw Colin sitting there. Colin's carpentry was really the only queer thing about him. We never saw what he made and yet he seemed to spend hours there. My mother made jokes about it, and Colin smiled, and took the jokes placidly. I thought of the shed as his hide-out and I sympathised with him. My mother, being a woman, wouldn't understand the need for a hide-out.

When I reached the door it stood open and I saw my father sitting on a low bench looking at another small bench which he had upside down on the floor in front of him. I stopped at the door and leaned against the jamb.

'*Colin!*' I said. My voice was beginning to break and the name came out in a sort of squawk. He didn't look up. Suddenly then, without having planned it, I poured out everything I had been thinking since the morning the sergeant came to the house; I uttered all the questions that had been plaguing me, and the few remarks that I had heard, getting hoarser, I think, and more emphatic as I went along.

'There's *something* wrong, Colin! There's something that doesn't make sense! If she *was* simple, if Mrs Toomey wasn't just talking vague gossip, if she really knew her, then *she couldn't have done it*! She couldn't have *done* it, she could have *dreamed* it, but she wouldn't have had the head to carry it out! She'd have forgotten something, or she'd have made a noise . . . do you remember that loony girl Josie, how she stumped about as if she had two wooden legs? And if her mind was weak *how* would she have had the *resolution* to carry it through even if she could plan it . . .'

My face was hot and I was panting.

I looked down at the top of Colin's head. He stopped, took hold of one of the legs of the little bench and waggled it. Then he clasped his hands.

'I agree with you,' he said mildly. 'It all turns on the word "simple" – what it means and whether it was correctly applied.'

I was taken by surprise. He was taking what I said seriously, and at the same time quite calmly! How could he?

'Well then . . . what do you think, Colin? What's your conclusion?'

He took so long then that I thought he wasn't going to answer.

'I have no conclusion,' he said. 'We can't hope to understand other people's lives. Lives are really very private. They are mysterious. They are hermetic . . .'

I didn't know what hermetic meant. His leisurely, almost dreamy voice was cooling me down, but his words disappointed me.

'We'll never know what went on in that house,' he said. 'Why should we? It's not our business.'

'But—' I said and stopped. I found it awkward to say what it seemed to me had to be said; the one thing, in fact, that I had come to say to Colin.

'You don't think . . .' I began; and stopped, panting with nervousness.

'You don't think,' I said, desperately: 'You don't think that . . . that justice . . . well, that justice *matters*?'

'Oh, *justice*!' said Colin. He got up, turned round and began picking up small tins from a shelf and peering into them.

'Justice,' he said, 'is for grocers . . .'

Then he sat down and started to try different screws from one of the tins for the loose leg of the little bench.

'Mercy,' he said vaguely. 'Mercy might be a better thing . . . considering what man is . . .'

His voice was only a murmur. There was silence then except for the little sounds his hands made.

There had been a light misting shower. It was gone now, but the cobblestones were wet and gleaming. There was a sort of glimmer over the yard that wasn't quite sunshine. The fresh, wet air was cooling my cheeks. I began to feel calm, almost happy. A sort of strain had gone just as the rain had. I was always happy when I was with Colin. He didn't talk down to me, he never said, *Let me explain to you*, as my tutor did. As I stood in the doorway and watched the light brighten over the yard my heart grew light. I wanted to jump about and shout like a small boy.

I said suddenly: 'I think I'll go and meet mother.'

'Do,' said Colin. 'She should be on the road by now.'

I ran off at once and went down the back avenue in leaps and bounds. I came out on the road and turned to go over the bridge, for my mother was coming from Clonmore. There was a fresh on the river, and I stopped for a minute to look down into the water.

It might be worthwhile taking a rod down for a try. Then I heard the sharp trot of a pony's hoofs on the road and I looked up to see my mother coming down the valley.

Anne Leaton

The Passion of Marco Z—

'I think it's a lousy title,' Janet said. 'Where's the passion?'

'You simply don't understand,' Edward said. 'Passion doesn't have to refer to jumping into bed with this or that person, as you seem to construe. Marco's is intellectual passion, about which you obviously know nothing.'

'I know about intellectual passion,' she said. 'I knew somebody once who suffered from that.'

'The hell you did,' Edward said.

'George Wade. In Albuquerque.'

'George Wade,' he said, 'was obsessed with Indian rugs. That doesn't constitute intellectual passion, not by a long shot.'

'He studied patterns. He could talk for hours about patterns. He chased weavings the way some men chase blondes,' Janet said.

'You just don't get it,' Edward said.

'You ought to master A before you go on to W,' Janet said. 'That's just common sense. This Marco guy is a eunuch. If what he's got is passion, I'd hate to see a dead goose.'

Edward felt faint with deprivation. For three years he had devoted himself to Marco Z—'s passion. He knew every wart in Marco's delicate skull. When acquaintances asked, 'and what do you do for kicks?' —Edward smiled wearily, remembering the intensity of ratiocination. He had 120 perfectly typed pages attesting to the vigor of perception. To have married in a fit of error a woman who could not understand the subtlety of his exploration made him feel as isolated as a bear on an ice-floe. What remedy could there be?

I was distracted, he explained to himself, by the demands of Marco Z—'s lucubrations, machinations and concatenations. My eye was wholly fixed then as now upon that singular behavior (is anything less required of the artist?). It was not surprising to him that he had failed to see Janet Staines in the fullness of her inadequacy. The wonder was he had noticed her at all.

Maybe, he said to himself, it will all work out, in the end.

'I see no reason for you to come home roaring drunk from the cantina,' he said. 'What is the reason for this excess?'

'I've always been a heavy drinker,' Janet said. 'My father's liver was cirrhosed before he was forty.'

'Are you saying that drunkenness is hereditary?'

'He set me a good example,' she said. 'I don't like living alone on the Southern Anatolian seashore. I might as well be in Albuquerque. You knew about my father. You also knew about my mother, before you married me. You also knew chances were good I wouldn't like drawing water from a village well, in the company of women speaking an unknown tongue.'

'Can't you learn a little Turkish?' he said. 'Are you of such feeble intelligence that you cannot learn to say, that is my bucket you have there, in Turkish?'

'Why should I learn?' she said. 'Someday I'll go back to Albuquerque. In Albuquerque the water runs out of a spigot in the wall.'

He shook his head, defeated.

'You knew my mother was a person of easy virtue . . . I told you my father chased little girls, with gin on his breath . . . what made you think I could learn Turkish . . .?'

'We'll work it out,' he said, returning to Marco Z——.

How could he have been expected to perceive, in the early days (he asked himself while sharpening his pencils with a very fine penknife), that Janet Staines was neurotic? That she drank whisky before breakfast? That she neither liked to draw water, nor to poach fish, nor to scrub tile floors from a kneeling position? That travel beyond the suburbs of Albuquerque was anathema? She might have been more explicit in her confessions. After all, she knew there was Marco Z——. The thing to do now was to hope for the best. The 120 typed pages had grown to 150.

Their sexual relationship was reasonably good, Edward thought one afternoon, as he rested between pyrotechnic chapters. He liked to make love about twice a week, preferably after a light supper. He didn't care for the more experimental aspects of the encounter. He thought there was very little that couldn't be satisfactorily expressed in the traditional postures. In his personal life (he smiled knowledgeably), he was a conservative; in Marco

Z——, he was an icon-smasher, an idiosyncrast, an adumbrator of things to come. One should discriminate baby from bathwater, before opening the window to hurl something-or-other out.

'How can you join,' he asked, 'an amateur theatrical group in a country the language of which you speak not a word?'

'It's in Adebei, at the airbase,' Janet said, looking slightly glazed. 'They're English. We're doing "Death of a Salesman".'

He cleaned the keys of his Smith-Corona. 'Well, it's the best of Miller,' he said. 'How will you get to Adebei?'

'On the People's Bus. Twice a week. We open in May.'

'I'm glad you've found something to occupy yourself with,' he said, digging sludge out of the E with a pin. 'Who'll draw the water while you're away? Who'll poach the fish?'

'The pot is not my province,' she said thickly. 'I've never wanted to cook anything but fried tomatoes. I don't suppose you've noticed how often fried tomatoes are served here?'

'I've noticed,' he said, replacing the top of the Smith-Corona. 'I thought it would resolve itself, in time.'

'It's probably because my father never drew a sober breath except for the sake of eating a fried tomato.'

'I don't see what your father's got to do with it.'

She wept, clutching a tomato not yet fried. Edward sighed with irritation. How had this happened? She was to have led distractions away from his door, as the Pied Piper fluted away the rats. As it was, she had sold out to the rats.

'Who is this man?' Edward said, flexing his tired fingers as he entered the sitting room in response to the random giggles and clinking of glasses he heard there, late one night.

'This is Reginald,' Janet said, rising unsteadily from the carpet-swathed divan. 'Reginald is a theatrical friend of mine.'

'How'd you do . . .' Reginald said, prone.

'Theatrical?' Edward said, massaging his fingers.

'The Adebei Art Players?' Reginald said. 'I believe you know of us. Your wife here's the crackerjack of our little group.'

'You don't say,' Edward said. 'Are you rehearsing?'

'Rehearsing?' Reginald said.

'I gather Janet's playing the mother,' Edward said. 'I was trying to recall the scene in the play where the mother comforts one of the sons. I didn't remember it looking so incestuous.'

'The mother?' Reginald said.

'We're doing "Streetcar Named Desire",' Janet said, refilling her glass. 'I play Stella.'

'She's a crackerjack Stella,' Reginald said, patting Janet on the cheek. 'I suppose I should be off. Getting late . . .'

'Playing Stella?' Edward said, cracking his knuckles to relax them. 'What happened to "Death of a Salesman"?'

'It was too depressing,' Janet said, seeing Reginald to the door. 'I'll just be a minute.'

Edward thought about drinking a little wine, to soothe his nerves, but he decided it wasn't worth the risk of a thick unproductive head the following day. He had to remain vigilant in these critical stages: Marco Z——'s passion had risen to its zenith. He sighed and crept up the ladder to his bed. Towards morning he thought he heard Janet come in. He supposed it was Janet. Someone, a female, was singing "The White Cliffs of Dover". He turned over again, to sleep.

'Little is asked of you, but you seem unable . . .' he began.

'You knew about my ginny father, my easy-virtued mother, when you married me.'

Had she told him? She had talked a great deal in Albuquerque. But of course there was always the counterpointed monologue of Marco Z——, buzzing blissfully in his head. Perhaps she had spoken of the perpetual pursuit of the little girls by the gin soaked father through the back streets of the city . . . But in the great ninth wave of female saying, who could discern a trickle here, a rivulet there? If only semaphores could be flung up to draw attention to some telling detail! Should he ask her, now, how easy was the virtue of her mother?

'I'm going away for the weekend,' she said, swaying a little in the doorway.

Edward stiffened at his Smith-Corona. 'This is very unwifely behavior.'

'I know,' she said, sadly. 'But it's me, it's me. Didn't I tell you about my passion for fried tomatoes, my boozy father lurching after pigtails, my—'

'What has that got to do with your present unwifely behavior?'

She considered. 'I wish I could get to the bottom of that. Maybe you could help. You're very clever sometimes.'

He sighed again. The wish that she could understand the exigencies of his life passed through his head, as he listened to her footsteps leaving his house.

'I just don't understand how this happened,' Edward said, to the Turkish official—caparisoned like a parade horse—who had caused him to be summoned to the Adebei Hospital and now stood next to him like a bright fiction in the grey foyer.

Parade Horse offered Edward a gold-tipped oval cigarette, which he took, to soothe his nerves. 'The woman,' he said, 'drinks graceless the liquor. Allah alone know the reason to this.'

Edward flopped down exhausted on a grey bench in the grey foyer. The drive to Adebei wth a monolingual constable had been arduous. 'Where is the doctor?' he said.

'Worry not,' Parade Horse assured him. 'Your spouse remain. There is the one arm only who dangle.'

'Dangles?' Edward said. 'Dangles?'

The doctor, when he appeared, said (through the graceful interpretation of Parade Horse) that the dangling arm dangled in fact because it was broken, at the shoulder. The other victim plucked from the inferno of the small Fiat which had pitched over a cliff near Adebei was in much more lamentable shape. 'A man named Reginald Baldsworth,' Parade Horse offered. 'He, regrettable, remain not.'

'What in hell were they doing in a Fiat, near a cliff!' Edward said.

Parade Horse cleared his throat noisily and looked knowingly at the doctor. The doctor put both hands into the large front pockets of his dingy white coat and left, discreetly. Parade Horse said: 'While was take place some regrettable festivities in the Fiat—this little car is very small for do such regrettables, a foot unknown to us alas, maybe she foot, maybe he foot—ruin the brake and this little car progress over cliff. No person see this progress alas. Praise Allah, is very small cliff only. If she runned Fiat over close by cliff of my acquaintance, your spouse is be small stain only.'

Edward felt dizzy. Nausea grew in him like mushrooms after rain. How long had she been away? 'How long has she been here?' he asked Parade Horse.

'Since two weeks, I hear it say. She was be since two weeks by the Adebei Palas.'

'My god,' Edward said.

Parade Horse nodded piously. 'Yes . . . thank the God, your spouse dangle only.'

'I don't know what to do about her,' he said, to Tom Barnes, an old friend on his first visit to Southern Anatolia. 'I just despair of the situation.'

Tom Barnes shook his head, closing his eyes a little in sympathy. He rotated the raki in his glass. The two men were sitting in one of the village's two earth-colored men's coffee houses. The other men sat in a distant corner, playing a dice game and surreptitiously watching the two strangers in their tweed jackets and thick brogans. 'It's a very difficult situation,' Tom said. 'I can see that. You certainly can't just go on as usual.'

Edward grimaced. 'I've done all I can,' he said. 'I can do no more.'

'Perfectly natural,' Tom Barnes said. 'A woman like Janet—I mean, whatever a man does is the wrong thing, isn't it?'

'I simply can't *depend* on her for anything,' Edward said. 'Except the drinking. And the incoherence. And now of course it's come to this . . . running around with . . .' Edward couldn't go on.

Tom Barnes sighed. 'Well Edward, it's just as well this happened as it did, that's what I think. Just as well you found out the whole truth of the matter.'

'I suppose so,' Edward said.

'No one could blame you for getting out, you know. After all, you can't go on like this. You're getting nowhere, are you? How's the book coming along, by the way?'

'I would have finished this month, if it hadn't been for . . .'

Tom Barnes nodded understandingly.

'I can't help wondering what will happen to her, when she's all alone,' Edward said.

'Well, you know,' Tom Barnes said, 'you can't be responsible for everybody else's life, now can you? No man is strong enough for that.'

'I guess not,' Edward said. 'Would you like to go to Adebei to eat something? After all, we have to eat, tragedy or not.'

I was glad (she wrote) to see the book in print—thanks for the autographed copy! I had never heard of the Oahu Tech Press before, but the dust jacket should help sales, although I don't remember any nude woman in old Marco Z——'s life! But then as you know I never got past page ten, since you tucked all the rest away after I failed the first test, you might say. Anyway, I've finished the whole thing now, and believe me it had to be a labor of love since my shoulder still twinges when I turn anything over, including pages. Maybe I overlooked something, but I still didn't find a woman in there even partially undressed. Are you sure Oahu Tech didn't pull a switcheroo on the dust jackets?

Albuquerque is the same as ever. I don't know why I'm so sad all the time, it's just me I guess. Pop had a little run-in with a pair of pigtails last week and he's out on bail now. Mom's out right now (he's a real sweet guy with the longest sideburns in Albuquerque!) but if she was here, I'm sure she'd send you a big hello.

How is Teheran? George Wade told me the other night that he'd heard from a guy in oil that it's a fascinating place. I know you don't think Albuquerque is fascinating, but in a funny kind of way it is to me, I wish I knew. Maybe I'll get to the bottom of it one of these days. If you ever get back here, look me up. For old time's sake.

Sincerely, Janet.

'The Passion of Marco Z—— (*Publisher's Weekly*) is 175 pages of dense twaddle.'

'If an author (*New York Magazine*) wants to write pornography, the least he can do is have the courage to come out with it (snicker).'

'What is Oahu Tech Press up to, anyway?' (Book Editor, *New York Times*——privately.)

'I've never read anything so unreadable.' (Virginia Kirkus, at the beach.)

What do they want? Edward said. I give them complex perception. I give them close observation of singular behavior. I give them an anguish of awareness . . . Is anything more required of the artist?

Nadine Gordimer

A City of the Dead, A City of the Living

You only count the days if you are waiting to have a baby or you are in prison. I've had my child but I'm counting the days since he's been in this house.

The street delves down between two rows of houses like the abandoned bed of a river that has changed course. The shebeen-keeper who lives opposite has a car that sways and churns its way to her fancy wrought-iron gate. Everyone else, including shebeen customers, walks over the stones, sand and gullies, home from the bus station. It's too far to bicycle to work in town.

The house provides the sub-economic township planner's usual two rooms and kitchen with a little yard at the back, into which his maquette figures of the ideal family unit of four fitted neatly. Like most houses in the street, it has been arranged inside and out to hold the number of people the ingenuity of necessity provides for. The garage is the home of sub-tenants. (The shebeen-keeper, who knows everything about everybody, might remember how the house came to have a garage—perhaps a taxi owner once lived there.) The front door of the house itself opens into a room that has been subdivided by greenish brocade curtains whose colour had faded and embossed pattern worn off before they were discarded in another kind of house. On one side of the curtains is a livingroom with just space enough to crate a plastic-covered sofa and two chairs, a coffee table with crocheted cover, vase of dyed feather flowers and oil lamp, and a radio-and-cassette-player combination with home-built speakers. There is a large varnished print of a horse with wild orange mane and flaring nostrils on the wall. The floor is cement, shined with black polish. On the other side of the curtains is a bed, a burglar-proofed window, a small table with candle, bottle of anti-acid tablets and alarm clock. During the day a frilly nylon nightgown is laid out on the blankets. A woman's clothes are in a box under the bed. In the dry cleaner's plastic sheath, a man's suit hangs from a nail.

A door, never closed, leads from the livingroom to the kitchen.

There is a sink, which is also the bathroom of the house, a coal-burning stove finned with chrome like a 1940s car, a pearly-blue formica dresser with glass doors that don't slide easily, a table and plastic chairs. The smell of cooking never varies: mealie-meal burning, curry overpowering the sweet reek of offal, sour porridge, onions. A small refrigerator, not connected, is used to store margarine, condensed milk, tinned pilchards; there is no electricity.

Another door, with a pebbled glass pane in its upper half, is always kept closed. It opens off the kitchen. Net curtains reinforce the privacy of the pebbled glass; the privacy of the tenant of the house, Samson Moreke, whose room is behind there, shared with his wife and baby and whichever of their older children spends time away from other relatives who take care of them in country villages. When all the children are in their parents' home at once, the sofa is a bed for two; others sleep on the floor in the kitchen. Sometimes the sofa is not available, since adult relatives who find jobs in the city need somewhere to live. Number 1907 Block C holds—has held—eleven people; how many it could hold is a matter of who else has nowhere to go. This reckoning includes the woman lodger and her respectable succession of lovers behind the green brocade curtain, but not the family lodging in the garage.

In the backyard, Samson Moreke, in whose name tenancy of Number 1907 Block C is registered by the authorities, has put up poles and chicken wire and planted Catawba grapevines that make a pleasant green arbour in summer. Underneath are three metal chairs and matching table, bearing traces of white paint, which—like the green brocade curtains, the picture of the horse with orange mane, the poles, chicken wire and vines—have been discarded by the various employers for whom Moreke works in the city as an itinerant gardener. The arbour is between the garage and the lavatory, which is shared by everyone on the property, both tenants and lodgers.

On Sundays Moreke sits under his grapevine and drinks a bottle of beer brought from the shebeen across the road. Even in winter he sits there; it is warmer out in the midday winter sun than in the house, the shadow of the vine merely a twisted rope—grapes eaten, roof of leaves fallen. Although the yard is behind the house and there is a yellow dog on guard tied to a packing-case shelter, there is not much privacy. A large portion of the space of the family living in the garage is taken up by a paraffin-powered refrigerator filled with soft-drink cans and pots of flavoured yoghurt: a useful little business that serves the community and supplements the earnings of the breadwinner, a cleaner at the city slaughter-house. The sliding metal shutter meant for the egress of a car from the garage is permanently bolted down. All day Sunday children come on errands to buy, knocking at the old kitchen door, salvaged from the city, that Moreke has set into the wall of the garage.

A street where there is a shebeen, a house opposite a shebeen cannot be private, anyway. All week drunks wander over the ruts that make the gait even of the sober seem drunken. The children playing in the street take no notice of men fuddled between song and argument, who talk to people who are not there.

As well as friends and relatives, acquaintances of Moreke who have got to know where he lives through travelling with him on the buses to work walk over from the shebeen and appear in the yard. He is a man who always puts aside money to buy the Sunday newspaper; he has to fold away the paper and talk instead. The guests usually bring a cold quart or two with them (the shebeen, too, has a paraffin refrigerator, restaurant-size). Talk and laughter make the dog bark. Someone plays a transistor radio. The chairs are filled and some comers stretch on the bit of tough grass. Most of the Sunday visitors are men but there are women, particularly young ones, who have gone with them to the shebeen or taken up with them there; these women are polite and deferential to Moreke's wife, Nanike, when she has time to join the gathering. Often they will hold her latest—fifth living—baby while she goes back into the kitchen to cook or hangs her washing on the fence. She takes a beer or two herself, but although she is in her early thirties and knows she is still pretty—except for a missing front tooth—she does not get flirtatious or giggle. She is content to sit with the new baby on her lap, in the sun, among men and women like herself, while her husband tells anecdotes which make them laugh or challenge him. He learns a lot from the newspapers.

She was sitting in the yard with him and his friends the Sunday a cousin arrived with a couple of hangers-on. They didn't bring beer, but were given some. There were greetings, but who really hears names? One of the hangers-on fell asleep on the grass, a boy with a body like a baggy suit. The other had a yellow face, lighter than anyone else present, narrow as a trowel, and the irregular pock-marks of the pitted skin were flocked, round the area where men grow hair, with sparse tufts of black. She noticed he wore a gold ear-ring in one ear. He had nothing to say but later took up a guitar belonging to someone else and played to himself. One of the people living in the garage, crossing the path of the group under the arbour on his way to the lavatory with his roll of toilet paper, paused to look or listen, but everyone else was talking too loudly to hear the soft plang-plang, and the after-buzz when the player's palm stilled the instrument's vibration.

Moreke went off with his friends when they left, and came back, not late. His wife had gone to bed. She was sleepy, feeding the baby. Because he stood there, at the foot of the bed, did not begin to undress, she understood someone must be with him.

'Mtembu's friend.' Her husband's head indicated the other side of the glass-paned door.

'What does he want here now?'

'I brought him. Mtembu asked.'

'What for?'

Moreke sat down on the bed. He spoke softly, mouthing at her face. 'He needs somewhere to stay.'

'Where was he before, then?'

Moreke lifted and dropped his elbows limply at a question not to be asked.

The baby lost the nipple and nuzzled furiously at air. She guided its mouth. 'Why can't he stay with Mtembu. You could have told Mtembu no.'

'He's your cousin.'

'Well, I will tell him no. If Mtembu needs somewhere to stay, I have to take him. But not anyone he brings from the street.'

Her husband yawned, straining every muscle in his face. Suddenly he stooped and began putting together the sheets of his Sunday paper that were scattered on the floor. He folded them more or less in order, slapping and smoothing the creases.

'Well?'

He said nothing, walked out. She heard voices in the kitchen, but not what was being said.

He opened their door again and shut it behind him. 'It's not a business of cousins. This one is in trouble. You don't read the papers . . . the blowing up of that police station . . . *you* know, last month? They didn't catch them all . . . It isn't safe for Mtembu to keep him any longer. He must keep moving.'

Her soft jowls stiffened.

Her husband assured her awkwardly. 'A few days. Only for a couple of days. Then—(a gesture)—out of the country.'

He never takes off the gold ear-ring, even when he sleeps. He sleeps on the sofa. He didn't bring a blanket, a towel, nothing—uses our things. I don't know what the ear-ring means; when I was a child there were men who came to work on the mines who had ear-rings, but in both ears—country people. He's a town person; another one who reads newspapers. He tidies away the blankets I gave him and then he reads newspapers the whole day. He can't go out.

The others at Number 1907 Block C were told the man was Nanike Moreke's cousin, had come to look for work and had nowhere to stay. There are people in that position in every house. No one with a roof over his head can say 'no' to one of the same blood—everyone knows that; Moreke's wife had not denied that. But she wanted to know what to say if someone asked the man's name. He himself answered at once, his strong thin hand twisting the gold hoop in his ear like a girl. 'Shisonka. Tell them Shisonka.'

'And the other name?'

Her husband answered. 'That name is enough.'

Moreke and his wife didn't use the name among themselves. They referred to the man as 'he' and 'him'. Moreke addressed him as 'Mfo', brother; she called him simply 'you'. Moreke answered questions nobody asked. He said to his wife, in front of the man, 'What is the same blood? Here in this place? If you are not white, you are all the same blood, here.' She looked at her husband respectfully, as she did when he read to her out of his newspaper.

The woman lodger worked in the kitchen at a Kentucky Fried Chicken shop in the city, and like Moreke was out at work all day; at weekends she slept at her mother's place, where her children lived, so she did not know the man Shisonka never left the house to look for work or for any other reason. Her lover came to her room only to share the bed, creeping late past whatever sleeping form might be on the sofa, and leaving before first light to get to a factory in the white industrial area. The only problem was the family who lived in the garage. The man had to cross the yard to use the lavatory. The slaughter-house cleaner's mother and wife would notice he was there, in the house; that he never went out. It was Moreke's wife who thought of this, and told the woman in the garage her cousin was sick, he had just been discharged from hospital. And indeed, they took care of him as if he had been—Moreke and his wife Nanike. They did not have the money to eat meat often but on Tuesday Moreke bought a pluck from the butchery near the bus station in the city; the man sat down to eat with them. Moreke brought cigarettes home—the man paid him—it was clear he must have cigarettes, needed cigarettes more than food. And don't let him go out, don't ever let him go to the shop for cigarettes, or over to Ma Radebe for drink, Moreke told his wife; *you* go, if he needs anything, *you* just leave everything, shut the house—go.

I wash his clothes with our things. His shirt and pullover have labels in another language, come from some other country. Even the letters that spell are different. I give him food in the middle of the day. I myself eat in the yard, with the baby. I told him he should play the music, in there, if he wants to. He listens to Samson's tapes. How could I keep my own sister out of the house? When she saw him I said he was a friend of Samson—a new friend. She likes light-skinned. But it means people notice you. It must be very hard to hide. He doesn't say so. He doesn't look afraid. The beard will hide him; but how long does it take for a beard to grow, how long, how long before he goes away.

Every night that week the two men talked. Not in the room with the sofa and radio-and-cassette player, if the woman lodger was at home on the other side of the curtains, but in the room where the Morekes slept. The man had a kitchen chair Moreke brought in, there was just room for it between the big bed and the wardrobe. Moreke lay on the bed with a pillow stuffed under his nape. Sometimes his wife stayed in the kitchen, at other times she came in and sat with the baby on the bed. She could see Moreke's face and the back of the man's head in the panel mirror of the wardrobe while they talked. The shape of the head swelled up from the thin neck, a puff-ball of black kapok. Deep in, there was a small patch without hair, a skin infection or a healed wound.

His front aspect—a narrow yellow face keenly attentive, cigarette wagging like a finger from the corner of his lips, loop of gold round the lobe of one of the alert pointed ears—seemed unaware of the blemish, something that attacked him unnoticed from behind.

They talked about the things that interested Moreke; the political meetings disguised as church services of which he read reports but did not attend. The man laughed, and argued with Moreke patiently. 'What's the use, man? If you don't stand there? Stand with your feet as well as agree with your head . . . Yes, go and get that head knocked if the dogs and the *kerries* come. Since '76, the kids've showed you how . . . You know now.'

Moreke wanted to tell the man what he thought of the Urban Councils the authorities set up, and the Committees people themselves had formed in opposition, as, when he found himself in the company of a sports promoter, he wanted to give his opinion of the state of soccer today. 'Those Council men are nothing to me. You understand? They only want big jobs and smart cars for themselves. I'm a poor man, I'll never have a car. But they say they're going to make this place like white Jo'burg. Maybe the government listens to them . . . They say they can do it. The Committees—eh?—they say like I do, *those Council men are nothing*—but they themselves, what can they do? They know everything is no good here. They talk; they tell about it; they go to jail. So what's the use? What can you do?'

The man did not tell what he had done. 'The police station' was there, ready in their minds, ready to their tongues; not spoken.

The man was smiling at Moreke, at something he had heard many times before and might be leaving behind for good, now. 'Your Council. Those dummies. You see this *donga* called a street, outside? This place without even electric light in the rooms? You dig beautiful gardens, the flowers smell nice . . . and how many people must shit in that shinking hovel in your yard? How much do you get for digging the ground white people own? You told me what you get. "Top Wages": ten rands a day. Just enough for the rent in this place, and not even the shit-house belongs to you, not even the mud you bring in from the yard on your shoes . . .'

Moreke became released, excited. 'The bus fares went up last week. They say the rent is going up . . .'

'Those dummies, that's what they do for you. You see? But the

Committee tells you don't pay that rent, because you aren't paid enough to live in the "beautiful city" the dummies promise you. Isn't that the truth? Isn't the truth what you *know*? Don't you listen to the ones who speak the truth?'

Moreke's wife had had, for a few minutes, the expression of one waiting to interrupt. 'I'll go to Radebe and get a bottle of beer, if you want.'

The two men gave a flitting nod to one another in approval.

Moreke counted out the money. 'Don't let anybody come back with you.'

His wife took the coins without looking up. 'I'm not a fool.' The baby was asleep on the bed. She closed the door quietly behind her. The two men lost the thread of their talk for a moment; Moreke filled it: 'A good woman.'

We are alone together. The baby likes him. I don't give the breast every time, now; yesterday when I was fetching the coal he fed the bottle to her. I ask him what children he has? He only smiles, shakes his head. I don't know if this means it was silly to ask, because everyone has children.

Perhaps it meant he doesn't know, pretends he doesn't know—thinks a lot of himself, smart young man with a gold ring in his ear has plenty of girl-friends to get babies with him.

The police station was never mentioned, but the man spent one of the nights describing to the Moreke couple foreign places he had been to—that must have been before the police station happened. He told about the oldest city on the African continent, so old it had a city of the dead as well as a city of the living—a whole city of tombs like houses. The religion there was the same as the religion of the Indian shopkeepers, here at home. Then he had lived in another kind of country, where there was snow for half the year or more. It was dark until ten in the morning and again from three o'clock in the afternoon. He described the clothes he had been given to protect him against the cold. 'Such people, I can tell you. You can't believe such white people exist. If our people turn up there . . . you get everything you need, they just give it . . . and there's a museum, it's out in the country, they have ships there their people sailed all over the world more than a thousand years ago. They may even have come here . . . This pullover is still from them . . . full of holes now . . .'

'Look at that, *hai*!' Moreke admired the intricately-worked bands of coloured wools in a design based upon natural features he did not recognize—dark frozen forms of fir forests and the constellation of snow cystals. 'She'll mend it for you.'

His wife was willing but apprehensive. 'I'll try and get the same colours. I don't know if I can find them there.'

The man smiled at the kindness of his own people. 'She shouldn't take a lot of trouble. I won't need it, anyway.'

No one asked where it was the pullover wouldn't be needed; what kind of place, what continent he would be going to when he got away.

After the man had retired to his sofa that night Moreke read the morning paper he had brought from an employer's kitchen in the city. He kept lowering the sheets slowly and looking around at the room, then returning to his reading. The baby was restless; but it was not that he commented on.

'It's better not to know too much about him.'

His wife turned the child onto its belly. 'Why?'

Her face was innocently before his like a mirror he didn't want to look into. He had kept encouraging the man to go on with his talk of living in foreign places.

The shadows thrown by the candles capered through the room, bending furniture and bodies, flying over the ceiling, quieting the baby with wonder. 'Because then . . . if they question us, we won't have anything to tell.'

He did bring something. A gun.

He comes into the kitchen, now, and helps me when I'm washing up. He came in, this morning, and put his hands in the soapy water, didn't say anything, started cleaning up. Our hands were in the grease and soap, I couldn't see his fingers but sometimes I felt them when they bumped mine. He scraped the pot and dried everything. I didn't say thanks. To say thank you to a man—it's not man's work, he might feel ashamed.

He stays in the kitchen—we stay in the kitchen with the baby most of the day. He doesn't sit in there, anymore, listening to the tapes. I go in and turn on the machine loud enough for us to hear it well in the kitchen.

By Thursday the tufts of beard were thickening and knitting together on the man's face. Samson Moreke tried to find Mtembu to hear what plans had been made but Mtembu did not come in response to messages and was not anywhere Moreke looked for him. Moreke took the opportunity, while the woman in whose garden he worked on Thursdays was out, to telephone Mtembu's place of work from her house, but was told that workshop employees were not allowed to receive calls.

He brought home chicken feet for soup and a piece of beef shank. Figs had ripened in the Thursday garden and he'd been given some in a newspaper poke. He asked, 'When do you expect to hear from Mtembu?'

The man was reading the sheet of paper stained with milky sap from the stems of figs. Samson Moreke had never really been in jail himself—only the usual short-term stays for pass offences—but he knew from people who had been inside a long time that there was this need to read every scrap of paper that might come your way from the outside world.

'—Well, it doesn't matter. You're all right here. We can just carry on. I suppose Mtembu will turn up this weekend.'

As if he heard in this resignation Moreke's anticipation of the usual Sunday beer in the yard, the man suddenly took charge of Moreke and his wife, crumpling the dirty newspaper and rubbing his palms together to rid them of stickiness. His narrow yellow face was set clear-cut in black hair all round now, like the framed face of the king in Moreke's worn pack of cards. The black eyes and ear-ring were the same liquid-bright. The perfectly-ironed shirt he wore was open at the breast in the manner of all attractive young men of his age. 'Look, nobody must come here. Saturday, Sunday. None of your friends. You must shut up this place. Keep them all away. Nobody walking into the yard from the shebeen. That's *out*.'

Moreke looked from the man to this wife; back to the man again. Moreke half-coughed, half-laughed. 'But how do I do that, man? How do I stop them? I can't put bars on my gate. There're the other people, in the garage. They sell things.'

'*You* stay inside. Here in this house, with the doors locked. There are too many people around at the weekend. Let them think you've gone away.'

Moreke still smiled, amazed, helpless. 'And the one in there, with her boy-friend? What's she going to think?'

Moreke's wife spoke swiftly. 'She'll be at her mother's house.'

And now the plan of action fell efficiently into place, each knew his part within it. 'Oh yes. Thank the Lord for that. Maybe I'll go over to Radebe's tonight and just say I'm not going to be here Sunday. And Saturday I'll say I'm going to the soccer.'

His wife shook her head. 'Not the soccer. Your friends will want to come and talk about it afterwards.'

'*Hai, mama!* All right, a funeral, far away . . .' Moreke laughed, and stopped himself with an embarrassed drawing of mucus back through the nose.

While I'm ironing, he cleans the gun.

I saw he needed another rag and I gave it to him.

He asked for oil, and I took cooking oil out of the cupboard, but then I saw in his face that was not what he wanted. I went to the garage and borrowed Three-in-One from Nchaba's wife.

He never takes out the gun when Samson's here. He knows only he and I know about it.

I said, what happened there, on your head at the back—that sore. His hand went to it, under the hair, he doesn't think it shows. I'll get him something for it, some ointment. If he's still here on Monday.

Perhaps he is cross because I spoke about it.

Then when I came back with the oil, he sat at the kitchen table laughing at me, smiling, as if I was a young girl. I forgot—I felt I was a girl. But I don't really like that kind of face, his face—light-skinned. You can never forget a face like that. If you are questioned, you can never say you don't remember what someone like that looks like.

He picks up the baby as if it belongs to him. To him as well, while we are in the kitchen together.

That night the two men didn't talk. They seemed to have nothing to say. Like prisoners who get their last mealie-pap of the day before being locked up for the night, Moreke's wife gave them their meal before dark. Then all three went from the kitchen to the Morekes' room, where any light that might shine from behind the curtains and give away a presence was directed only towards a blind: a high corrugated tin fence in a lane full of breast-high khakiweed. Moreke shared his newspaper. When the man had read it, he tossed through third-hand adventure comics and the sales promotion pamphlets given away in city supermarkets Nanike Moreke kept; he read the manual 'Teach Yourself How to Sell Insurance' in which, at some stage, 'Samson Moreke' had been carefully written on the fly-leaf.

There was no beer. Moreke's wife knew her way about her kitchen in the dark; she fetched the litre bottle of coke that was on the kitchen table and poured herself a glass. Her husband stayed the offer with a raised hand; the other man's inertia over the manual was overcome just enough to move his head in refusal. She had taken up again the cover for the bed she had begun when she had had some free time, waiting for this fifth child to be born. Crocheted roses, each caught in a squared web of a looser pattern, were worked separately and then joined to the whole they slowly extended. The tiny flash of her steel hook and the hair-thin gold in his ear signalled in candlelight. At about ten o'clock there was a knock at the front door. The internal walls of these houses are planned at minimum specification for cheapness and a blow on any part of the house reverberates through every room. The black-framed, bone-yellow face raised and held, absolutely still, above the manual. Moreke opened his mouth and, swinging his legs over the side, lifted himself from the bed. But his wife's hand on his shoulder made him subside again; only the bed creaked slightly. The slenderness of her body from the waist up was merely rooted in heavy maternal hips and thighs; with a movement soft as the breath she expelled, she leant and blew out the candles.

A sensible precaution; someone might follow round the walls of the house looking for some sign of life. They sat in the dark. There was no bark from the dog in the yard. The knocking stopped. Moreke thought he heard laughter, and the gate twang. But the shebeen is noisy on a Friday, the sounds could have come from anywhere. 'Just someone who's had a few drinks. It often happens. Sometimes we don't even wake up, I suppose, ay, Nanike.' Moreke's hoarse whisper, strangely, woke the baby, who let out the thin wail that meets the spectre in a bad dream, breaks through into consciousness against a threat that can't be defeated in the conscious world. In the dark, they all went to bed.

A city of the dead, a city of the living. It was better when Samson got him to talk about things like that. Things far away can't do any harm. We'll never have a car, like the Councillors, and we'll never have to run away to those far places, like him. Lucky to have this house; many, many people are jealous of that. I never knew, until this house was so quiet, how much noise people make at the weekend. I didn't hear the laughing, the talking in the street, Radebe's music going, the terrible screams of people fighting.

On Saturday Moreke took his blue ruled pad and an envelope to the kitchen table. But his wife was peeling pumpkin and slicing onions, there was no space, so he went back to the room where the sofa was, and his radio-and-cassette player. First he addressed the envelope to their twelve-year-old boy at mission school. It took him the whole morning to write a letter, although he could read so well. Once or twice he asked the man how to spell a word in English.

He lay smoking on his bed, the sofa. 'Why in English?'

'Rapula knows English very well . . . it helps him to get letters . . .'

'You shouldn't send him away from here, *baba*. You think it's safer, but you are wrong. It's like you and the meetings. The more you try to be safe, the worse it will be for your children.'

He stared quietly at Moreke. 'And look, now I'm here.'

'Yes.'

'And you look after me.'

'Yes.'

'And you're not afraid.'

'Yes, we're afraid . . . but of many things . . . when I come home with money . . . Three times tsotsis have hit me, taken everything. You see here where I was cut on the cheek. This arm was broken. I couldn't work. Not even push the lawnmower. I had to pay some young one to hold my jobs for me.'

The man smoked and smiled. 'I don't understand you. You see? I don't understand you. Bring your children home, man. We're shut up in the ghetto to kill each other. That's what they want, in their white city. So you send the children away; that's what they want, too. To get rid of us. We must all stick together. That's the only way to fight our way out.'

That night he asked if Moreke had a chess set.

Moreke giggled, gave clucks of embarrassment. 'That board with the little dolls? I'm not an educated man! I don't know those games!'

They played together the game that everybody knows, that is played on the pavements outside shops and in factory yards, with the board drawn on concrete or in dust, and bottle-tops for counters. This time a handful of dried beans from the kitchen served, and a board drawn by Moreke on a box-lid. He won game after game from the man. His wife had the Primus stove in the room, now, and she made tea. The game was not resumed. She had added three completed squares to her bed-cover in two nights; after the tea, she did not take it up again. They sat listening to Saturday night, all round them, pressing in upon the hollow cement units of which the house was built. Often tramping steps seemed just about to halt at the front or back door. The splintering of wood under a truncheon or the shatter of the window-panes, thin ice under the weight of the roving dark outside, waited upon every second. The woman's eyelids slid down, fragile and faintly greasy, outlining intimately the aspect of the orbs beneath, in sleep. Her face became unguarded as the baby's. Every now and then she would start, come to herself again. But her husband and the man made no move to go to bed. The man picked up and ran the fine head of her crochet hook under the rind of each fingernail, again and again, until the tool had done the cleaning job to satisfaction.

When the man went to bed at last, by the light of the cigarette lighter he shielded in his hand to see his way to the sofa, he found she had put a plastic chamber-pot on the floor. Probably the husband had thought of it.

All Sunday morning the two men worked together on a fault in Moreke's tape-player, though they were unable to test it with the volume switched on. Moreke could not afford to take the player to a repair shop. The man seemed to think the fault a simple matter; like any other city youngster, he had grown up with such machines. Moreke's wife cooked mealie-rice and made a curry gravy for the Sunday meal. 'Should I go to Radebe and get beer?' She followed her husband into their room to ask him alone.

'You want to advertise we are here? You know what he said.'

'Ask him if it matters, if I go—a woman.'

'I'm not going to ask. Did he say he wants beer? Did I?'

But in the afternoon, she did ask something. She went straight to the man, not Moreke. 'I have to go out to the shop.' It was very hot in the closed house; the smell of curry mixed with the smell of the baby in the fug of its own warmth and wrappings. He wrinkled his face, exposed clenched teeth in a suppressed yawn; what shops—had she forgotten it was Sunday? She understood his reaction. But there were corner shops that sold essentials even on Sundays; he must know that. 'I have to get milk. Milk for the baby.'

She stood there, in her over-trodden slippers, her old skirt and cheap blouse—a woman not to be noticed among every other woman in the streets. He didn't refuse her. No need. Not after all this past week. Not for the baby. She was not like her husband, big-mouth, friendly with everyone. He nodded; it was a humble errand that wouldn't concern him.

She went out of the house just as she was, her money in her hand. Moreke and the baby were asleep in their room. The street looked new, bright, refreshing, after the dim house. A small boy with a toy machine-gun covered her in his fire, chattering his little white teeth with rat-a-tat-tttt. Ma Radebe, the shebeen-keeper, her hair plaited with blue and red beads, her beautiful long red nails resting on the steering wheel, was backing her car out of the gateway. She braked to let her neighbour pass and leaned from the car window. '*My dear* (in English), I was supposed to be gone from this place two hours ago. I'm due at a big wedding that will already be over . . . How are you? Didn't see your husband for a few days . . . nothing wrong across the road?'

Moreke's wife stood and shook her head. Radebe was not one who expected or waited for answers when she greeted anyone. When the car had driven off Moreke's wife went on down the street and down the next one, past the shop where young boys were gathered scuffling and dancing to the shopkeeper's radio, and on to the purplish brick building with the security fence round it and a flag flying. One of her own people was on guard outside, lolling with a sub-machine-gun. She went up the steps and into the office, where there were more of her own people in uniform, but one of *them* in charge. She spoke in her own language to her own kind, but they seemed disbelieving. They repeated the name of that other police station, that was blown up, and asked her if she was sure? She said she was quite sure. Then they took her to the white officer and she told in English—'There, in my house, 1907 Block C. He has been there a week. He has a gun.'

I don't know why I did it. I get ready to say that to anyone who is going to ask me, but nobody in this house asks. The baby laughs at me while I wash her, stares up while we're alone in the house and she's feeding at the breast, and to her I say out loud: I don't know why.

A week after the man was taken away that Sunday by the security police, Ma Radebe again met Moreke's wife in their street. The shebeen-keeper gazed at her for a moment, and spat.

Ruth Rendell

The Convolvulus Clock

'Is that your own hair, dear?'

Sibyl only laughed. She made a roguish face.

'I didn't think it could be,' said Trixie. 'It looks so thick.'

'A woman came up to me in the street the other day,' said Sibyl, 'and asked me where I had my hair set. I just looked at her. I gave a tiny little tip to my wig like this. You should have seen her face.'

She gave another roar of laughter. Trixie smiled austerely. She had come to stay with Sibyl for a week and this was her first evening. Sibyl had bought a cottage in Devonshire. It was two years since Trixie had seen Sibyl and she could detect signs of deterioration. What a pity that was! Sibyl enquired after the welfare of the friends they had in common. How was Mivvy? Did Trixie see anything of the Fishers? How was Poppy?

'Poppy is beginning to go a bit funny,' said Trixie.

'How do you mean, "funny"?'

'You know. Funny. Not quite *compos mentis* any more.'

Sibyl of all people ought to know what going funny meant, thought Trixie.

'We're none of us getting any younger,' said Sibyl, laughing.

Trixie didn't sleep very well. She got up at five and had her bath so as to leave the bathroom clear for Sibyl. At seven she took Sibyl a cup of tea. She gave a little scream and nearly dropped the tray.

'Oh my conscience! I'm sorry, dear, but I thought that was a squirrel on your chest of drawers. I thought it must have come in through the window.'

'What on earth was that noise in the middle of the night?' When Sibyl wasn't laughing she could be downright peevish. She looked a hundred without her wig. 'It woke me up, I thought the tank was overflowing.'

'The middle of the night! I like that. The sun had been up a good hour, I'm sure. I was just having my bath so as not to be a nuisance.'

They went out in Sibyl's car. They had lunch in Dawlish and tea in Exmouth. The following day they went out early and drove across Dartmoor. When they got back there was a letter on the mat for Trixie from Mivvy, though Trixie had only been away two days. On Friday Sibyl said they would stay at home and have a potter about the village. The church was famous, the Manor House gardens were open to the public and there was an interesting small gallery where an exhibition was on. She started to get the car out but Trixie said why couldn't they walk. It could hardly be more than a mile. Sibyl said it was just under two miles but she agreed to walk if Trixie really wanted to. Her knee hadn't been troubling her quite so much lately.

'The gallery is called Artifacts,' said Sibyl. 'It's run by a very nice young couple.'

'A husband and wife team?' asked Trixie, very modern.

'Jimmy and Judy they're called. I don't think they are actually married.'

'Oh my conscience, Sibyl, how can one be "actually" married? Surely one is either married or not?' Trixie herself had been married once, long ago, for a short time. Sibyl had never been married and neither had Mivvy or Poppy. Trixie thought that might have something to do with their going funny. 'Thankfully, I'm broad-minded. I shan't say anything. I think I can see a seat ahead in that bus shelter. Would you like a little sit-down before we go on?'

Sibyl got her breath back and they walked on more slowly. The road passed between high hedges on high banks dense with wild flowers. It crossed a stream by a hump-backed bridge where the clear brown shallow water rippled over a bed of stones. The church appeared with granite nave and tower, standing on an eminence and approached, Sibyl said, by fifty-three steps. Perhaps they should go to Artifacts first?

The gallery was housed in an ancient building with bow windows and a front door set under a Georgian portico. When the door was pushed open a bell tinkled to summon Jimmy or Judy. This morning, however, they needed no summoning for both were in the first room, Judy dusting the dolls' house and Jimmy doing something to the ceiling spotlights. Sibyl introduced Trixie to them and Trixie was very gracious towards Judy, making no difference in her manner than she would have if the young woman had been properly married and worn a wedding ring.

Trixie was agreeably surprised by the objects in the exhibition and by the items Jimmy and Judy had for sale. She had not expected such a high standard. What she admired most particularly were the small pictures of domestic interiors done in embroidery, the patchwork quilts and the blown glass vases in colours of mother-of-pearl and butterfly wings. What she liked best of all and wanted to have was a clock.

There were four of these clocks, all different. The cases were ceramic, plain and smooth or made in trellis work, glazed in blues and greens, painted with flowers or the moon and stars, each incorporating a gilt-rimmed face and quartz movement. Trixie's favourite was blue with a green trellis over the blue, a convolvulus plant with green leaves and pale pink trumpet flowers climbing the trellis and a gilt rim round the face of the clock which had hands of gilt and blue. The convolvulus reminded her of the pattern on her best china tea service. All the clocks had price cards beside them and red discs stuck to the cards.

'I should like to buy this clock,' Trixie said to Judy.

'I'm terribly sorry but it's sold.'

'Sold?'

'All the clocks were sold at the private view. Roland Elm's work is tremendously popular. He can't make enough of these clocks and he refuses to take orders.'

'I still don't understand why I can't buy this one,' said Trixie. 'This is a shop, isn't it?'

Sibyl had put on her peevish look. 'You can see the red sticker, can't you? You know what that means.'

'I know what it means at the Royal Academy but hardly here surely.'

'I really do wish I could sell it to you,' said Judy, 'but I can't.'

Trixie lifted her shoulders. She was very disappointed and wished she hadn't come. She had been going to buy Sibyl a pear carved from polished pear wood but now she thought better of it. The church was also a let-down, dark, poky and smelling of mould.

'Things have come to a pretty pass when shopkeepers won't sell their goods to you because they're upset by your manner.'

'Judy wasn't upset by your manner,' said Sibyl, puffing. 'It's more than her reputation is worth to sell you something she's already sold.'

'Reputation! I like that.'

'I mean reputation as a gallery owner. Artifacts is quite highly regarded round here.'

'You would have thought she and her—well, partner, would be glad of £62. I don't suppose they have two half-pennies to bless themselves with.'

What Sibyl would have thought was never known for she was too out of breath to utter and when they got home had to lie down. Next morning another letter came from Mivvy.

'Nothing to say for herself of course,' said Trixie at breakfast. 'Practically a carbon copy of Thursday's. She's going very funny. Do you know she told me sometimes she writes fifty letters in a week? God bless your pocket, I said. It's fortunate you can afford it.'

They went to Princetown in Sibyl's car and Widecombe-in-the-Moor. Trixie sent postcards to Mivvy, Poppy, the Fishers and the woman who came in to clean and water the plants in the greenhouse. She would have to buy some sort of present for Sibyl before she left. A plant would have done, only Sibyl didn't like gardening. They went to a bird sanctuary and looked at some standing stones of great antiquity. Trixie was going home on Tuesday afternoon. On Tuesday morning another letter arrived from Mivvy all about the Fishers going to see the Queen Mother open a new arts centre in Leighton Buzzard. The Fishers were crazy about the Queen Mother, watched for her engagements in advance and went wherever she went within a radius of 150 miles in order just to catch a glimpse of her. Once they had been at the front of the crowd and the Queen Mother had shaken hands with Dorothy Fisher.

'We're none of us getting any younger,' said Sibyl, giggling.

'Well, my conscience, I know one thing,' said Trixie. 'The days have simply flown past while I've been here.'

'I'm glad you've enjoyed yourself.'

'Oh, I have, dear, only it would please me to see you a little less frail.'

Trixie walked to the village on her own. Since she couldn't think of anything else she was going to have to buy the pear-wood pear for Sibyl. It was a warm sunny morning, one of the best days she'd had, and the front door of Artifacts stood open to the street. The exhibition was still on and the clocks (and their red 'sold' discs) still there. A shaft of sunlight streamed across the patchwork quilts on to the Georgian dolls' house. There was no sign of Jimmy or Judy. The gallery was empty but for herself.

Trixie closed the door and opened it to make the bell ring. She picked up one of the pear-wood pears and held it out in front of her on the palm of her hand. She held it at arm's length the way she did when she had helped herself to an item in the supermarket just so that there couldn't be the slightest question of anyone suspecting her of shoplifting. No one came. Trixie climbed the stairs, holding the pear-wood pear out in front of her and clearing her throat to attract attention. There was no one upstairs. A blue Persian cat lay sleeping on a shelf between a ginger jar and a mug with an owl on it. Trixie descended. She closed the front door and opened it to make the bell ring. Jimmy and Judy must be a heedless pair, she thought. Anyone could walk in here and steal the lot.

Of course she could just take the pear-wood pear and leave a £5 note to pay for it. It cost £4.75. Why should she make Jimmy and Judy a present of 25p just because they were too idle to serve her? Then she remembered that when she had been here with Sibyl a door at the end of the passage had been open and through that door one could see the garden where there was a display of terracotta pots. It was probable that Jimmy and Judy were out there, showing the pots to a customer.

Trixie went through the second room and down the passage. The door to the garden was just ajar and she pushed it open. On the lawn, in a cane chair, Judy lay fast asleep. A ledger had fallen off her lap and lay on the grass alongside a heap of books. Guides to the management of tax they were and some which looked like the gallery account books. It reminded Trixie of Poppy who was always falling asleep in the daytime, most embarrassingly sometimes, at the table or even while waiting for a bus. Judy had fallen asleep over her book-keeping. Trixie coughed. She said 'Excuse me' very loudly and repeated it but Judy didn't stir.

What a way to run a business! It would serve them right if someone walked in and cleared their shop. It would teach them a lesson. Trixie pulled the door closed behind her. She found herself tiptoeing as she walked back along the passage and through the second room. In the first room she took the ceramic clock with the convolvulus on it off the shelf and put it into her bag and she took the card too with the red sticker on it so as not to attract attention to the clock's absence. The pear-wood pear she replaced among the other carved fruit.

The street outside seemed deserted. Trixie's heart was beating rather fast. She went across the road into the little newsagent's and gift shop and bought Sibyl a teacloth with a map of Devonshire on it. At the door, as she was coming out again, she saw Jimmy coming along the street towards the gallery with a bag of groceries under one arm and two pints of milk in the other. Trixie stayed where she was until he had gone into Artifacts.

She didn't much fancy the walk back but there was no help for it. When she got to the bridge over the stream she heard hooves behind her and for a second or two had a feeling she was pursued by men on horseback but it was only a girl who passed her, riding a fat white pony. Sibyl laughed when she saw the teacloth and said it was a funny thing to give someone who *lived* in Devonshire. Trixie felt nervous and couldn't eat her lunch. Jimmy and Judy would have missed the clock by now and the newsagent would have remembered a furtive-looking woman skulking in his doorway and described her to them and soon the police would come. If only Sibyl would hurry with the car! She moved so slowly, time had no meaning for her. At this rate Trixie wouldn't even catch her train at Exeter.

She did catch it—just. Sibyl's car had been followed for several miles of the way by police in a Rover with a blue lamp on top and Trixie's heart had been in her mouth. Why had she done it? What had possessed her to take something she hadn't paid for, she who when shopping in supermarkets held 17p pots of yoghurt at arm's length?

Now she was safely in the train rushing towards Paddington she began to see things in a different light. She would have paid for that clock if they had let her. What did they expect if they refused to sell things they had on sale? And what *could* they expect if they went to sleep leaving their shop unattended? For a few moments she had a nasty little qualm that the police might be waiting for her outside her own door but they weren't. Inside all was as it should be, all was as she had left it except that Poppy had put a pint of milk in the fridge and someone had arranged dahlias in a vase—not Poppy, she wouldn't know a dahlia from a runner bean.

That would be just the place for the clock, on the wall bracket where at present stood a photograph of herself and Dorothy Fisher at Broadstairs in 1949. Trixie put the photograph away in a drawer and the clock where the photograph had been. It looked nice. It transformed a rather dull corner of the room. Trixie put one of the cups from her tea service beside it and it was amazing how well they matched.

Mivvy came round first thing in the morning. Before letting her in Trixie quickly snatched the clock off the shelf and thrust it inside the drawer with the photograph. It seemed so *exposed* up there, it seemed to tell its history in every tiny tick.

'How did you find Sibyl?'

Trixie wanted to say, I went in the train to Exeter and got out at the station and there was Sibyl waiting for me in her car . . . Only if you started mocking poor Mivvy where would you end? 'Very frail, dear. I thought she was going a bit funny.'

'I must drop her a line.'

Mivvy always spoke as if her letters held curative properties. Receiving one of them would set you up for the winter. After she had gone Trixie considered replacing the clock on the shelf but thought better of it. Let it stay in the drawer for a bit. She had read of South American millionaires who have Old Masters stolen for them which they can never show but are obliged, for fear of discovery, to keep hidden away for ever in dark vaults.

Just before Christmas a letter came from Sibyl. They always sent each other Christmas cards. As Trixie said, if you can't get around to writing the rest of the year, at least you can at Christmas. Mivvy wrote hundreds. Sibyl didn't mention the theft of the clock or indeed mention the gallery at all. Trixie wondered why not. The clock was still in the drawer. Sometimes she lay awake in the night thinking about it, fancying she could hear its tick through the solid mahogany of the drawer, through the ceiling and the bedroom floorboards.

It was curious how she had taken a dislike to the convolvulus tea service. One day she found herself wrapping it in tissue paper and putting it away in the cupboard under the stairs. She took down all the trellis work round the front door and put up wires for the clematis instead. In March she wrote to Sibyl to enquire if there was a new exhibition on at Artifacts. Sibyl didn't answer for weeks. When she did she told Trixie that months and months back one of those ceramic clocks had been stolen from the gallery and a few days later an embroidered picture had also gone and furniture out of the dolls' house. Hadn't Sibyl mentioned it before? She thought she had but she was getting so forgetful these days.

Trixie took the clock out of the drawer and put it on the shelf. Because she knew she couldn't be found out she began to feel she hadn't done anything wrong. The Fishers were bringing Poppy round for a cup of tea. Trixie started unpacking the convolvulus tea service. She lost her nerve when she heard Gordon Fisher's car door slam and she put the clock away again. If she were caught now she might get blamed for the theft of the picture and the dolls' house furniture as well. They would say she had sold those things and how could she prove she hadn't?

Poppy fell asleep halfway through her second buttered scone.

'She gets funnier every time I see her,' Trixie said. 'Sad, really. Sibyl's breaking up too. She'll forget her own name next. You should see her letters. I'll just show you the last one.' She remembered she couldn't do that, it wouldn't be wise, so she had to pretend she'd mislaid it.

'Will you be going down there again this year, dear?' said Dorothy.

'Oh, I expect so. You know how it is, you get to the stage of thinking it may be the last time.'

Poppy woke up with a snort, said she hadn't been asleep and finished her scone.

Gordon asked Trixie, 'Would you like to come with us to see Her Majesty open the new leisure complex in Rayleigh on Monday?'

Trixie declined. The Fishers went off to do their shopping, leaving Poppy behind. She was asleep again. She slept till six and, waking, asked Trixie if she had put something in her tea. It was most unusual, she said, for her to nod off like that. Trixie walked her back to the bus stop because the traffic whipped along there so fast you had to have your wits about you and drivers didn't respect zebra crossings the way they used to. Trixie marched across on the stripes, confident as a lollipop lady but without the lollipop, taking her life in her hands instead.

She wrote to Sibyl that she would come to Devonshire at the end of July, thinking that while there it might be best to make some excuse to avoid going near Artifacts. The clock was still in the drawer but wrapped up now in a piece of old flannel. Trixie had taken a dislike to seeing the colour of it each time she opened the drawer. She had a summer dress that colour and she wondered why she had ever bought it, it didn't flatter her, whatever it might do for the Queen Mother. Dorothy could have it for her next jumble sale.

Walking back from posting a letter, Mivvy fell over and broke her ankle. It was weeks getting back to normal. Well, you had to face it, it was never going to be *normal*. You wouldn't be exaggerating, Trixie wrote to Sibyl, if you said that obsession of hers for writing letters had crippled her for life. Sibyl wrote back to say she was looking forward to the last week of July and what did Trixie think had happened? They had caught the thief of the pieces from Artifacts trying to sell the picture to a dealer in Plymouth. He had said in court he hadn't taken the clock but you could imagine how much credence the magistrate placed on that!

Trixie unwrapped the clock and put it on the shelf. Next day she got the china out. She wondered why she had been so precipitate in pulling all that trellis off the wall, it looked a lot better than strands of wire on metal hooks. Mivvy came round in a taxi, hobbling up the path on two sticks, refusing the offer of the taxi driver's arm.

'You'll be off to Sibyl's in a day or two, will you, dear?'

Trixie didn't know how many times she had told her not till Monday week. She was waiting for Mivvy to notice the clock but at this rate she was going to have to wait till Christmas.

'What do you think of my clock?'

'What, up there? Isn't that your Wedgwood coffee pot, dear?'

Trixie had to get it down. She thrust it under Mivvy's nose and started explaining what it was.

But Mivvy knew already. 'Of course I know it's a clock, dear. It's not the first time I've seen one of these. Oh my goodness, no. The young man who makes these, he's a friend of my nephew Tony, they were at art school together. Let me see, what's his name? It will come to me in a minute. A tree, isn't it? Oak? Ash? Peter Oak? No, Elm is his name. Something Elm. Roland Elm.'

Trixie said nothing. The glazed surface of the clock felt very cold against the skin of her hands.

'He never makes them to order, you know. He just makes a limited number for a few selected galleries. Tony told me that.

Where did you get yours, I wonder?'

Trixie said nothing. There was worse coming and she waited for it.

'Not around here, I'm sure. I know there are only two or three places in the country they go to. It will come to me in a minute. I shall be writing to Tony tomorrow and I'll mention about you having one of Richard's—no, I mean Raymond's, that is, Roland's, clocks. I always write to him on Tuesdays. Tuesday is his day. I'll mention you've got one with bindweed on it. They're all different, you know. He never makes two alike.'

'It's convolvulus, not bindweed,' said Trixie. 'I'd rather you didn't write to Tony about it if you don't mind.'

'Oh, but I'd like to mention it, dear. Whyever not? I won't mention your name if you don't want me to. I'll just say that lady who goes down to stay with Auntie Sibyl in Devonshire.'

Trixie said she would walk with Mivvy up to the High Street. It was hopeless trying to get a taxi outside here. She fetched Mivvy's two sticks.

'You take my arm and I'll hold your other stick.'

The traffic whipped along over the zebra crossing. You were at the mercy of those drivers, Trixie said, it was a matter of waiting till they condescended to stop.

'Don't you set foot on those stripes till they stop,' she said to Mivvy.

Mivvy didn't, so the cars didn't stop. A container lorry, a juggernaut, came thundering along, but a good way off still. Trixie thought it was going much too fast.

'Now if we're quick,' she said. 'Run for it!'

Startled by the urgency in her voice, Mivvy obeyed, or tried to obey as Trixie dropped her arm and gave her a little push forward. The lorry's brakes screamed like people being tortured and Trixie jumped back, screaming herself, covering her face with her hands so as not to see Mivvy under those giant wheels.

Dorothy Fisher said she quite understood Trixie would still want to go to Sibyl's for her holiday. It was the best thing in the world for her, a rest, a complete change, a chance to forget. Trixie went down by train on the day after the funeral. She had the clock in her bag with her, wrapped first in tissue paper and then in her sky-blue dress. The first opportunity that offered itself she would take the clock back to Artifacts and replace it on the shelf she had taken it from. This shouldn't be too difficult. The clock was a dangerous possession, she could see that, like one of those notorious diamonds that carry a curse with them. Pretty though it was, it was an *unlucky* clock that had involved her in trouble from the time she had first taken it.

There was no question of walking to Artifacts this time. Sibyl was too frail for that. She had gone downhill a lot since last year and symptomatic of her deterioration was her exchange of the grey wig for a lilac-blue one. They went in the car though Trixie was by no means sure Sibyl was safe at the wheel.

As soon as they walked into the gallery Trixie saw that she had no hope of replacing the clock without being spotted. There was a desk in the first room now with a plump smiling lady sitting at it who Sibyl said was Judy's mother. Trixie thought that amazing—a mother not minding her daughter cohabiting with a man she wasn't married to. Living with a daughter living in sin, you might put it. Jimmy was in the second room, up on a ladder doing something to the window catch.

'They're having upstairs remodelled,' said Sibyl. 'You can't go up there.' And when Trixie tried to make her way towards the garden door, 'You don't want to be had up for trespassing, do you?' She winked at Judy's mother. 'We're none of us getting any younger when all's said and done, are we?'

They went back to Sibyl's, the clock still in Trixie's bag. It seemed to have grown heavier. She could hear it ticking through the leather and the folds of the sky-blue dress. In the afternoon when Sibyl lay down on the sofa for her rest, the lilac wig stuck on top of a Poole pottery vase, Trixie went out for a walk, taking the clock with her. She came to the hump-backed bridge over the stream where the water was very low, for it had been a dry summer. She unwrapped the clock and dropped it over the low parapet into the water. It cracked but the trellis work and the convolvulus remained intact and the movement continued to move and to tick as well for all Trixie knew. The blue and green, the pink flowers and the gilt, gleamed through the water like some exotic iridescent shell.

Trixie went down the bank. She took off her shoes and waded into the water. It was surprisingly cold. She picked up a large flat stone and beat at the face of the clock with it. She beat with unrestrained fury, gasping and grunting at each blow. The green trellis and the blue sky, the glass face and the pink flowers, all shattered. But they were still there, bright jewel-like shards, for all to see who came this way across the bridge.

Squatting down, Trixie scooped up handfuls of pebbles and buried the pieces of clock under them. With her nails she dug a pit in the bed of the stream and pushed the coloured fragments into it, covering them with pebbles. Her hands were bleeding, her knees were bruised and her dress was wet. In spite of her efforts the bed of the stream was still spread with ceramic chips and broken glass and pieces of gilt metal. Trixie began to sob and crawl from side to side of the stream, ploughing her hands through the blue and green and gold gravel, and it was there that one of Sibyl's neighbours found her as he was driving home over the bridge.

He lifted her up and carried her to his car.

'Tick-tock,' said Trixie. 'Tick-tock. Convolvulus clock.'

Elizabeth Jolley

Paper Children

Clara Schultz lying alone in a strange hotel bedroom was suddenly confronted by the most horrible thoughts. For a woman accustomed to the idea that she would live for ever, having lived, it seemed for- ever, these thoughts were far from welcome. For instead of being concerned with her immortality they were, without doubt, gravely about her own death.

Perhaps it was the long journey by air. She had travelled from Vienna, several hours in an aeroplane with the clock being altered relentlessly while her own body did not change so easily. She was on her way to her daughter. She had not seen her since she was a baby and now she was a grown woman, a stranger, married to a farmer. A man much younger than herself and from a background quite unknown to Clara and so somewhat despised by her. She confided nothing of this thought, rather she boasted of her daughter's marriage.

'I am going to visit Lisa, my daughter, you know,' she told her neighbour Irma Rosen. Sometimes they stopped to talk on the stairs in the apartment house in the Lehar Strasse and Clara would impress on Irma forcefully, 'My daughter is married to an Australian farmer and expecting her first child. All these years I have only a paper daughter and now my paper children, my daughter and son-in-law, they want me to come, they have invited me!' And Irma whose smooth face was like a pink sugar cake on the handworked lace collar of her dress nodded and smiled with admiration.

It was only when she was alone Clara despised the farmer husband, she was able to overlook completely that her despising was in reality a kind of fear of him and his piece of land.

'We are in a valley,' Lisa wrote to her mother. Clara tried to imagine the valley. She had in her mind a picture of a narrow green flower-splashed place with pine trees on the steep slopes above the clusters of painted wooden houses, like in the Alps, very gay and always in holiday mood. She tried to alter the picture because Lisa described tall trees with white bark and dry leaves which glittered in the bright sunshine, she wrote also of dust and corrugated iron and wire netting and something called weather-board. Clara found it hard to imagine these things she had never seen.

No one can know when death will come or how. Alone in the hotel, Clara thought what if she should go blind before dying. She thought of her room at home, what if she had to grope in that familiar place unable to find her clothes, unable to see where her books and papers were. She lay with her eyes closed and tried to see her desk and her lamp and her silver inkwell, trying to place things in order in her mind so that she would find her way from one possession to the next.

What if she should go blind now here in this strange room, not knowing any other person here? In a sudden fear she pushed back the bedclothes and put her small white fat feet out of the bed and stood on the strange floor and groped like a blind person for the light switch.

'Lisa,' she said to her daughter gently so as not to startle the girl. Lisa turned, she had a very white face, she moved awkwardly and her face was small as if she was in pain. She was much younger than her mother expected her to be. Beside her was a little girl of about two years, she had fair hair cut square across a wan little forehead. The child had been crying.

'What a dear little girl,' Clara said as pleasantly as she knew how. 'What do you call her?'

'Sharon.'

'Cheri?'

'No Sharon.'

'Ach! What a pretty name. Come here to Grossmutti my darlink,' but the little girl hid behind the half open door.

'What a pretty place you have Lisa,' Clara tried. 'Pretty! Pretty!' She waved her short plump arm towards the desolate scene of the neglected hillside, cleared years ago, scraped and never planted; patches of prickly secondary growth littered the spaces between collapsing sheds and the tangles of wire netting where some fowls had lived their lives laying eggs.

The house, in decay, cried out for mercy, it was a place quite uncherished. The rust on the iron roof was like a disease, scabs of it scaled off and marked the verandah as if with an infection.

Clara wondered why. Poverty perhaps or was Lisa feckless? Clara had no patience with a feckless woman. If they were poor, well she had money, and she would find out the best way to spend it. She wanted to help Lisa. All the tenderness stored up over the empty years was there to be poured forth, now on her child and her child's property.

'Have you hurt yourself Lisa?' Clara tried again, softly gently as if speaking in a dream. She had not expected a little girl. She knew only that her daughter was pregnant.

'Lisa wants me to be near when she has her baby, my paper children want me,' Clara told Irma on the stairs and Irma nodded her approval. 'So I burn up my ships as they say in English and go.' Clara had taken many big steps in her life but never such a final one as this might be. Australia was such a long way off from Vienna, it almost could not exist it was so remote.

'They have fifty cows and sheeps and chickens.' Such space was not to be imagined on the dark stairs of the apartment. 'Such a long way!' Clara said 'But air travel, you know, makes the world so much smaller.'

'Have you hurt yourself Lisa?' Gently she approached the pale young woman who was her unknown daughter.

'Aw it's nuthin',' the girl replied. 'He threw me down the other night, I kept tellin' him "You're hurtin' my back!" but he took no notice. "You're hurtin' my back," I shouted at him!' She rubbed the end of her spine.

Clara flinched with a real hurt.

'Pete, this is my mother,' Lisa said as a short thick-set young man, very sunburned and bullet shaped came round the side of the house. He threw a bucket to his wife. 'Mother this is Pete.'

As they stood together the sun slid quickly into the scrub on the far hillside and long shadows raced one after the other across and along the sad valley. Clara had never seen such a pair of people and in such dreary hopeless surroundings. She felt so strange and so alone in the gathering darkness of the evening.

The little muscular husband shouted something at Lisa and marched off with hardly a look at his new mother-in-law. Clara couldn't help remembering the Gestapo and their friend, they thought he was their friend, the one who became a Gauleiter. That was it! Gauleiter Peter Gregory married to her daughter Lisa.

'This man is my father's friend,' proudly Clara had introduced the friend to her husband only to experience in a very short time a depth of betrayal and cruelty quite beyond her comprehension. Friends became enemies overnight. Lisa's husband somehow reminded Clara unexpectedly of those times.

'Have you something to put on your back?' Clara asked.

'Like what?' the girl looked partly amused and partly defiant.

'Menthol Camphor or something like that,' Clara felt the remoteness between them, a kind of wandering between experience and dreams. She moved her hand in a circular movement. 'Something to massage, you know.'

At first Lisa didn't understand, perhaps it was the unusual English her mother spoke. Clara repeated the suggestion slowly.

'Aw No! Had a ray lamp but he dropped it larst night! Threw it down most likely but he said he dropped it. "The lamp's died," he said. I thought I'd die laughin' but I was that mad at him reely I was!'

'Should we, perhaps, go indoors?' Clara was beginning to feel cold. The Gauleiter was coming back. 'I just have these few packages,' Clara indicated her luggage which was an untidy circle about her. But the young couple had gone into the cottage leaving her to deal with her baggage as well as she could.

Trying to hear some sort of sound she heard the voice of Gauleiter Peter Gregory shouting at his wife, her daughter Lisa, and she heard Lisa scream back at her husband. Voices and words she couldn't hear and understand properly from the doorway of the asbestos porch. She heard the husband push the wife so that she must have stumbled, she heard Lisa fall against a piece of furniture which also fell, a howl of pain from Lisa and the little child, Sharon, began to cry.

Clara entered the airless dishevelled room. Because of all she was carrying it was difficult, so many bundles. 'One cannot make such a journey without luggage,' Clara explained to Irma as, buried in packages, she said goodbye to her neighbour, 'Goodbye Irma. Goodbye for ever dear friend.'

Besides she had presents for Lisa and even something for that husband.

Lisa looked up almost with triumph at her mother.

'I'm seven months gone', she said 'and he wouldn't care if he killed me!' The husband's sunburned face disappeared in the gloom of the dirty room.

'Oh,' Clara said pleasantly, 'she is too young to die and far too pretty.'

'Huh! me pretty!' Lisa scoffed and, awkwardly, because of the pain in her back, she eased herself into a chair.

'Who's young!' the husband muttered in the dark. Clara didn't know if he was sitting or standing. 'Well, we women must back each other up,' she said, wasting a smile. Whatever could she do about Lisa's pain.

Clara fumbled with the straps of her bag.

'Come Sharon, my pretty little one. See what your Grossmutti has brought for you all across the World.' The child stood whimpering as far from Clara as possible while the parents watched in silence.

And Clara was quite unable to unfasten the bag.

She had never been frightened of anything in her whole life. Dr Clara Schultz (she always used an abbreviation of her maiden name), Director of the Clinic for Women (Out Patients' Department), University Lecturer, wife of the Professor of Islamic Studies, he was also an outstanding scholar of Hebrew. Clara Margarethe Carolina, daughter of a Baroness, nothing frightened her, not even the things that frightened women, thunder and mice and cancer.

Even during the occupation she had been without fear. They were living on the outskirts of the city at that time. One afternoon she returned early from the clinic intending to prepare a lecture and she noticed there was a strange stillness in the garden. The proud bantam cock they had then was not crowing. He was nowhere in sight. Usually he strutted about, an intelligent brightly coloured little bird, and the afternoons were shattered by his voice as he crowed till dusk as if to keep the darkness of the night from coming too soon. The two hens, Cecilia and Gretchen, stood alone and disconsolate like two little pieces of white linen left by the laundress on the green grass.

Clara looked for the little rooster but was unable to find him. His disappearance was an omen.

Calmly Clara transferred money to Switzerland and at once, in spite of difficulties and personal grief, she arranged for her two-year-old baby daughter to be taken to safety while she remained to do her work.

A few days later she found the bantam cock, he was caught by one little leg in a twisted branch among the junipers and straggling rosemary at the end of the garden. He was hanging upside down dead. Something must have startled him Clara thought to make him fly up suddenly into such a tangled place. When she went indoors, missing her baby's voice so much, she found her husband hanging, dead, in his study. She remained unafraid. She knew her husband was unable to face the horror of persecution and the threat of complete loss of personal freedom. She understood his reasons. And she knew she was yearning over her baby but she went on, unafraid, with her work at the clinic. Every day, day after day, year after year, in her thick-lensed spectacles and her white coat she advised, corrected, comforted and cured, and, all the time, she was teaching too, passing on knowledge from experience.

But now, this fearless woman trembled as she tried to unfasten two leather straps because now years later, when all the horror was over for her, she was afraid of her daughter's marriage.

As Clara woke in the strange bedroom, it was only partly a relief.

There was still this possibility of blindness before death, because of course she would die. Ultimately everyone did. For how long would she be blind, if she became blind? Both her grandmothers had lost their sight.

'But that was a cataract,' Clara told herself. 'Nowadays one can have operation.'

Again in imagination, she blundered about her room at home trying to find things, the treasures of her life. But alone and old she was unable to manage.

And another thing. What if she should go deaf and not be able to listen to Bach or Beethoven any more? She tried to remember a phrase from the Beethoven A Minor String Quartet. The first phrase, the first notes of caution and melancholy and the cascade of cello. She tried to sing to herself but her voice cracked and she could not remember the phrase. Suppose she should become deaf now at this moment in this ugly hotel with no music near and no voices. If she became deaf now she would never again be able to hear the phrase and all the remaining time of her life be unable to recall it.

Again she put her small fat white feet out of the bed and stood on the strange floor and began like a blind and deaf person to grope for the light switch.

'Travelling does not suit everyone,' she told herself and she put eau de Cologne on her forehead and leaving the light on, she took her book, one she had written herself, *Some Elementary Contributions to Obstetrics and Gynaecology*, and began to read.

This time it really was Lisa, with joy in her heart Clara went towards her. The real Lisa was much older and Clara saw at once that the pregnancy was full term. Lisa walked proudly because of the stoutness of carrying the baby. Though Clara knew it was Lisa, she searched her daughter's face for some family likeness. The white plump face was strange however, framed in dark hair, cut short all round the head. Mother and daughter could not have recognized each other.

'Oh Lisa you have a bad bruise on your forehead,' Clara gently put out a hand to soothe the bruise. Supposing this husband is the same as the other one, the thought spoiled the pleasure of the meeting.

'It's quite clear you are a doctor, Mother,' Lisa laughed. 'Really it's nothing! I banged my head on the shed door trying to get our cow to go inside.'

'One cow and I thought they had many,' Clara was a little disappointed but she did not show it. Instead she bravely looked at the valley. It was not deep like the wooded ravine in the Alps, not at all, the hills here were hardly hills at all. But the evening sun through the still trees made a changing light and shade of tranquillity, there was a deep rose blue in the evening sky which coloured the white bark and edged the tremulous glittering leaves with quiet mystery. Clara could smell the sharp fragrance of the earth, it was something she had not thought of though now she remembered it from Lisa's letters. All round them was loneliness.

'Where is your little girl?' Clara asked softly. Lisa's plain face was quite pleasant when she smiled, she had grey eyes which were full of light in the smile.

'Little girl? Little boy you mean! He's here,' she patted her apron comfortably. 'Not born yet. I wrote you the date. Remember?'

'Oh yes of course,' Clara adjusted her memory. 'Everyone at home is so pleased,' she began.

'Here's Peter,' Lisa said. 'Peter this is my mother,' Lisa said.

'Mother this is Peter.'

The husband came to his mother-in-law, he was younger than Lisa so much so that Clara was startled. He seemed like a boy, his face quite smooth and it was as if Lisa was old enough to be his mother.

Peter was trying to speak, patiently they waited, but the words when they came were unintelligible. His smile had the innocence of a little child.

'He wants to make you welcome,' Lisa explained. She took her husband's arm and pointed across the cleared and scraped yard to a small fowl pen made of wire netting. Beside the pen was a deep pit, the earth, freshly dug, heaped up all round it.

'GO AND GET THE EGGS!' she shouted at him. She took a few quick steps still holding his arm and marched him towards the hen house. 'QUICK! MARCH!' she shouted. Gauleiter Lisa Gregory. Clara shivered, the evening was cold already. Her own daughter had become a Gauleiter.

'QUICK! MARCH! ONE TWO! ONE TWO!' Lisa was a Führerin. The valley rang with her command. 'DIG THE PIT!'

The sun fell into the scrub and the tree tops in the middle distance between earth and sky became clusters of trembling blackness, silent offerings held up on thin brittle arms like starved people praying into the rose deep, blue swept sky.

Mother and daughter moved in the shadows to the door of the weatherboard and iron cottage.

'I am very strong mother,' Lisa said in a whisper and in the dusk Clara could see her strength, she saw too that her mouth was shining and cruel.

In the tiny house there was no light. Clara was tired and she wondered where they could sleep. In a corner a cot stood in readiness for the baby, there seemed no other beds or furniture at all.

'When my sons are born,' Lisa said in a low voice to her Mother, 'it is to be the survival of the fittest!' She snapped her thick fingers. Clara had no reply. 'Only the strong and intelligent shall live,' Lisa said. 'I tell my husband to dig the pit. I have to. Perhaps it will be for him, we shall see. Every day he must dig the pit to have it ready. There will be no mercy.'

Clara reflected, in the past she had overlooked all this, she had taken no part in the crimes as they were committed but, ignoring them, she had continued with her work and because her work was essential no one had interfered. Clara reflected too that Lisa had never known real love, taken away to safety she had lost the most precious love of all. Clara took upon herself the burden of Lisa's cruelty now. She wanted to give Lisa this love, more than anything she wanted to overlook everything and help Lisa and love her. She wanted to open her purse to show Lisa before it was too dark that she had brought plenty of money and could spend whatever was necessary to build up a nice little farm. She wanted to tell Lisa she could buy more cows, electricity, sheds, pay for hired men to work, buy pigs, two hundred pigs if Lisa would like and drains to keep them hygienic. Whatever Lisa wanted she could have. She tried to tell her how much she wanted to help her. She tried to open her purse and Lisa stood very close and watched Clara in severe silence. The cottage was cold and quite bare, Clara longed to be warm and comfortable and she wanted to ask Lisa to unfasten her purse for her but was quite unable to speak, no words came though she moved her mouth as if trying to say something.

She had never been so stupid. Of course she would feel better in the morning. Women like Dr Clara Schultz simply did not fall ill on a journey. It was just the strange bed in the rather old-fashioned hotel. Tomorrow she would take her cold bath as usual and ask for yoghurt at breakfast and all she had to do then was to wait for Lisa and Peter.

The arrangement was that they were driving the two hundred miles to fetch her to their place. Of course it was natural to be a little curious. Lisa was only two years old when she was smuggled out of Vienna. The woman Lisa had become was a complete stranger, and so was the husband. Even their letters were strange, they wrote in English because Lisa had never learned to speak anything else.

Clara knew she would feel better when she had seen them. All these years she had longed to see Lisa, speak with her, hear her voice, touch her and lavish love and gifts on her. She still felt the sad tenderness of the moment when she had had to part with her baby all those years ago.

'Lisa, my bed is damp,' Clara said 'The walls are so thin. I never expected it to be so cold.'

Lisa had been quite unable to imagine what her mother's visit would be like. In spite of the heat and her advanced pregnancy she cleaned the little room at the side of the house. She washed the louvres and made white muslin curtains. There was scarcely any furniture for the narrow room but Lisa made it as pretty as she could with their best things, her own dressing table and a little white-painted chair and Peter fetched a bed from his mother's place.

Lisa tried to look forward to the visit, she knew so little about her mother, an old lady now after a life of hard work as a doctor. Every year they threw away the battered Christmas parcel which always came late, sewn up in waterproofed calico. There seemed no place in the little farmhouse with its patterned linoleum and plastic lamp shades for an Adventskranz and beeswax candles. And the soggy little biscuits, heart shaped or cut out like stars, had no flavour. Besides they ate meat mostly and, though Peter liked sweet things, his choice of pudding was always tinned fruit with ice cream. The meaningless little green wreath with its tiny red and white plaster mushrooms and gilded pine cones only served to enhance the strangeness between them and this mother who was on her way to them.

Of course her mother was ill as soon as she arrived. She had not expected the nights to be so cold she explained and it was damp in the sleepout.

'My bed is damp,' she said to Lisa. So they moved her into the living room.

'No sooner does your mother arrive and the place is like a "C"-Class Hospital,' Peter said. He had to sit for his tea in the kitchen because Clara's bed took up most of the living room. She had all the pillows in the house and the little table beside her bed was covered with cups and glasses and spoons and bottles and packets of tablets.

'It is only a slight inflammation in my chest,' she assured Lisa. 'A few days of rest and warm and I will be quite well, you will see!'

Lisa worried that her mother was ill and unable to sleep. She tried to keep Peter friendly, but always a silent man, he became more so. She stood in the long damp grass outside the cowshed he had built with homemade concrete bricks, waiting for him at dusk, she wanted to speak to him alone, but he, knowing she was standing there, slowly went about his work and did not emerge.

From inside the asbestos house came Clara's voice. 'Lisa! Another hot water bottle please, my feet are so cold.'

Lisa could not face the days ahead with her mother there. She seemed suddenly to see all her husband's faults and the faults in his family. She had never before realized what a stupid woman Peter's mother, her mother-in-law, was. She felt she would not be able to endure the life she had. Years of this life lay before her. Fifteen miles to the nearest neighbour, her mother-in-law, and the small house, too hot in summer and so cold and damp once the rains came, and the drains Peter had made were so slow to soak away she never seemed able to get the sink empty. This baby would be the first of too many. Yet she had been glad, at her age, to find a husband at last and thought she would be proud and happy to bear a farmer a family of sons.

'A spoonful of honey in a glass of hot water is so much better for you!' Clara told them when they were drinking their tea. She disapproved of their meat too. She was a vegetarian herself and prepared salads with her own hands grating carrots and shredding cabbage for them.

Peter picked the dried prunes out of his dinner spoiling the design Clara had made on his plate.

'I'm not eating that!' he scraped his chair back on the linoleum and left the table.

'Oh Peter please!' Lisa implored, but he went out of the kitchen and Lisa heard him start up the utility with a tremendous roar.

'He will come back!' Clara said knowingly nodding her head.

'Come eat! Your little one needs for you to eat. After dinner I show you how to make elastic loop on your skirt,' she promised Lisa. 'Always I tell my patients, "an elastic loop, not this ugly pin!"' she tapped the big safety pin which fastened Lisa's gaping skirt. 'After dinner I show you how to make!' Lisa knew her mother was trying to comfort her but she could only listen to Peter driving down the track. He would drive the fifteen miles to his mother and she would, as usual, be standing between the stove and the kitchen table and would fry steak for him and make chips and tea and shake her head over Lisa and that foreign mother of hers.

She listened to the car and could hardly stop herself from crying.

Living, all three together became impossible and, after the birth of the baby, Lisa left Peter and went with her mother to live in town. Clara took a small flat in a suburb and they went for walks with the baby. Two women together in a strange place trying to admire meaningless flowers in other people's gardens.

Lisa tried to love her mother, she tried to understand something of her mother's life. She realized too that her mother had given up everything to come to her, but she missed Peter so dreadfully. The cascading voices of the magpies in the early mornings made her think as she woke that she was back on the farm, but instead of Peter's voice and the lowing of the cows there were cars on the road outside the flat. She missed the cows at milking time and the noise of the fowls. And in the afternoon she longed to be standing at the edge of the paddock where the long slanting rays of the sun lit up the tufted grass and the shadows of the coming evening crept from the edges of the Bush in the distance.

'Oh Liserl! Just look at this rose,' her mother bent over some other person's fence. 'Such a fragrance and a beautiful deep colour. Only smell this rose Lisa!' And then slowly, carrying the baby, on to the next garden to pause and admire where admiration fell lost on unknown paving stones and into unfamiliar leaves and flowers unpossessed by themselves. The loneliness of unpossession waited for them in the tiny flat where a kind of refugee life slowly unpacked itself, just a few things, the rest would remain for ever packed. Only now and then glimpses of forgotten times came to the surface, an unwanted garment or a photograph or an old letter reminding of the reasons why she had grown up in a strange land cared for by people who were not hers.

In the evenings they shaded the lamp with an old woollen cardigan so that the light should not disturb the baby and they sat together. Lisa listened to the cars passing, in her homelessness she wished that one of the cars would stop, because it was Peter's. More than anything she wished Peter would come. Tears filled her eyes and she turned her head so that her mother should not see.

'Oh Peter!' Lisa woke in the car, 'I was having such an awful dream!' She sat up close to the warmth of her husband feeling the comfort of his presence and responsibility.

'Oh! It was so awful!'

She loved Peter, she loved him when he was driving, especially at night. She looked at his clear brow and at the strong shape of his chin. He softly dropped a kiss on her hair and the car devoured the dark road.

'You'll feel better when you actually meet her,' he said. 'It's because you don't know her. Neither of us do!'

Lisa agreed and sat in safety beside her husband as they continued the long journey.

Clara was able to identify Lisa at once. She had to ask to have the white sheet pulled right down in order to make the identification. Lisa had two tiny deep scars like dimples one on the inside of each thigh.

'She was born with a pyloric stenosis,' Clara explained softly. 'Projectile vomiting you know.' The scars, she explained, were from the insertion of tiny tubes.

'Subcutaneous feeding, it was done often in those days,' she made a little gesture of helplessness, an apology for an old-fashioned method.

In the mortuary they were very kind and helpful to the old lady who had travelled so far alone and then had to have this terrible shock.

Apparently the car failed to take a bend and they were plunged two hundred feet off the road into the Bush. Death would have been instantaneous, the bodies were flung far apart, the car rolled. They tried to tell her.

Clara brushed aside the clichés of explanation. She asked her question with a professional directness.

'What time did it happen?' she wanted to know. She had been sitting for some time crouched in a large armchair, for some hours after her yoghurt, wondering if she could leave the appointed meeting place. Outside it was raining.

'Should I make a short rain walk?' she asked herself. And several times she nearly left the chair and then thought, 'But no, any moment they come and I am not here!'

A few people came into the vestibule of the hotel and she looked at them through palm fronds and ferns, surreptitiously refreshing herself with eau de Cologne, wondering, hopeful. Every now and then she leaned forward to peer to see if this was Lisa at last, and every time she sat back as the person went out again. Perhaps she was a little relieved every time she was left alone. She adjusted her wiglet.

Back home in Vienna she was never at a loss as to what to do. Retirement gave her leisure but her time was always filled. She never sat for long hours in an armchair. Back home she could have telephoned her broker or arranged with her dentist to have something expensive done to a tooth.

'Time? It's hard to say exactly,' they said. 'A passing motorist saw the car upside down against a tree at about five o'clock and reported the accident immediately.'

There were only the two bodies in the mortuary. Beneath the white sheets they looked small in death. Dr Clara Schultz was well acquainted with death, the final diagnosis was the greater part of her life's work. And wasn't it after all she herself who, with her own hands, cut the dressing-gown cord from her own husband's neck. She had to put a stool on his desk in order to reach as she was such a short person, and furthermore, his neck had swollen, blue, over the cord making the task more difficult.

They supported the old lady with kind hands and offered her a glass of water as she looked at the two pale strangers lying locked in the discolouration of injury and haemorrhage and the deep stillness of death.

Clara looked at her daughter and at her son-in-law and was unable to know them. She would never be able to know them now.

'I have a photograph, and I have letters,' she said. 'They were my paper children you know.' She tried to draw from the pocket of her travelling jacket the little leather folder which she took with her everywhere.

In the folder was a photograph of them standing, blurred because of a light leak in the camera, on a track which curved by a tree. And on the tree was nailed a small board with their name on it in white paint. Behind the unknown people and the painted board was a mysterious background of pasture and trees and the light and shade of their land. She pulled at the folder but was unable to pull it from her pocket.

Not being able to speak with them and know them was like being unable ever again to hear the phrase of Beethoven, the cascade of cello. It was like being blind and deaf for the rest of her life and she would not be able to recall anything.

Dr Clara had never wept about anything but now tears slowly

forced themselves from under her eyelids.

'My daughter, Lisa you know, was pregnant,' she managed to say at last. 'I see she is bandaged. Does this mean?'

'Yes, yes,' they explained gently, 'That is right. Owing to the nature of the accident and the speed with which it was reported they were able to save the baby. A little girl, her condition is satisfactory. It was a miracle.'

Dr Clara nodded. In spite of the tears she was smiling. As well as knowing about death she understood miracles.

As soon as it was decently possible she would ring for the chambermaid and ask for a glass of hot water. Of course she wasn't blind or deaf and no one had come in with any news of an accident. She was only a little upset with travelling. Her fear of the failure of her body was only the uneasiness of stomach cramp and the result of bad sleep. She would have her cold bath early and then only a very short time to wait after that. Country people had to consider their stock that was why they were driving overnight to fetch her. It might be a good idea to start getting up now, it would never do to keep them waiting. She put her fat white feet out of the bed and walked across the strange floor to ring the bell. It was a good idea to get up straight away because the telephone was ringing. Dr Clara, in the old days was used to the telephone in the night. Often she dressed herself with one hand and listened to the Clinic Sister describing the intervals between the labour pains and the position of the baby's head. A little breathless, that was all, she sat on the chair beside her telephone, breathless just with getting up too quickly.

'Dr Clara Schultz,' she said and she thought she heard a faint voice murmur.

'Wait one moment please. Long distance.' And then a fainter sound like a tiny buzzing as if voices were coming from one remote pole to another across continents and under oceans as if a message was trying to come by invisible wires and cables from the other side of the world. Clara waited holding the silent telephone. 'Clara Schultz here,' she said alone in the dark emptiness of her apartment for of course she had sold all her furniture.

'I have burn up my ships,' she told Irma. 'Clara Schultz here,' her voice sounded strange and she strained into the silence of the telephone trying to hear the other voice, the message, her heart beat more quickly, the beating of her heart seemed to prevent her listening to the silence of the telephone.

'Lisa!' she said, 'Is it you Lisa?'

But there was no sound in the telephone, for a long time just the silence of nothing from the telephone. 'Lisa speak!' But there was no voice.

Clara longed to hear her daughter's voice, of course the voice could not be the same now as the laughter and incoherent chatter of the little two year old. Now as an old woman holding a dead telephone she remembered with a kind of bitterness that she sent away her little girl and continued her work at the clinic paying no attention to the evil cruelty of war. She knew she was overlooking what was happening to people but chose to concern herself only with the menstrual cycle and the arched white thighs of women in labour.

'It's a means to an end,' she said softly to her frightened patients when they cried out. 'Everything will be all right, it's a means to an end,' she comforted them.

Clara knew she had neglected to think of the end. Now she wanted, more than anything, to hear Lisa speak. But there was no sound on the telephone. She went slowly out on to the dark stairs of the apartment house. On the second landing she met her neighbour.

'Irma is that you?'

'Clara!'

'Irma you are quite unchanged.'

Irma's pink sugar cake face sat smiling on the lace collar which was like a doily. 'Why should I change?' Irma asked.

Clara took Irma's hand, grateful to find her friend. 'Only think, Irma,' she said, 'I am bringing home my daughter's baby!' she laughed softly to Irma. 'My paper children had a baby daughter,' she said, 'I shall call her Lisa.'

When Lisa and Peter arrived at the hotel they were unable to understand how it was that Clara must have been crying and laughing when she died.

Irma Rosen tried to explain to them as well as she could with her little English, and of course she was very tired with making the long journey by air at such short notice.

'When I find her you know, outside my door,' Irma said. 'I know, as her friend, I must come to you myself to tell. On her face this lovely smile and her face quite wet as if she cry in her heart! While she is smiling.'

They were as if encapsulated in the strange little meeting in the hotel vestibule. Lisa tried to think of words to say to this neat little old lady, her mother's friend. But Irma spoke again. 'Your mother is my friend,' she said, 'Always she speak of you. Her paper children and she so proud to be preparing to come to you. She would want me to tell you. Now I suppose I go back. Your mother say always "But air travel, you know, makes the world so much smaller." Is true of course, but a long way all the same!' She smiled and nodded, pink, on her lace collar. 'Sorry my Enklisch iss not good!' she apologized. 'Oh you speak beautifully,' Lisa was glad to be able to say something. 'Really your English is very good,' Lisa shouted a little as if to make it easier for Irma to understand her.

The young couple wanted to thank Irma and look after her but as Lisa's labour pains had started during the long journey, Peter had to drive her straight to the hospital.

ALICE MUNRO

Miles City, Montana

My father came across the field carrying the body of the boy who had been drowned. There were several men together, returning from the search, but he was the one carrying the body. The men were muddy and exhausted, and walked with their heads down, as if they were ashamed. Even the dogs were dispirited, dripping from the cold river. When they all set out, hours before, the dogs were nervy and yelping, the men tense and determined, and there was a constrained, unspeakable excitement about the whole scene. It was understood that they might find something horrible.

The boy's name was Steve Gauley. He was eight years old. His hair and clothes were mud-colored now and carried some bits of dead leaves, twigs, and grass. He was like a heap of refuse that had been left out all winter. His face was turned in to my father's chest, but I could see a nostril, an ear, plugged up with greenish mud.

I don't think so. I don't think I really saw all this. Perhaps I saw my father carrying him, and the other men following along, and the dogs, but I would not have been allowed to get close enough to see something like mud in his nostril. I must have heard someone talking about that and imagined that I saw it. I see his face unaltered except for the mud—Steve Gauley's familiar, sharp-honed, sneaky-looking face—and it wouldn't have been like that; it would have been bloated and changed and perhaps muddied all over after so many hours in the water.

To have to bring back such news, such evidence, to a waiting family, particularly a mother, would have made searchers move heavily, but what was happening here was worse. It seemed a worse shame (to hear people talk) that there was no mother, no woman at all—no grandmother or aunt, or even a sister—to receive Steve Gauley and give him his due of grief. His father was a hired man, a drinker but not a drunk, an erratic man without being entertaining, not friendly but not exactly a troublemaker. His fatherhood seemed accidental, and the fact that the child had been left with him when the mother went away, and that they continued living together, seemed accidental. They lived in a steep-roofed, gray-shingled hillbilly sort of house that was just a bit better than a shack—the father fixed the roof and put supports under the porch, just enough and just in time—and their life was held together in a similar manner; that is, just well enough to keep the Children's Aid at bay. They didn't eat meals together or cook for each other, but there was food. Sometimes the father would give Steve money to buy food at the store, and Steve was seen to buy quite sensible things, such as pancake mix and macaroni dinner.

I had known Steve Gauley fairly well. I had not liked him more often than I had liked him. He was two years older than I was. He would hang around our place on Saturdays, scornful of whatever I was doing but unable to leave me alone. I couldn't be on the swing without him wanting to try it, and if I wouldn't give it up he came and pushed me so that I went crooked. He teased the dog. He got me into trouble—deliberately and maliciously, it seemed to me afterward—by daring me to do things I wouldn't have thought of on my own: digging up the potatoes to see how big they were when they were still only the size of marbles, and pushing over the stacked firewood to make a pile we could jump off. At school, we never spoke to each other. He was solitary, though not tormented. But on Saturday mornings, when I saw his thin, self-possessed figure sliding through the cedar hedge, I knew I was in for something and he would decide what. Sometimes it was all right. We pretended we were cowboys who had to tame wild horses. We played in the pasture by the river, not far from the place where Steve drowned. We were horses and riders both, screaming and neighing and bucking and waving whips of tree branches beside a little nameless river that flows into the Saugeen in southern Ontario.

The funeral was held in our house. There was not enough room at Steve's father's place for the large crowd that was expected because of the circumstances. I have a memory of the crowded room but no picture of Steve in his coffin, or of the minister, or of wreaths of flowers. I remember that I was holding one flower, a white narcissus, which must have come from a pot somebody forced indoors, because it was too early for even the forsythia bush or the trilliums and marsh marigolds in the woods. I stood in a row of children, each of us holding a narcissus. We sang a children's hymn, which somebody played on our piano: 'When He Cometh, When He Cometh, to Make Up His Jewels.' I was wearing white ribbed stockings, which were disgustingly itchy, and wrinkled at the knees and ankles. The feeling of these stockings on my legs is mixed up with another feeling in my memory. It is hard to describe. It had to do with my parents. Adults in general but my parents in particular. My father, who had carried Steve's body from the river, and my mother, who must have done most of the arranging of this funeral. My father in his dark-blue suit and my mother in her brown velvet dress with the creamy satin collar. They stood side by side opening and closing their mouths for the hymn, and I stood removed from them, in the row of children, watching. I felt a furious and sickening disgust. Children sometimes have an access of disgust concerning adults. The size, the lumpy shapes, the bloated power. The breath, the coarseness, the hairiness, the horrid secretions. But this was more. And the accompanying anger had nothing sharp and self-respecting about it. There was no release, as when I would finally bend and pick up a stone and throw it at Steve Gauley. It could not be understood or expressed, though it died down after a while into a heaviness, then just a taste, an occasional taste—a thin, familiar misgiving.

Twenty years or so later, in 1961, my husband, Andrew, and I got a brand-new car, our first—that is, our first brand-new. It was a Morris Oxford, oyster-colored (the dealer had some fancier name for the color)—a big small car, with plenty of room for us and our two children. Cynthia was six and Meg three and a half.

Andrew took a picture of me standing beside the car. I was wearing white pants, a black turtleneck, and sunglasses. I lounged against the car door, canting my hips to make myself look slim.

'Wonderful,' Andrew said. 'Great. You look like Jackie Kennedy.' All over this continent probably, dark-haired, reasonably slender young women were told, when they were stylishly dressed or getting their pictures taken, that they looked like Jackie Kennedy.

Andrew took a lot of pictures of me, and of the children, our house, our garden, our excursions and possessions. He got copies made, labelled them carefully, and sent them back to his mother and his aunt and uncle in Ontario. He got copies for me to send to my father, who also lived in Ontario, and I did so, but less regularly than he sent his. When he saw pictures he thought I had already sent lying around the house, Andrew was perplexed and annoyed. He liked to have this record go forth.

That summer, we were presenting ourselves, not pictures. We were driving back from Vancouver, where we lived, to Ontario, which we still called 'home,' in our new car. Five days to get there, ten days there, five days back. For the first time, Andrew had three weeks' holiday. He worked in the legal department at B. C. Hydro.

On a Saturday morning, we loaded suitcases, two thermos bottles—one filled with coffee and one with lemonade—some fruit and sandwiches, picture books and coloring books, crayons, drawing pads, insect repellent, sweaters (in case it got cold in the mountains), and our two children into the car. Andrew locked the house, and Cynthia said ceremoniously, 'Goodbye, house.'

Meg said, 'Goodbye, house.' Then she said, 'Where will we live now?'

'It's not goodbye forever,' said Cynthia. 'We're coming back. Mother! Meg thought we weren't ever coming back!'

'I did not,' said Meg, kicking the back of my seat.

Andrew and I put on our sunglasses, and we drove away, over the Lions Gate Bridge and through the main part of Vancouver. We shed our house, the neighborhood, the city, and—at the crossing point between Washington and British Columbia—our country. We were driving east across the United States, taking the most northerly route, and would cross into Canada again at Sarnia, Ontario. I don't know if we chose this route because the Trans-Canada Highway was not completely finished at the time or if we just wanted the feeling of driving through a foreign, a very slightly foreign, country—that extra bit of interest and adventure.

We were both in high spirits. Andrew congratulated the car several times. He said he felt so much better driving it than our old car, a 1951 Austin that slowed down dismally on the hills and had a fussy-old-lady image. So Andrew said now.

'What kind of image does this one have?' said Cynthia. She listened to us carefully and liked to try out new words such as 'image.' Usually she got them right.

'Lively,' I said. 'Slightly sporty. It's not show-off.'

'It's sensible, but it has class,' Andrew said. 'Like my image.'

Cynthia thought that over and said with a cautious pride, 'That means like you think you want to be, Daddy?'

As for me, I was happy because of the shedding. I loved taking off. In my own house, I seemed to be often looking for a place to hide—sometimes from the children but more often from the jobs to be done and the phone ringing and the sociability of the neighborhood. I wanted to hide so that I could get busy at my real work, which was a sort of wooing of distant parts of myself. I lived in a state of siege, always losing just what I wanted to hold on to. But on trips there was no difficulty. I could be talking to Andrew, talking to the children and looking at whatever they wanted me to look at—a pig on a sign, a pony in a field, a Volkswagen on a revolving stand—and pouring lemonade into plastic cups, and all the time those bits and pieces would be flying together inside me. The essential composition would be achieved. This made me hopeful and lighthearted. It was being a watcher that did it. A watcher, not a keeper.

We turned east at Everett and climbed into the Cascades. I showed Cynthia our route on the map. First I showed her the map of the whole United States, which showed also the bottom part of Canada. Then I turned to the separate maps of each of the states we were going to pass through. Washington, Idaho, Montana, North Dakota, Minnesota, Wisconsin. I showed her the dotted line across Lake Michigan, which was the route of the ferry we would take. Then we would drive across Michigan to the bridge that linked the United States and Canada at Sarnia, Ontario. Home.

Meg wanted to see, too.

'You won't understand,' said Cynthia. But she took the road atlas into the back seat.

'Sit back,' she said to Meg. 'Sit still. I'll show you.'

I could hear her tracing the route for Meg, very accurately, just as I had done it for her. She looked up all the states' maps, knowing how to find them in alphabetical order.

'You know what that line is?' she said. 'It's the road. That line is the road we're driving on. We're going right along this line.'

Meg did not say anything.

'Mother, show me where we are right this minute,' said Cynthia.

I took the atlas and pointed out the road through the mountains, and she took it back and showed it to Meg. 'See where the road is all wiggly?' she said. 'It's wiggly because there are so many turns in it. The wiggles are the turns.' She flipped some pages and waited a moment. 'Now', she said, 'show me where we are.' Then she called to me, 'Mother, she understands! She pointed to it! Meg understands maps!'

It seems to me now that we invented characters for our children. We had them firmly set to play their parts. Cynthia was bright and diligent, sensitive, courteous, watchful. Sometimes we teased her for being too conscientious, too eager to be what we in fact depended on her to be. She was fair-haired, fair-skinned, easily showing the effects of the sun, raw winds, pride, or humiliation. Meg was more solidly built, more reticent—not rebellious but stubborn sometimes, mysterious. Her silences seemed to us to show her strength of character, and her negatives were taken as signs of an imperturbable independence. Her hair was brown, and we cut it in straight bangs. Her eyes were a light hazel, clear and dazzling.

We were entirely pleased with these characters, enjoying the contradictions as well as the confirmations of them. We disliked the heavy, the uninventive, approach to being parents. I had a dread of turning into a certain kind of mother—the kind whose body sagged, who moved in a woolly-smelling, milky-smelling fog, solemn with trivial burdens. I believed that all the attention these mothers paid, their need to be burdened, was the cause of colic, bed-wetting, asthma. I favored another approach—the mock desperation, the inflated irony of the professional mothers who wrote for magazines. In those magazine pieces, the children were splendidly self-willed, hard-edged, perverse, indomitable. So were the mothers, through their wit, indomitable. The real-life mothers I warmed to were the sort who would phone up and say, 'Is my embryo Hitler by any chance over at your house?' They cackled clear above the milky fog.

We saw a dead deer strapped across the front of a pickup truck.

'Somebody shot it,' Cynthia said. 'Hunters shoot the deer.'

'It's not hunting season yet,' Andrew said. 'They may have hit it on the road. See the sign for deer crossing?'

'I would cry if we hit one,' Cynthia said sternly.

I had made peanut-butter-and-marmalade sandwiches for the children and salmon-and-mayonnaise for us. But I had not put any lettuce in, and Andrew was disappointed.

'I didn't have any,' I said.

'Couldn't you have got some?'

'I'd have had to buy a whole head of lettuce just to get enough for sandwiches, and I decided it wasn't worth it.'

This was a lie. I had forgotten.

'They're a lot better with lettuce.'

'I didn't think it made that much difference.' After a silence, I said, 'Don't be mad.'

'I'm not mad. I like lettuce on sandwiches.'

'I just didn't think it mattered that much.'

'How would it be if I didn't bother to fill up the gas tank?'

'That's not the same thing.'

'Sing a song,' said Cynthia. She started to sing:

'Five little ducks went out one day,
Over the hills and far away.
One little duck went
"Quack-quack-quack"
Four little ducks came swimming back.'

Andrew squeezed my hand and said, 'Let's not fight.'

'You're right. I should have got lettuce.'

'It doesn't matter that much.'

I wished that I could get my feelings about Andrew to come together into a serviceable and dependable feeling. I had even tried writing two lists, one of things I liked about him, one of things I disliked—in the cauldron of intimate life, things I loved and things I hated—as if I hoped by this to prove something, to come to a conclusion one way or the other. But I gave it up when I saw that all it proved was what I already knew—that I had violent contradictions. Sometimes the very sound of his footsteps seemed to me tyrannical, the set of his mouth smug and mean, his hard, straight body a barrier interposed—quite consciously, even dutifully, and with a nasty pleasure in its masculine authority—between me and whatever joy or lightness I could get in life. Then, with not much warning, he became my good friend and most essential companion. I felt the sweetness of his light bones and serious ideas, the vulnerability of his love, which I imagined to be much purer and more straightforward than my own. I could be greatly moved by an inflexibility, a harsh propriety, that at other times I scorned. I would think how humble he was, really, taking on such a ready-made role of husband, father, breadwinner, and how I myself in comparison was really a secret monster of egotism. Not so secret, either—not from him.

At the bottom of our fights, we served up what we thought were the ugliest truths. 'I know there is something basically selfish and basically untrustworthy about you,' Andrew once said. 'I've always known it. I also know that that is why I fell in love with you.'

'Yes,' I said, feeling sorrowful but complacent.

'I know that I'd be better off without you.'

'Yes. You would.'

'You'd be happier without me.'

'Yes.'

And finally—finally—racked and purged, we clasped hands and laughed, laughed at those two benighted people, ourselves. Their grudges, their grievances, their self-justification. We leapfrogged over them. We declared them liars. We would have wine with dinner, or decide to give a party.

I haven't seen Andrew for years, don't know if he is still thin, has gone completely gray, insists on lettuce, tells the truth, or is hearty and disappointed.

We stayed the night in Wenatchee, Washington, where it hadn't rained for weeks. We ate dinner in a restaurant built about a tree—not a sapling in a tub but a tall, sturdy cottonwood. In the early-morning light, we climbed out of the irrigated valley, up dry, rocky, very steep hillsides that would seem to lead to more hills, and there on the top was a wide plateau, cut by the great Spokane and Columbia rivers. Grainland and grassland, mile after mile. There were straight roads here, and little farming towns with grain elevators. In fact, there was a sign announcing that this county we were going through, Douglas County, had the second-highest wheat yield of any county in the United States. The towns had planted shade trees. At least, I thought they had been planted, because there were no such big trees in the countryside.

All this was marvellously welcome to me. 'Why do I love it so much?' I said to Andrew. 'Is it because it isn't scenery?'

'It reminds you of home,' said Andrew. 'A bout of severe nostalgia.' But he said this kindly.

When we said 'home' and meant Ontario, we had very

different places in mind. My home was a turkey farm, where my father lived as a widower, and though it was the same house my mother had lived in, had papered, painted, cleaned, furnished, it showed the effects now of neglect and of some wild sociability. A life went on in it that my mother could not have predicted or condoned. There were parties for the turkey crew, the gutters and pluckers, and sometimes one or two of the young men would be living there temporarily, inviting their own friends and having their own impromptu parties. This life, I thought, was better for my father than being lonely, and I did not disapprove, had certainly no right to disapprove. Andrew did not like to go there, naturally enough, because he was not the sort who could sit around the kitchen table with the turkey crew, telling jokes. They were intimidated by him and contemptuous of him, and it seemed to me that my father, when they were around, had to be on their side. And it wasn't only Andrew who had trouble. I could manage those jokes, but it was an effort.

I wished for the days when I was little, before we had the turkeys. We had cows, and sold the milk to the cheese factory. A turkey farm is nothing like as pretty as a dairy farm or a sheep farm. You can see that the turkeys are on a straight path to becoming frozen carcasses and table meat. They don't have the pretense of a life of their own, a browsing idyll, that cattle have, or pigs in the dappled orchard. Turkey barns are long, efficient buildings—tin sheds. No beams or hay or warm stables. Even the smell of guano seems thinner and more offensive than the usual smell of stable manure. No hints there of hay coils and rail fences and songbirds and the flowering hawthorn. The turkeys were all let out into one long field, which they picked clean. They didn't look like great birds there but like fluttering laundry.

Once, shortly after my mother died, and after I was married—in fact, I was packing to join Andrew in Vancouver—I was at home alone for a couple of days with my father. There was a freakishly heavy rain all night. In the early light, we saw that the turkey field was flooded. At least, the low-lying parts of it were flooded—it was like a lake with many islands. The turkeys were huddled on these islands. Turkeys are very stupid. (My father would say, 'You know a chicken? You know how stupid a chicken is? Well, a chicken is an Einstein compared with a turkey.') But they had managed to crowd to higher ground and avoid drowning. Now they might push each other off, suffocate each other, get cold and die. We couldn't wait for the water to go down. We went out in an old rowboat we had. I rowed and my father pulled the heavy, wet turkeys into the boat and we took them to the barn. It was still raining a little. The job was difficult and absurd and very uncomfortable. We were laughing. I was happy to be working with my father. I felt close to all hard, repetitive, appalling work, in which the body is finally worn out, the mind sunk (though sometimes the spirit can stay marvellously light), and I was homesick in advance for this life and this place. I thought that if Andrew could see me there in the rain, red-handed, muddy, trying to hold on to turkey legs and row the boat at the same time, he would only want to get me out of there and make me forget about it. This raw life angered him. My attachment to it angered him. I thought that I shouldn't have married him. But who else? One of the turkey crew?

And I didn't want to stay there. I might feel bad about leaving, but I would feel worse if somebody made me stay.

Andrew's mother lived in Toronto, in an apartment building looking out on Muir Park. When Andrew and his sister were both at home, his mother slept in the living room. Her husband, a doctor, had died when the children were still too young to go to school. She took a secretarial course and sold her house at Depression prices, moved to this apartment, managed to raise her children, with some help from relatives—her sister Caroline, her brother-in-law Roger. Andrew and his sister went to private schools and to camp in the summer.

'I suppose that was courtesy of the Fresh Air fund?' I said once, scornful of his claim that he had been poor. To my mind, Andrew's urban life had been sheltered and fussy. His mother came home with a headache from working all day in the noise, the harsh light of a department-store office, but it did not occur to me that hers was a hard or admirable life. I don't think she herself believed that she was admirable—only unlucky. She worried about her work in the office, her clothes, her cooking, her children. She worried most of all about what Roger and Caroline would think.

Caroline and Roger lived on the east side of the park, in a handsome stone house. Roger was a tall man with a bald, freckled head, a fat, firm stomach. Some operation on his throat had deprived him of his voice—he spoke in a rough whisper. But everybody paid attention. At dinner once in the stone house—where all the dining furniture was enormous, darkly glowing, palatial—I asked him a question. I think it had to do with Whittaker Chambers, whose story was then appearing in the *Saturday Evening Post*. The question was mild in tone, but he guessed its subversive intent and took to calling me Mrs. Gromyko, referring to what he alleged to be my 'sympathies.' Perhaps he really craved an adversary, and could not find one. At that dinner, I saw Andrew's hand tremble as he lit his mother's cigarette. His Uncle Roger had paid for Andrew's education, and was on the board of directors of several companies.

'He is just an opinionated old man,' Andrew said to me later. 'What is the point of arguing with him?'

Before we left Vancouver, Andrew's mother had written, 'Roger seems quite intrigued by the idea of your buying a small car!' Her exclamation mark showed apprehension. At that time, particularly in Ontario, the choice of a small European car over a large American car could be seen as some sort of declaration—a declaration of tendencies Roger had been sniffing after all along.

'It isn't that small a car,' said Andrew huffily.

'That's not the point,' I said. 'The point is, it isn't any of his business!'

We spent the second night in Missoula. We had been told in Spokane, at a gas station, that there was a lot of repair work going on along Highway 2, and that we were in for a very hot, dusty drive, with long waits, so we turned onto the interstate and drove through Coeur d'Alene and Kellogg into Montana. After Missoula, we turned south toward Butte, but detoured to see Helena, the state capital. In the car, we played Who Am I?

Cynthia was somebody dead, and an American, and a girl. Possibly a lady. She was not in a story. She had not been seen on television. Cynthia had not read about her in a book. She was not anybody who had come into the kindergarten, or a relative of any of Cynthia's friends.

'Is she human?' said Andrew, with a sudden shrewdness.

'No! That's what you forgot to ask!'

'An animal,' I said reflectively.

'Is that a question? Sixteen questions!'

'No, it is not a question. I'm thinking. A dead animal.'

'It's the deer,' said Meg, who hadn't been playing.

'That's not fair!' said Cynthia. 'She's not playing!'

'What deer?' said Andrew.

I said, 'Yesterday.'

'The day before,' said Cynthia. 'Meg wasn't playing. Nobody got it.'

'The deer on the truck,' said Andrew.

'It was a lady deer, because it didn't have antlers, and it was an American and it was dead,' Cynthia said.

Andrew said, 'I think it's kind of morbid, being a dead deer.'

'I got it,' said Meg.

Cynthia said, 'I think I know what morbid is. It's depressing.'

Helena, an old silver-mining town, looked forlorn to us even in the morning sunlight. Then Bozeman and Billings, not forlorn in the slightest—energetic, strung-out towns, with miles of blinding tinsel fluttering over used-car lots. We got too tired and hot even to play Who Am I? These busy, prosaic cities reminded me of similar places in Ontario, and I thought about what was really waiting there—the great tombstone furniture of Roger and Caroline's dining room, the dinners for which I must iron the children's dresses and warn them about forks, and then the other table a hundred miles away, the jokes of my father's crew. The pleasures I had been thinking of—looking at the countryside or drinking a Coke in an old-fashioned drugstore with fans and a high, pressed-tin ceiling—would have to be snatched in between.

'Meg's asleep,' Cynthia said. 'She's so hot. She makes me hot in the same seat with her.'

'I hope she isn't feverish,' I said, not turning around.

What are we doing this for, I thought, and the answer came—to show off. To give Andrew's mother and my father the pleasure of seeing their grandchildren. That was our duty. But beyond that we wanted to show them something. What strenuous children we were, Andrew and I, what relentless seekers of approbation. It was as if at some point we had received an unforgettable, indigestible message—that we were far from satisfactory, and that the most commonplace success in life was probably beyond us. Roger dealt out such messages, of course—that was his style—but Andrew's mother, my own mother and father couldn't have meant to do so. All they meant to tell us was 'Watch out. Get along.' My father, when I was in high school, teased me that I was getting to think I was so smart I would never find a boyfriend. He would have forgotten that in a week. I never forgot it. Andrew and I didn't forget things. We took umbrage.

'I wish there was a beach,' said Cynthia.

'There probably is one,' Andrew said. 'Right around the next curve.'

'There isn't any curve,' she said, sounding insulted.

'That's what I mean.'

'I wish there was some more lemonade.'

'I will just wave my magic wand and produce some,' I said. 'Okay, Cynthia? Would you rather have grape juice? Will I do a beach while I'm at it?'

She was silent, and soon I felt repentant. 'Maybe in the next town there might be a pool,' I said. I looked at the map. 'In Miles City. Anyway, there'll be something cool to drink.'

'How far is it?' Andrew said.

'Not far,' I said. 'Thirty miles, about.'

'In Miles City,' said Cynthia, in the tones of an incantation, 'there is a beautiful blue swimming pool for children, and a park with lovely trees.'

Andrew said to me, 'You could have started something.'

But there was a pool. There was a park, too, though not quite the oasis of Cynthia's fantasy. Prairie trees with thin leaves—cottonwoods and poplars—worn grass, and a high wire fence around the pool. Within this fence, a wall, not yet completed, of cement blocks. There were no shouts or splashes; over the entrance I saw a sign that said the pool was closed every day from noon until two o'clock. It was then twenty-five after twelve.

Nevertheless I called out, 'Is anybody there?' I thought somebody must be around, because there was a small truck parked near the entrance. On the side of the truck were these words: 'We have Brains, to fix your Drains. (We have Roto-Rooter too.)'

A girl came out, wearing a red lifeguard's shirt over her bathing suit. 'Sorry, we're closed.'

'We were just driving through,' I said.

'We close every day from twelve until two. It's on the sign.'

She was eating a sandwich.

'I saw the sign,' I said. 'But this is the first water we've seen for so long, and the children are awfully hot, and I wondered if they could just dip in and out—just five minutes. We'd watch them.'

A boy came into sight behind her. He was wearing jeans and a T-shirt with the words 'Roto-Rooter' on it.

I was going to say that we were driving from British Columbia to Ontario, but I remembered that Canadian place names usually meant nothing to Americans. 'We're driving right across the country,' I said. 'We haven't time to wait for the pool to open. We were just hoping the children could get cooled off.'

Cynthia came running up barefoot behind me. 'Mother. Mother, where is my bathing suit?' Then she stopped, sensing the serious adult negotiations. Meg was climbing out of the car—just wakened, with her top pulled up and her shorts pulled down, showing her pink stomach.

'Is it just those two?' the girl said.

'Just the two. We'll watch them.'

'I can't let any adults in. If it's just the two, I guess I could watch them. I'm having my lunch.' She said to Cynthia, 'Do you want to come in the pool?'

'Yes, please,' said Cynthia firmly.

Meg looked at the ground.

'Just a short time, because the pool is really closed,' I said. 'We appreciate this very much,' I said to the girl.

'Well, I can eat my lunch out there, if it's just the two of them.' She looked toward the car as if she thought I might try to spring some more children on her.

When I found Cynthia's bathing suit, she took it into the changing room. She would not permit anybody, even Meg, to see her naked. I changed Meg, who stood on the front seat of the car. She had a pink cotton bathing suit with straps that crossed and buttoned. There were ruffles across the bottom.

'She *is* hot,' I said. 'But I don't think she's feverish.'

I loved helping Meg to dress or undress, because her body still had the solid unself-consciousness, the sweet indifference, something of the milky smell, of a baby's body. Cynthia's body had long ago been pared down, shaped and altered, into Cynthia. We all liked to hug Meg, press and nuzzle her. Sometimes she would scowl and beat us off and this forthright independence, this ferocious bashfulness, simply made her more appealing, more apt to be tormented and tickled in the way of family love.

Andrew and I sat in the car with the windows open. I could hear a radio playing, and thought it must belong to the girl or her boyfriend. I was thirsty, and got out of the car to look for a concession stand, or perhaps a soft-drink machine, somewhere in the park. I was wearing shorts, and the backs of my legs were slick with sweat. I saw a drinking fountain at the other side of the park and was walking toward it in a roundabout way, keeping to the shade of the trees. No place became real till you got out of the car. Dazed with the heat, with the sun on the blistered houses, the pavement, the burned grass, I walked slowly. I paid attention to a squashed leaf, ground a Popsicle stick under the heel of my sandal, squinted at a trash can strapped to a tree. This is the way you look at the poorest details of the world resurfaced, after you've been driving for a long time—you feel their singleness and precise location and the forlorn coincidence of your being there to see them.

Where are the children?

I turned around and moved quickly, not quite running, to a part of the fence beyond which the cement wall was not completed. I could see some of the pool. I saw Cynthia, standing about waist-deep in the water, fluttering her hands on the surface and discreetly watching something at the end of the pool, which I could not see. I thought by her pose, her discretion, the look on her face, that she must be watching some byplay between the lifeguard and her boyfriend. I couldn't see Meg. But I thought she must be playing in the shallow water—both the shallow and deep ends of the pool were out of my sight.

'Cynthia!' I had to call twice before she knew where my voice was coming from. 'Cynthia! Where's Meg?'

It always seems to me, when I recall this scene, that Cynthia turns very gracefully towards me, then turns all around in the water—making me think of a ballerina on point—and spreads her arms in a gesture of the stage. 'Dis-ap-peared!'

Cynthia was naturally graceful, and she did take dancing lessons, so these movements may have been as I have described. She did say 'Disappeared' after looking all around the pool, but the strangely artifical style of speech and gesture, the lack of urgency, is more likely my invention. The fear I felt instantly when I couldn't see Meg—even while I was telling myself she must be in the shallower water—must have made Cynthia's movements seem unbearably slow and inappropriate to me, and the tone in which she could say 'Disappeared' before the implication struck her (or was she covering, at once, some ever-ready guilt?) was heard by me as quite exquisitely, monstrously self-possessed.

I cried out for Andrew, and the lifeguard came into view. She was pointing toward the deep end of the pool, saying, 'What's that?'

There, just within my view, a cluster of pink ruffles appeared, a bouquet, beneath the surface of the water. Why would a lifeguard stop and point, why would she ask what that was, why didn't she just dive into the water and swim to it? She didn't swim; she ran all the way around the edge of the pool. But by that time Andrew was over the fence. So many things seemed not quite plausible—Cynthia's behavior, then the lifeguard's—and now I had the impression that Andrew jumped with one bound over this fence, which seemed about seven feet high. He must have climbed it very quickly, getting a grip on the wire.

I could not jump or climb it, so I ran to the entrance, where there was a sort of lattice gate, locked. It was not very high, and I did pull myself over it. I ran through the cement corridors, through the disinfectant pool for your feet, and came out on the edge of the pool.

The drama was over.

Andrew had got to Meg first, and had pulled her out of the water. He just had to reach and grab her, because she was swimming somehow, with her head underwater—she was moving toward the edge of the pool. He was carrying her now, and the lifeguard was trotting along behind. Cynthia had climbed out of the water and was running to meet them. The only person aloof from the situation was the boyfriend, who had stayed on the bench at the shallow end, drinking a milkshake. He smiled at me, and I thought that unfeeling of him, even though the danger was past. He may have meant it kindly. I noticed that he had not turned the radio off, just down.

Meg had not swallowed any water. She hadn't even scared herself. Her hair was plastered to her head and her eyes were wide open, golden with amazement.

'I was getting the comb,' she said. 'I didn't know it was deep.'

Andrew said, 'She was swimming! She was swimming by

herself. I saw her bathing suit in the water and then I saw her swimming.'

'She nearly drowned,' Cynthia said. 'Didn't she? Meg nearly drowned.'

'I don't know how it could have happened,' said the lifeguard. 'One moment she was there, and the next she wasn't.'

What had happened was that Meg had climbed out of the water at the shallow end and run along the edge of the pool toward the deep end. She saw a comb that somebody had dropped lying on the bottom. She crouched down and reached in to pick it up, quite deceived about the depth of the water. She went over the edge and slipped into the pool, making such a light splash that nobody heard—not the lifeguard, who was kissing her boyfriend, or Cynthia, who was watching them. That must have been the moment under the trees when I thought, Where are the children? It must have been the same moment. At that moment, Meg was slipping, surprised, into the treacherously clear blue water.

'It's okay,' I said to the lifeguard, who was nearly crying. 'She can move pretty fast.' (Though that wasn't what we usually said about Meg at all. We said she thought everything over and took her time.)

'You swam, Meg,' said Cynthia, in a congratulatory way. (She told us about the kissing later.)

'I didn't know it was deep,' Meg said. 'I didn't drown.'

We had lunch at a take-out place, eating hamburgers and fries at a picnic table not far from the highway. In my excitement, I forgot to get Meg a plain hamburger, and had to scrape off the relish and mustard with plastic spoons, then wipe the meat with a paper napkin, before she would eat it. I took advantage of the trash can there to clean out the car. Then we resumed driving east, with the car windows open in front. Cynthia and Meg fell asleep in the back seat.

Andrew and I talked quietly about what had happened. Suppose I hadn't had the impulse just at that moment to check on the children? Suppose we had gone uptown to get drinks, as we had thought of doing? How had Andrew got over the fence? Did he jump or climb? (He couldn't remember.) How had he reached Meg so quickly? And think of the lifeguard not watching. And Cynthia, taken up with the kissing. Not seeing anything else. Not seeing Meg drop over the edge.

Disappeared.

But she swam. She held her breath and came up swimming.

What a chain of lucky links.

That was all we spoke about—luck. But I was compelled to picture the opposite. At this moment, we could have been filling out forms. Meg removed from us, Meg's body being prepared for shipment. To Vancouver—where we had never noticed such a thing as a graveyard—or to Ontario? The scribbled drawings she had made this morning would still be in the back seat of the car. The plump, sweet shoulders and hands and feet, the fine brown hair, the rather satisfied, secretive expression—all exactly the same as when she had been alive. The most ordinary tragedy. A child drowned in a swimming pool at noon on a sunny day. Things tidied up quickly. The pool opens as usual at two o'clock. The lifeguard is a bit shaken up and gets the afternoon off. She drives away with her boyfriend in the Roto-Rooter truck. The body sealed away in some kind of shipping coffin. Sedatives, phone calls, arrangements. Such a sudden vacancy, a blind sinking and shifting. Waking up groggy from the pills, thinking for a moment it wasn't true. Thinking if only we hadn't stopped, if only we hadn't taken this route, if only they hadn't let us use the pool. Probably no one would ever have known about the comb.

There's something trashy about this kind of imagining, isn't there. Something shameful. Laying your finger on the wire to get the safe shock, feeling a bit of what it's like, then pulling back. I believed that Andrew was more scrupulous than I about such things, and that at this moment he was really trying to think about something else.

When I stood apart from my parents at Steve Gauley's funeral and watched them, and had this new, unpleasant feeling about them, I thought that I was understanding something about them for the first time. It was a deadly serious thing. I was understanding that they were implicated. Their big, stiff, dressed-up bodies did not stand between me and sudden death, or any kind of death. They gave consent. So it seemed. They gave consent to the death of children and to my death not by anything they said or thought but by the very fact that they had made children—they had made me. They had made me, and for that reason my death—however grieved they were, however they carried on—would seem to them anything but impossible or unnatural. This was a fact, and even then I knew they were not to blame.

But I did blame them. I charged them with effrontery, hypocrisy. On Steve Gauley's behalf, and on behalf of all children, who knew that by rights they should have sprung up free, to live a new, superior kind of life, not to be caught in the snares of vanquished grownups, with their sex and funerals.

Steve Gauley drowned, people said, because he was next thing to an orphan and was let run free. If he had been warned enough and given chores to do and kept in check, he wouldn't have fallen from an untrustworthy tree branch into a spring pond, a full gravel pit near the river—he wouldn't have drowned. He was neglected, he was free, so he drowned. And his father took it as an accident, such as might happen to a dog. He didn't have a good suit for the funeral, and he didn't bow his head for the prayers. But he was the only grownup that I let off the hook. He was the only one I didn't see giving consent. He couldn't prevent anything, but he wasn't implicated in anything, either—not like the others, saying the Lord's Prayer in their unnaturally weighted voices, oozing religion and dishonor.

At Glendive, not far from the North Dakota border, we had a choice—either to continue on the interstate or head northeast, toward Williston, taking Route 16, then some secondary roads that would get us back to Highway 2.

We agreed that the interstate would be faster, and that it was important for us not to spend too much time—that is, money—on the road. Nevertheless we decided to cut back to Highway 2.

'I just like the idea of it better,' I said.

Andrew said, 'That's because it's what we planned to do in the beginning.'

'We missed seeing Kalispell and Havre. And Wolf Point. I like the name.'

'We'll see them on the way back.'

Andrew's saying 'on the way back' was a surprising pleasure to me. Of course, I had believed that we would be coming back, with our car and our lives and our family intact, having covered all that distance, having dealt somehow with those loyalties and problems, held ourselves up for inspection in such a foolhardy way. But it was a relief to hear him say it.

'What I can't get over,' said Andrew, 'is how you got the signal. It's got to be some kind of extra sense that mothers have.'

Partly I wanted to believe that, to bask in my extra sense. Partly I wanted to warn him—to warn everybody—never to count on it.

'What I can't understand,' I said, 'is how you got over the fence.'

'Neither can I.'

So we went on, with the two in the back seat trusting us, because of no choice, and we ourselves trusting to be forgiven, in time, for everything that had first to be seen and condemned by those children: whatever was flippant, arbitrary, careless, callous —all our natural, and particular, mistakes.

BIOGRAPHICAL NOTES

Toni Cade Bambara (1939–) was born and brought up in Harlem, New York and now lives in Atlanta, Georgia. She has worked in the Theatre of the Black Experience and as a social worker and teacher. She has published two volumes of stories, *Gorilla, My Love* (1972) and *The Seabirds Are Still Alive* (1982). She has also written a novel, *The Salt Eaters* (1980) and a book on the Atlanta murders of 1980–82, *Those Bones Are Not My Child*.

Marjorie Barnard (1897–1987), novelist, children's writer, historian and biographer, was born in Sydney and in recent years lived in New South Wales. She graduated from the University of Sydney in 1918, and wrote from the 1920s to 1950s in collaboration with Flora Eldershaw. She became increasingly politicized and in the late 1930s became a pacifist. Her outstanding novel *Tomorrow and Tomorrow and Tomorrow* (1947) was belatedly honoured with the Patrick White Prize in 1983. Her collection of short stories, *The Persimmon Tree*, was published in 1943. She has also written historical and children's books.

Elizabeth Bowen (1899–1973) was born in Dublin and brought up there and in the Anglo-Irish family home, Bowen's Court in County Cork. She spent most of the rest of her life in Oxford and London and in later years visited America regularly. Her novels include *The Last September* (1929), *The Death of the Heart* (1938) and *The Heat of the Day* (1949), and she published seven volumes of stories, including *Look At All Those Roses* (1941) and *The Demon Lover* (1945). Her non-fiction, edited by Hermione Lee, was published as *The Mulberry Tree* in 1986.

Kay Boyle (1902–1993), novelist, short story writer, poet and academic, was born in St. Paul, Minnesota, and studied music and architecture. In 1923 she travelled to Europe where she lived for thirty years, mingling in the 1920s with the famous American expatriates living in Paris. This story is told in *Being Geniuses Together 1920–1930* (1968, with Robert McAlmon). She was involved on the Left with civil rights, Amnesty, and anti-war movements all her life. From the 1940s she taught at various American universities and from 1963 to 1979 she was English Professor at San Francisco State University. Her first novel, *Plagued by the Nightingale* (1931) was followed by thirteen more, and by numerous volumes of short stories. Her essays, *Words That Must Somehow Be Said*, were published in 1985.

KATE CHOPIN (1851–1904), novelist and short story writer, was born in St. Louis of a part-French family, and lived in New Orleans and on a plantation in Louisiana. Her stories, *Bayou Folk* (1894) and *A Night in Acadie* (1897) were sketches of Creole and Cajun life. Her novel *At Fault* (1890) was followed by *The Awakening* (1899), the story of Edna Pontellier's resistance to her conventional marriage. It was greeted with a storm of disapprobation and censorship which silenced the writer.

MAVIS GALLANT (1922–), the distinguished Canadian writer, was born to an English father and a European mother in Montreal, Quebec. She attended 17 different schools in Canada and the U.S. and became a journalist. In 1950 she went to live in Paris. She has published numerous collections of short stories including *Home Truths* (1981) and *Overhead in a Balloon* (1985) and two novels, *Green Water, Green Sky* (1959) and *A Fairly Good Time* (1970). Her *Paris Notebooks: Essays and Reviews* were published in 1988.

JANE GARDAM (1928–), novelist and short story writer, was born at Coatham in North-east Yorkshire. She read English Literature at London University and worked as a journalist. Her books include *God on the Rocks* (shortlisted for the 1978 Booker Prize), *Black Faces, White Faces* (1975), *Bilgewater* (1976), *The Sidmouth Letters* (1980), *The Pangs of Love* (1983), *Crusoe's Daughter* (1985) and *The Queen of the Tambourine* (1991).

NADINE GORDIMER (1923–), who was awarded the Nobel Prize for Literature in 1991, and is the recipient of prizes, honorary degrees and awards world-wide, lives in Johannesburg, the city near where she grew up, though she has travelled widely in Europe and the USA. Among her novels are *A World of Strangers* (1958), *Occasion for Loving* (1963), *The Conservationist* (1974), *Burger's Daughter* (1979), *July's People* (1981), *A Sport of Nature* (1987), *My Son's Story* (1990) and *Jump* (1991). Her collections of stories include *The Soft Voice of the Serpent* (1952), *Six Feet of the Country* (1956), *Friday's Footprints* (1960), *Livingstone's Companions* (1971), *Some Monday For Sure*

(1976), *Something Out There* (1984), and *Crimes of Conscience* (1991). She has also written essays (including *The Essential Gesture* (1988) and television plays.

CAROLINE GORDON (1895–1981), novelist, short story writer and critic, was born in Kentucky, taught and reviewed, and was married (twice, between 1924 and 1959) to the Southern 'Fugitive' poet and critic Allen Tate. Many of her novels, including *Aleck Maury, Sportsman* (1934) and *None Shall Look Back* (1937) are set in Kentucky. She has published several volumes of short stories including *The Forest of the South* (1946) and *Old Red and Other Stories* (1963).

BESSIE HEAD (1937–1986) was born in Pietermaritzburg, near Natal in South Africa. The child of a white mother and a black father, she left South Africa to live in Serowe, a village in Botswanaland. Her painful experiences of exile and racial oppression went into her novels, *When Rain Clouds Gather* (1969), *Maru* (1971) and the autobiographical *A Question of Power* (1973). She also wrote a sequence of interconnected stories, *The Collector of Treasures* (1977), a book about her village, *Serowe: Village of the Rain Wind* (1981) and a narrative oral history, *A Bewitched Crossroad: An African Saga* (1984).

PATRICIA HIGHSMITH (1921–), one of America's leading psychological crime writers, was born in Fort Worth, Texas, moved to New York as a child, and has been living in Europe since 1963. Her first novel, *Strangers on a Train* (1950) was made into a film directed by Alfred Hitchcock. Her anti-hero, the killer Tom Ripley, features in many of her novels, including *The Talented Mr Ripley* (1955), *The Boy Who Followed Ripley* (1980) and *Ripley Under Water* (1991). Among her other novels are *Edith's Diary* (1977), *People Who Knock on the Door* (1983) and *Carol* (1990). *Tales of Natural and Unnatural Catastrophes* were published in 1987.

RACHELL INGALLS (1940–) grew up in New England, was educated partly in Germany and has lived in London since 1965. She has worked as a librarian, theatre-dresser, publisher's reader and ballet critic. Her fiction includes the novels *Mrs Caliban* (1982) and *Binstead's Safari* (1983), a novella, *Theft* (1970), and the stories, *Three of a Kind* (1985), *The Pearl Killers* (1986), *The End of Tragedy* (1987) and *Black Diamond* (1992).

ELIZABETH JOLLEY (1923–), novelist, radio playwright and poet, was brought up in the English Midlands in a German-speaking family and moved to Western Australia with her husband and family in 1959. She has worked as a nurse and salesperson, and teaches writing in prisons and community centres. Her novels include *Mr Scobie's Riddle* (1983), *Miss Peabody's Inheritance* (1983), *Foxybaby* (1985) and *The Sugar Mother* (1988). Her stories include *Woman in a Lampshade* (1983).

'ANNA KAVAN' (1901–1968) was born in Cannes and grew up in California, England and France. She began writing conventional novels under the name Helen Ferguson, but after an unsuccessful marriage she radically altered her style of writing and began to publish as Anna Kavan with *Asylum Piece* (1940), which reflected her sense of isolation and alienation. Though she developed a small cult following, she lived an increasingly reclusive life. Her books include *Let Me Alone* (1930), *A Stranger Still* (1935), *A Scarcity of Love* (1956), *Sleep Has His House* (1958), *A Bright Green Field* (1958), *Who Are You?* (1963) and *Ice* (1967), a fantasy novel.

JAMAICA KINCAID (1949–) is West Indian and was born in St. John's, Antigua. She is on the staff of the *New Yorker* and lives in New York. She has published one collection of stories, *At the Bottom of the River* (1984) and two novels, *Annie John* (1985) and *Lucy* (1991).

ANNE LEATON (1932–) was born and now lives in Texas, but has travelled widely in Europe, South Africa, the Middle East and Canada. She has published short stories, poems, radio plays and novels, including *Good Friends, Just* (1983), *Mayakovsky, My Love* (1984) and *Pearl* (1985).

KATHERINE MANSFIELD (1888–1923), one of the world's greatest short story writers, was born in Wellington, New Zealand, and came to live in London in 1908, though her search for a cure for tuberculosis took her frequently to Europe, where she died. Short stories published in her lifetime were *In a German Pension* (1911), *Prelude* (1918), *Bliss and Other Stories* (1920), and *The Garden Party and Other Stories* (1922). *The Dove's Nest and Other Stories* (1923), as well as letters and journals, were published posthumously.

ALICE MUNRO (1931–) was born in Wingham, Ontario, and went to the University of Western Ontario. She started writing in her teens and her first collection of stories was *Dance of the Happy Shades* (1968). Since then she has published *Lives of the Girls and Women* (1971), a series of linked stories; *Something I've Been*

Meaning to Tell You (1974), *Who Do You Think You Are?* (1978), *The Moons of Jupiter* (1982), *The Progress of Love* (1986) and *Friend of My Youth* (1990).

SUNITI NAMJOSHI (1941–) was born in Bombay, India. Since 1972 she has been Professor of English at the University of Toronto, Canada, and she now lives in Devon. Her *Feminist Fables* was published in 1981 and she has also published poems, articles, reviews and fiction, *The Conversations of Cow* (1985), *Aditi and the One-eyed Monkey* (1986) a children's book, *The Brothers of Maya Diip* (1989), the poems and fables in *Because of India* (1989) and the lesbian poems *Flesh and Paper* (1986, with Gillian Hanscombe).

FLANNERY O'CONNOR (1925–1964) was born in Savannah, Georgia, and spent most of her life, cut short by illness, on her mother's farm in Milledgeville, Georgia. She wrote two novels, *Wise Blood* (1952) and *The Violent Bear It Away* (1960), and two brilliant collections of stories, *A Good Man is Hard to Find* (1955) and *Everything that Rises Must Converge* (1965). Her essays and letters were published posthumously. Her collected stories were published by Faber in 1991.

JULIA O'FAOLAIN (1932–), the daughter of the Irish writer Sean O'Faolain, was born in London, brought up in Dublin, and has lived in Rome, Paris, Florence, London and California. Her books include *Women in the Wall* (1975), *No Country for Young Men* (1980), *The Obedient Wife* (1982), *The Irish Signorina* (1984) and the stories *Man in the Cellar* (1974) and *Daughters of Passion* (1982).

CYNTHIA OZICK (1928–), the Jewish-American writer, lives in her native town, New York, graduated from New York University, and has taught literature and writing there and at Indiana University. Her first book of fiction, *Trust* (1966) was followed by the novels *The Cannibal Galaxy* (1983) and *The Messiah of Stockholm* (1987). She has written four collections of stories, *The Pagan Rabbi* (1971), *Bloodshed and Three Novellas* (1976), *Levitation: Five Fictions* (1982), and *The Shawl* (1991), and two volumes of essays, *Art and Ardor* (1983) and *Messiah of Stockholm* (1987). Her latest novel is *What Henry James Knew* (1993).

K. ARNOLD PRICE was born in Connaught and grew up in Munster, Ireland. She read Modern Literature at Dublin University and has lived for a time in Greece. She now lives in Dublin. She has been writing since the 1940s; her work includes a novel, *The New Perspective* and a collection of short stories, *The Captain's Paramours* (1985).

RUTH RENDELL (1930–) was born in Bristol and began her career as a journalist. Her first crime novel, *From Doon with Death* (1964) introduced her character, Inspector Wexford, who appears in several of her later novels. Among her crime works are *The Secret House of Death* (1968), *Shake Hands Forever* (1975), *Put On By Cunning* (1981), *Live Flesh* (1986), *Talking to Strange Men* (1987), *The Bridesmaid* (1989), and *Going Wrong* (1990). She has written several collections of short stories including *The Copper Peacock* (1991) and *King Solomon's Carpet* (1991). In 1986 she published her novel, *Dark-Adapted Eye,* under a pseudonym, Barbara Vine. Further novels have followed under the same pseudonym, including *Gallowglass* (1990) and *Asta's Book* (1992).

'HENRY HANDEL RICHARDSON' (1870–1946), pseudonym of Ethel Florence Lindesay Richardson, was born in Melbourne, the daughter of an English mother and an Irish father, both early emigrants to Australia. She left Australia at the age of seventeen to study the piano at the Conservatorium of Leipzig, where she spent three years. Later she married a Professor of German at London University and though she travelled to Europe, she spent much of her life in England. Her books include *Maurice Guest* (1908), *The Getting of Wisdom* (1910), her famous Australian trilogy, *The Fortunes of Richard Mahoney* (1917–1929), a collection of short stories, *The End of Childhood* (1934) and her autobiography, *Myself When Young* (1948).

'STEVIE SMITH' (1902–1971), pseudonym of Florence Margaret Smith, was born in Hull and moved to Palmers Green in North London in 1905, where she lived for the rest of her life. She worked as a secretary for a publishing firm. She wrote three novels, *Novel on Yellow Paper* (1936), *Over the Frontier* (1938) and *The Holiday* (1949), and some short stories and reviews. Her first volume of poetry, *A Good Time Was Had By All*, was published in 1937 and was followed by seven subsequent volumes, all with her own illustrations. Since her death her genius has been fully recognised and marked by the appearance of her *Collected Poems* (1975), an anthology of her unpublished work, a play and a film of her life, and two biographies.

ELIZABETH SPENCER (1921–), novelist and short story writer, was born in Carollton, Mississippi, went to Vanderbilt University and later moved to Montreal, Canada. Her early novels, such as *The Voice at the Back Door* (1956), were about Mississippi; some later works, including *Knights and Dragons* (1965) were set in Italy, and many of her stories use her Montreal experience. Her volume of stories, *Ship Island* (1968) was dedicated to Eudora Welty.

ROSE TREMAIN (1943–) grew up in London, took a BA at the University of East Anglia, and has worked as a teacher, editor and creative writing fellow at the Universities of Essex and East Anglia. Her novels include *The Cupboard* (1975), *Letter to Sister Benedicta* (1978), *Restoration* (1989) and *Sacred Country* (1992). Her collections of stories are *The Colonel's Daughter* (1984) and *The Garden of the Villa Mollini* (1987). She has also written radio and TV plays, a book on the suffrage movement and a biography of Stalin (1975).

FAY WELDON (1931–), novelist, short story writer, dramatist, adaptor and prolific writer for television and radio, was born in Worcestershire and grew up in New Zealand. She went to St. Andrew's University, took an MA in economics and psychology and worked in advertising. Her novels include *Female Friends* (1975), *Praxis* (1978), *Puffball* (1980), *The Life and Loves of a She-Devil* (1983), *The Shrapnel Academy* (1986), *The Hearts and Lives of Men* (1987), *The Cloning of Joanna May* (1989), *Darcy's Utopia* (1990) and *Moon Over Minneapolis or Why She Couldn't Stay* (1991).

EUDORA WELTY (1909–), novelist, short story writer, and recipient of many awards including the Pulitzer Prize, was born in Jackson, Mississippi, where she has lived all her life. Her short story collections include *A Curtain of Green* (1941), *The Wide Net* (1943) and *The Golden Apples* (1949); her *Collected Stories* were published in 1980. She has published five novels, including *Delta Wedding* (1946), *Losing Battles* (1970) and *The Optimist's Daughter* (1972). Her non-fiction work includes a volume of essays, *The Eye of the Story* (1978) and an autobiography, *One Writer's Beginnings* (1984).

EDITH WHARTON (1862–1937), the American novelist, also well known for her ghost stories, was born into a wealthy New York family, emerged from an unhappy marriage to a life as an American expatriate in France, a close friend of Henry James, and one of the greatest American fiction writers of the twentieth century. Her best novels are *The House of Mirth* (1905), *The Custom of the Country* (1913), *Ethan Frome* (1911) and *The Age of Innocence* (1920).

ANTONIA WHITE (1899–1980), novelist, short story writer and translator from the French (in particular of Colette), wrote a tetralogy of novels, *Frost in May* (1933), *The Lost Traveller, The Sugar House* and *Beyond the Glass* (1950–1954) which gave a version of her Catholic convent upbringing, and her periods of breakdown. She published her stories, *Strangers,* in 1954 and also wrote an account of her reconversion to Catholicism, *The Hound and the Falcon* (1965). Her diaries were edited by Susan Chitty and published in 1991 as *The Diaries of Antonia White 1926–1957.*

VIRGINIA WOOLF (1882–1941), daughter of the Victorian man of letters Leslie Stephen, sister of the painter Vanessa Bell, wife of the left-wing political writer and editor Leonard Woolf, central figure in the 'Bloomsbury Group', her essays, letters, diaries, stories and novels, from *The Voyage Out* (1915) to *Between the Acts* (1941, published posthumously after her suicide) make up one of the greatest collections of writings in the century.

ACKNOWLEDGEMENTS

The editor would like to thank John Barnard, Philip Hobsbaum, Pat Kavanagh, Jenny Uglow, and, in particular, Robyn Sisman, for advice and suggestions.

Acknowledgements are due to the following for permission to include the stories which appear in this book: Louisiana State University Press for 'The Storm' (1899) from *The Complete Works of Kate Chopin*, edited by Per Seyersted (Louisiana State University Press, 1969); Quentin Bell, Angelica Garnett and the Hogarth Press for 'Lappin and Lapinova' (1939) by Virginia Woolf from *A Haunted House and Other Stories* (The Hogarth Press Ltd 1949); William R Tyler and A P Watt Ltd for 'Atrophy' by Edith Wharton from *Certain People* (Appleton, 1930); Kay Boyle, Lawrence Pollinger Ltd and Watkins Loomis Agency for 'Natives Don't Cry' from *The White Horses of Vienna* (Penguin Books 1937); Angus & Robertson Ltd for 'Two Hanged Women' (1934) by Henry Handel Richardson from *The Adventures of Cuffy Mahoney* (Angus & Robertson, 1981); The Estate of Antonia White and Virago Publishers for 'The House of Clouds' (1928) by Antonia White from *Strangers* (Virago, 1981); Eudora Welty and Marion Boyars Publishers Ltd for 'Why I Live at the P.O.' (1937) from *Collected Stories* (Marion Boyars, 1981); The Estate of Elizabeth Bowen and Jonathan Cape Ltd for 'The Happy Autumn Fields' (1944) from *Collected Stories* (Jonathan Cape, 1980); Marjorie Barnard and Curtis Brown Ltd for 'The Lottery' (1943) from *The Persimmon Tree* (Virago, 1985); Peter Owen Ltd for 'An Unpleasant Reminder' (1940) by Anna Kavan from *Asylum Piece*, (Michael Kesand, 1981) Caroline Gordon for 'The Petrified Woman' from *Old Red and Other Stories* (Scribners, 1963); The Estate of Stevie Smith and Virago Publishers for 'Sunday at Home' (1949) from *Me Again* (Virago, 1981); Mavis Gallant and Jonathan Cape Ltd for 'The Ice Wagon Going Down the Street' (1963) from *Home Truths* (Jonathan Cape, 1985); A D Peters & Co Ltd for 'Everything that Rises Must Converge' (1965) by Flannery O'Connor from *Everything that Rises Must Converge* (Faber, 1980); Penguin Books Ltd for 'The Adult Holiday' (1965) by Elizabeth Spencer from *The Stories of Elizabeth Spencer* (Penguin Books, 1983); Toni Cade Bambara and The Women's Press Ltd for 'The Lesson' (1972) from *Gorilla, My Love* (Women's

Press, 1984); Patricia Highsmith and William Heinemann Ltd for 'One for the Islands' from *Slowly, Slowly in the Wind* (Heinemann, 1979); Jane Gardam and David Higham Ltd for 'The Weeping Child' from *Black Faces, White Faces* (Hamish Hamilton, 1975); Bessie Head and Heinemann Educational Books Ltd for 'Looking for a Rain God' from *The Collector of Treasures* (Heinemann, 1977); Julia O'Faolain and Deborah Rogers Ltd for 'Diego' from *Daughters of Passion* (Penguin Books, 1982); Cynthia Ozick and Secker & Warburg Ltd for 'Levitation' from *Levitation* (Secker & Warburg, 1982); Fay Weldon and Hodder & Stoughton Ltd for 'Weekend' (1978) from *Watching Me, Watching You* (Hodder & Stoughton, 1981); Rachel Ingalls and Richard Scott Simon Ltd for 'Third Time Lucky' from *The Pearl Killers* (Faber, 1986); Jamaica Kincaid and Pan Books Ltd for 'What I Have Been Doing Lately' from *At the Bottom of the River* (Picador, 1984); Rose Tremain and Richard Scott Simon Ltd for 'My Wife is a White Russian' (first published in *Granta)* from *The Colonel's Daughter* (Hamish Hamilton, 1984); Suniti Namjoshi and Sheba Feminist Publishers for 'The Giantess', 'Of Cats and Bells' and 'Svayamvara' from *Feminist Fables* (Sheba, 1984); K. Arnold Price and Hamish Hamilton Ltd for 'The White Doll' from *The Captain's Paramours* (Hamish Hamilton, 1985); Anne Leaton and A D Peters & Co Ltd for 'The Passion of Marco Z' from *Transatlantic Review* No.55/56, 1976; Nadine Gordimer and A P Watt Ltd for 'A City of the Dead, A City of the Living' (1982) from *Something Out There* (Cape, 1984); Ruth Rendell and A D Peters & Co Ltd for 'The Convolvulus Clock' from *The New Girlfriend* (Hutchinson, 1985); Elizabeth Jolley and Penguin Books Australia Ltd for 'Paper Children' from *Woman in a Lampshade* (Penguin, 1983, 1986); Alice Munro and Chatto & Windus Ltd for 'Miles City, Montana' from *The Progress of Love* (Chatto & Windus, 1987).

The copyright in the individual stories is as follows: 'The Storm' © 1969 by Louisiana State University Press; 'Lappin and Lapinova' Copyright 1949 The Estate of Virginia Woolf; 'Atrophy' Copyright 1930 The Estate of Edith Wharton; 'Natives Don't Cry' Copyright Kay Boyle 1937; 'Two Hanged Women' Copyright The Estate of Henry Handel Richardson 1934; 'The House of Clouds' copyright Antonia White 1954, The Estate of Antonia White 1980; 'Why I Live at the P.O.' © Eudora Welty 1965-1980; 'The Happy Autumn Fields' Copyright The Estate of Elizabeth Bowen 1944, 'The Lottery' Copyright Marjorie Barnard 1943; 'An Unpleasant Reminder' Copyright The Estate of Anna Kavan 1940; 'The Petrified Woman' Copyright Caroline Gordon; 'Sunday at Home' Copyright The Estate of Stevie Smith 1949; 'The Ice Wagon Going Down the Street' © Mavis Gallant 1963; 'Everything that Rises Must Converge' © 1961, 1965 The Estate of Mary Flannery O'Connor; 'The Adult

Holiday' Copyright Elizabeth Spencer 1983; 'The Lesson' © Toni Cade Bambara 1972; 'One for the Islands' © Patricia Highsmith 1979; 'The Weeping Child' © Jane Gardam 1975; 'Looking for a Rain God' © Bessie Head 1977; 'Diego' © Julia O'Faolain 1982; 'Levitation' © Cynthia Ozick 1982; 'Weekend' © Fay Weldon 1981; 'Third Time Lucky' © Rachel Ingalls 1986; 'What I Have Been Doing Lately' © Jamaica Kincaid 1984; 'My Wife is a White Russian' © Rose Tremain 1982; 'The Giantess' 'Of Cats and Bells' and 'Svayamvara' © Suniti Namjoshi 1984; 'The White Doll' © K. Arnold Price 1985; 'The Passion of Marco Z' © Anne Leaton 1976, 'A City of the Dead, A City of Enterprises 1985; 'Paper Children' © Elizabeth Jolley, 1983, 1986; 'Miles City, Montana' © Alice Munro 1987.